Redemption of the Sorcerer
The Crystalon Saga
Book One
By Ralph L Angelo Jr.

This book is dedicated to my Parents, who in recent years have endured much. I love you both, thank you.

--Ralph L. Angelo (proudly) Jr.

This book was a long time in coming to completion. Approximately seven years. Along the way I had help from three people who read each chapter, commented on them and pretty much told me what worked and what didn't. Thanks Ron Angelo (My Brother) Jerry Zuckerman (my good friend) and Demi Arceneaux (My friend and fellow CoHer). I could not have completed this journey without the three of you. Your help was invaluable.

Ralph

Redemption of the Sorcerer
The Crystalon Saga
Book One

Cosmic Comet Publishing
Story Copyright 2012 By Ralph L. Angelo Jr.
Published By Cosmic Comet Publishing

Edited By Deborah Richardson @ Dre&m services

Cover by Gustav Barta

Contents

Redemption of the Sorcerer: The Crystalon Saga, Book I

Part One

Chapter 1

Another when, another now...

The battle raged all about the capitol of the great city, the great empire. Men with weapons, which spit blasts of light against those whose hands glowed and spit it back upon them. Hundreds of thousands of warriors, battling each other beneath a dark and miasmic sky. Clouds roiled with fury and thunder overhead, striking out with precision, dealing devastating blows of lightning to one side of the battle but not the other. Yet, on the ground, great fissures opened and swallowed entire regiments of the opposing side. And so it went...

The battle raged for days, weeks, and more, leaving blood and ichor calf deep beneath the combatants. A warrior would fall next to one of his comrades and immediately be replaced by another from behind. Some wore brightly colored armor, some were bare-skinned with war paints streaked on their quivering, sweat-covered flesh. Some bore cruel, horrific blades that would rend skin horribly, others muttered incantations beneath their breath and released huge bursts of energy from spasming fingertips. Incinerating flesh, leaving the very air tainted with a smell of burned meat.

And slowly they crept forward; the renegades, the rebels, those who had lived through enough tyranny for the past thousand, thousand years. They pressed forward. Their hands curled with effort to cast one more spell, to swing their blade one more time, their heads covered in blood and

1

sweat and grime, and yes, tears. Tears for their brothers, their fathers, their sisters and their mothers, as well as tears for the ones next to them who died in their tracks.

But never for the enemy. No, not for those who they slowly pressed back. Not those who had given in and reaped the benefits of working under the yoke of the Oppressor. For that sin there was no forgiveness. He was a harsh taskmaster, but he gave momentous gifts to those loyal to him. He insisted on complete and utter respect and subservience, upon promise of punishment and never ending misery if failure was the result.

This world, this Earth quivered beneath their feet, as warriors arrived from a hundred outlying worlds to lend aid to their cause. For such was the fear this malignant cancer, this Oppressor had instilled across the galaxy.

The weeks pressed on; still there was no telling of the difference between day and night, for both were black as pitch with heat and humidity as oppressive as a blanket of fire laid upon the skin. The seemingly endless battle raged on. Never slowing, never abating. The only sound, that of men grunting and screaming in exertion or death.

Then one day, seemingly without warning, the fighting stopped, the skies cleared, and both sides, both great armies looked skywards, apprehensively, while huge ships dropped from the sky like gigantic insects, their landing legs bending like the knee of some praying mantis upon landing. More troops wearing great suits of armor, crimson in color, disembarked. An honor guard of sorts exited the largest of the ships, bearing banners of great color and length. At its center, an old, wizened man, head held regally stepped forth. A knurled walking stick in his hand, the sun gleamed on his bald head; his own golden armor glistening brightly in the sunlight, he stepped forward, walking like a conqueror surveying his conquests.

In truth this was partly correct. He was known as the Sehr. Not because it was his name, for he no longer had a name. When he ascended to his position as leader of his race, he took a title that rose above all names. The duly elected leader of the people known as the Sehriens walked regally towards the citadel that rose from the sky a half-mile in the distance. He could have ridden in any vehicle, or upon the back of any number of creatures. But he did not. He chose to walk. It was both a sign of his respect towards his troops, as well as a sign that his forces had won the war, and that he was now commander of all he surveyed.

The crimson suited troopers opened the doors to the citadel, and in a great, cathedral shaped room, huge and majestic, knelt a man in glowing, mystical chains surrounded by dozens of men in ragged, bloodied garb. Most were as old and as wizened as the Sehr. All stood proud and strong, pointing either sharp blades and pikes, or unwavering energy weapons at the figure before them, face turned down, on his knees, unable to move. He raised his head and stared with anger and deep-seated hatred at the newcomer.

He was not a particularly special looking man. His height slightly under six feet, he wore his black hair neatly, and of no great length. A small, black goatee adorned his chin. His clothing, a red and black tunic with mystic symbols scrawled across it, with a similarly colored cloak sprawled behind him, was in tatters. Armored pieces adorned each shoulder, though one was cracked and broken now. Knee height boots of black leather covered his feet. His pants were the same red material as his tunic.

The Sehr approached him, touching his warriors gently, ushering them aside, as he tried to pass. One stopped him.

The man, obviously an officer in the Sehr's great army, spoke. "Please Sehr; you should not approach him any closer. We know not the strength of his powers as of yet. It takes the concentration of everyone here to maintain the bonds we have conjured to keep him thus subdued."

The Sehr smiled gently and laid his hand upon his subordinates shoulder. "Tufor, the battle, the war is over. Not even the mighty Crystalon could hold out forever against the power of so many worlds. Our coalition has defeated the Oppressor, and he will be dealt with by his peers. Isn't that correct Crystalon?"

The man on the floor of his own castle snarled incoherently as he lifted his face up to meet that of his enemy.

"You are a fool Sehr. I will yet have your head upon a platter for this effrontery. When I break free of these bonds – and make no mistake, I will be free of them – yours will be the first life I take as I begin my return to my rightful place above the cattle."

"And what is that place, Crystalon?" The Sehr asked as he turned his back on the downed man and began walking around the large room.

"You know as well as I do, fool. As their leader, their King, their God."

The Sehr spun quickly and pointed at Crystalon with his staff. "You are no God. You are a powerful, but petty man who terrorized a galaxy with his petulance for far too long. You were given the greatest mystical abilities ever known. You were a natural sorcerer of untold power; you could have helped shape the universe into a thing of great beauty, ushered in an age of galactic utopia. Instead you chose to create an empire that strangled its citizens and broke their backs with the weight of its aggression."

"I created a world where those who were loyal to me prospered. I gave their lives meaning!" Crystalon roared, his voice reverberating within the great hall.

"You enslaved them," the Sehr answered quietly. "Ponder all of this. In one day hence, you will be sentenced for your crimes against the universe, against decency itself.

4

Pray that our judgment of you is less severe than you would impose upon one who committed a far lesser aggression."

The Sehr turned to leave as the man upon the floor fought mightily to stand. Energy painfully coruscated about his bonds, driving him back to the floor in a heap. All present stared at him with vehemence, save the Sehr who merely shook his head sadly and muttered, "Such promise, wasted," as he left the citadel.

The sorcerer Crystalon watched his enemy leave his home and sneered. For even as a prisoner here, this was still his castle. Earlier as a precaution, when the battle was not going his way and he knew he would fall to these men and their treachery, he silently sent an immeasurable portion of his power into the void, so none of these present would be able to claim it. In that at least he had a victory. The rest though? He sank to the floor, feeling true defeat for the first time in many millennia.

***

The next day the great hall filled to overflowing with spectators, as the Sehr and eleven other men of great power sat at a half circle table. In the center of the room, facing the half circle was the shackled Crystalon. He stared at the men, at everyone in the room, with the disgust of one so far above his enemies, of a God among lower beings who meant nothing to him. He stared as if he could snuff out their lives with but a thought. And at one time he could have...

The Sehr stood, staring down at Crystalon. "Have you anything to say this day, Crystalon, lord of the thousand, thousand year realm, to those who bested you and your forces in fair combat? Say it now before we pass our just and fair judgment upon thee."

"Your judgment? How can cattle judge a God? How can you sheep judge one who is the master of the universe? Yes, you have gained the upper hand for now, but you know as well as I do that this is all a momentary

5

inconvenience. Soon I will shatter these shackles of power and then I will crush you all, and laugh as I exact my vengeance."

"Perhaps, if given the chance, that would be so, Crystalon." The Sehr began, "But we are not so foolish as to give you that chance. Understand this, Crystalon. Thy time here has ended. The thousand, thousand year realm is now free of your scourge. The universe is free of you, and we intend to keep it that way."

"You pontificate greatly, Sehr. There is no prison that can hold me. You know this as well as I. I am as one with the very fabric of reality. I draw mystic strength from the very air, ground and sea. Soon these mystic shackles will burn out from the strain of holding my power in check. Soon your many weak fools who dare to call themselves 'Sorcerers' will weaken and fail against my already returning might. Then we will battle anew, and I promise you, the outcome will be different."

"Again, Crystalon, perhaps, but only if we give you the chance. Only one item has saved you from never ending death, Crystalon – the simple fact that you have never killed your own people. In war people die, there can be no arguing of that, so we do not judge you for that. But even your own enemies amongst your people begrudgingly admit you have never had one of their number put to the sword. No one amongst your native empire has ever had to die at your angered hand. You were a stern ruler, but at times a fair one. This alone saves you from utter annihilation."

"Annihilate me?" Crystalon snorted imperiously, "You have not the power."

"That is where you are mistaken, Crystalon. You see, amongst the many sorcerers here, one spell has been learned by all. The spell of ultimate dissolution. Every Mage here can invoke this power at once, all aimed in your direction. You would be torn asunder to a molecular level before you would even be able to fight back. Even in your fully powered, non-weakened state, you would be hard pressed against it. As you are now, you would stand not a chance."

Crystalon paused at this, fear actually beginning to show upon his face. "Do as you will to me. I do not fear your petty judgments. I stand ready for whatever foolishness you seek to bestow upon me."

The other men seated near the Sehr began to excitedly speak amongst themselves. The Sehr joined in the conversation, and then rose once again to stare directly at the great enemy who stood shackled and weak before them all.

"Our decision has been made, Crystalon. You will be sent for all eternity, or as long as you may live, to dwell as a normal, mortal man on a world where no magic exists. On a world where you cannot wield any power. You will be sent there coinless and poor, with naught save the clothes on your back. You will in truth live as a pauper, a beggar amongst these people till you die a death of natural, or forced causes. You will be cut off from this reality forever. Your time here as a God amongst men is over, Crystalon. Now it is time for you to truly live and learn what it means to be a man among many."

Crystalon turned his head towards a woman in one of the viewing stands. She stared at him, pain etched on her face at his plight. But she did nothing, save grip the railing before her tighter, turning her knuckles white.

"You did this to me, woman. Your poisoning of me weakened me to the point where these fools could gain the upper hand. How could you do this to me? You were my wife!" He almost shrieked his lament, as all about him stared emotionlessly.

"Your sentence will be carried out immediately, Crystalon. Stare about you at this realm for the final time, usurper. Your days here are ended."

7

Then, fourteen men stepped forth and began to make esoteric movements with their hands, each of which started to glow one at a time, causing the air to vibrate between them with a deep, thrumming resonance. Slowly a pinprick of light formed between them all. It grew from a pinprick to a coin-sized circle, and then grew more. Slowly at first, then quicker until it finally reached man sized proportions.

Two armored guards grabbed the former dictator, and half dragged him towards the now fully irised portal. He stared about the great hall one last time, taking in the thousands of beings that stared at him, and his gaze once again settled on his wife. Her long, flowing blonde hair cascading about her shoulders and bosom, a gold circlet enwraps her left arm. She wore a flowing white and gold trimmed gown. He would remember her always thusly. She finally raised her eyes to meet the stare she had long felt upon her. Immediately her eyes welled up with tears, but she held firm to his gaze.

Then he was shoved roughly into the portal, he fought back momentarily, not breaking her gaze. He mouthed three silent words in her direction before being pushed through, and immediately she began to cry openly.

The portal closed with a thunderous snap and immediately the crowd dispersed, most very happily. A new era was beginning for them, one free from a tyrannical boot upon their spines. But one woman continued to sob in the now mostly empty hall.

The Sehr approached and lay his hand upon her shoulder. "You did what was right, Amera. There was no other choice. He was evil in a way most cannot ever begin to understand. Your actions alone freed untold worlds from his domination. You should be happy."

She turned to him, anger coloring her face a bright red and spoke, her words venom, "I did as you bade me. I poisoned my very husband, who, no matter his faults, I did truly love. I have rid the realm of the despot, but at a personal cost I will never be able to repay. The truth is I lost more than my husband today, oh Sehr. I lost my father as well. Never speak to me again, old one. For you are now and evermore dead to my eyes. Of this you can be certain."

She stood quickly and then haughtily walked towards the exit. The Sehr stood, watching her, his lips quivering in anger and regret. Then she stopped and turned quickly back to him, before speaking one final time. "Do you know what he said to me father? Do you know what words Crystalon, the so called *scourge of the universe,* spoke as he was being shoved through the portal?"

The Sehr merely shook his head in anguish.

"His words were 'I forgive you.' That is what the oppressor of billions said as he was being sent to a lifetime of torment. Think on this my former father, for the rest of your life, no matter how long, or short it may be."

And then she was gone, in a flourish of white and gold. Leaving a lonely old man to think about what he had wrought for the greater good.

Chapter 2

The dream begins with a long spiraling scream down a vortex – a tunnel of winding thunder and light. Then ends after a seemingly endless tumble through said vortex, with a throat raw from screaming in distorted agony. There is a dull and painful thud upon landing on a strange black surface, which seems as hard and unyielding as steel.

With a pained look upon his face, he stood, dusted himself off, and looked around.

"By the seven moons, where am I?" Crystalon muttered.

"Brrraaaap!" He turned towards the loud offending sound accosting him, and saw a dull-eyed metallic beast braying at him as it thundered towards him.

"What madness is this?" The Sorcerer swore as he raised an arm to unleash a bolt of energy that would eradicate the beast from this world with but a thought. Would, if he were still in his own reality.

To his eternal consternation, nothing happened. Instead he barely threw himself out of the way, as the metal beast actually hit him, tossing him aside without any effort at all. Pain roared through his body as he fought to stand and ran from the beast, but surprisingly, in a squeal of seeming delight, the beast stopped and a panel of sorts opened on its side, disgorging a strangely garbed human.

"Hey Mister! You alright?" The man asked "Didn't mean to scare you there, definitely didn't mean to hit you, but you came outta nowhere real sudden like." Then after a second the man continued. "Where did you come from anyway? A Halloween party? You got a few months before Halloween buddy." He grabbed Crystalon by the elbow trying to help steady the Mage.

"Unhand me, you witless cur." Crystalon roared imperiously, as he snapped his elbow out of the man's grip.

"Hey buddy! I said I was sorry, I'm tryin' ta help now. Relax an' let me get you an ambulance."

"I-I do not...need your help, you fool. I am Crys...Talon" Crystalon stammered as a wave a nausea and pain flared through his body. He reached up and held his head with his left hand, and for the first time, realized his head was bleeding. He turned to stare incredulously at the man next to him who has once again grabbed Crystalon by the elbow to help steady him.

Then the world suddenly started going dark around him once again. At first he thought it was another transportation, to yet another world, as his last journey had begun much like this one.

But then he realized he was merely passing out, as he crumpled like a balloon whose helium was released, his pained and blurring gaze turning to the face of the man who gently lowered him down on the ground, and he saw something there in the man's face he has not seen reflected towards him for many, many years. Genuine concern for his well-being. One thought raced through Crystalon's delirious mind as consciousness passed.

"You idiot"

And then the world went black.

For a time...

The light outside his eyelids was suddenly bright. He crunched them tighter to ward off the offending light source, muttering a small incantation that would defuse the light in the room about him. But nothing happened. It was an instinctive reaction. One born of centuries of power and abuse of that power.

But it was meaningless right now. He remembered what happened to him, how he was banished to this strange world of no magic, and more he remembered, in a teeth gritting blast of agony, why he succumbed to the sleeping world. He had passed out from pain, from agony when the metallic beast had attacked him.

Then a rather annoying female voice intruded upon his thoughts "Wake up, sleepy head. C'mon I know you're awake. I heard you mutter something when I opened the drapes a minute ago. Rise and shine, Chris."

Crystalon warily opened his eyes, one at a time actually. First the left, then the right. He was in a light green colored room. Austere would be a good word for it he supposed. He was on a bed, with tubes going into his arms, and his right leg heavily bandaged. He slowly tried to push himself up to a sitting position and look towards the window, where the bright sunshine beamed through.

The woman who had spoken to him, a middle aged, brown haired, unspectacular looking woman who he thought had a high caloric content to her diet, helped him up to his sitting position and swung a tray in front of him with a beverage on it.

"Here you go Chris, drink a little of this orange juice, see how that feels."

Silently he did as he was bid, simply because it seemed like a good idea at the time. After he drank the contents of the glass, he turned towards her. "How do you know my name?"

"Honey," she began, "it's right here on your medical chart. Mr. Chris Talon. Address unknown, social security number unknown. Date of birth unknown. Nothing is known about you BUT your name. Care to fill in the blanks?" She handed him a clipboard with a piece of paper attached to it with strange symbols scattered all over it.

"I -I do not know," he answered, stammering and only half-lying. For one, he had no idea how to read the gibberish on the page before him, beyond that he had no idea what he would write if he could. What would he write? That he was an out of work sorcerer who used to rule an entire reality before being overthrown by the forces of a hundred worlds?

"Hhhmm," the woman muttered. "Memory loss? Possible with a conk to the noggin like you took, honey. Best to rest a while. You've been asleep a long time. Things'll come back to you." Then she added, "We hope."

"Wait!" he blurted out as she started to leave the room, surprising no one more then himself. "How long was I unconscious? How long have I been here?"

"You've been here for four days, sugar."

"What is your name, healing woman?"

"I'm not the 'healing woman' Chris. I'm just your nurse. My name is Debbie. You can call me Nurse Debbie. I have this shift today, and every day. I'll make sure you're comfy, Chris."

"What is wrong with me?" he asked, while running his hand up through his hair, wondering about the small bumps he was feeling on his scalp.

"You took a bad bang to the head requiring stitches, and somehow broke a small bone in your foot too. Your leg got scraped up a bit in the accident. The Doctors say it looks like two separate occurrences though. The leg somehow being the first of the two."

Crystalon's mind raced backwards to when he fell from his own dimension to land with a thud on this world's hard, black surface, and then the subsequent attack of the metal beast that disgorged the human from the side of its mouth. He turned his head towards the window, and listened to the stunning cacophony coming through the open panes. Turning his head just so he was able to glimpse the street far below him, he saw it filled with metal beasts.

"What madness?" He murmured aloud.

"What's that Chris?" The woman asked him.

He turned towards her and spoke, "Nurse Debbie, where are my clothes? "

"Right here Chris." she answered, opening a small closet door next to his bed.

"Good, when can I leave here?"

"Chris, you can't leave here, at least not for several days yet, until the Doctors feel you're well enough to go home, if you can even remember where home is. That's another issue for you. Do you remember where you live?"

"I-I do not remember much of anything before awaking here, to your kindness." He genuinely meant that too. Her kindness struck him, as a man who was not used to this from his subjects – from people in general – as somehow refreshing.

But still the malevolent voice within coaxed him with words of anger and fury

'*She is a cow and a fool. She would be cleaning your stables back on our Earth.*'

Even as the thoughts occurred to him, he regretted them, to a point. This woman was nice to him, and she seemed to honestly care for his well being, and for no other reason than that she wanted to. He had no doubt she was being compensated for her work, but she was more than just going through the motions of dealing with an ailing monarch, and she was not acting through fear, something his lesser subjects did on a daily basis. No, this woman called *Nurse Debbie* was performing her daily chores, the aiding of those who required medical care, because she liked doing it, of that he had no doubt.

"The Doctor will be in shortly to see you, Chris. Relax until he arrives." She smiled at him as she left the room, and then returned a second later, obviously forgetting something. "Oh Chris, that's Mr. Myers next to you, in the other bed. He should be okay, he was just released from the intensive care unit, and needs a few days to get back on his feet."

15

Crystalon looked at the man next to him, and then turned his gaze back to Nurse Debbie. "What is wrong with him?" he asked quietly.

"He had a heart attack a few days ago, but he's on the road to recovery he had a bypass operation, and should be home in a matter of days."

Crystalon stared at her incredulously, suddenly realizing that Myers had stitches across his chest, where his heart was located. In his universe when someone was sick, healers applied a few herbs and performed some minor incantations, and the sick were healed. In this world, it seemed they barbarically tore the body of the afflicted open, physically tending to organs needing repair. Crystalon was aghast. These people had no true way of dealing with medical injuries. How could one heal the sick without magic? The thought alone confounded and perplexed him, and actually made him a little bit afraid for his own well-being.

But the simple fact that they did survive, and that they found a way to overcome this obvious shortcoming was incredible to him!

Debbie's voice shook him from his silent reverie once again "Chris, like I said, the Doctor will be in to see you in a few minutes. Relax and see if you can remember anything at all. I'll be back to check on you in an hour or so. If you need anything, press the nurses' station button next to your bed." He stared where she pointed, at a glowing, backlit button; then nodded emotionlessly.

Debbie exited the room, shaking her head slowly to herself as she meandered towards the nurse's station. Another nurse standing nearby walked towards her, clipboard in hand.

"What's the matter Debs? Is the mystery patient making you crazy in there?"

"Hhhm? What? No Cherise." Debbie replied, "He seems nice enough, but there's something odd about him,

16

and I can't place my finger on it. Almost like I feel like I'm dealing with some kind of royalty or something. He seems almost condescending, but then he was concerned about the man in the next bed. He definitely seems like a strange guy."

Cherise wrinkled her nose and laughed. She was a heavyset black woman with long curly hair and a pleasant smile, "Sugar, if he seems like a strange guy to you, then it's just another day in good ol' Brooklyn, New York." She continued walking, laughing to herself pleasantly. Nearby a young Doctor eavesdropped on the entire conversation, his face stoic, keeping his own counsel; he continued to listen, intently...

Chapter 3

Crystalon sat staring out his hospital window, repeatedly fighting back his growing anger at the feelings of helplessness that he was drowning in. The patient next to him, Mr. Meyers, was a steady conversationalist, who badgered the former sorcerer constantly. Finally after several days of this, Crystalon shut the curtain between them with vehemence, announcing "I do not want to be disturbed for the nonce!"

Paul Meyers replied, "What's a nonce?"

Crys groaned and pulled a pillow over his head, imploring every being he had ever invoked for just one spell of silence to wrap the room, and especially the bed next to him, in.

But no such spell or power was forthcoming.

A knocking occurred on the doorsill of the room, as Dr. Singh, Crystalon's physician, entered once again with chart in hand.

"Hello Mr. Chris, how are you feeling today hhmm?" Dr. Singh continued to look at the chart as he walked, seemingly using radar of some kind to navigate the room, until he arrived next to Crys's bed. "I have to be telling you, Mr. Chris, that you are looking to be well, but we have a problem. We do not know what to do with you. You should be released, but you have no money, and no memory of where you are to be living. So what are we to do with you hhhm?"

"I-I wish I could answer that for you, physician, but my mind is a blank. I do not remember where I came from, or where I should be going. I do not even remember how to read. What should I do, physician? Where should I go?"

The Doctor smiled as he flipped pages on his clipboard. "There is a Police officer who would like to talk to you. He will take pictures of you, and speak to you at

19

length. Then he will be talking to the missing persons bureau and they will be sending that picture and description of you around to all the other agencies in the country until we find where you came from. My thoughts are that you are a local man. But the clothing you were wearing, perhaps you are a magician for children's birthday parties?"

Crystalon practically bristled at this; he fought to make himself stay in the bed, gripping the sheets with such ferocity that his knuckles turned a bright, bleached white. Then he spoke, fighting to reply in a low voice without displaying emotion, "No physician Singh, I assure you whatever I am, I am NOT a child's party prestidigitator."

"Okay Mr. Chris, whatever it is you say. This Policeman will be coming to see you later today, and hopefully we'll be able to move you to your home, wherever that may be. But if we cannot locate your home, we will find and move you into a facility nearby where you can stay until you are well enough to move on back where you belong."

"Thank you for your caring, physician." He answered as pleasantly as he could through gritting teeth.

Dr. Singh smiled and left the room humming a tune to himself as he closed the door.

"Idiot." Crystalon grumbled as he reached to turn the television on with the remote. He had been here several days now, and the differences and similarities between his world and this one were staggering.

On his Earth, when one wanted to view entertainment, one gestured and a scrying field appeared before the eyes of all present where entertainment was pre-stored, or in this world's vernacular, recorded on mystic stones that held memories of recorded events. Much like a – what do they call it here? – a DVD? He bristled at the thought of archaic methods through which this world carried on a daily existence.

But he would have to get used to it, he supposed. As much as he tried, he could find no evidence of mystic properties here to bind to his iron clad will.

Try he did though, and on a daily basis. He stretched his mind and will outwards, seemingly trying to touch the fabric of this world's reality, but to no avail. All his training, all his years of dedication to his craft were for naught. Once, several nights earlier, he had thought he felt a murmur of magic, a faint echo that replied to him in a hush of breath, as if it were a warm breeze upon the cheek at night beneath a tree, but then it was gone and at this point, he realized, it could very well have been his imagination.

'*Am I going mad?*' He thought to himself in frustration. '*No.*' an inner voice answered. '*You are paying for your sins.*'

Angrily he gripped the television remote in his hand, flipping channels with a fire he had not felt in days. He was trapped on a world where he was useless, when mere days before; he ruled an empire that stretched beyond imagining. Now the only thing he was able to control was this television. He was annoyed to say the least.

For days he'd been pushed and prodded for information about his past and he had to lie like a thief in the night to these fools, telling them he had no recollection of his past, telling them he did not even remember how to read (That was at least partly true, this worlds written language was far removed from his own Earth's elegance.) He continued flipping channels and then stopped as one in particular grabbed his eye, he raised the volume as his roommate, Mr. Meyers grumbled at him.

"Hey! Lower that, c'mon they don't need to hear it next door."

"Quiet you oaf! Tell me, what is that place displayed on the screen?" Crystalon answered in a quiet, almost reverent voice.

Meyers, a small, balding, round man with large eyes, pulled himself to a sitting position and stared at the screen a moment, squinting until he affixed his eyeglasses in place. He smoothed back his balding head of gray hair and looked closer before speaking.

"That? That's Stonehenge," he answered. "Ain't you never seen anything before?"

"I did not ask your opinion of my knowledge of this world Meyers, but tell me where this place is?"

"England, it's in England. Now lower it, will ya? I'm trying ta get some rest before I go home tomorrow. My Shelly will keep me awake for the rest of my life with her yammering. At least let me get some peace and quiet here, will ya?"

Crystalon smiled at this. In this at least, all earths it seemed were identical. Women the world over harangued their men. Then his attention was once again riveted to the screen before him. He watched intently for the next two hours, listening to the history of the place, shaking his head at some theories, and nodding knowingly at others.

"What are you going on about?" Meyers asked him at some point.

"This is a place of magic." he spoke softly in answer.

"It's a place where they sacrificed people ta some kinda sewer God or somethin'. " Meyers replied.

"You do not know what you speak of my friend. There is magic in this world, or at least there was at one time. Those towers, the way they were originally aligned, was to focus mystical energies in a nexus at the center point. Over the years they have been destroyed by nature's ravages, but their history remains for those who can see beyond such things. There was magic here."

"What do you know about magic?" Meyers asked Crystalon inquisitively, and with some genuine fascination.

"A lot." Another voice answered, before Crystalon could, from the doorway to their room. Both men turned towards the source of the voice to see a rumpled man in a poor fitting suit with short black hair, who looked like he just rolled out of bed fully dressed, standing there. "My names O'Malley. Detective O'Malley. I've been assigned to your case to find out who you really are Mr. Talon. I came in here when you were sleepin' for a few days and took a couple of pictures of you. This is what I found out. Your name really is Chris Talon, you're a stage magician-"

"Ah-HA! I knew it!" Meyers blurted out, as both Crystalon and the Detective turned towards him and cast him icy gazes.

"A stage magician from Jersey who disappeared about a week ago, about the time you showed up here. My best guess is that you were mugged and then dumped over here. They probably thought you were dead. They bonked ya so hard on the head that it messed up your memories. When you came to, you wandered out into the street and got hit by that truck. Which brings us to here."

Crystalon furrowed his brow in thought, '*Were these two earths so similar that even a double of himself was present here? One who disappeared at precisely the moment he arrived?*' The vagaries of the Universe were known to him, but this was beyond anything he imagined.

"Anyways," The Detective continued, "When you're good enough to go home, we'll get you a ride to your place." Then he stopped and looked at Crystalon shaking his head side to side with his left palm facing upwards, "Does any of this sound familiar to you?"

Crystalon sighed before answering "Detective, it is as if you were describing to me the life of someone's who I have never met. None of this is even vaguely familiar."

"Well keep your chin up Chris, hopefully all this will suddenly make sense to ya soon enough."

"What does keeping my chin up have to do with anything?" Crys mused aloud after watching the detective leave the room.

"It's a sayin', ya knucklehead! Don't you know anything?" Meyers screeched from the next bed. Crystalon merely rolled his eyes in anger and made the television even louder.

***

"Something is familiar about this place," Crystalon thinks to himself. He stands upon a dark and furious plain. Wind whips the air at a frenzied pace, burned grasses stretches as far as the eye can see, over hill and dale. The scent of burned flesh, as well as wood, assails his nostrils.

Then he sees them. Blackening the dark horizon, seemingly to the periphery of the world. A massive shadow at first, then indistinct figures against the dark sky, turning it darker still. His gaze carries down to his clothes. He is wearing the hospital garment he so despised. "That is not right." He speaks aloud, snapping his fingers. His garb turns to his royal raiments. "Ah, better." Again he turns towards the distant horizon as the...things before him grow more distinct.

"I know this place." he speaks again, and then decides on a course of action. "I must get closer to those. I recognize them, but must be certain." with a thought, he is airborne. No leaping or jumping, or running start. Merely a thought. His body seemingly becomes light as a feather and he gracefully flies towards his targets in the distance. Then they suddenly shift in clarity, becoming distinct, and dangerous!

Dragons. Thousands of them. Flying wing tip to wing tip, tail to nose. Aboard them are warriors, mystics wielding swords that breath fire or lightning, or staffs that whip the very wind to a frenzied pace.

"No.," he breaths almost wordlessly as he watches them approach. "Not here, not now, not again."

He flies at them now, picking up his pace to levels beyond measure, crossing the distance between them in a nano second. Once there, he unleashes a roaring blast of pure fury, pure power that would turn an entire city to dust.

But it passes through them as if it never existed, and then they in turn pass through him, as if he were but a ghost, an immaterial phantasm beneath their notice. As if he does not matter.

"I know this place! The battle of the plain of Worlot!" he rages aloud. Turning, he followed the dragon riders, all five thousand of them to the small city of Worlot, where five hundred men stood to defend their city from the hordes of the evil Emperor Maceyis.

"Why is Maceyis described as 'Evil'?" The question burns in Crystalon's mind as he darts downwards, faster than the dragon riders, to the warriors below. Five hundred men, armed with rudimentary magic and farm implements against one hundred thousand of the emperor's best. They had no doubt to their fate, but they would fight to the last. Landing as light as a feather, Crystalon runs through the crowds of farmers turned soldiers, looking for two, make that one in particular, and then he sees him, them both.

"Papa." he speaks aloud, but no one hears him. A strong man, who bears a striking resemblance to Crystalon himself, but with harder, more deeply cut features, seemingly stares back at him. Next to him is a young boy of no more than sixteen. The boy stares sternly at the dragons beginning to descend towards them, with seemingly no fear in his eyes or his heart.

But Crystalon knows better "I was shaking inside that day, like a leaf in a winter's wind. Fear gripped me in its stone hard hand and choked the very thoughts from my body. But I stood my ground. Side by side with my father,

25

my Papa, knowing our battle here would allow the women of the city, my mother and sister among them, the time required to escape to the border region, where King Garalu's forces were forming ranks. We all knew there was no hope of survival. Not for any of us. Death was waiting mere instances away." He continues to speak aloud as the dragons slowly arc towards their position, circling once overhead in a show of power, before beginning their final run of death. "And then it happened. I remember it vividly, even though it was a thousand, thousand years ago."

He watches now as his younger self runs screaming alongside his father towards the attacking monsters, with a turn of his head and a sharp inhalation of breath, Crystalon watches as his father dies a second time before his eyes on the spear of a dragon rider, watches as his younger self grips a mystic sword dropped from the hands of one of the riders who had fallen to the thrown spear of a farmer, as suddenly his anger, his pain at his father's death triggers something within him. He had been tested for magic at a young age, and deemed to not possess more than a rudimentary affinity for it. Those who deemed him so were wrong. Very wrong.

Tears streaming down his face, a battle raging all around him, with great winged beasts spitting flame at those beneath them, Crystalon watches as his younger self grips the weapon he had just recovered, tightly in his hand and screams his anger and despair in an inarticulate curse to the heavens themselves. As he does, a cold, blue fire races first down the sword, enveloping his entire body, then up his body and back out, reaching across the sky like icy fingers of death, sweeping through the hundred thousand dragons and their riders, a wave of power and fury, unseen ever before on this world of magic. Instantly every rider, and their steeds, are disintegrated, as if they never were. And across a now barren and blasted plain only one being remains alive, the sole survivor of the battle of Worlot.

26

"I lived. I alone. Down on my knees in the dirt, exhausted and passing out from the exertion, I lived. And thus began my life anew, as leader, as ruler of this world. It took me years to cement my crown upon my head. The thought to never have another child watch their father die in battle was the driving force behind my kingship."

"Now you see how that turned out."

Crystalon turns towards the voice to see his father standing before him, spear protruding from his neck still, blood running down his chest. Crystalon draws in a sharp breath. "Papa?" he almost whispers.

"Perhaps. Or perhaps just your memory of him. You have displeased me, boy. You turned our world into a place where people feared for their lives, from you. Is that what you really wanted?"

"My people, our people were happy. They had a good life. An existence free of pain and fear of attack."

"Yes from others, but not from their king. Their ruler who ignored them, or drove them to work feverishly to create and power his mighty war machines, which in turn, brought a galaxy to its knees, and under his subjugation. To speak ill of the king was treasonous. To ask 'Why all of this?' was treasonous. You made men's own thoughts treason. While they were never killed, many were never seen again, sent to some barren world to fend for themselves. Are you happy with what that wrought?"

"The Sehr." Crystalon answers, his eyes turning black with anger.

"Yes you fool, the Sehr, and his entire race. Men who were forced off Earth eons ago, who fought and conquered their worlds, where you left them. They finally bonded together after many centuries and formed an alliance of planets, in small movements taking years to do so, so as not to draw your notice. They banded together and found a way to destroy you, to defeat and exile the Usurper. You."

27

"Amera" he speaks aloud.

"Yes, your very wife, the daughter of the Sehr. Are you proud of this? Proud knowing that these men had to plan and scheme for centuries and generations to finally overthrow your rule? One that had become far more feared then that of the evil Maceyis. Maceyis who stole their very land, and their cattle and yes, their daughters. But you stole something else. Their dignity. They had no reason to exist other than to feed your machine of power. They were naught but Cogs in a wheel."

"They had good lives." Crystalon replies angrily,

"Good lives? You turned them into slaves, for all practical purposes. They became in life what you and your advisors told them they had to be. They had no imagination or free spirit. No freedoms whatsoever. They became your playthings, and nothing more. They were well fed and nourished, yes, but their lives had little meaning beyond that which you told them they would do or become. You stole their individuality, their free will"

"Help me!" A pained voice cried out

"What was that?" Crystalon asks, his head spinning around the now expressionless white expanse he and his father suddenly stand in. There was no floor; there was no sky only white everywhere the eye could see.

"Somebody please help me!" The agonized voice beseeched again

"There it is again. What is that? It sounds like a voice of someone I know crying out in pain."

"Perhaps it is that and perhaps it is so much more, my wayward son. Perhaps it is a chance for your redemption."

And with that the world around Crystalon turns black.

Then the voice returned, weaker this time, "Help, please..."

The horrible sound remained. A sound of a soul in torment. He forced himself up. His eyes opened with a great effort as he struggled to turn his head towards the sound, fighting to turn his gaze to where the sound came from.

He had been asleep, dreaming, but this he was sure, was no dream. Through the curtain between his and Meyer's beds, he saw two glowing forms, he pushed the curtain aside, and beheld a scene as if from nightmare.

"Am I sleeping yet? Can this be?" The thoughts rang about his mind as he struggled to his feet.

Astride Meyers, who lay there with a wide eyed look of total and abject fear on his face were two ghostly white, winged monstrosities, who could best be described as demons. Neither have legs or lower bodies, only skeletal torsos and wings. One had its hand in Meyers chest, seemingly grasping his heart, while the other forced Meyers mouth wide, as a vaporous essence escaped the old man's throat, rising upwards to be sucked into the demon-things own open maw.

"Leave him!" Roared Crystalon as he threw himself at the horrific creatures crashing through them as if they were gossamer, to land in a heap besides Meyer's bed. In pain, he forced himself upwards and struck at them again, ineffectively.

Suddenly both stopped, turned towards him, then to each other and speak. Their words could best be described as water burbling mixed in with a serpent's sibilant hiss.

"This one sees us." spoke the one whose hand remained in Meyer's chest

"How can this be?" Asked the one who was sucking Meyer's soul out.

"I do not know, but I sense great power about him, or perhaps there was at one time."

"Now he seems more pathetic then dangerous. Perhaps we'll consume his soul next. It could be tasty."

29

"Get away from him, demon scum." Crystalon roared as he frantically pushed the help button for the nurse's station.

The demon with his hand in Meyer's chest laughed at him. "No one can help either of you, human. We saw to that. The door is locked with a mystic glamour, and the room is silenced with another. No one knows this is happening, and no one heard you."

Crystalon then felt something he had not felt in centuries, the same feeling of helplessness he had felt at Worlot. Anger filled his breast, and fear, an emotion he had not felt since that very day. Deep within him, something stirred, something dangerous.

Suddenly the door burst open, and a young Doctor stood silhouetted in the darkness, he ripped his shirt open and removed a pendant that glowed mightily. A beam of light shone from it upon both demons, who screamed agonized cries of horrific pain before dissolving before Crystalon's very eyes.

"That was magic." Crystalon whispered with an almost reverent sound to his voice.

The Doctor scowled and reached into his jacket, removing a syringe which he quickly plunged into Crystalon's arm in one fast movement that took the former Sorcerer by total surprise.

"You're having a nightmare, Mr. Talon. Go back to sleep."

Crys watched as the Doctor exited the room, which then turned dark all too quickly for him.

Chapter 4

Braap

"We're losing him."

"The paddles, again."

Braap

"Still no pulse."

"Adrenaline."

"Paddles again."

Braap

Crystalon immediately awoke; startled and stunned he pulled the curtain next to him open, only to have Nurse Debbie pull it back closed.

"Stay there, Chris." she spoke while not looking at him. "We're losing Mr. Meyer."

"W-what?" Crystalon stammered. "He was fine last night? What happened?"

He was ignored.

After several minutes of this a man's voice spoke. "Call it, he's gone."

"I'll inform the staff to call the next of kin," Nurse Debbie's voice answered.

Crystalon pulled the curtain aside once more and stared at Paul Meyers motionless form, with a twinge of sadness. Debbie turned to him once again.

"We did all we could for him, Chris. He must have had another heart attack during the night. Did you hear anything?"

His mind raced back to fuzzy, half remembered events that suddenly, shakily, buzzed into focus.

"I-I think I remember a sound. Of a man, of him calling out for aid, but I cannot be certain." Then he continued, "Was there a Doctor on duty last night, a young physician, with brown hair, perhaps my length? I seem to remember him in here last night."

"Dr. Walker was on duty last night, but he's gone now."

"He will return tonight?"

"He's scheduled to. Do you want to talk to him when he returns to duty?"

"Yes, Nurse Debbie, I would like that very much."

"Very well, Chris. I have to go now and arrange to have Mr. Meyers next of kin called."

"You mean his wife, Shelly."

"Yes, I suppose so." she turned and took a step towards the door then stopped and turned back towards Crystalon. "I didn't think you even liked Mr. Meyers, I'm kind of surprised that you even seem, I dunno, saddened by his passing?"

"Debbie, I have spent the better part of a week here in close quarters with the man, and as much as he prattled on about this or that, he was in truth a harmless man who seemed good natured enough, and even, dare I say it, likeable. The thought that he was going home to a woman he described to me as annoying, was somehow a comfort to me, but it was also a comfort to know that he loved someone who obviously enjoyed his company as well. So yes, to answer your surprisingly roundabout question, yes I mourn his passing. No man should have to die as he did, even the most wicked, or one who is at least thought of in that way."

"What do you mean? He died quickly, and probably in his sleep. Did something happen here we're not aware of?"

"No Debbie, I simply seem to remember hearing him thrashing about in my sleep. Perhaps I am mistaken or simply being morose." He turned and faced out the window, then continued to speak as sunshine poured through the hospital window, lighting up the rather austere room. "Please ask Dr. Walker to see me as soon as he is able, I will be awaiting his company."

Debbie turned and shut the door behind her. She walked to the nurse's station where her friend Cherise stood looking at some computer records. She immediately noticed the strange look on Debbie's face. "What is it sugar? Mr. Weird acting up again?"

"He's never acted up, Cherise. But he continues to surprise me, our mysterious Mr. Talon."

"In what way, hon?" Cherise asked while looking Debbie in the eyes.

"He just became all, oh I don't know, melancholy would be a good word for it, about poor Mr. Meyers. Something I didn't expect of him. He seems too stoic, too tough to be that way. But he seems to actually have grown to like Mr. Meyer."

"Yeah right! Like a cat likes a mouse before he eats it, you know what I'm talkin' about, how they play with them and all." Cherise answered, perhaps a bit too loud.

Debbie looked around at the surprised looks on the Doctors and Nurses who were walking through the busy hospital corridor, and smiled weakly at them before turning back to Cherise.

"No Cherise, you're wrong about that. He treated Meyers more like a, I guess like a king would treat subjects he really cared about."

"You think this guy is a king? He's from Bayonne, Sugar! Last I looked Jersey ain't had no kings."

"You're missing the point, Cherise."

"No I'm not, girl. Debbie, you're acting all weird, hanging on every word this guy says. If I didn't know better I'd think you had a schoolgirl crush on a patient. It's like he put some kinda magic spell on you."

"That's the furthest thing from the truth Cherise, and you know it. Enough of this garbage, I have to get back to my rounds." Turning curtly, Debbie walked off, more than a little angry at Cherise, and at herself.

***

In his room, Crystalon stood staring out the window, leaning on a cane he'd been given to aid his walking. He looked down at the wooden stick and angrily cast it aside, forcing himself to stand gingerly on his broken foot. He stared out the window silently, and slowly clasped his hands behind his back.

Crystalon had refused food for the day and had asked to be left alone, assuring the staff that came to see him that he was fine, and that he simply wanted to be left alone with his thoughts. After a quick exam by Dr. Singh, who could find nothing wrong with him, he was allowed his day of reflection.

But that was not what Crystalon was doing. While the death of Paul Myers was something he had not relished the thought of; he had more important matters to attend to. What had he seen last night? What were the implications of what transpired before his very eyes? He would know, or there would be hell to pay.

Hours later, with the sky speckled with starlight, a man walked into the doorway of Crystalon's room. Without turning his head, Crystalon spoke. "Enter." One word that was all.

"You must have good ears, Mr. Talon, to know I was standing there." Dr. Walker announced.

"Perhaps, Dr. Walker." Crys replied as he turned to face the man for the first time, "Or perhaps it was something more." He continued. "Close the door please, I would like none to be privy to our conversation."

Walker reached behind him and clicked the door shut slowly, and then turned back to Crystalon. "So what is it you would like to see me about, Mr. Talon?"

"I suggest we stop with the pretenses, Dr. Walker. I want you to tell me what I saw here last night."

Walker looked genuinely surprised. "I don't understand the question, Mr. Talon. What do you think you saw?"

"We are both aware of what transpired here, Walker. A man's death by nether worldly means. I believe you tried to stop that death, and in doing so at least saved the man's soul. But I want to know everything about what transpired here last night."

Walker simply shook his head, "I don't know what you are referring to, Mr. Talon. Perhaps you had a nightmare, and it has clouded your reasoning after Mr. Meyer's death."

"This was NO nightmare." Crystalon suddenly roared, loud enough and with enough force to startle Walker momentarily. "I would know, and know now, what...I...saw!"

Walker regained his composure quickly then spoke. "Mr. Talon, I assure you that-"

"Shut up, you fool." Crystalon snapped imperiously, feeling like himself for the first time in days, "You will explain everything, including this!" As he spoke he gestured with his right hand, clawing at the air, his eyes close, his brow furrowed with concentration, lips curled upwards and his teeth gnashing together noisily, when suddenly Walkers shirt began to jump, and with a snap of a chain breaking, the metal pendant he wore around his neck leapt from its hiding spot beneath his shirt and into Crystalon's hand, which he closed, claw-like around the pendant.

"How did you-" Walker began wide-eyed.

"Like yourself, Dr. Walker, I am more than I seem. This parlor trick which you just witnessed would have required nary a thought for me, mere days ago. You see Dr.

35

Walker," Crystalon said wryly, with a slight smile and a tip of his head, "I am not from around here."

"Who are you Mr. Talon, really?" Walker asked in a hushed tone.

"My name is not Mr. Chris Talon. It is actually Crystalon. I am from a different plane of existence, a different dimension, and in my universe, on my Earth, I was like unto a God. My power literally could move Heavens and Earth, but here it takes all my concentration to just move a minor mystic bauble that I spent all day attuning myself to. Before last night I believed I had lost all my mystic abilities, but upon seeing those demonic creatures killing poor Mr. Meyers, and then your subsequent use of your mystic pendant, I realized there must be magic in some form on this world."

"Attuning yourself?"

"That pendant," he tossed it back to Walker as he spoke, "has minor mystic properties throughout it. It oscillates on a mystic frequency heretofore unknown to me. But I heard its 'Voice' last night and sought it out all day. That is how I knew you were in the doorway. I felt the pendants presence the moment you entered the hospital. In this dimension I am powerless, for the moment. But that will change, I assure you. Now you will tell me of yourself, and what I saw last night."

Walker sighed resignedly, and sat himself in a metal chair in the room, then gestured for Crystalon to do the same. Both men sat facing each other for a moment; Walker sighed again, shook his head, and then began.

"There are forces in this world, of good, and of evil. There is no balance between them occurring naturally. Evil vies to destroy good. Good must counter, forcing evil back until it grows again. Mystic forces embodying all the vile, evil, and depraved alliances of this world constantly seek out those that are pure of soul and good, and seek to devour them."

36

"That is what I witnessed last night." It was a statement, not a question.

"Yes Mr. Ta-, Uhh Crystalon, that is what you witnessed. Those creatures are called Wraith Lords. They are beings that exist to devour the souls of the good and pure. They use them to power their black designs to the souls everlasting torment. The pendant in my hand is a blessed object empowering the light of the Golden Dawn. An order of which I am a knight."

"The Knights of the Golden Dawn, eh? Interesting. Go on." Crystalon nodded while stroking his goatee.

"You do understand with organizations such as mine, even its very existence is sworn to secrecy. By confiding in you, I am taking a very large risk."

With a wave of his hand Crystalon continued asking questions "What does your organization do? What is its purpose?"

"We stand against the evil, the dark, in the alleys and the boardrooms of the world. Our order has been in existence since before the time of Christ. We become aware of a demonic infiltration in an area through our own mystic means, and then we use that knowledge to save souls, and blockade the Wraith lords."

"Interesting, again. My next question is why are you divulging so much information to me? You could have lied, or you could have gleaned over the truth."

Dr. Walker paused a moment and stared out the window before speaking, Then he continued. "I was sent here not to save Mr. Meyers, Crystalon, but to watch you. We were alerted to your presence immediately when you arrived here."

"My presence? Why? Am I considered a threat by your order?"

"Not necessarily. But you are an enigma. We do not know what you are all about, or where you are from, and your latent power registered higher than anything we have ever seen before."

"How did you become assigned to this facility so quickly?"

"That is no great feat for the Knights of the Golden Dawn, Crystalon. We have agents in all walks of life."

"So what is it you want of me then, Dr. Walker?"

"Our order would like to offer you membership within the Knights of the Golden Dawn itself. This is an honor beyond measuring, and it is not so freely given."

"Ah, now I understand. You are recruiting me. How quaint. I am afraid I must refuse your offer, Dr. Walker. You see, now that I know there is magic in this world, I must begin to master it, to regain my powers and abilities, and that will take up my every waking moment."

"You're refusing us? You don't really understand what I have offered you then. To be a Knight of the Golden Dawn is practically like being blessed. You become a solemn guard against mystic evils. You could do much good in this world, Crystalon, Much good. You should really consider this more thoroughly."

"I will consider it, Doctor. But I will not join you as of now. That is my decision for the moment."

Walker looked at the floor, and then shook his head before standing and offering his hand to Crystalon. "Thank you for your time, I trust our conversation will remain between the two of us."

Crystalon took the man's hand awkwardly, not used to being touched in such a manner and shook it. "Our conversation, I assure you, was private and will remain that way. Now be gone Dr. Walker. I need rest, as I am told I will be returning to a home I've never been to tomorrow."

"Yes, you are being released, that is correct. If you need to contact me, you can here." He handed Crystalon a business card with a number etched into it, and nothing more.

The Doctor walked out the door, and Crystalon stood staring at the card in his hand, then reluctantly, but with a quickened pace, he opened the door and called for the Doctors return.

"Dr. Walker, a moment more, please." The word "Please" rolled off his tongue in an unaccustomed way. Over the centuries, he had used it less and less, and was beginning to realize that was an error in judgment.

The Doctor returned, looking at his patient quizzically. "What is it, Mr. Talon?"

"This card, what do these symbols mean? What am I to do with this?"

"You can't read?" Walker asked, surprised as he walked back into the room, and shut the door behind them both.

"Sadly, not this worlds written word. Who can assist me in learning, who can... teach me to read your...what do you call it? English?"

"I'll get you a tutor to come to your home, starting Monday." He stepped towards the exit once more then stopped and stared at Crystalon a moment.

"What is it Dr. Walker?" The Mage asked.

"You really are from a different world, a different Earth, aren't you?"

"Did you think I lied?" Crystalon answered, slightly displeased and showing it.

"Actually, I had the inkling you might be insane, and had made all that up in your delirious mind."

"But you were not sure of that." It was a statement, not a question.

"No, Mr. Talon, I was not sure. The largest reason for my belief in what you said, was this." He pulled the pendant and chain from beneath his shirt once more. "If you had not shown me what you could do, I would have simply believed you were a crackpot, one of literally hundreds who roam through Brooklyn on a daily basis. But

39

you have convinced me, totally. Oh, and those numbers on the card, you use the telephone with them." He pointed to the phone next to the bed.

"Ah, I saw Mr. Meyers use that on several occasions. Now I understand. You enter the corresponding hieroglyph from the card into the phones depressible nodes."

"We call them buttons Chris, buttons."

"Very well. Buttons. Now I will take my rest, thank you for answering my rather inane questions."

"Your questions are not inane at all, rather you are a stranger in a strange land. Think about what I offered you, Crystalon. It wouldn't hurt you to have friends here." And with that he was gone, leaving the former master mage with naught but his own thoughts.

Chapter 5

The morning came all too quickly for Crystalon. His night had been spent tossing and turning for one final time in the hospital bed. Thoughts of his former home, and how things had been for him for a millennia, bombarded his sleeping mind all through the night with the uncertainty of the forthcoming day's events figuring prominently in his thoughts.

He awoke in the hospital for the final time at 7:25, perhaps a half-hour plus before he had actually wanted to awaken. He got out of bed and stepped towards the closet where his torn and tattered sorcerers garb had been stored, but when he opened it he found his favored uniform, plus a package addressed to him. He opened it and found a change of clothes, a pair of blue jeans and a short sleeved button down shirt inside, in a slight off-yellow color. There was a note attached: "*Mr. Talon, this is just a gift to you from the girls on the floor, you've been intriguing to say the least, but we've all enjoyed talking to you, and found you quite charming, We hope everything fits, and we hope you make it back to your home safely, wherever that may be. May your memories return to you faster than you had hoped, good luck, Nurse Debbie and the staff.*"

"Incredible." he thought, "They actually seemed to have grown affectionate towards me. If only they had seen me a few weeks past. The affection would surely have turned to hatred. But no matter. A new life beckoned for me, so be it. Whatever the future may hold for me, it is my destiny to take command of my life and steer it where I want it to be."

He showered and dressed silently, then had a quiet breakfast alone as he placed his sorcerers garb into the box the new clothing had come in, as he did there was a knock at his open door. He turned his head and saw the police officer that had visited him earlier along with another man who, for some reason, was vaguely familiar to him.

"Detective O'Malley, good day sir." Crystalon began. "What can I do for you today?"

"Hello Mr. Talon, I got someone here who wants to talk to you. Go ahead Carboneri." He addresses the man standing next to him.

The man scowled at the Detective, and then turned towards Crystalon. "My name is Joe Carboneri, you may or may not remember me, but I was the guy who almost ran you over that day you dropped outta the sky."

The Detective immediately interrupted him "Hey! How many times do I have to tell you to stop that cock and bull story?"

"It ain't bull O'Malley, and Mr. Talon here knows it, too."

Crystalon said nothing but merely folded his arms across his chest and stared with a glint of anger at Carboneri.

"Anyways," Joe Carboneri continued, "I just wanted to say I'm sorry for what happened, and I want ta offer ya a ride home."

Once more, the populace of this world astounded the sorcerer. This man had no reason to come to him, it was clearly a mistake, or an act of the Gods that he had dropped to this world in that vehicles path, but being a man of the mystic ways he knew nothing happened unless there was a purpose for it, a reason for it to have happened.

"Mr. Carboneri, I will gladly take your offer of a ride home, now if I knew where I lived that would be another matter entirely."

O'Malley stepped forward and digs a crumpled piece of paper out of his pocket, "That's where I come in, Talon. Here's your address. Carboneri will drive you home, and you should be all set."

Crystalon shook each man's hand in turn, with the detective handing him a business card with his name and the number to his desk in his precinct house.

"If you need to discuss anything about your case with me, feel free to contact me. Otherwise I'll consider this case closed."

"Indeed, Detective, closed it is to myself as well. Thank you for your time and effort on my behalf."

"All part o' the job, Mr. Talon. Take care and good luck gettin' your noggin squared away." O'Malley tapped his own head as he spoke.

Shaking hands one last time all around, the detective left whistling a happy tune. Crys and Joe Carboneri watched as the man entered the elevator at the end of the hall and disappeared through its doors, then turned back towards each other.

"Why do you wish to help me, Mr. Carboneri?" Crystalon asked.

"Uh, cause I feel bad I ran ya over, even though it ain't my fault, but no one believes me when I tell 'em all you fell outta the sky like some kinda goofy superhero who fergot how ta fly."

"I assure you my good man, I am not a 'Superhero'. I am just a man who was in the wrong place at the wrong time. Be that as it may I have decided to take you up on your generous offer of a ride home. I assume the Detective gave you my proper address as well?"

"Uh yeah, Mr. Talon, he did."

"Very well, Let us leave then."

The two men walked out of the room, past the nurse's station where Crystalon glanced around looking for Nurse Debbie, who was nowhere to be seen. Furrowing his brow he continued on. He did not recognize any of the women on duty, but thought nothing of it, as he walked toward the elevator. He hesitated a second before entering.

"Wassamatter Mr. Talon? It's just an elevator."

"Perhaps to you, Joseph Carboneri. To me it is an unknown device. Something I have never seen before recently, much less entrusted my life to."

"You are one weird dude, Mr. Talon. I gotta tell ya."

"So I have been told, but remember Joseph, I have no memory of anything beyond a scant few days ago," he lied. "So in a very real sense, everything here is new to me." That part was the truth, and even though he hated lying to this man, Crystalon knew no one should know the truth save those already 'in the know' about such things, such as Dr. Walker.

The two men walked silently out of the hospital, the medical insurance of this worlds Chris Talon having already paid the bill for Crystalon's stay.

They exited into the hustling, bustling Brooklyn streets. Crystalon stopped for a moment and just absorbed it all. Buildings taller then anything he ever had seen sprawl in the distance. Flying machines he had seen spoken of on the picture box called a 'television' carrying hundreds of souls in their rail-like stomachs flew overhead. So called 'cars' streamed past him one after another at a dizzying rate through the street. Simply put, he was overwhelmed.

"This way Mr. Talon." Joe Carboneri implored as he guided Crystalon towards his car.

Crystalon looked at the vehicle parked in the spot that they walked to. "Why is this vehicle so...shabby?" The car was a mess. Rot covered both doors, the paint was faded a dull blue, and the fabric on the inside of the roof was falling down inside.

"She don't look like much Mr. Talon, but she runs great, hop in."

Wrinkling his nose in anticipation, Crystalon entered the vehicle and sat down, surprised at the lack of odor he was expecting.

"Buckle yerself in there, Mr. Talon." Carboneri advised.

"What? What are you referring to?" Crystalon had no idea what the man was talking about.

Joe Carboneri held his hands up in a 'wait a minute' gesture, and showed Crystalon how he buckled himself in.

"You think you can do that? Or you want me to do it for you?" the rumpled man asked.

Crystalon grimaced a moment then began grabbing the seat belt and rummaging around with its end until finally, after looking at Carboneri's own belt and where it attached, he clicked the two sections together.

"Okay Mr. Talon, are you ready now?" Carboneri asked.

"I suppose I am Mr. Carboneri, proceed."

Joe Carboneri turned the key the car started with a cough; he nodded with a smile towards Crystalon, who merely turned his head towards the window, rolling his eyes in the process. The car backed out of the space under Carboneri's control and off they went.

Soon they were crossing the Verrazano-Narrows Bridge, into Staten Island, and Crystalon was awed. "Men built this bridge?" he asked Carboneri while slowly looking around at the skyline of New York City. "With their hands?"

"Well, who else? If men didn't build this it's not gonna just appear from thin air, like magic."

Crystalon considered his answer slowly then merely nodded his head in understanding. He was not home. This was not his home, his land, nor his world. Not even his universe. He was a mortal man here. Unremarkable from anyone else. Had his own selfishness and shortsightedness really driven those around him to hate him so? Even now he could not believe it, after everything that had happened to him. But it must be true.

The rest of the ride continued in silent thought for the former arch mage. He barely noticed all of the new sights as they passed by his window.

After a seemingly interminable amount of time, the car pulled into the driveway of a modest home, in a modest community. Trees line both sides of the street; the old houses were all two stories tall on either side of the street. Children played on bicycles and the sounds of birds chirping occasionally filled the air. *'When was the last time I listened to birds sing?'* Crystalon thought to himself.

Carboneri, exited his side of the car, and walked around to Crystalon's. The sorcerer's leg was still not healed, but the bone had been fractured in such a way that it could not be put into a cast. So he walked with a slight limp for now, relying on a cane provided by the hospital.

"Here, O'Malley gave me these. Said they were yours. He musta had them made up for you, 'cause they look new." He handed Crystalon a key set, which the wizard stared at quizzically. Impatiently Carboneri took them back out of Crystalon's hand and showed him how the door opened.

"All yours, Mr. Talon." He said, swinging the door wide open, and the wizard walked inside. The dark wood of the place was surprisingly homey to him. It was something he had always liked, at least in his younger years. Now it seemed to be something he merely had forgotten. Wood floors and carpeting intermingled in the modest, old home. Breathing deeply of the stale air, he started walking around the long closed house.

"How do I open these windows?" He asked Carboneri.

"I dunno, let's look," the smaller man answered him.

Together they figure out how to open the latches and within minutes several windows are open, airing out the closed up house, allowing fresh air to permeate it's musty, enclosed confines.

"All right Mr. Carboneri, you may go now. I...thank you for your time."

"Yeah it's okay Mr. Talon, an' if you need anything feel free to call me." He handed Crys a crumpled wad of paper with his phone number scrawled across it.

"Thank you Joseph, now please go, I need time to meditate on my position, and condition."

"Okay Mr. Talon, take it easy." And with that Carboneri was gone. Entering his car and driving away.

Crystalon shut his door, looked around and then called out. "You may show yourself now."

The sound of slow handclapping was his reply from a room he had not entered yet. He made his way towards it, purposely taking his time as he walked. He pushed the dark wooden door open and entered a study. Again all in dark wooden tones. A high-backed, black leather desk chair was turned so the back of it faced him. As he entered the room the chair slowly turned towards him. A man was seated in the chair. Thin, almost gaunt, wearing a pinstriped dark gray suit, with a black rose pinned to his left lapel. His slicked back black hair was neat and tidy. His thin mustache, barely a wisp on his upper lip, and the gray of his suit matched his eyes. An air of...evil permeated his very essence, chilling Crystalon to the bone.

'*Is this what others thought of me?*' The Sorcerer thought to himself.

"Who are you and what do you want in my home?" Crys intoned dramatically, "And be quick about it." He added with more than a hint of venom in his voice.

"You may call me Monsieur Épine-noire." was the man's reply, in a voice like honey and arsenic combined.

Light streamed through the half-closed blinds into the room from outside, casting shadows and columns of sun light between the two men. Crystalon paused only an instant before speaking.

"What do you want, Mr. Black Thorn?"

"Ah you know your French, Monsieur Talon."

"I am fluent in over two hundred languages, some not even spoken on this planet. Now again I ask, what do you want here?"

Epine-Noir was taken aback momentarily by Crystalon's reply, he knew that Crystalon had answered truthfully concerning the two hundred plus languages, but more importantly he was concerned with the latter part of his answer. The '*some not even spoken on this planet*' part.

He continued "I have come to make an offer to you. My associates would very much like to meet with you and discuss options and possibilities for you in this brave new world you find yourself in. You will be paid handsomely, and your every need will be taken care of, forever. We will help you reclaim your lost power, and then some. You will be treated like a prince, and all will bow before you in time."

"I have been a king. A mere prince-ship is of no interest to me. Entire civilizations bowed before me, on over fifty worlds, across the known universe. You have nothing to offer me. But it is what you want of me that you are not saying. You represent those soul thieves, the Wraith Lords who killed Paul Meyers. Word of what I might be capable of has returned to you by some arcane means, and make no mistake of it Monsieur Epine-Noire, the stink of dark forces is all about you. I sensed your presence the moment I entered this home. I knew you did not belong here. You seek to make use of my now nascent abilities for your side of this eternal battle. You believe that when my powers return I will turn the tide from one side to the other, or obliterate the losing side entirely. You have no idea who you are dealing with, Epine-Noir. Now be gone from my home, and do not return."

Epine-Noir sprang from the desk chair he was seated in, closing his right hand slowly in a fist, and raising it high in the air. Instantly Crystalon was grasped by invisible fingers around his throat, and flung towards the ceiling, his face smashing into it brutally, and held there by hands of invisible magic.

Then the gray suited man spoke, "You know not who you speak to in such a manner, fool. I sense you once had great power about you, perhaps greater than any being in this world has ever wielded.

"But that was on your world, on this one you are a powerless, weak mortal like all the rest. I offer you a chance to redeem your power, to rise again above the rabble, and you refuse me? Again, I offer this to you. If you are indeed as intelligent as you seem you will not refuse me twice. I will be in touch."

He left the room, with Crystalon still pinned to the ceiling by an invisible hand. Agonizing moments pass, Crys considering if he'll ever get down from where he was, as blood from some facial wound ran down his cheek, and then finally he was released, dropping to the floor like dead weight.

Breathing heavily, Crystalon lay still for many moments, anger and frustration welling up within him. Pain echoed across his face in steady throbs as he realized his nose must be broken, for that was where the blood was coming from. After several more minutes he raised himself up from the floor, and was about to seat himself in the leather chair when he looked at it. The leather was rotting before his eyes, as if acid were poured upon it, all accomplished by Epine-Noir's foul touch. Grasping it by the top of the chairs back, the part so far untouched by the vile rot, he dragged it quickly out of his house and with an angry grunt heaved it to the lawn like a madman. Neighbors stopped what they were doing and looked on, stunned at his display.

49

He looked at them, sliding his head from side to side with anger, frustration and more then a little indignation running through his blood, and walked back inside, slamming the door behind him.

Now he must plan...

Chapter 6

Crystalon sat at the desk in the small study, a new leather desk chair beneath him. Next to him was Joe Carboneri, who was showing him how to use the computer that sat atop the desk. Or rather, Joe's ten-year-old son was. "And you push this button on the right side of the mouse to bring up menus"

"Menus, yes. Got it." Crystalon mumbled while deep in thought, fascinated by what the young boy was showing him. It was two days later, Monday morning to be exact. The Mage was getting his first computer lesson, because he had seen a commercial on the television for a home study course that explained this seemingly magic box. When he called Carboneri about it, the man explained that anything the course could show Crys, his son could explain better. Reluctantly, Crys agreed to the boy demonstrating what he knew about the computer.

So far, the former sorcerer was more than impressed. The boy was opening doors for him.

He knew he was very far away from regaining his power, but every tool he acquired made the job that much easier. He knew in his heart that this tool was going to aid him mightily.

"Joey," Crystalon began speaking to Joe's son, Joe Jr. as it were; "can you show me magical places? Can you use this wondrous machine to show me the places where magic takes place?"

The boy beams. "Sure Mr. Talon. I'll just type in 'Magic' and we'll see where it takes us." His black hair was cut short and tosseled in that way all little boys get by midday, otherwise he looked very much like his father.

"Here ya go Mr. Talon." The boy smiled excitedly as he spoke, "Stuff about David Copperfield, an' Houdini, an' a buncha others too."

"Yes, yes, very interesting indeed young Joseph, but what about places I've heard of like this 'Stonehenge'? Are there many more like that?"

"Uh I don't know Mr. Talon. I never looked up stuff like that before. I mean I could, sure. Let's see what we can find."

Within minutes they had thousands of search results, literally ninety thousand plus to sort through. Crystalon stroked his chin as he thought. "How do we, what is the word for it? Pare them down? To something more manageable, perhaps?"

"You mean maybe filterin' them Mr. Talon?" The enthusiastic boy answered.

"Yes, yes Joey. That is indeed what I mean. Now filter these by, say, using the words 'sorcery', and perhaps 'witchcraft' anything like that."

Joe senior shot Crys a look, obviously he did not like his son getting involved in anything like this, at least where this seems to be pointing. Crys returned the glance, then nodded and smiled, trying to ease the man's tensions.

"Joey, understand that I am trying to research these...historical occurrences to refresh my memory of all I have lost, for my magic act. Nothing more."

"That's cool Mr. Talon. I know there's no such thing as real magic."

Joe nodded to Crys behind the child's back and smiled.

"Okay Mr. Talon, I got it down to about a thousand pages an' websites now. All boring, historical stuff."

"Excellent Joey, most excellent. I thank you both for your time." Then added silently within the confines of his own thoughts *'If only I knew how to read them.'*

"Naaah, my pleasure Mr. Talon. If there's anything else you need ta help ya get yer memory back, let me know." Joe senior replied.

"Joey, please leave your father and I alone a moment I have something to discuss with him in private. The television is in the living room. Go and watch whatever you would like for a moment."

The boy smiled, nodded and turned the Yankee cap atop his head backwards with the brim facing his neck and ran off.

"What'd you want ta ask me Mr. Talon?"

"Joseph, how much money do I have?"

"Uhh, you don't know?"

"I haven't the faintest clue. I noticed an, what did your son call these? An 'Icon'? On my computer screen for a, a bank account I believe it is referred to."

"Oh, uh yeah Mr. Talon hang on, I can help ya with that." Joe seated himself in the desk chair and started to click on the screen and type numbers; a moment later the screen they were looking for popped up. "Hey, ya had some kinda password manager in here that had your stuff all stored. Good thing too, cause I'm sure ya didn't remember that."

"Undoubtedly, Joseph. So what does it show?"

Suddenly Joe stopped short and rubbed his eyes, then looked again. Slowly he turned towards Crystalon before speaking. "Uh, you sure all you did was magic acts at kid's parties? Cause if that's the truth, you gotta get me a gig like that."

"What? Why? What did you discover?"

"Mr. Talon. You're rich. I mean, like not comfortable, I mean like filthy stinkin' loaded.'

"How much in monetary terms?"

"Like a hundred million bucks in your bank account. An' this ain't no regular bank account either, it's some bank on the Cayman Islands."

"I do not understand. Are you saying I have an inordinately large sum of money?"

"Yer freakin' loaded." Joe's reply came in a hushed tone; nervously looking around and making sure his son did not hear.

"But how?" was Crys's stunned answer.

"Yer askin' me?"

Crystalon shook off the shock and sat for a moment, steepling his fingers in thought. Joe was in his desk chair, and he himself was sitting on a folding chair they had found in the basement.

"Joseph, how much... money do you make per year?" He asked quietly.

"Me? Drivin'? If I put in some good OT I end up okay, like fifty five thousand a year or so. Why?"

"OT? What is that?"

"Overtime. Like I work more then normal hours. A few extra hours a day, maybe an extra day a week. Stuff like that. Why are ya askin'?"

Crys sat there a moment longer in thought before answering.

"Joseph, I need someone to be my man in the street, someone who knows his way around this strange New World I find myself in. Someone who can help me understand the way of this world, as you and your son did today here," he motioned at the computer as he spoke. "How would you like to come to work for me? I will make you a very wealthy man. You in turn will be my right hand. If I require you to travel with me you shall."

Joe sat there stunned. He was wearing a navy blue T-Shirt and a pair of faded blue jeans; a Yankee cap similar to his sons, just older and more faded, sat atop his head. "How much you offerin' me, Mr. Talon?"

"A one-time payment of, hhhmm what is adequate? Does five million dollars sound about right for a year's worth of your time?"

"A year? Hell yeah!" the man shouted then hushed himself as he looked around the corner and through the doorway towards where his son sat and watched the television.

"Good then it is settled. Now I require a car to begin with. It seems the one you drive has seen its better days. Go and pick one out for me. A car that is shiny and large. Comfortable, yet not to ostentatious. I do not want to draw undo attention. Now return here on Wednesday and we shall begin our work."

Okay, uh, thanks I think, Mr. Talon. I'm like flabbergasted. I really don't know what ta say to ya about this. Ya really stunned me here. Thanks again. Now I gotta break this to the Mrs. Wow, me a millionaire. Who woulda thunk it? C'mon Joey time ta go" The man called to his son as he walked through Crys's home towards the door. The small boy jumped up and ran to his father's side, noticing his father's now jaunty step.

"What's up daddy?" the boy asked.

"Not much kid, just the chance of a lifetime. C'mon, I gotta go talk to ya ma."

"G'bye Mr. Talon." the boy called as they leave the house.

Crystalon smiled, it was somewhat forced, but not entirely so. The boy and his father had been a great help so far. In fact they were probably the best things to have happened to him in this strange New World since he arrived here. But one thing bothered the former arch mage. It was this money thing, in his 'account'. He did not even know what an account is. The way it was described to him it sounds like a repository for one's wealth. In his world, one's wealth is kept in one's home. The penalty for robbery is banishment to the outer worlds. Worlds which spawned such beings as the Sehr and his ilk. A red-hot flash of anger overcame Crystalon at this moment, flooding him with hatred for what the Sehr and those around him had done to

Crystalon, and his life. Angrily he slammed the bottom of his fist down on the desk, sending items on it, including a cup of coffee, flying. He rose from his seat and entered his kitchen for paper towels to clean up the mess when the doorbell rang.

"Oh, who is this now?" he grumbled angrily as he dropped the roll of paper towels and angrily made his way to his front door.

"Yes? What is it?" He began vehemently as he threw the door open, and then stopped short, his heart suddenly stopping its movement in his chest as he looked on in utter disbelief and shock.

"Amera?" he almost whispered.

Before him stood his wife.

It was her, of that he had no doubt. Her beauty was exactly as he remembered it, how could he forget? That fateful day in his palace he etched her memory into his mind's eye for all eternity as he was being roughly pushed into that portal. She had changed her hair color, it was now a light brown as opposed to the color of the sun on a summer morning, and the style was new, but it was her, he was sure of it.

"Amera!" He shouted as he hugged the woman passionately.

"Hey! What are you doing? Back off Mister!" was her reply as she shoved him away.

"What?" He took a step back, shocked by her reaction. It was as if she had never seen him before in her life.

"My name's not 'Amera' Mr. Talon, It's Amanda. I was sent here at Dr. Walker's request. He said you needed help with your reading. But if you're some kind of pervert, or other freak, this tutoring will end right here and now."

Crystalon was taken aback momentarily. He knew this was his wife, his Amera. Yet it so obviously was not, as well. He was stunned, and for the first time in centuries was at a loss. He truly did not know what to do.

And then the ruler, the sorcerer of old took over. He merely straightened himself up and smiled in a slightly imperious, almost condescending way, and then spoke. "I apologize. I merely mistook you for a long lost friend, who you bare an uncanny resemblance to. Most uncanny, actually. Please accept my...apologies." The word dripped over his tongue like poison, but he continued. "I did not mean to upset you in any way. You look so much like someone I used to be very close to. Again my apologies."

"Well I guess that could happen to anyone." She fidgeted, and tossed her hair with her right hand as she spoke nervously. You seem like you're okay, but I'm going to warn you now, people know where I am, so if anything happens to me, they're going to know who to look for." as she spoke she pointed her finger at him. All the body language, all the speech patterns, everything screamed at him, *'Amera'*.

But this was not her. This was this world's version of her. Of the woman who stole his heart, and made him feel more alive than any he had ever met. The woman he loved more than life itself.

The woman who had betrayed him.

And now she was going to become his tutor, and teach him how to read this worlds language. It was almost laughable; the cruel tricks fate was playing upon him.

"Please, excuse my rather inappropriate greeting, and accept my sincerest apology. I need your help, as I'm sure Dr. Walker told you, I recently suffered a traumatic event, and lost most of my memory, including little things like how to read the English language. This is what I require your help with."

"Well all right Mr. Talon, let's give it a shot."

"Please enter." He held the door wide for her and stepped back, his left arm held open in a welcoming gesture.

She entered and walked past him looking around at the dark wood and warm surroundings.

As she walked in front of him she leaned over and picked up the roll of paper towel Crystalon had dropped on his way to the door.

"You drop something?"

"The coffee." He replied, not really to her, but just as a statement, twisting his mouth in anger as he walked past her to the den, where she followed, still holding the paper towel roll.

"Oh man, what a mess." She uttered as she knelt down and pulled paper towel from the roll, soaking up the spilled coffee with it.

"Again, I apologize Amanda. You caught me at an awkward moment."

"I can see that Mr. Talon." She answered as she was down on the floor now, cleaning up the coffee spill with him, handing him sheets of paper.

"Please, call me" he hesitated, because he was beginning to grudgingly accept the name, but hated it as well for that acceptance. "Chris."

"Very well Mr. Talon, or Chris whatever you prefer is fine. Let's get started, shall we?"

Crystalon, mistakenly called Chris Talon here on this Earth, which was not his own, was hesitant, so much was happening to him so very fast. But he was used to rolling with the punches of life, especially lately. He smiled and moved them both towards the leather couch in his den. Between them was a coffee table where she opened several books. Then looked up at him before speaking. "Okay, let's start with the alphabet."

Thus began the re-education of Crystalon.

Chapter 7

The first education of Crystalon began a million years ago, back before man on this Earth was crawling out of the trees, and trying to walk upright, Crystalon's Earth boasted a thriving medieval civilization. The difference could be summed up in one word. Magic.

Magic was prevalent on Crystalon's Earth, it was real, it was powerful, and most of the citizenry was able to practice it in one form or another. When the young boy devastated the opposing armies of his kingdom in one small moment, while everyone was surprised by the sheer power he possessed, no one was surprised by the deed itself.

Magic was an everyday tool, in use by just about everyone on his Earth.

So it came to pass that a sixteen-year-old, near man was brought before the lord of his land as well as that lord's sorcerers.

"So boy," The Lord spoke, "You struck down over one hundred thousand of Maceyis's soldiers in one moment. Something no one would imagine was possible. How do you account for this?"

"I do not know my Lord," was Crystalon's only answer.

"Are you possessed by some malevolent spirit as some have said?" The Lord continued, "Or perhaps you have aligned yourself with dark Gods, who have given you the power to do this thing? What is it boy? We will know for sure when this day is done." The Lord assured Crystalon as he leaned forward on his throne, surrounded by fineries from other lands as well as his own, with the men of his court scowling towards the boy-man.

Crystalon looked up; his young, clean-shaven face wore a furrowed brow as he stared back into the lord's eyes. For the first time, Crystalon's haughty nature was about to be seen. He had had enough of the poking and the posturing. Five days ago his father had died before his eyes and his rage had exploded within him, like unto a thunderclap that shook the Earth for miles around, like unto a volcano that spewed hot, poisonous, molten death everywhere, so had his rage enacted. And now he felt that rage building again.

And then he spoke.

"Lord of the Land, know ye this." Crystalon spoke imperiously, for he was not an uneducated fool, but a learned student who preferred knowledge over roughhouse play, "Five days ago my father perished before my eyes, killed by a madman whose greed knows no bounds. No sorcerous or Godly entity or force did this deed. I did. Simply put, great sir. I did. I watched as men died around me, and I knew we were all doomed. Everyone here would be dead or incarcerated this very moment if not for me. Yourself included."

The Lord bristled at this, stirring in his throne and shifting from one side to the other as his viziers and counselors all shifted uneasily where they stood, lining the throne room at the boy's haughty proclamation.

"If not for my actions, this land would be the villain Maceyis' now , and you all would be in chains or dead. For five long, agonizing days, you and your men have studied me as if I were some strange farm animal brought in for the first time for study. I say to you good Lord, enough. I have had enough of the poking and the prodding and the tests. My father is dead, yet I was not given the chance to mourn." He spoke in a wise voice seemingly beyond his years, "While you have sat here drinking your wine and eating your fine meals, I, the savior of this land, have been remanded to a veritable prison. No more my Lord. I am no demon; I am no evil God. I am a man who has had enough. I do not know how I destroyed those dragon riders that day,

60

but I know I did. Maceyis will not soon recover from that defeat, as your own advisors have told you. Now the time has come for me to be allowed to mourn."

He stood silently staring at the Lord of the Land, his mind set, his young eyes meeting the Lord's head on, locked together with his in some unknowable grip. A grip the youth controlled by sheer force of his own impenetrable, indomitable will.

Finally the Lord spoke. "Here is my decree. You will be given seven days to mourn your loss, after that time you will return here, to begin your education as a sorcerer. This will not be easy for you, but your rewards will be great. You are older than any who have started the training, by some twelve years. Never in our history has a man-child been inducted into the sorcerous ranks at such a late age. Twenty years you will toil, and at that time you will be able to join your brethren here, as one among the few, the mystical guardians of this land."

Four years after Crystalon began his studies he had surpassed even his instructor's aptitude. The student became the teacher. Fifteen years later, he had stopped the aging process in his own body, turning himself immortal, a feat never before accomplished.

But his thirst for knowledge was not satisfied. Soon he was forcibly stepping through dimensions to other worlds, other planes of existence that others only theorized existed, but never could access. Yet he did. And he learned. Learned all that these other realms had to offer, and more. Year after year he spent in strict study, learning the magic of a thousand different worlds and realities. On his world, kingdoms faded and new ones were born. The Lord of the Land faded to dust, to be replaced by his descendants.

Yet still Maceyis lived on, his life extended through mystical means, as was Crystalon's. In the time after Crystalon had discovered the secret of extending his existence indefinitely, the secret was somehow stolen by

Maceyis' spies and, where Crystalon himself administered the spell to himself and was unharmed at its passing, it took well over a dozen of the best sorcerers Maceyis had available to create the magic and to make it work on their king.

But there was a price to be paid this time. Whereas Crystalon's will controlled the spell, his sheer magical might holding the forces of nature in check, all twelve of these men who performed the spell for Maceyis died instantly, horribly immolated on the spot, burned to death with a scream on their lips that was never uttered.

But they succeeded; Maceyis lived now, as eternally as Crystalon. And for a time, all was silent between the Emperor Maceyis' domain and the Lord of the Lands own far more humanely run kingdom. Years passed, and Maceyis merely sneered at the man who defeated his entire army in one moment, afraid of Crystalon, but hating him with every fiber of his being at the same time.

And so it went for decades, until one day exactly one hundred years after the Battle of Worlot, when it all changed.

Crystalon now lived in a manor. Almost as large as the Lord's. At this point in his life, castles and riches were meaningless. Knowledge and mystical power was all that mattered. His daily routine was spent in intensive study. His mind was a sponge, his thirst for knowledge of the mystic ways was an unabated hunger, one he sought to satiate every moment he could. He was at his oaken table in the dark wooden hall, light shining through glass panes above, reading an old manuscript that had recently come into his possession, when a servant interrupted him.

"Master, there is a courier at the door. He bears a package for you and will only turn it over to you."

"What nonsense is this Zerfam?"

"I do not know sir. He said he has been riding for days and the courier who he received it from said only that you were the only person who was to take possession of it. He seems agitated."

Crystalon turned his head to the side and snorted angrily, slapping the old parchment on to the table before him as he stood angrily.

"Very well, let me be done with this foolishness."

He followed Zerfam out through the hall, to his main entrance. The eleven-foot tall double oak doors were swung wide at his approach, revealing a horseman, filthy with road dirt and debris. Mud caked in spots, his hair brown with road dust as well.

"Gods, man. What happened to you?" Crystalon intoned, surprised at the man's condition. "Zerfam, get the man some cool water."

"T-thank you my lord." Was the man's surprised reaction. He stood about six feet tall, and was wiry to a fault, looking gaunt in the morning sun streaming through the trees in the manor's front yard.

"Well? What do you have for me, rider?" Crys pressed on with impatience and wanting to continue with what he was doing.

"O-oh yes m'lord. Here. This is for you. I rode hard and fast the past several days to get it to you. The rider who entrusted it to me was told it must be in your care today, no matter what. I did my best to get it to you in due time, m'lord."

"Yes, yes you did. Now drink your water and be gone."

The man was momentarily taken aback by Crystalon's dismissal.

"M'lord, an additional wage of some type is customary when one goes out of ones way for another."

"A tip? You mean? You require me to tip you? I already have, rider." Crys nodded towards the fresh wineskin filled with water that Zerfam handed the man an instant before.

"Water? That is all you have for me? I am bone-tired, and rode as if my life depended on it for you, to bring you your package in the allotted time, and this is all I get for my troubles?"

"Do not be so quick to dismiss that skin of water. I demand you drink of it now." Crys spoke sternly.

The rider stared at him with a slight tilt of his head and a narrowing of his eyes as he took a long drink from its contents. Suddenly the man's entire demeanor changed, a smile broke out broadly across his face as he stared at Crystalon in shock and delight.

"W-what is in here m'lord? I have never felt so good in m'life. What magical elixir is this bag holdin'?"

"That bag contains the water of Elueceus. It will revitalize you in every way with each long drink you take of it. You will be as fresh and as strong, as vital as you were on the best day of your life."

"M-m'lord, please tell me, how can I get more o' this water? I-I never want to drink anything else again."

Crystalon smiled a thin-lipped knowing smile and nodded to the wineskin in the man's hand. "Drain its contents now, do as you are commanded, do not question me."

The man nodded in the affirmative so quickly his face seemed to almost blur in anticipation. He placed the water skin to his lips and drained it dry. When the skin was empty, he held it up towards Crystalon, seeking more.

"Now watch." Was Crystalon's reply.

As the three men stood at the door, the wineskin suddenly inflated itself, refilling with the magical water as if from thin air. The man was shocked, his eyes wide, he drank more from it, with the same desired result.

"T-this is a miracle! You mean I'll have this forever?"

"Only as long as you never divulge where you received it from to anyone else. I think you should consider

64

never talking of this to anyone. You now have a rather unfair advantage to all your compatriots in the courier business. Now you can never tire, will require shorter rest periods, and can go far further in a day then they can. I also highly recommend you pour a little of that water into your horse's water as well. Do not let him drink from public horse watering sources. Add some of that to his drinking water, and he will go further as well."

"T-thank you m'lord, thank you!" The man bowed and shook Crystalon's hand whole-heartedly as he quickly ran back to his waiting horse, a tired old stallion he had flogged for too long and too far. A few scant moments later the horse thundered out of the manor grounds like a young thoroughbred, having drank of the magic water.

Zerfam closed the manor doors, then walking beside his master he spoke. "Will you require anything else of me at the moment, master?"

"No Zerfam, go back to your duties. I will open this in my study."

The two men parted, and Crystalon reentered his study, sitting down at the huge oaken table, the high backed wood and leather chair pressed against him as he cut through the roughhewn cord, which had been wrapped tightly around the package. The thick paper that had enwrapped the object fell away easily, revealing one object and a note inside. The object looked familiar to Crystalon, but he could not place where he had seen it. It was a woman's pendant. He laid the pendant warily on his table, and picked up the note, Only a few words were scrawled across it, but they froze his heart.

"*I have her, and have for one hundred years. Today, the anniversary of the Battle of Worlot, she dies.*" And scrawled at the bottom of the note was a large stylized "*M*".

"Maceyis" he spoke aloud, and then he remembered where he had seen the pendant, why it was so familiar.

"Mother," he spoke aloud again in a hushed voice.

Chapter 8

Crystalon flew, literally, to the Lord of the Lands manor, touching down lightly on the steps of the lord's home. He was immediately met by two armed guards, brandishing swords and pikes, with a wave of his hand he dismissed them, summoning a powerful wind that blew them both to opposite sides of the manors well-kept grasses.

Waving his hand yet again, the huge oaken doors swung wide for him as he wrapped himself within his cloak, and then continued forward.

Again he waved his hand and a second set of twenty-foot tall doors opened on their own. Within this chamber, the throne room, the current Lord of the Land stood immediately, anger furrowing his brow as he saw Crystalon.

"How dare you enter my home in such a manner! I should have you flogged for such an effrontery!"

"Stop your pompous grandstanding, Lord Izzulus. My needs are most urgent and I must speak to you now, alone." Crystalon replied.

Izzulus stared at him a moment then settled back into his throne, with a wave he dismissed everyone else in the room, including his guards. They all left quickly. Once they were gone Crystalon waved his hand again closing the double doors once more, and barring them mystically.

"What is it you want Crystalon?" Izzulus asked. He was a young man, perhaps thirty, with neat, long brown hair. He was of average build, and wore fine raiments. The typical, lazy monarch in training. His father's father was a warrior who wrested the throne from the previous ruling family, who were related to Maceyis. Thus the battle a century earlier. His own father also was a proud, strong ruler following in his own father's footsteps. But Izzulus

67

was a softer man, too used to everything being given to him, and not requiring him to fight for anything.

Crystalon sighed while looking at the monarch before speaking. "I am going to war with Maceyis."

"WHAT? YOU are going to war? You are not the ruler here, my friend. Need I remind you who is?"

"You do not understand, he has my mother." As he spoke he pulled the pendant from the confines of his night dark cloak.

"What is this?" Izzulus asked as he looked at the object Crystalon handed to him.

"It is a pendant I gave my mother over a hundred years ago. Maceyis sent it to me this morning with this note."

"As your courts royal sorcerer, I am informing you that I am going to be attacking Maceyis' realm shortly to free my mother. I am asking you to do nothing, merely stay clear of what I am about to do."

"We have been at peace with Maceyis for a hundred years. You cannot attack him."

"I can and I will. If he is holding my mother captive."

"It is obviously a trap. I know today is the anniversary of the Battle of Worlot. The celebrations are just beginning across our realm."

"Yes it is Lord Izzulus, and it is a celebration only possible because of my efforts. If I had not been able to eradicate his forces, you, most likely, would not have been born. Think on that"

Crystalon stared angrily at the man before him, who matched his gaze, but finally relented, his demeanor cracking.

"Very well Crystalon, do what you must, but this is not an officially sanctioned incursion. You do this thing on your own."

"I would have it no other way Lord Izzulus."

Crystalon spun and exited the throne room wordlessly. Stepping outside he immediately glided up into the air, rocketing away, towards Maceyis' lands.

Green pastures and fields passed beneath Crystalon as he soared at great speed towards Maceyis' country.

But behind the mage, the skies turned at his passing, as if the very forces of nature were mirroring his demeanor. He paused momentarily at the border to Maceyis' lands, floating grim faced, staring daggers at the heart of his enemy. He knew it was a trap he ventured into, but he cared not. If what he suspected was true, that Maceyis had lengthened his mother's life to torment and torture her, he would destroy the evil one in such a way as to make him pay for all eternity.

Then he was off, soaring into Maceyis' land. Almost immediately he saw them. Dragon riders, perhaps five thousand strong. A hundred years ago he obliterated them. This time, with a mere furrowing of his brow he created massive sky-born tornadoes that sucked every rider and mount into its maw, spitting them out in pieces, a thousand miles away.

He would not be deterred. The momentary annoyance dealt with; he arrived at Maceyis' gates to his kingdom proper. There a legion of armed men stood ready to lay down their lives against him.

Now Crystalon spoke, in a voice heard throughout Maceyis' land. "You men will leave now. Return to your families, or never see them again. I give you that choice. If you do not know who I am, think on this: not a scant five moments ago, your liege sent five thousand dragon riders against me. Now those men's bodies are fertilizing fields a thousand miles from here. Go back to your families. Maceyis began this, but I will end it. You were given your warning, you shan't be given another."

The men beneath him grumbled amongst themselves as he floated above them, his cape billowing in the wind. They uneasily stepped side to side, and a few dropped their weapons and ran, others called them cowards as they did. But the runners were the smart ones. Crystalon was now a force of nature, so angry in his heart that his coming fierce retribution was a palpable thing, sensed on a feral, raw level, as if from a distant, ancestral memory. This was what these men felt, sensed in the primitive, animal parts of their brains. And that was why they fled. When a tiger ignores you and goes after another prey, you run. When he who could destroy the tiger, and all his kin, effortlessly ignores you, you run fast.

Suddenly, one of the braver warriors threw a spear, seeking to impale Crystalon with its polished point. The spear burst into flame and melted as it left the man's hand, and the flame followed the spears arc, back to the hand, engulfing the man's body, turning him to ash on the spot.

Then two things happened. Men so frightened by what they saw fled, dropping their weapons immediately, and others too brave, brainwashed or stupid to realize what just happened, attacked.

The result was sheer chaos. Men scrambling in two directions at once falling over each other amid screams of fear, while some fired bows and arrows that led to immediate burnings as the spell Crys had mentally cast when he arrived simply followed the arrows paths back to the hand that fired the bow, burning its shooter to death instantly.

The army of Maceyis was routed in mere seconds, and Crystalon did not have to raise a finger to do so.

He allowed himself a momentary, slight smile as he soared off. Now he was above the City of Verelious, Maceyis' Throne City, and speeding towards the castle looming above all else. He set his eyes as something caught his attention, a great winged beast circling the parapets of the castle. The body was oddly shaped, thick and heavy, with long arm-like protrusions set up high, and what appeared to be claws on rear-set hind legs. He was still far enough away where none of this could be noted for certain. He ignored the creature for now – if it attacked him, he would obliterate it.

"Maceyis." Crystalon's magically amplified voice boomed out, reverberating through every mind in the city, "You have taken someone dear to me and held her for many years. Now you taunt me with her. Return her to me, now or know deep despair. The choice is yours, madman. You have only your own foolishness and greed to blame for what will happen if you do not heed my warning."

"Warning?" A voice replied, with a hint of sarcasm. "You would warn the king of this land in his own castle? You are a fool, wizard. No man speaks to me as such and is allowed to live." Maceyis stood on the uppermost parapet and stared at Crystalon, who was still above the ruler's head.

"What you allow, and what become fact are two different occurrences, despot. The only reason I do not obliterate you on the spot is because you are a duly recognized ruler, and to do so would throw this region into bloody chaos, though I am sure no one in your kingdom would miss your iron hand. Consider yourself lucky that I have no reason to see your people suffer for your vainglorious foolishness."

"You have no right to be here Crystalon, I could cut you down where you stand, and no one could stop me, nor say I was not within my rights to do so."

"Do not feign innocence, Maceyis, not when you sent me this." Crystalon pulled the pendant from the inside of his cloak, and waved it for all the world to see.

"Oh. That." Maceyis replied snidely, his cruel beard wrapping into a smile. He was a tall, stocky man, with black hair tied into a ponytail, and a full beard covering a battle scarred face. "Yes I have her here. Your mother has been my...guest for well unto a hundred years now. She has

71

been kept alive by means similar to what you and I have used to extend our lives. Similar, but not entirely the same. In fact, I have to say that the process she was subjected to has driven her quite mad as a result, but you can judge that for yourself."

As he spoke, Maceyis turned his head away from Crystalon, and pointed it upwards. The mage warily followed the arc that Maceyis looked in and was suddenly shocked to his core. Descending towards him, with claws outstretched and huge wings beating the air with a power that seemingly shook the foundation of the great castle itself with the reverberations in the air they created, was a grotesque monstrosity, the one he had espied earlier circling the castle. A monstrosity seemingly part lion, part winged eagle, and part woman, and the woman wore the face of his mother as it descended towards him, blood stained claws outstretched to shred him to pieces upon contact.

And below him, Maceyis laughed heartily, the laugh of a man who had finally achieved victory in a long protracted battle.

Chapter 9

Crystalon stared in horror at the descending harpy, he was aghast at the sight of it. The sight of his mother's face on this horrific thing. The great beast roared into him, slashing him with its claws. He dove to one side, narrowly avoiding instant death in place of a gash across this chest. He winced in pain immediately, feeling the blood begin to trickle down his chest. But there was no time for a healing spell now, not with the beast returning for a second pass. Catapulting upwards, Crystalon soared over the beast, and sought a way to slow it, or hamper its movements, until he could discern if it was, in truth, his long missing mother.

But he would be allowed no time for such research, again the beast rocketed towards him, teeth and claws slashing the air frantically, seeking to tear him apart.

"Ah family reunions. Aren't they pleasant Crystalon?" Maceyis jibed from below, laughing as he spoke.

"Maceyis, know this. If this is in truth my mother, your fate will be darker then anything you can imagine. That I promise you."

"Please Crystalon, just kill the beast and be done with it. Kill your Mother. Then we can get on with our proper battle."

'*He has more planned then this?*' Crystalon thought to himself as he frantically flew to avoid the beasts rending claws. '*So he spent the past century planning well for this day then. And in truth he did take me by surprise at the depths of depravity he would sink to.*'

"What was that Crystalon?" Maceyis shouted once more, laughing as he did, "I can't quite make out what you said above the roar of the beast. Do silence her, will you?"

'He wants me to kill her, and in truth I may have no choice, for all my power I do not know what caused this transformation, nor how I go about reversing it. Even so, I must find out truthfully if this is my mother or not.' He thought to himself once again.

Crystalon and the harpy darted around the castle in a flight of death, he barely avoided her outstretched claws on numerous occasions, until finally he flew too low, too slow and she connected with a powerful tearing of flesh across his back, and knocked him from the sky like a stone.

With a dull plop he landed in the moat. Floating there with his bloodied back facing upwards, and his face down in the mire.

Above, on the tallest parapet, Maceyis rejoiced immediately, "Oh ho! The mighty have fallen; mightily I might add, hahaha. Finally the so-called master sorcerer is dead. Killed by his own kin, his mother who brought him into the world like a plague, has sent him from it, and I for one can finally rejoice."

The Harpy hovered in the air above Crystalon's still form, its wings beating the air slowly, methodically, as it awaited the orders it needed to go in for the final rending of flesh. The beast looked at Maceyis, seeking his approval. In reply, and with a smile, the emperor nodded affirmatively. The creature then dove, as a hawk hunting prey, instantly arcing downwards, claws outstretched for the kill. It soared to the still form of Crystalon, shrieking horrifically on its descent, as people throughout the city covered their ears in agony from the sound.

And then, just as it was about to plunge its nightmarish claws into the sorcerers still flesh, the beast stopped. But not just the Harpy, everything stopped. In the world. The harpy hung, as if from strings above the sorcerers still form, suspended not by beating wings, but by some unknown means. Above Crystalon, on the highest parapet, Maceyis was stopped in mid-sentence, his mouth

74

frozen open, and his hands held still as they were about to raise above his head in triumph. Birds, likewise, were suspended in flight all across the land; animals in mid run were frozen in place. Not a breath was taken, anywhere. Drinks were stopped in the air in mid-pour from pitchers.

On the ground, in the moat, Crystalon stirred, the only being on the planet moving, or so it seemed. He stood painfully, favoring his wounded back. Shuffling out of the moat, he flew painfully over its side, to land on his feet, and then he collapsed to his knees for a moment in obvious pain. After a short pause of ragged breath, Crystalon stood, he concentrated inwardly, and his body glowed, bathed with a radiance from within himself. The wounds across his body healed miraculously, instantly, and he was whole again. Now he turned towards Maceyis, anger and venom in his eyes and soul. He snapped his fingers haughtily.

"Get down here." Crystalon commanded, and instantly Maceyis appeared at his side, still frozen in position.

He stared at Maceyis, pondering what to do with this man, then slapped his hands together with a loud crack, and Maceyis suddenly stumbled forward, moving again.

"Wha? What did you do to me? You should be dead!"

Maceyis lunged at Crys, who made a backhand motion with his right hand, and an invisible hand smashed Maceyis back into the moat, with a loud splash.

"I did nothing to you, tyrant. Nothing. What I did was to step between seconds, to stand between time, and now I pulled you as well into this between instants moment, a moment that could last forever."

Maceyis stumbled out of the moat, climbing the heavy chain from the drawbridge to the ground. Soaked with muck and looking more like a rogue barbarian then a ruler, he stared daggers at Crystalon.

"Why don't you just die?" He screamed angrily, throwing his hands into the air in frustration.

"You will have your chance now to affect my death, madman."

As Crystalon spoke, two gleaming objects hurtled through the sky, glinting reflected sunlight menacingly, they appeared to be small stars hurtling towards both men, when suddenly their images grew sharper, more distinct, and Maceyis threw himself to the ground cowering in fear, as the point of a four foot long sword stopped mere inches from his throat, and hung suspended in midair before him, by an invisible hand.

He turned his head towards Crystalon, and watched as another blade floated into the master sorcerer's hand. Maceyis stared incredulously at Crystalon, as the blade pointed at Maceyis' throat flipped around slowly, offering its handle to Maceyis.

"Take it." Crystalon commanded. "You claim to be the greatest swordsman in the land, now is your chance to prove it."

"You will use your dark sorcery; I would stand no chance with a mere blade against you."

"No, there will be no magic, no sorcery. Nothing but these two blades I borrowed from the abandoned battlefield where I dispersed all of your dragon riders scant moments ago. This will be you versus me, with no witnesses, no one to see. An instant frozen in time. The winner walks away, the loser faces death. What say you, tyrant?"

Maceyis smiled a thin-lipped, nasty grin, before leaping towards Crys, gripping the blade before him from the mid-air where it had hung motionless. "I say you will die this day, sorcerer. No man in the land can best me, especially not some pampered magician who has never gotten his hands dirty wielding a blade."

He attacked with a powerful, savage downward slash while leaping at Crys, who deftly, surprisingly parried it easily.

Maceyis' eyes practically bulged from his head. "How? You have no blade skill?"

"Who told you that, you fool?" Crys replied, attacking as he spoke, "My training included extensive swordsmanship lessons, and I daily train with a weighted blade as part of my exercise regimen. You face no pampered dandy here Maceyis, you face your better." His words were an animal's growl as he attacked, driving back Maceyis, who suddenly redoubled his own effort, turning the tide upon the sorcerer, slashing and hacking maniacally, breathing heavily as he forced Crystalon backwards.

"No man may best Maceyis in sword combat, fool, no matter what his training is! I am the world's greatest swordsman, and you will feel my blades kiss!"

Crys smiled as he parried and then hacked against Maceyis' blade once again, deftly jumping sideways to avoid a cut. "You are a pompous ass Maceyis. That alone will prove your undoing."

"You would speak to me of being pompous? You frilly fool, I'll slice you in twain!" Maceyis slashed down from Crys' head to his toes, only throwing himself backwards saved Crys from getting sliced in two by a hair.

With a growl Crystalon attacked anew, slashing and hacking at his foe, from left to right, again and again, and each time Maceyis parried the blow. Suddenly he kicked at Crys in the groin, catching him by surprise.

Crystalon doubled over in pain, but reflexively jammed his sword out, blocking a decapitating blow, as he did he swept his left foot out knocking Maceyis' own leg out from beneath him, dumping him on the hard packed ground with a puff of dirt.

Maceyis rolled away and leapt to his feet, as Crys did the same in an opposite direction. Both men sneered at each other as they circle. Both were breathing heavily, like two caged beasts.

"I'll split you in two, you skinny twit." Maceyis roared as he bounded towards Crys, his sword raised high.

"You can try, you barbaric scum, but... you... shall...fail!"

As he spoke Crys ducked low, and jammed his sword upwards, under Maceyis' downwards chop, his blade found pay dirt, embedding itself in Maceyis' chest. The warlord dropped his blade and growled, struggling to rip himself free, grasping the blade and cutting his hands up at the same time as he sought to tear himself off its point. Crys stood, still grasping the hilt of the blade, and he commenced forcing Maceyis down to the ground, by applying just the right amount of pressure to bring him down, yet not to drive the blade any deeper. He stared eye to eye with Maceyis, and then down at him as he forced himself above the mortally wounded king, while he kept downward pressure upon his sword.

Crystalon brought his nose scant inches from his enemies, then he reared back and spit in Maceyis' face, before stepping on his chest, and ripping his sword out of Maceyis' body, the warlord screamed in pain as the blade left him. He crawled on the ground, his breath a ragged thing filled with agony.

"Did you think you would actually best me, Maceyis? Did you think you had a chance against me? What do you believe I am, Barbarian? Some simple magician? A powerful sorcerer perhaps? I am far more than your paltry mind could imagine. I am not some learned magic user, some gifted mage. No, you idiot, I am far more. I *am* magic. My abilities have transcended description. No one in the history of the universe has the sheer powers I command. Do you not understand, Maceyis? I have virtually become a God. Who else could stop time around us and allow our little century old drama to play itself out? Who else but a God indeed."

Maceyis choked, blood dribbling from his mouth as he spit. "You are no God. I should have killed you a century ago. You're a madman. Tell me O God, if you are so almighty powerful, why don't you change your mother back to her proper form?"

"You will not speak of her again, Maceyis. What you did to her will earn you a special kind of hell, of which there can be no escape."

"Haha, you idiot. I am dying, and will soon be out of your reach."

"That is where you are incorrect, Maceyis. Yes, you are dying, but you will not die."

Maceyis stared blankly at Crystalon and said nothing. But he felt his heart pounding, and fear gripped his guts, overpowering the almost all encompassing pain he now felt.

"No words Maceyis?" Crystalon asked as he walked around the despot, circling him slowly, keeping their eyes locked. "No sharp retort to my proclamation? Nothing to say for once, oh so mighty king? You should have left me alone. I was willing to leave you as you were. Our paths need never have crossed again. But you saw fit to first capture and corrupt that poor woman, whose only sin was birthing me."

"You are a monster, this world will hate you, far more than it will ever despise me." Maceyis choked out, blood turning his mouth and teeth red with every word, as on the ground, he laid on his belly staring upwards at the sorcerer, his long, black, damp hair fell all about his face.

"You are a fool if you believe so, Maceyis. None can be despised as you are. Further, I see now my destiny is to unite this world and be its guiding force to an era of greatness and prosperity never before seen in the annals of humankind. This moment, right here is that turning point.

The moment history will view with fond, loving eyes. The day Crystalon slew the great evil, and freed a world from fear and oppression. I see now I should have done this years ago."

"So. You do intend to finish your dirty work here and kill me. So be it. I face you with no fear, I merely weep for the rest of the world that I failed in destroying you."

"You misunderstand, Maceyis. I will not be killing you, but the world will think I did. To be sure, you have suffered a mortal blow. Any other time or place you would already be dead. But not here, not now." And then with finality, "Not ever."

"Wh-what?" Maceyis stammered aloud.

"This is your new home, for all eternity. This moment stolen between seconds. You will exist here, forever. Never healing, never dying. You will exist in mortal agony, forever. Your world is now this place, this stolen instant. You are a ghost, existing as you are. Never being able to touch another being, to speak to another being, and always, eternally and forever, in brutal agony from a wound that will not heal. Welcome to your own immortal nightmare."

"Y-you can't mean this. I am a man of the sword; to die in battle is something I would be proud to do. It is... an honorable death."

"Which is precisely why you will not die. You have no honor, monster. You deserve no 'honorable death'. This is what you deserve, for what you did a hundred years ago, and even more so, for what you did to my mother. This is my vengeance upon you, usurper. This is your doom." Crystalon turned and walked away, towards his mother's transfigured form, suspended in midair.

"Nooooooo! Let me die! I want to go to my ancestors! Let me leave this plane! I curse you Crystalon! I curse you and your heirs!" Maceyis howled in agony, a man knowing his destiny, and no longer able to affect it.

Crys approached the harpy thing that was his mother. It's claws reaching towards the spot he had lain previously, it's mouth distended in a biting motion. A beast now, and nothing more. He caressed the creature's face, and felt a deep, sorrowful remorse. He laid his head against her. "I am sorry mother. When you had disappeared so long ago I should have realized he had taken you. I assumed you were killed in the Great War, and lost to me forever. I never even considered otherwise. What of my sister? What of Shaleeya? Does she yet live? Or did she suffer a fate as horrific as yours, mother? I know not. I know that despite all my great and momentous power, that I do not know how to cure you, how to return you to your proper state." He stroked the hideous creature's face as he spoke, and his eyes welled up in tears. "There is nothing more I can do for you, Mother. Nothing but release you from this hideous existence. I know your mind is no more. That Maceyis has rendered you into nothing more than an animal. I wish I could save you. I wish I knew the spells needed to return you to humanity. But I do not. He hid the magic's used well. I can either leave you frozen in time somewhere, while I fight for the Gods know how long to find a way to reverse this evil, or I can release you, and give you peace. The peace you so richly deserve. Goodbye my beloved mother. I will always bear the scars of my failure in knowing you were yet alive. It will be no balm to you I know, but I will make sure no child ever again has to be concerned with his parent's well-being, or to fear their demise. I do this in your name and honor. Goodbye mother, I love you."

Crystalon waved his hand over her form, and suddenly, and slowly, the harpy beast that was his mother dissolved, fading from sight, forever.

He turned towards Maceyis who still shouted and railed at him. Pain and anger etched in his face, and his fists clenched and unclenched repeatedly, as he fought the impulse to end Maceyis' life right here and now, but he did not. He merely turned his back on the screaming tyrant, and stepped back into the time stream, at the moment he left it.

Chapter 10

"Uhhhhhnnn!" Crystalon awoke with a start, bathed in sweat; he bolted upright in his bed, his bare chest gleaming in the moonlight as it filtered through the blinds in his bedroom. He rubbed his eyes and face, and glanced at the clock on his nightstand.

"5 AM." He muttered aloud. "Nightmares, memories, old feelings all are appearing at once. Why am I being haunted by things that happened a million years ago?" He asked aloud. No answer was forthcoming.

"Why am I dreaming of my mother now, of at all times? To remind myself of my failures?" Again, no answer. Not that he was expecting one either.

He rolled over and buried his face in his pillow" Breathing heavily, he was back asleep within minutes. He needed his rest, Today was to be a big day for Crystalon.

***

Hours later, Crystalon was up and moving, packing a bag and readying himself for the first part of a long planned journey of mystical discovery. He had been on this Earth, his new home, three months now. He had learned much about the world, and what was expected of him in it. Now was the time to venture forth in it and rediscover magic. Today was truly the first day of the rest of his life.

'Beep, Beep'

The sound of a car horn erupted from the street at eight AM. Crys grumbled to himself, as he furrowed his brow, he stomped angrily towards the front door "Damned fool, it is too early yet to be using automobile horns, the neighbors..."

He flung the door open and quieted the limo driver with a wave of his hand as Joe bound up the short steps to his doorway. "Hey Mr. Talon you ready yet?"

"Yes I am awake and ready Joseph, as are all the neighbors for three blocks around with that fools incessant horn blowing."

"Geeze Louise Mr. T, give it a break, the guy only tooted a couple times."

"Joseph, there are people sleeping on this street. Show some consideration." and then he stopped himself, hesitating only for a second, and reflected upon his own words. It had been so long, so very long, since he cared about others in a simple regard like this. Their right to sleep a little bit later without being disturbed, just the thought of it gave him momentary pause, and almost – almost – brought a smile to his lips.

He patted Joe on the back "Come my friend, help me with the bags, the airport awaits." Both men hurriedly filled the limousine's trunk, along with the driver, with Crys' bags, and they were off.

Crystalon watched his home of the past three months recede into the distance of the neighborhood, and then turned his gaze to the road ahead.

"Y'know Mr. Talon, my wife, she wasn't too enthused about all a this, what with me goin' away for so long wit' you on this here adventure o' yours."

"Understandable, Joseph, but you advised her of the necessity of the matter I'm sure?"

"Yeah, yeah, I did Mr. T."

"And?"

"And, 'have a good time runnin' around wit' yer crazy, rich boss,' is what she said Mr. Talon."

"As I expected she would. Very well Joseph, adventure awaits us both. Let us go find it."

A seemingly interminable limousine ride later the two men exited from the vehicle in front of John F. Kennedy International Airport.

"Joseph, you handle our bags. I must see to..."

"Is she here yet?" Joe blurted out before Crys could finish his sentence.

"I do not know. I hope that she is. That woman can be frustrating to say the least."

"Yeah, but you wouldn't have asked her along if ya didn't want her here."

"As always, Joseph, you are a master of the obvious."

Joe smiled to himself as he pulled his Yankee Cap down lower while simultaneously grabbing a bag in each hand and hurrying to the waiting skycap.

Crystalon walked through the automatic doors of the airport and scanned about, slowly looking for someone in particular, but not seeing her, he first stopped at a newspaper vending machine, and then moved to the waiting area and sat down in an empty seat. He unfolded the paper and scanned the headlines for the day. He was nervous, his stomach twitched, but he ignored it. This was the beginning of a great adventure for him. He would continue to reclaim his power in this world now, with this trip.

Crys slowly read through the first few pages, still having minor difficulty with some words and how the English language was written on this Earth. But he was making tremendous progress, and he knew he must continue to practice his reading so that soon he would be able to read this worlds written English as if it were his own.

"Ah Jack and Jill went up the hill, Monsieur?"

The voice froze his heart, but only for an instant. He looked over the edge of the paper; his eyes glaring daggers at the sound of the voice, the voice that seemed to slide the words out like an oil covered snake.

"Epine-Noir." was all Crys said, in a tone filled with venom.

All around them, the busy airport terminal hustled and bustled as people moved about their business, but here, seated across from each other, two men filled the space between them with vehemence.

"What do you want, maggot?" Crystalon intoned haughtily.

"Tsk, tsk. Such anger Mr. Talon. Between two old friends, such as we, words like that should never pass, *Vous Convenez*? How is your nose by the way? Healed up nicely I presume?"

The slender Frenchman asked sarcastically as he played with the end of his white handled walking cane. His slicked back hair and slender mustache give him almost a comical, 'Dick Dastardly'(A character Crys had seen on something called 'Cartoon Network' quite a bit in the past month.) type of look, though he was anything but funny. He was evil, and the space between them was permeated with that evil.

Undaunted, Crystalon repeated, "I said what do you want, maggot."

"You know what we want Talon, what we paid for. Your assistance, your power."

Crys was taken aback a moment as he leaned back into the chair he was sitting in and eyed his enemy through narrowed lids.

"What you paid for? Of course. You had some sort of...arrangement with the other Mr. Talon, and assumed I am he when I returned from the hospital. Is that where the money came from Epine-Noir?"

The Frenchman stood up slowly, and angrily he closed in on Crystalon.

"You know full well where the money came from, and what is expected of you. Are we aware you are not the same Mr. Talon who began this endeavor? Of course, we realized that the moment the Wraith-Lords attempted to steal Meyers soul in your hospital room. That is why I met

86

with you and made you an offer to come to our...side, peacefully."

"You assume much, Epine-Noir. I do not know what you expect or what arrangement you had with my doppelganger, wherever he might be. But I do know his arrangement is not my arrangement. I owe you nothing, now be gone from my sight, little man, and do not sully my air with your foul stench again."

"You speak out of turn, monsieur, perhaps a reminder of our last meeting is in order no? Oh and do not concern yourself with others hearing your screams for help. To all around us we appear to be two men reading newspapers across from each other, not paying the other any heed"

Epine-Noir gestured and Crystalon merely smiled.

"*Quoi?*" Epine-Noir was stunned momentarily.

"Surprised Epine-Noir? Expected me to go sailing to the ceiling once again? My abilities may be a mere hint of what they used to be, but I can still easily block a novice like you from the same sorry attempt a second time. Here, let me give you something to wrestle with."

Crystalon narrowed his eyes and concentrated a moment, and the walking stick in Epine-Noir's hand suddenly became a coiled and hissing viper that quickly wrapped itself around his arm. The man dropped to the floor and screamed in fright trying to pull the venomous snake off of himself.

"Oh and Epine-Noir, do not be concerned about others around you being disturbed by your cries of agony, I took the liberty of masking your presence to everyone the moment you appeared. You are not even here to all around you."

Crystalon rose as Epine-Noir writhed on the floor seeking to extricate himself from the snake.

"Have a good day Epine-Noir."

As Crys walked away, he smiled. Walking into the men's room he entered a stall, and nearly collapsed from the exertion. His face broke out in a terrible sweat, and his knees crumpled. Maintaining a simple illusion as the one he had just performed on Epine-Noir was child's play to him not long ago. Now it took all his concentration and resolve. He knew that Epine-Noir was already free and exiting the airport hurriedly, in embarrassment, and he knew his enemy would seek revenge for the humiliation Crystalon had just heaped upon him, especially when the first illusion dropped and everyone in the airport saw this dapper, gray suited Frenchman rolling around on the floor with his walking stick like a deranged fool.

Still, it was a small victory for Crystalon, but it was one he would cherish for a long time to come.

He smiled to himself, as he exited the stall in the men's room, still thrilled with his minor victory.

And then the back of his head exploded in agony, as he dropped to the floor, his consciousness faded quickly into a boiling red miasma of pain, the last thing he saw was Epine-Noir holding up the handle of his now bloodied steel tipped walking stick, as he was about to bring it down on Crystalon's skull a second time, for the killing blow...

Chapter 11

Joe Carboneri was getting annoyed. Which was not an easy thing for Joe Carboneri to do. Just about everyone who knew Joe thought of him as just about the most even-tempered person they had ever met. But right now that even temper was turning sour.

First, he had been walking around for fifteen minutes looking for the last member of their little adventuring band who was joining he and Mr. Talon on their trip, and he still hadn't found this person, and now, he couldn't find Mr. Talon either.

"What the heck is going on here?" Joe thought to himself as he decided to make a stop in the men's room.

As he pushed the door open, he stopped dead in his tracks for all of half a second. On the floor he saw his boss, and his friend, Mr. Talon on his knees, clutching the back of his head with bloodied hands. Standing above him, walking stick dripping blood, was this thin, evil-looking man with a pencil thin mustache who looked like he just fell out of some show on the Bravo network. The man grunted and turned towards Joe. Without a second thought, Joe leapt towards him.

Now as men go, Joe Carboneri was not considered a huge man. He stood about five feet eight inches tall, and weighed about two hundred pounds. Some of that weight was because of his wife's fine Italian cooking, and a lot of that weight was muscle Joe had developed over the years in the streets, playing sports and lifting weights. Joe was no pansy. He may be a nice guy by anyone's account, but he was also known in the mean streets of Brooklyn as a tough guy when he had to be. This was one of those times.

Joe collided with Epine-Noir, hard, catching him in the middle of his body with a hard thrown, football style

89

tackle, his shoulder slamming very hard into the thin man's gut. With bone crushing force, Epine-Noir choked hard and gasped for air as Joe threw a left elbow into the man's face as a follow up. Then, as a matter of exclamation, he heaved his right arm back, and unloaded a powerful right cross to the pencil necks face. Epine-Noir went down like a sack of potatoes hitting the ground, only after his head connected with the fine white ceramic tile on the wall of the men's room.

"You okay boss?" Joe asked as he helped Crystalon to his feet.

"Y-yes Joseph, Much better, in fact, since you wandered in." Crys replied touching the back of his head gingerly.

"We gotta get you to a Doc, get that stitched up, but first we get airport cops to take this crazy lookin' pansy away."

Joe turned back towards Epine-Noir who lay crumpled in a heap on the men's room floor.

"Yes Joseph, let us do just that. A few nights in a cell would do this man's disposition some good I believe."

Both men exited the men's room, and Joe shouted "Hey! We need some help over here! Someone get a Cop, an' fast! My pal was assaulted in the men's room."

Crys looked at him with a stern look of small annoyance, but that quickly turned to a smile. An instant later no less than five burly security men appeared with hands on their pistols.

"What happened here?" the first officer asked both men.

"Some creep attacked my buddy, Mr. Talon here, and I caught him in the act in the men's room. I got him locked in here, that's why I'm standin' in front o' the door, so the bum can't get out."

"Okay," A second officer nodded, "Let us past."

90

Both Joe and Crys stepped out of the way, Crys still holding a wad of paper towel to the back of his head he had grabbed from a dispenser on his way out of the men's room.

An instant later all five officers returned. "You two better come in here."

Crys' eyes narrowed suspiciously as he entered the men's room once again.

"There's no one here." The lead officer announced. "Are you sure this was the men's room you were attacked in?"

"What kinda question is dat? O' course we're sure." Joe answered with more then a little annoyance to his voice. "How could this guy get away? We was standin' here the whole time."

"Well sir, the room is empty." The officer answered, annoyance of his own coloring his voice.

"Not quite." Crys replied softly as he walked towards the mirror covering one side of the wall. There, stuck between two of the tiles, was a black rose.

"Guess this guy left us his calling card. How the hell'd he get outta here? Dat's what I wanna know." Joe exclaimed in exasperated anger. "I mean who is he? Houdini?"

"Something like that I suppose." Crys answered quietly.

"Hey Mr. Talon. Is he a competitor a yours?" Joe asked. "You know, another magician? That would explain how he got away I guess. He pulled a Copperfield on us."

"Again Joseph, something like that." Crys replied, now more than a little annoyed his companion did not know when to talk and when to shut his mouth.

"You're a magician?" One of the officers asked. "Do you know this guy?"

"Only in passing. We had met once, and the meeting was indeed...unfriendly. I suppose he followed me

91

in here after he saw me sitting outside, awaiting my flight. His name is Epine-Noir, at least that is what he calls himself."

"Does that name mean anything?" The officer asked as he grabbed the black rose from the mirror. "Ouch!" He exclaimed, as he looked at his hand and saw blood trickling down his finger.

"His name means 'Black Thorn', officer." Crys replied.

"Yeah well let's get some more information about this 'Mr. Black-Thorn and get an APB out on him, but first we have to get you to the airport Doctor, and have the back of your head looked at."

"I do not want to miss my flight, officer, I assure you, I am fine. It is only a little blood."

"No good Mr. ... Talon was it?" One officer asked.

Crys merely nodded, his brow slightly furrowed.

"The airline and the airport will put you on a later flight, you have nothing to worry about there, but you have to be looked at by a physician. This way sir."

The entire entourage walked towards the airport infirmary, basically a small room akin to a school nurse's office. Suddenly, a woman hurriedly ran up to them, papers held in her hands loosely, in a nervous manner.

"What happened?" Amanda Serros asked as she stared at the bloody rag held to the back of Crystalon's head.

"The boss was attacked by some nut job, 'Manda." Joe answered as they all entered the small office.

"I-is he all right?" she asked, more than a little nervously.

"I will indeed be shortly, Amanda. Please, see to our flight with this officer's help. We will have to change our arrangements to a later one today."

"O-okay Chris, sure." Amanda replied, as she watched him walk into the office and the door shut behind them all. "They're not going to like this." She mumbled aloud. "Not one bit."

Chapter 12

High above the Atlantic Ocean, the big plane flew in calm silence. It was night, the sky outside the windows was brilliant with stars, a sight Crystalon had not seen since his arrival on this Earth. He had often flown to the worlds ceiling as he called it, to view the stars, the night sky, and all manner of objects in the celestial heavens. It was his secret passion, his joy. One of only a few he allowed himself when no one was looking. Now he had to compensate for this by flying inside the belly of a metal beast.

'*That too will change,*' Crystalon thought to himself.

After the nonsense with Epine-Noir, the rest of the day had progressed smoothly. His head still ached slightly but the pills they had given him, 'aspirin' he believed they were called, eased that dull thudding to a mere whisper of annoyance, and the stitch that was administered to his neck pained him more than the thudding in his head from Epine-Noirs' attack.

'*How could I have been so foolish?*' He thought to himself. '*I only supposed that the man was beaten and down. I should have made certain. He could have killed me. I shan't make the same mistake again.*'

Next to him were both Amanda and Joe, who were turning into the perfect traveling companions. He smiled to himself as he swiveled his head back towards the window from staring at his two associates. Both of them were sleeping; Joe snoring slightly, Amanda merely sleeping quietly. She shifted slowly and leaned her head on his shoulder in her sleep, a slight smile crept over her face, one of comfort. Crystalon's soul ached at this. She was so much like his beloved wife in almost every way. This small, unconscious gesture pained him to his core, as few things

95

had in life. He wanted to take her in his arms, but knew better than to do that. Perhaps someday, when his powers and abilities were returned, but not now. This was not his wife, not his world, and just being in this great metallic winged beast reminded him of that fact all too well.

He was no stranger to technology, his universe had it too, some of it far advanced of this worlds, but his reality had always been built around magic, something that was in scarce supply here, but it did exist, and he would command it as he had once before. What he would do with it once he did command it was the question.

It did not matter though. He would find the sources of magic and once again command them all.

He stared out the window of the plane, watching the black night sky roll by. The vastness of it all broken by the lights of another plane in the distance or a stray cloud reflecting moonlight. This all seemed so...slow to him. Almost interminable in its complexity. On his world he could fly far faster than this lumbering ship. He could teleport great distances with but a thought and a huge expenditure of energy. And yet here he was, trapped like a small fish in a tin, slowly making his way towards 'Great Britain' as it was called here.

For there lay his destiny. His future.

Hours later, the plane touched down at London's Heathrow airport without incident. Passengers disembarked and Crystalon immediately delegated responsibilities.

"Joseph, retain our automobile. Amanda, see to our accommodations. I will retrieve our luggage. Quickly now, both of you, I want out of this madhouse as quickly as possible."

Joe grabbed Crys by the arm and spoke to him in a low voice "Hey boss, take it easy. This ain't nothin' to get upset about. Everything'll be okay. Let me an' 'Manda deal with this junk. You go grab the bags, but relax. We'll be in our rooms in no time."

Crystalon looked at Joe Carboneri slowly and then nodding slightly, relaxing, and unwinding like a spring.

"You are correct my friend. I am indeed under stress here. This great quest of ours will change my future and it is beginning to rack my nerves with anxiety."

Joe turned his face and looked oddly at Crystalon, cocking his head slightly to the side as the hustle and bustle of the airport all around them disappeared momentarily. "Boss, I ain't got no idea what you're goin' on about at all. But if it makes you feel any better, then that's fine. Go get the bags, okay? I'm goin' ta get the car." Joe started walking away, but turned his head back towards Crys, smiling a moment before adding, "An boss, relax!" He repeated, noticeably concerned.

***

Nearby two sets of eyes watched Crystalon and Joe's conversation with intent. Each man turned towards the other and nodded knowingly. Both were dark skinned, obviously of mid-eastern descent.

Across the room, between rows of people claiming luggage and the ever-present murmur of an airport in full use, another man, blonde haired and blue eyed, watched intently the two men who were watching Crystalon. His eyes narrowed purposefully, and then he turned and disappeared into the crowd.

***

Outside Heathrow airport, Joe secured the car, a largish four door in black. Crystalon and Amanda filled the trunk and then they were off.

"Remember to make sure you're on the other side of the road here Joe." Amanda cautioned.

"Hey 'Manda, how many times you gonna remind me o' that? Geeze yer worse 'an my wife!"

"I'm just making sure you don't kill us all Joe." She snickered.

97

"Yeah, yeah Blondie. Keep it up. Your time'll come."

Under her breath while turning toward the cars window, Amanda almost silently agreed "You have no idea Joe."

Rain spattered the car lightly as they made their way into London proper; the eighteen-mile trip passing quickly.

The car pulled up in front of the large hotel, and they all exited.

"I suggest you both get some rest. We have a two hour ride ahead of us tomorrow, and I need you both fresh." Crystalon ordered. He took a step forward, and then stopped and relaxed himself, shaking his head slightly as the light rain spattered about him. "Excuse my abruptness my...friends. I am trying to change my demeanor, and have failed again to break old habits. Like they say, they do die hard, but that is no excuse for my rudeness. Come let us go to dinner, I will, of course, treat."

Joe smiled at Amanda, and they both turned towards Crystalon. Each had luggage in their hands then Joe walked towards Crys and Amanda followed.

"Sure boss, no problem. Here take these." Joe smiled and handed the bags to the bewildered Crystalon. Then Amanda followed suit and handed hers to him as well.

Crystalon stood before them both, his hands filled with luggage, as he watched them both walk away, laughing quietly to themselves as Amanda leaned into Joe, placing her left arm across his shoulders.

There he stood, the most powerful man in his universe, reduced to a bellhop in the soaking steady rain. His hair was soaking wet now, his clothes dripping, and he was fumbling with luggage, as finally all the bags he had been holding dropped to the ground in a heap. Angrily he looked at the luggage, and then at the receding backs of his

cohorts, and suddenly he did something he would never
have done before. He laughed. It started small, then burst
into a loud guffaw, as Crystalon plopped down into the wet,
empty street. A moment later both Joe and Amanda
returned to help him carry the bags in, each laughing as
well.

Chapter 13

The next morning, all three were seated in their rental car, heading out of the city and towards the enigmatic Stonehenge.

"Sun's out today. I thought this place was always cloudy, boss?" Joe asked as he drove along.

"Hhhmm. I'm not sure what you mean Joseph." Crys answered distractedly.

"I heard it was always rainin' in this country, is what I meant, boss."

"It doesn't rain nonstop here Joe. They just get their share of it, that's all." Amanda answered.

Crystalon sat in the front seat of the large car and was studying a few items he had removed from his pockets.

"You okay Mr. T? You seem like you're a million miles away from here." Joe pressed.

"A million miles and more, Joseph." Crystalon replied quietly.

"How come?" Joe asked innocently enough.

"This land reminds me very much of my home."

"Yeah? Nice lookin' place here. Really country-ish here. Reminds me of Vermont or some parts o' upstate New York."

Crystalon smiled, he had been studying so hard the past few months to learn the lay of the land and the way of life here that he was familiar with both those places from pictures he had seen. But this, this was home to him, yet it was not. The rolling countryside, the ancient buildings, a flock of sheep being shepherded across the road. All these things remind the deposed ruler of his own world, his own home somewhere in the ether of time and space.

Amanda sat in the back seat. She wore a set of small sunglasses perched on her nose and silently kept her own council. The rest of the ride was small talk broken by minutes of silence by all in the car. The scenery was breathtaking, especially when they cleared the last rise in the road some two hours after they had left London.

All three take a collective gasp as they spied the stone monoliths that comprised Stonehenge rising out of the ground ahead of them.

"Wow. That's pretty damned awesome," Joe mouthed, almost too low to hear.

"Indeed it is, Joseph. Indeed it is."

"I have to get a picture of this." Amanda commented as she got out of the back door of the car.

Crystalon exited the passenger door and walked up the hill towards the ancient monoliths, leaving the car door open and forgotten as he slowly made his way up the hill, almost reverently.

"Joseph, the item?" He held his hand out to his side where Carboneri stood, not looking at him, but just staring intently at Stonehenge.

Joe fumbled around in his jacket pockets, and then simply said "Oops."

Crystalon turned on him, his nostrils flaring in the sunlight, as his eyebrows rose in anger.

"Hehe, only kidding boss, here it is." Joe removed a small, ornately crafted box from one of his pockets and handed it to Crystalon. Small gems shone and sparkled in the sunlight all over the box.

Crys examined the box closely, smiled slightly and nodded towards Joe. Then he walked forwards, and opened the box's lid, speaking in a voice too low to hear. After several seconds Crystalon shut the box's hinged cover, abruptly turned and walked away. "We are done here." He hesitated a moment, then continued "My friends. Let us be off and back to our hotel." He re-entered the car and shut the passenger door.

"What's his big rush?" Amanda asked Joe as both headed back to the car.

"Ya got me 'Manda. You know how he gets. He's done here so the world has ta roll over. Least he called us his 'friends'. "

"True. I guess he's loosening up some. Goodie for us." She replied sarcastically.

"Aw 'Manda, it ain't like that. He's really a good guy, you know that."

"Yeah Joe, I do." She answered, "He's a stiff at times, but a good guy. Still, he's a little weird."

"Yeah I hear ya. He is fer sure. But that's the boss."

She stared at Joe and nodded slowly before turning and returning to the car.

***

Across the parking lot, the two men who had been watching Crystalon, Joe and Amanda at the airport sat in their own vehicle, again watching intently. After Joe, Amanda and Crystalon have gotten back in their car and Joe was backing the car out of its space, only then did the two men start their own vehicle, dropping into line several cars behind Crys' car and began following.

***

"So boss, I don't get it. What'd you do out there? It just looked like you opened up the lid on that little box we picked up in Chinatown last week and closed it again."

Crystalon smiled, then turned his head towards the window, watching the scenery of Great Britain go by before he replied. "Yes Joseph, that is precisely what I did."

"OK, but what'd that do for you?"

"Joseph, what that did was for me to understand and know."

"In udder words 'Joe, shut yer yap', right?"

"More or less correct Joseph."

"That's wonderful Mr. T." Joe grunted as he continued to drive, obviously displeased to not be getting the entire story.

103

"I really like being here. I never thought I'd get to England." Amanda noted as the car passed down a winding road.

"Indeed, the scenery is..." Crys paused a second before continuing, letting out a short sigh, "Relaxing. Yes I believe that is the word I am looking for. It is bucolic."

"Huh what?" Joe asked turning towards Crystalon as he drove.

"It is rustic, Joseph. Pleasantly provincial. To me, it is also soothing in an odd way, because it reminds me of home."

"You live in Jersey." Joe answered, quizzically.

"I believe our Mr. Talon is again referring to where he is originally from, aren't you Crys?" Amanda asked.

"That is indeed a... possibility, Amanda."

"Man, you are one vague guy." Joe commented, shaking his head slightly as he drove.

"Sometimes vagaries are meant for the protection of those around oneself, Joseph."

"Hhhmph, if you say so Boss." Joe quieted down and continued driving.

A moment later he spoke again in the quiet car. "Hey Boss, you got anybody who might have something against you? I mean besides that jerk in the airport the other day?"

"Why do you ask?"

"Well," Joe continued, "We're bein' followed."

"What? Are you certain?"

"Yeah o'course I'm certain. There's a silver four-door three cars back of us. I seen it last night near the hotel, pulled in after us when we left you ta get wet. An' I thought I saw it behind us this mornin', but thought nothin' of it. But like they say, third times da charm, and this ain't too charmin'. Two guys in the car, and I think I seen one o' those faces in the airport last night, too. From what I can see from here, this far ahead o' them, at least."

"Turn at the next corner, the more obscure a spot the better." Crystalon commanded.

"A-are you sure Chris" Amanda asked, fear coloring her voice.

"Indeed I am certain Amanda. Trust in me."

She nodded slightly and turned to look out the rear window.

"Do not turn around Amanda, sit looking straight ahead. We do not want to tip them off to the fact that we are aware that they are following us."

"Obscure turn spot up here boss-man." Joe announced.

"Very well Joseph, Turn in, then get past those trees. Stop for a moment to let me out, then continue ahead. Then immediately pull the car across the road as if you are making a U-turn and act as if you cannot get the car started again, as if you were stuck."

"Okay boss, your call."

Joe turned the corner; a corner with high hedges on each side lining a thin road of gravel and sand, as he made his turn he slowed to five miles per hour and Crystalon exited the passenger door at a lope, disappearing into the hedges. Then Joe sped up slightly to make up for lost time, traveled half a block further, then commenced to turning the car into its U-turn, stopping in the center of it.

Immediately he exited the car door, and popped the hood. Thirty-five seconds later the silver sedan that they had espied from a distance turned into the street behind them, tentatively. The driver passed the spot Crystalon had secreted himself, and slowly pulled up near Joseph and Amanda, who had remained in the car while Joe fiddled under the hood.

Joe lifted his head and waved slightly at the car approached, smiling sheepishly as if to say 'What can I do? I'm stuck?' The driver of the car, a swarthy, heavy man with a heavy beard – obviously of Middle Eastern lineage –

rolled down his window. Looking sternly at Joe, he asked in a heavily accented voice "Are you stuck? Do you need help?"

"Uhh, yeah chief. I can't get 'er started." Joe replied.

"How did this happen?" the other man asked as he exited the car, a thinner, clean-shaven man also of Middle Eastern descent. Both men walked up to Joe, one on either side of him.

The driver looked in the car and then asked, "Where is your third traveling partner?"

"Samir!" The thin man blurted out in surprise and anger.

"Yeah bub, how'd you know there were three of us?" Joe asked with a smile as he stood up straight from under the hood.

"They know because they have been following us for quite some time, haven't you gentlemen?" All heads turned towards the spot behind the two cars, where Crystalon stood in the road. Legs spread slightly, and arms crossed on his chest.

'*For an average guy, he is imposing,*' thought Joe as he smiled genuinely impressed with the image Crys had struck behind the startled strangers. Then it hits Joe, like a hammer between the eyes. It wasn't so much the image the man he knew as Chris Talon portrayed, it was the way he carried himself. He was commanding to say the least. Powerful, and more then a little awe-inspiring. It was now after months of knowing the man, that Joe Carboneri was suddenly and most assuredly aware of the aura of strength, not just strength, but power, he displayed. All of this passed in a heartbeat, as the two men facing Crystalon suddenly pull guns from beneath their ill-fitting sport jackets, and aimed them at Crystalon.

"You! You will come with us now." The heavy set man ordered, his hand shaking slightly as he held the gun nervously.

Amanda sat in the car, forgotten and frightened, but still holding herself together.

Crystalon smiled as he stared at the two men before him. "I think not gentlemen. Both of you, put your guns down, immediately."

Surprisingly both men began to comply, then the thinner man stopped and raised himself up again aiming the pistol back at Crys. "No Mr. Talon, you do not play the mind tricks with me so easily. Samir may be weak, but I am not." As he spoke he smacked Samir across the back of his head with his open hand.

"Very well then. We shall do this another way." Crys answered, instantly beginning to gesture, and as he did the air around him became filled with two horrific fanged monstrosities, large in size with grasping claws and ravenous mouths, and long barbed tails, all a deep, blood red in color. Horrendous bat-like wings beat the air with a nauseating heat from their backs. They suddenly dove at the two men who screamed in horror and began shooting at the creatures, but the bullets passed right through them as they attacked the two strangers, driving them to the ground in terror and pain.

"Get in the car." Crystalon ordered Joe, who merely shook his head in surprise and shock, entering the driver's door. Crys entered the passenger door and Joe drove away quickly, leaving the two men writhing on the dirt road with the horrible creatures attacking them.

Minutes passed in silence in the car as they headed back to their hotel. No one spoke until Joe finally uttered "Uhh, Boss, those were illusions, right? Mind tricks you played on those two punks?"

Crys looked straight ahead and answered quietly. "Perhaps Joseph, perhaps," was all the former master mage replied tiredly as he turned to face the side window of the car.

Chapter 14

"Chris, wait" Amanda asked, quietly at first.

"Chris, slow down!" She asked a little louder as he continued walking, ignoring her.

"Chris Talon! Stop and talk to me!" She shouted now. All the heads within the palatial hotel lobby turned her way, curious what all the yelling was about.

Crystalon bristled slightly. He turned his head haughtily towards her, and angrily motioned her to follow him into the elevator.

"What are you cackling about woman? Do you want the entire hotel to know my business?"

"I couldn't care less what they know, Mr. Bigshot. I want to know what happened out there. You scared the living hell out of me on that road. I want to know what and who I'm dealing with."

"Amanda, You do not have to know everything that transpires around you concerning myself. Needless to say I will make sure you are safe at all times."

"Bull! I was scared for my life out there. We all could have been killed by those two creeps. You took some chance doing what...whatever it was you did to them. What did you do to them? Were those monsters real? Or something you made us all see?"

He shook his head in disgust, looked at the blank wall of the elevator, and then turned towards her. "You will have to trust me in saying I will never put you into danger. I give you my word of that"

"How can I trust you when you already put me into danger? Damn you, you piss me off sometimes."

"Amanda!" Crystalon was genuinely stunned by her reaction, momentarily taken aback.

"What you don't like my language? Too damned bad. If I'm going to stay with you on this little adventure of yours I want to start being 'in the know' about what we're actually doing, and why. Your 'word' doesn't hold much water with me."

He looked her in the eyes then, anger beginning to brew behind his own eyes, as he turned away, obviously trying to calm his growing temper. "So much like her." He muttered aloud.

"Like who? Who am I like?" Amanda asked, her face red with her own frustration.

The elevator door opened then, and a group of tourists stepped forward to enter, when Crystalon held out his hand and ordered, "Stop! This elevator is not taking any more passengers." Then he stabbed the 'door close' button and jabbed his floor again, coaxing the elevator upwards, as the stunned travelers merely stared in open-jawed surprise as the doors slid shut in front of them.

"Th-that was unbelievable! Just who do you think you are?" A stunned Amanda asked.

"I am your employer, period. That is the only answer you will receive. Those men on the road meant me harm. You would have been harmed as well as Joseph. I dealt with them, expediently."

"You scared the crap out of me, Chris!"

"Amanda!" Again her mouth and the spirit of her temerity surprised him. "At least try to act like a lady."

"What? Does every minor act of me being 'unladylike' annoy you? Where the hell are you from anyway? The way back machine where women don't curse, ask questions, or vent their frustrations?"

"You are beginning to try my patience, woman."

"Good. It looked like you need some of that, to keep you in line, Mr. Bigshot, because nothing else is. Who do you think you are anyway? King of the world?"

"More so than you realize, woman." He answered loudly, staring her directly in the face. His presence overwhelmed her for a moment as she physically took a step backwards, but ended up bumping into the wall of the elevator.

He stared at her, his face red with anger. She met his gaze for a moment then to faltered and turned away. He then touched her chin with his right hand, turning her gently towards him. She didn't fight his touch, she faced him and their lips drew close as the elevator doors slid open.

"Hey! There you two are! I was wonderin' where you had gone off to. I-" Joe Carboneri stopped short when he realized what they were about to do, the kiss that did not happen, as both turned towards him, slight annoyance in both their faces. "Oops sorry folks, I –uh-"

"Never mind, I still want answers, Mr. Wizard." Amanda barked as she stepped from the elevator, pushing her way past Joe, and marching off indignantly towards her room.

"Uhh, sorry boss. Didn't mean to interrupt."

"I know Joseph. I am glad you did though. You stopped me from making the same mistake twice in my life."

"Huh?"

"Never mind, Joseph." Then Crys stopped and turned towards his friend. "I suppose you want answers too, about what just happened?"

"With those two thugs? Yeah that'd be nice. I'm kinda in the dark about a lot o' that."

Crystalon exhaled, giving in to fate. "Very well then Joseph. Gather up Amanda, would you please? We will meet for dinner at six. I will explain everything then."

"Okay boss, I'm lookin' forward to hearin' what you got to say about what we saw out there."

"You will have your answers, Joseph. I promise."

111

'*Now*' Crystalon thought to himself, "*I have to decide if I am going to tell you the truth or not.*"

Chapter 15

Six PM came quickly for Crystalon. He showered and shaved, wishing again for the seeming one thousandth time he was at his full omnipotent power levels once again, as he fit his watch to his left wrist.

'*I never needed one of these things to tell the time of day.*' He mused. '*I just knew. Perhaps one day again soon I will no longer need a watch once again.*'

Moments later he exited his room, pulling the door shut behind him and descending in the elevator to the Restaurant level of the opulent hotel.

He was greeted by staff at every doorway, genially, and it reminded him of his old life, the way others would give him respect for his position and power. Here it seemed, money talked, and was what empowered this world. He had a seemingly large amount of money, and as such, had a seemingly large amount of power. But he knew where that money came from now, and that bothered him to no small degree.

Seating himself at the table he had reserved, he disdainfully checked his watch once again. Five fifty-five PM. He was five minutes early. '*Good,*' he thought. '*Best to show a position of power in these matters, even if with my newfound friends.*'

Three minutes later both Joe and Amanda exited the elevator and made their way to him, at a waiters direction, through the crowded restaurant.

"Joseph, Amanda. You look lovely Amanda." Crys noted with a slight smile.

"Thank you." She replied straight-faced, and without warmth.

The two seated themselves, and Crys started to speak, controlling the conversation's direction.

"How are you both enjoying your stay here?" Crys inquired to begin.

"Hey Mr. T I ain't stayed in a swankier place my whole life. Damn straight I'm enjoyin' it." Joe replied with a smile.

"And you, Amanda?"

"It's fine." She softly answered.

"Indeed it is. I myself used to live in a home that was perhaps six times as large as this entire building. As fine as everything is here, my life before this was almost infinitely superior."

"What are you talking about?" Amanda asked, annoyance coloring her tone. "You come from Jersey. Are you really insane?"

Crys laughed slightly then turned towards her. "No Amanda, Chris Talon was from New Jersey. Crystalon, spelled C-R-Y-S-T-A-L-O-N, is not."

"Huh? What are you talkin' about boss?" Joe asked, surprised and befuddled by what he had just heard.

Crys turned towards him and spoke, "Joseph, do you remember the day you claimed I fell out of the sky in front of your truck?"

"O'course I do. It was the day we met. I still say you appeared outta nowhere, wearin' that funky suit."

"You were right."

"Wha? Whadayamean I was right?"

"I did drop out of the sky in front of you. I mistook your truck at the time for some foul smelling beast whose grill were teeth ready to swallow me whole."

"What kind of stupidity is this?" Amanda asked, more then a little annoyed.

"Not stupidity Amanda, the truth. You claimed you wanted it. Now you shall have it. But beware of what you are not yet ready to understand."

114

"Oh I understand it all right. This is more mental sleight of hand on your part. You're always playing mind games with us, yet you claim we are your friends."

"You two are. You are my only friends on this world."

"Wha' da ya mean 'On this world'?"

"I mean Joseph, precisely that. Since I arrived on this world, you two have become my closest companions, and are the only two I can trust."

"Trust, funny word coming from a man who is trying to feed two people a line about himself."

"There is no 'line' here Amanda. I am speaking the truth. You wanted to know what you were involved in, now you will."

He paused and looked back and forth between them. Joe was more mystified then anything, listening raptly. Amanda was incredulous and seemingly angry, as he had thought they both would be.

"You really mean to tell us that you are an alien from another planet?" Amanda blurted out, her voice rising in pitch and volume.

Joe looked around nervously, but no one seems to have heard their discussion.

"No Amanda, I never said I am from another planet, nor any type of alien. I am from Earth, just not your Earth."

"Huh? You lost me." Joe answered, perplexed.

"I am from an Earth that is markedly different from yours."

"You mean ta tell me there's more than one Earth? How's that? An' how are ya from there? I gotta admit Boss, yer soundin' more and more like a nutcase to me too."

Crys took a drink of his wine that the waiter had brought over, and placed the fine stemware back on the table before continuing.

"I knew this would be difficult, and had, in fact, no intention of telling either of you my true identity. But be that as it may, after the two attacks against me in recent days I deemed it necessary to share everything with you both."

"Okay I'll bite. Tell me about yourself then, Oh high and mighty Crystalon. But I'm warning you, I wasn't born yesterday and will only listen to this crazy story so long." Amanda taunted sarcastically.

"Nor was I, Amanda. In truth I was born over a million of your years ago, though I now believe time flows differently on my world then yours. Joseph, you believe I am some sort of magician, correct?"

Joe nodded in agreement, taking a drink of his own wine, and making a face as he did.

Crys smiled and continued, "In truth you are incorrect Joseph. I am not a simple magician who performs parlor tricks for children and those of weak mind, I am a sorcerer. The most powerful of my home dimension. I ruled an empire there for almost a million years. The day we met, Joseph, was the day I was deposed. I was thrown out of my universe, my dimension, my kingdom, by those that deemed me unfit to rule, and sent here, where they believed no magic existed. But they were incorrect, my friends. Magic does exist here, but it is hidden beneath the surface. Grounded in things that no ordinary man will care to look at. Some of it hidden right before their eyes."

"Like today at Stonehenge?" Joe asked.

"Indeed Joseph, exactly like today." Crystalon answered, smiling.

"Say I buy into this for the moment, what did you do with that small box you pulled out of your pocket?" Amanda asked, still incredulous.

"That box is a magic gathering apparatus from ancient China. It absorbed the nascent power from Stonehenge and is used to transfer that power to myself."

"Wait, you already absorbed what ya grabbed from there?"

116

"Indeed Joseph. When I jumped from the car door to behind the hedges I performed a small spell that allowed me to transfer the power in the box to myself. Now that magic, that small amount of mystical force courses through my veins, and has made an affinity between myself and the magic of this land. It is the first step in my acquisition of power once again. It is as of nothing, compared with the power I once wielded, but it is indeed a start."

"You are so full of it, Mr. Chris Talon or whatever your name is." Amanda answered, standing, and throwing her napkin onto her plate, before she turned and walked away.

"Sit," was all Crystalon said, and she immediately complied, then an instant later turned towards him, surprise and anger, now tinged with fear and wonder coloring her face. "What did you do to me?" She whispered.

"A mere mental command, my dear. I want you to give me the courtesy of hearing my story. Then you can decide if you want to leave or not."

She said nothing but relaxed slightly in her chair; she nervously took her wine goblet and drank heavily from it.

"As I was saying, I absorbed the mystical energies the Chinese magic box had contained, and am now gaining an affinity to the magic of your world. Those two men who accosted us were thugs sent by either the group that Epine-Noir works for..."

"The guy in the airport?" Joe interrupted.

"Precisely Joseph, the guy in the airport, as you put it, or some other group who wants to put my abilities to their use. Whoever sent those men, obviously did not have the best interests of any of us in their minds."

"What did you do to them? Those things that attacked them, were they real?" Amanda asked, quietly.

"No they were mere illusions. I do not have the power to call such nether worldly demons to this plain of existence. At least not at the moment."

"But if you did, you would have." She finished for him.

"Indeed. If it were up to me, and had those creatures been real, they would have torn those two villains apart, Amanda. But such was not the case. Rest assured those men yet live, and are probably now cowering beneath their covers somewhere afraid to go out into the night, for fear of those beasts attacking them once again. Make no mistake about it Amanda, they were indeed villains who would have done us all grievous harm."

"Why were you deposed from your world? Were you an evil, bad ruler?" She asked.

" In my mind, I would say no, I was a just one. Though I admit not the easiest man to get along with. I demanded hard work from my subjects, but they were also repaid handsomely for their work. They all had full bellies and were never sick. It rained when I commanded it too, and the crops were good every year. My armies were large and powerful, and my empire was vast. But some wanted more. They wanted freedom to do whatever they wanted, whenever they wanted, no matter what that may be, or who it may harm."

"And you denied that to them?"

"Yes Amanda, I did. There have to be laws in place to govern and rule properly. Anarchy does not work. Ever. It merely leads to chaos and destruction. Perhaps my laws were too harsh? I do not know. But a growing resistance with a well-devised plan led to my eventual overthrow. It literally took them generations to enact their schemes but when they did, they defeated me, using one I loved as the instrument of my destruction."

"Sounds like you deserved it." She answered almost below her breath, then added, "Not that I believe any of this crazy story."

Crystalon sat back in his chair a moment before leaning forward once again and speaking. "What must I do to convince you?"

"More then you've showed me so far. Some hypnotist mumbo jumbo is not going to do it."

"Very well then. Let me ask you, what do you notice about this room at this very moment?"

She looked around, as did Joe, both looking perplexed momentarily.

Then Joe blurted out "Hey, it's quiet in here."

"No, not quiet." Amanda replied. "It's...silent."

"That is correct, my friends. No one within this room can hear our conversation, and I have silenced their conversations from our ears, unless someone specifically mentions us. They merely see us talking quietly and our voices seemingly intermingling with those around us into a steady background drone."

"Sounds like group hypnosis to me." Amanda answered, still unbelieving.

"Believe what you will Amanda. I have presented you with the facts. If your mind cannot comprehend what I have shown you, there is no reason to be embarrassed. Not many can comprehend the wonders of the mystical world."

"Can't comprehend?" She shouted, exasperated. "I can comprehend anything you can show me, including a line of garbage like this that you're wasting your time trying to sell me." She got up then, and left.

"Hey 'Manda, relax, where ya goin'? The boss is just talkin', why you puttin' an attitude on?" Joe asked, as she receded into the crowd in the restaurant.

"Let her go, Joseph. She obviously is filled with anger concerning my supposed deception here."

"Hey, I ain't seein' no deception, to be honest Boss. I see you bein' a little private with some weirdo stuff we could have you committed for."

"Do you believe I am insane, Joseph?"

"Naaah, I know what I been seein', and I believe ya, though I gotta tell ya, it's definitely a hard nut ta swallow."

"Thank you Joseph, I think."

"What about 'Manda?"

"I can only hope she'll want to talk more in the morning."

"Hey Boss, I gotta ask ya, why do you want your power back? An' believe me I'm havin' a hard time even sayin' these words, This thing sounds so outta this world ta me, but like I said, you convinced me."

"When I first arrived here, Joseph, I thirsted for revenge. My life's meaning was to return to my world and depose those who did the same to me."

"And now?"

"My reasons for re-empowering myself have...changed somewhat."

"Tell me more?"

Both men turned towards the sound of the voice and saw Amanda standing there smiling, slightly embarrassed.

"Amanda, why have you returned?" Crys asked, his face twisting quizzically.

"Because I've seen some crazy things the past few days, and the only explanation for any of it is your explanation. But I still would like to hear why you want your power back."

"Very well. Originally, as I said, I wanted to enact revenge upon my enemies, but now, that feeling and the anger that went with it has waned. Now I seek my powers back merely because they are a part of me, much like a limb that has gone missing. But furthermore, they will be necessary in defeating my enemies, who have dogged my trail for the past several months since I first arrived here."

"What enemies?" Joe inquired.

"In the time I spent in the hospital, I witnessed demons try to steal a man's soul, I was able to thwart them with the aid of a man who was more than he seemed to be. Since then I have been attacked and followed by representatives of the same organization that the demons represented, on several occasions."

"That guy in the men's room the other day in JFK, an' those two meatballs today?"

"Yes, though I am not certain if those thugs today were allied with the same group as Epine-Noir."

"You think someone else may be after ya?"

"I am indeed disposed to the fact that others may have sensed my latent abilities."

"Whazzat?"

"Yes, I believe others may have sensed my affinity to magic, and are seeking to profit from it."

"Ya coulda just said 'yes' you know."

"Though I am not sure if indeed there is anyone else. There only *may* be."

"Demons? You saw demons?" Amanda asked, shock coloring her face a pale white.

"Yes, they were called Wraith lords. Gossamer-like creatures with skeletal, legless bodies and monstrous wings upon their ghostly backs. Soul stealing demons who inhabit the underworld."

"And this is why you want your so-called powers back?"

"Yes Amanda, this is why."

"To help and protect us, and this world?"

"Amanda, even though I have of late begun to see myself through new eyes, and have begun to regret some past decisions, in my own mind, I have ever been fighting on the side of right. I have always thought of myself as one of the 'good guys' as it were."

121

"So you think these demon guys are some kinda major threat to this world, an' you may be the only guy who can stop 'em?"

"Precisely Joseph. These diabolical creatures, along with their nefarious bosses, and make no mistake about this, I am not exaggerating in the least when I say 'Diabolical' or 'Nefarious', for that is precisely what they are, they are indeed a threat to this entire world. Your Earth is grounded in science, whereas mine is grounded in sorcery. The differences are primal, meaning they go back to the time of each world's creation, and are inbred in every being upon either world. On my Earth, everyone uses sorcery to some degree. While science is studied, and advancements made, magic always plays a far, far larger role in the daily scheme of things, and always will. On your earth, magic is largely unheard of and laughed at by the more jaded in society who believe they know better. What they know in truth is insignificant."

"So we're all at risk then."

"Yes Amanda, we are. There is that opposing force that saved the soul of the man in the bed next to me, their name I will continue to conceal till a time of my choosing, as to not put you both in further danger. But they are a group I have decided to, at least for the moment, not outwardly ally myself with. If the need comes, I know they seem on the surface at the very least to be the lesser of the two evils, and even, I dare say from the small contact I have had with them, the heroes of the piece."

"You're talking about Dr. Walker's group aren't you? The Knights of the Golden Dawn? But you doubt they can get the job done against these Wraith lords, right?"

"Yes Amanda that is true. They have been in some sort of balanced battle with them for centuries, from what I have been able to discern, but the Wraith Lords have been seeking ways to break this impasse, and I believe they may have already. Or are about too."

"Then why'd they want you so badly?"

"Because if the other side did manage to gain my loyalty, The Wraith Lords fear they will be heavily overmatched. Right now I believe they are convinced they have some sort of advantage"

"But do you think they have the advantage as of now?"

"Yes I do, Amanda."

"So basically it's us three ta save the world?"

"That is what I surmise Joseph, yes."

"You sure you ain't hallucinatin'? 'Cause a lotta this seems like a stretch."

"Joseph, I have engineered military campaigns for centuries. I have learned to trust my own feelings on these things. This is what I believe. I may be wrong, but I surely doubt it."

"Okay then, I'm in." Joe announced with a smile. "I always did wanna save the world."

"Amanda?" Crys looked at her, awaiting her decision.

"I must be insane, at least crazier than you, but I'm in too." She replied sourly.

"Good then let us enjoy our dinner."

Chapter 16

The next morning found Crystalon, Joe and Amanda packing their car, with Joe and Amanda smirking as Crys brought his own bags down. They laughed slyly as he eyed them suspiciously, then he smiled himself and all three entered the car, and drove away with Joe behind the wheel.

"So we're headin' to France huh? I ain't got much use for those people ya know."

"That is alright Joseph. Keep your opinions to yourself while we are within their country and all will be fine."

"Whatever you say, boss."

"Why are we going to France?" Amanda asked flatly.

"That nation has had its share of mystical occurrences over the centuries. I will be absorbing some of those latent energies there as well."

"So this is your big quest? We're going from country to country wherever supposed 'Magic' may have been used and we're getting you some of it?"

"In layman's terms yes."

"Neat." Amanda smiled as she answered.

"Where exactly do ya wanna go in France, Boss?"

"We'll be visiting the cathedral of Notre Dame specifically, as well as a few lesser known spots."

"So that hunchback story was fer real?"

"There is some truth in most legends and tales, Joseph."

"Speakin' o' tails, I think we picked ours up again." Joe stated as he stared into the rearview mirror.

"Not those fools from yesterday again?"

"Yeah I'm afraid so Boss. Same car an' everythin'."

"This has got to end." Amanda angrily retorted.

125

"Indeed it does Amanda. But let us continue on. When they get too close I will deal with them. If they keep their distance we will merely keep watch on them."

"Can't you make them just go away, or forget about us?"

"There was a time, dear girl, when I could have sent them to another world with an eye blink. But now everything must be planned, and I have no true power as of yet, only shadows of it."

"So are we in danger?"

"I cannot say. For them to reappear means either they are complete imbeciles, if indeed it was the same two men again, or they have acquired some mystic abilities of their own they deem strong enough to deal with me."

"This oughta be interestin'."

"That it will indeed Joseph, that it will indeed."

They drove in silence for a few moments as Amanda continually looked nervously over her shoulder at the car shadowing them, some car lengths back.

"It does look like those same two guys." She offered.

"Indeed. Very well. Joseph slow down suddenly, try to get them close to us. I need to see their eyes."

"What're you gonna do?"

"Watch," was all Crys replied.

As Joe drove, Crys climbed over the front seat into the back of the car, as Amanda moved to the right side of the rear seat, looking at Crys perplexedly.

"Hey! Watch your hands, Mr. Talon, I'm not that kind of girl." She laughed, nervously.

Crystalon ignored her comment. Instead he stared pointedly at the driver of the car following them.

"Joseph, you need to slow down quickly, and I need to be in line of sight with the driver."

"Anythin' else you want, Boss? Maybe some cappuccino wit' that order?"

"Stop your fooling around Joseph, this is decidedly serious."

"If you say so, boss. Now hang on, both a you."

Joe slammed the brakes on, causing several cars behind him to lock up their brakes, including the one being driven by their pursuers.

"Excellent." Crys intoned icily, as he locked eyes with the driver. Concentrating, Crystalon arched his neck and pushed his face visibly forward, until it was almost touching the rear window of the car. A single bead of sweat dropped down past his temple, and then he urged Joe...

"Go quickly I have no idea how long this will last."

Joe sped away, zigzagging through London traffic, heading towards the shore and the Channel.

"What did you do to them?" Amanda asked breathlessly.

***

In the car being driven by their pursuers, the two men are suddenly confronted by something they cannot explain.

"Th-the cars, the-they all are identical! Even the tag numbers!" The driver stammered to his partner, who nodded quickly in the affirmative.

***

Back in Crystalon's car Joe asked, "So they're both seein' the same thing?"

"Yes Joseph both of them are seeing the identical car, over and over and over. It is an illusion that will last for some hours. We should be in Paris by then."

"Oooo. Paris, the city of love." Amanda Coos, as she sank back into the car's rear seat, contentedly.

"Bah." Crys replied disdainfully.

Joe snorted, while looking straight ahead at the road; "You are one weird chick, 'Manda."

Redemption of the Sorcerer

Chapter 17

The next morning, after a solid nights rest followed by breakfast, Joe and Crys left Amanda at the hotel they had chosen to stay at while in Paris and continued on by themselves to their destination, one out of folklore and legend!

"What're we doin' here, boss?" Joe asked.

"Gathering more power Joseph, as I explained earlier."

"But in a cathedral? I mean we're in Notre-Dame Cathedral, in France. What're we goin' ta get here? Hunchbacks?"

"Ha! Not everything is relevant to a movie, Joseph. I do know I have tracked great mystical energies here, from times past. Now I will harvest some of that power, in our Chinese gathering box."

Joe looked around him at the great cathedral, staring at its high ceilings and stained glass windows. "Lots o' history here, Boss."

"Indeed, but here is NOT where we need concern ourselves."

"What're you talkin' about?"

"We must gain egress to the sub-basement. It is there that our quest will end for today."

"An' how do ya figure on doin' that? We're in a Church. No. Let me rephrase that, we're breakin' into a Church. This ain't just wrong, it's sacrilegious."

Crystalon turned to face Joe, annoyance furrowing his brow, "Keep your voice down, Joseph. This must be done."

Joe looked at Crystalon, meeting his gaze with one of his own, but then nodded his head slowly, after thinking about it for a minute. "All right. You said the fate of the

129

world depends on us, and that somethin' big is happenin'. So I'm in. Let's just get this over with, before we get arrested." He paused a moment, then made the sign of the cross and whispered "I'm sorry God, for both of us."

Crys watched his friend silently, but softened his gaze, the corners of his mouth turning up slightly. "You are a good man, Joseph Carboneri."

"Yeah, that's what I hear."

"Now watch for anyone who may disturb us, Joseph, while I open this lock to the basement door."

"Yeah, yeah, already on it." Carboneri replied, grumbling.

Joe turned slightly to watch what Crys was doing, and his eyes went wide.

Crys' pointer finger was glowing as he aimed it at the old lock on the door before him, and similarly, the lock began to glow. Then with a soft 'pop' the lock opened, then fell apart. Joe caught it, and then juggled the hot metal lock before it could hit the floor loudly and bring unwanted curiosities to where they are standing.

"Holy cow! How'd you do that?" He whispered in a higher pitch then usual as he still bobbled the hot metallic lock from hand to hand.

"A minor spell, nothing more." Crys answered as he snatched the lock from Joe's hands in mid-air and deposited it into a pocket of the black leather jacket he was wearing. "Now enter, quickly. Now that the spell is over I have masked our presence as I did in the restaurant. No one will see us enter this door, but the instant we shut the door the spell ends, so we must be swift about it."

Joe nodded and entered; Crys turned around and faced the room, making sure no one was watching, breaking through his cloak of illusion, before shutting the door behind him.

***

In a pew nearby, a man raised his head and smiled. The thin mustache adorning his lip quivered slightly, as the black rose upon his lapel stood in stark contrast to the white suit it was attached too.

***

Inside the two men began descending down a long, winding stairway.

"How d' ya know where we're goin'?"

"I..hear what I am looking for calling me in a siren song of magic, Joseph."

"Huh? I don't hear nothin'"

"Nor would I expect you to. I am growing more and more attuned to the magic of this world. There is an item stored in the confines of this church, an item that was at one time, many centuries ago, a danger to the world until warriors led by a great holy man deposited it here for safe keeping."

"What're you talkin' about? I ain't never heard o' any o' this stuff."

"Nor would I have expected you to. This is something only a mystic of great power would have ascertained."

"If this thing is so dangerous, it must be evil. Why are you lookin' it up?"

"Because it is powerful. The magic contained within it is neither good nor evil. The difference is all in how it is used. A weaker man could become enamored with it, and fall prey to darker tendencies by its call. I assure you I am not weak. Beside the fact is that I do not want the item, I merely want to draw off some of its mystic energies to assimilate as I did it Stonehenge."

"So what is this thing?"

"It is a sword that was used to fell a mighty beast many centuries ago. It is called 'Ascalon'."

131

"Waitaminute. Ascalon, as in St. George and the dragon Ascalon? You're tellin' me that we're here to steal that sword?"

"No we are not stealing anything. Merely borrowing some mystic energy from it. The sword was used for good, to fell a great evil, but in the doing it became tainted with that evil. Now the destiny of the sword is tied to he who wields it. It can either do great good, or great evil, depending on the will of the bearer. The sword can 'choose' who it allows to wield it based on the strength of will of the combatants"

"So there was a dragon? That story is true?"

"I have told you before Joseph, there is a bit of truth in all such tales. This one especially."

"How'd you find this all out? You've only been here for three months."

"I lost my mystical powers upon this world, Joseph, not my intuitiveness for magic."

Finally the men stopped descending the long and winding staircase and came upon a level floor of locked doors in the sub-basement. The floor was lit poorly, merely by oil lamps set in the wall.

"Huh. Not even electricity down this low." Joe noticed. "This place must be ancient."

"It is almost a thousand years old. Construction began in 1163 AD."

"Whoa. So we're walkin' through history here."

Crys stopped, turned towards his companion and continued speaking. "No, we are making history here."

He placed a hand on Joe's arm, stopping him in front of a certain door. "We are here. This is where the sword rests."

Crystalon again pointed his finger at the door lock, again his finger glowed, and again the lock buckled from within. He grasped the ancient doorknob and turned it, with a satisfying click the door opened. "Now we may enter and be done with this."

They both entered the tiny room. Within it, dust covered everything. Parchments lay stacked in crude wooden cubicles, and one ancient wooden wall shelve was stacked with items rolled in cloth of varying lengths. It was on this shelf that Crystalon concentrated his search.

"Here, Joseph, we must search here."

Crystalon ran his hand over the items on the shelf, touching each one a moment, then moving on.

"Hurry it up boss. I feel bad enough about this as it is. I don't wanna hang around here any longer then I have to."

"Silence Joseph, I need a moment."

Crys closed his eyes and touched the remaining items slowly moving from one item to the next.

Joe continued to look around nervously, waiting for someone to discover them at any moment.

Then Crystalon smiled as his hand purposefully gripped an item rolled in an ancient blanket. With a tug, he pulled it off the shelf and kneeling upon the dusty floor, unwrapped it. Inside, an ancient sword gleamed as if it were newly forged.

"Wow. Will ya lookit that." Joe barely whispered in amazement.

"Wow indeed my friend, wow indeed."

As Crys spoke, he removed the magic box from inside his jacket, and undid the complex locks on its ornate hinged cover. Then he opened it and placed it upon the swords blade. Instantly light sparkled from the handle of the sword and seemed to flow into the box. Then just as suddenly as it started, the sparkling lights stopped, the box closed itself and its locks reengaged by themselves.

"Whoa, I don't know about you Boss, but I'm creeped out by that."

"Yes, I would see why Joseph. But fear not. The box cannot contain evil, so be assured only power for good has been caught."

"If you say so."

Crystalon placed the box into a pocket on the inside of his jacket, then wrapped the sword up, placing it neatly where it was on the shelf amidst the other items.

"Not so fast Monsieur, I'll take that."

The sound of the voice sent a chill down Crys's spine as he turned towards the voice's owner.

"Epine-Noir," Crystalon spit venomously.

"Indeed, minor sorcerer. Now give me that sword, or your little friend dies."

Crys allowed his gaze to drift upwards, and the sight that greeted him shocked him to his core. Joe Carboneri was pinned to the ceiling by an invisible hand, and was slowly being choked to death.

Chapter 18

"Release him!" Crystalon roared.

"Only after you hand me the blade." Epine-Noir answered as he toyed with the end of his mustache. A triumphant smile played across his wicked features as he watched Crystalon's reaction.

"Release him. Now!" an enraged Crystalon shouted as he leapt at his foe, smashing him across the jaw with a powerful right cross. Both men tumbled out of the small, storage room, and Joe fell from the ceiling, unconscious, but still breathing.

"I have had enough of you, you effete, evil man." Crys rumbled in anger as he pounded Epine-Noir across the face again and again. Suddenly Noir waved his left hand in a backhanded motion, and Crys sailed from him, as if he was gripped by a huge hand, to smash headfirst into the wall behind him. Stunned, Crys slid down the wall in a heap.

Epine-Noir rose from the floor, his mouth dripping blood. He savagely kicked Crys in the jaw, as he passed him to enter the storage room. He walked past Joe's unconscious form and grasped the sword rolled in cloth, and then exited the small room.

He walked over to Crys' barely conscious body and grabbed him by the hair, until their eyes met on the same level.

"You will join us, Monsieur. Of that there will be no doubt. It is only a matter of time. Time that is in our favor."

He released Crys' hair, and the sorcerer dropped to the floor, catching himself so he did not fall like a rag doll. Haltingly, in a pained voice, Crys spoke "You have made a mistake, Epine-Noir. You have dealt with me as you would an underling, or a spoiled child. I am, as you are about to find out, neither."

Epine-Noir turned to face Crystalon, and was momentarily shocked to find the sorcerer standing, facing him.

"We are not done here yet, you pretentious oaf." Crystalon growled as he spun his hands in concentric patterns before him, before suddenly stepping and stabbing forward with his right hand, while simultaneously drawing his left hand back to his ear in a fist. The first two fingers of his right hand side by side, the ring and pinkie finger curled into his palm, as a powerful burst of light, the same that he had used earlier to melt the door locks, leapt from his fingers, to slice a hole completely through Epine-Noir's torso.

Immediately the Frenchman staggered in pain, as blood slowly colored his white suit, red. He stumbled backwards, clutching the sword in surprise and sudden fear.

"This...is not...over so easily...Monsieur. See to your friend." Suddenly the room where Joe lay exploded in flame, at Epine-Noirs bidding. Crys paused momentarily, wanting to go after Epine-Noir, who was immediately shuffling away in pain, but unable to leave knowing Joe was unconscious inside the room.

Not hesitating, Crystalon ran into the room, and drew himself to an inner state of calm, he reached out with both hands as the flames surround him, sweat dotting his brow, he snapped fingers on both hands, and the flames died out instantly.

Quickly he grabbed Joe, lifting him onto his shoulder, and carried him out of the room, towards the staircase, but then he stopped, closed his eyes and concentrated, as if searching for something. His eyes opened and he ran as fast as possible with Joe across his back down another dimly lit hallway. At its end was a darkened door.

"Whas up?" Joe slurred as light filtered back into his eyes.

"Good, you are awake. Get up Joseph, quickly. We must get away from here. Epine-Noir set the storage room ablaze, and that is sure to draw attention."

Joe slumped against the wall, rubbing his throat painfully. "What happened to him? He got away?"

"Yes, but believe me, at great cost to himself. Now we must exit this door, and quickly."

Again Crys' finger glowed as he set the lock ablaze on this door as well, then he gingerly turned the handle and opened the lock, but not before he made sure they were both once again cloaked by illusion.

They exited the basement into an underground catacomb of sewers.

"Man, does this place stink. What is it?"

"An ancient catacomb that was used in centuries past for waste disposal." He turned towards Joe and smiled slightly, "Welcome to the sewers of Paris. There will be a ladder to the street level soon. We can exit from there. I will keep us cloaked from prying eyes, even though I am weakened at the moment."

Twenty long minutes later, both men exited a manhole cover on a small street, some blocks from the cathedral.

"That was some walk, Boss. We made more twists an' turns in that stinkin' sewer then I can remember."

"That was done purposefully, Joseph. I wanted to make sure, even though we are cloaked in illusion, that no one could follow us. Let us get back to our hotel, we are both in need of medical ministrations."

"I just want a month in the shower and a ton of aspirin." Joe replied while rubbing his neck

"Precisely as I said."

Both bedraggled men entered the sprawling hotel, and made their way to their adjacent rooms.

"Should we tell 'Manda what happened?"

"Not yet Joseph. There will be time for that later. Let us tend to our own wounds."

"He got the blade didn't he?" Joe asked, sourly with the realization that neither of them had brought this up before.

"Yes he did. I can only assume that he could not enter the Church and remove it himself because his purpose is nefarious at best."

"So we did his dirty work for him."

"This is not over, Joseph, believe me. There will come a reckoning, and it will be soon."

"All right. I hope so Boss, I really do. I want another crack at that freak. Seeya later."

Crystalon merely nodded wearily as both men entered their suites and closed their doors behind them.

Thirty seconds later they were both back in the hallway.

"Your room-?" Crys began

"Lookin' like someone went through it with a bulldozer!" Joe answered.

"Amanda!" Crys worriedly stared at her room's door.

Both men ran to her room and began pounding on the door worriedly.

" 'Manda, open up!" Joe shouted. "Aww the hell wit' this." He grunted as he kicked the door powerfully, smashing it open.

Both men entered the room, only to find it likewise ransacked.

"She's gone. They got her." Joe bemoaned in anguish.

"Yes, they did." Crys agreed as he picked up a single black rose from the bed. "I promised her I would keep her safe not two days ago, and I have already failed." He threw the rose down on the bed vehemently, his eyes showing his anguish, "But this madness will end, and soon my friend. We will rescue Amanda, and bring her to safety."

"You will need help for that, Crystalon." a somewhat familiar voice offered from the doorway's opening. Both Joe and Crys turned towards the sound of the voice, surprised by what they saw.

"You." Crystalon exclaimed warily with slit eyes...

Chapter 19

Amanda Serros struggled to open her eyes as light filtered through her pained eyelids.

"She is awakening." She heard a strangely hollow voice speak.

"Yes, we must tell the others." Another, equally hollow voice answered.

Amanda's eyes opened, and at first what she saw was white light, that slowly resolved itself into objects, and then, pure unadulterated horror.

She screamed in terror at the figures floating before her who merely laughed at her fright. Gossamer thin phantoms, legless with huge skeletal, but decidedly immaterial bat-like wings floated and hovered around her. Empty eye sockets regarded her from skulls with horn-like protrusions on their skinless skulls. She whipped her arms across her face to shoo them away in fright, and her hands merely went through them as they would through fog or mist. They laughed at her, making this all the more horrible.

"Enough, leave her now, I command it." A man, very solid and real, though somehow covered in an impenetrable darkness, ordered. With a sibilant hiss the Wraith Lords complied, floating out of the room laughing amongst themselves as they stared at her in turn, licking ghostly lips with tongues of mist.

"Ignore them." The darkened figure commanded. He was powerfully built, that at least Amanda could tell, but for some reason she could not see him clearly.

"W-who are you? " She stammered in almost a whisper.

"Someone who holds your life in his hands. Remember that, and we will get along fine." The figure answered as it paced back and forth in the room, hands clasped behind his back.

Amanda looked about her. The room was large, and decidedly old. Mahogany was the wood of choice in this room, as everything inside it was made from it. The ceiling was high, perhaps twice the height of a tall man, and a slight musky dampness filled her nostrils as she saw windows with sunlight pouring through. The slight sound of water splashing on rocks alerted her to there being a shore nearby.

"Where am I?" She asked, part in wonder, part in indignation, mostly in fear.

"You are safe for the moment, that is all you need know. Do not try to escape and you will remain that way. I have no desire to harm you, but if you disobey me, I will not hesitate to allow the Wraith Lords to harvest your screaming soul."

Amanda gulped hard at his proclamation, pulling a sheet on the bed she found herself in up to her neck tightly.

"Just so we are clear, Miss Serros, I want nothing from you personally. You are a tool, and you are merely being used to bring an enemy to me."

"Crys?" She asked, eyes wide in fear.

"Indeed. Behave yourself and you will have nothing to fear. Disobey, and my friends will return for a rather long snack."

"Who are you?" She repeated, this time slightly more indignantly then before. "Why can't I see you clearly? It's like I'm looking through a blurry lens when I try to see you."

"I am your captor, that is all you need concern yourself with. It is through my magical abilities that you do not see me, because I have deigned it so. Dinner will be served shortly in the main dining hall. I will send someone for you when the time arrives." He turned towards a closet at the far end of the room. "In there you will find clothes that are in your size. There is a certain gown in there you will wear tonight. You will know it when you see it; it is rather striking; though it will pale before your beauty. You have approximately one hour. Be ready, for I do not suffer tardiness from anyone."

"Well whoop de doo." Amanda replied as the door shut behind him. But once it did, her face turned stern and worrisome as she agonized about her fate. "Find me Crys." She intoned mournfully, while closing her eyes, and shaking her head from side to side. "Please find me."

Chapter 20

Crystalon stared at the man in the hotel room doorway, as unto a fox at the hens.

"Dr. Walker. I wondered when you would make your presence known."

"Hey I recognize this guy from the hospital in Brooklyn." Joe blurted out.

"You knew I was here?" Walker asked, surprised.

"I felt your presence, or rather the presence of this." Crys snapped his fingers and the pendant around Walkers neck snapped its chain and flew free, easily this time, and into Crys' waiting hand. "Since the airport in London," he continued. "Why are you following us?"

"I'm here to help you. The Knights of the Golden Dawn assigned me to aid you if you needed it." Then Walker added, "I see you have gotten a bit more powerful since the last time you pulled that trick."

"I told you already Walker, I do not need your assistance. I prefer to work alone, beholden to no one or no group."

"Hey Crystalon, we're the good guys. We're not asking for anything in return. We just want to help you defeat this great evil that is threatening all of us."

"So say you, Walker. I trust no one who seemingly has an ulterior motive."

"And what motive would that be, Crystalon?"

"You know full well you seek to gain my favor for your side of this eternal conflict."

"What's wrong with that? Like I said, we're the good guys. Why shouldn't we seek your help? 'Why should you hesitate?,' is the question that we should all ask."

"I am not hesitating, Dr. Walker. Merely I am seeking to remain my own man, as it were."

"Even if the fate of the world is tied into that decision?"

"You over-dramatize."

"And you underestimate. The Wraith Lords are evil, ancient beings that – through their human pawns like Epine-Noir and his ilk – are seeking nothing less then bringing Hell to Earth on a permanent, grand scale. You have incredible untapped power and potential here. I see you're on the right track trying to reclaim it, but you better realize you can't remain an unattached commodity for long. If you don't join the Wraith Lords they will try to kill you. The only reason they haven't already is because they want you to attain more power and they want to see how much. But the moment they fully realize your potential, and see that you are not going to their side, they will kill you. Or at least attempt to. That's when everyone around you is in danger, so you better think about this, Maybe where you come from you were the top dog, but here you're a little pup."

"Crystalon is no man's pup Dr. Walker, and anyone who underestimates me that way will be taught a lesson, and a very severe one."

"Perhaps so Crystalon, but it looks like someone in your party is already the first casualty."

"I will find Amanda, of that I can guarantee you, and do not forget you are the man who sent Amanda Serros to me."

"Yes, I suppose you will guarantee it, but will you make good on that guarantee? The woman is already missing, and in your enemies hands. What have you done to begin finding her?"

"I just discovered she was missing mere instants before you arrived."

"Yes, and what have you done about it? Argue with me about your freedoms? I can help you. I'm not asking anything in return, Like I said, we're the good guys."

Crys looked around the ransacked room. Curtains were pulled down and all over the floor; the beds sheets were strewn in a corner, dresser drawers emptied on the floor. "What were they looking for?" Crys asked himself, almost too quietly to hear.

"Maybe the Chinese magic box, boss?" Joe answered.

"Yes, probably so. But how did they know we had the item?"

"The vendor we bought it from back in Chinatown, back in New York?"

"Again, probably so. From past experience I have to assume men who would do something like this will stoop to whatever level is necessary to accomplish their goals."

"Includin' murder?" Joe asked, a bit of fear in his voice for Amanda.

"Don't make any mistake about it, Mr. Carboneri, for these men murder would be akin to brushing your teeth to you,." Walker answered.

Crystalon hesitated, and walked across the room staring out the windows on Paris as night hesitantly fell. Then after several long moments in thought he turned back to Walker.

"You sent Amanda to me, Walker. Do you not feel any responsibility for this? Help us locate her."

"Of course I feel responsibility for this, I will gladly help find Amanda. It's the least I can do, Crystalon." He walked towards Crystalon and outstretched his hand.

Crystalon shook it.

"This means that we are only allied in finding Amanda. I am not aligned with you for anything more then that. All other matters, well time will tell with them."

"Agreed, nothing is expected of you Crystalon. But we should leave here, and fast."

"Why?" Crys asked.

As if in answer, police sirens sounded nearby and were getting closer to the hotel.

"They comin' for us boss?" Joe asked.

"So it would seem, though I am not certain if this has to do with our visit to the Cathedral earlier or Amanda's disappearance and the rooms subsequent ransacking."

"How would they know the rooms have been ransacked?" Walker asked, deep in thought.

"Perhaps our enemies alerted the police to Amanda's disappearance and our visit to the Cathedral, and pointed them in our direction?"

"I'd think that would be about right, Crystalon. We should get out of here quickly. I have a car waiting behind the hotel."

"Very well Dr. Walker, so be it, we will join you, for now. Joseph, grab what you can of yours from your room. Take only items you need. Then let us be gone, and be quick about it."

Joe nodded and ran out of the room.

The sirens stopped in front of their hotel, as uniformed police ran from their vehicles towards the front of the building.

"They could be here for some other reason entirely." Walker offered.

"Yes and as it is said 'Pigs can fly'. I am no fool, Dr. Walker. These policemen are here for myself, Joseph and now you as well."

"I can just walk away anytime, Crystalon. They don't know me."

"Yes, except that our enemies will be more powerful with myself out of the way. In that event, your side loses."

"As does everyone on the planet, I guess."

"So it would seem, Walker."

Joe came running into the room, his hands full of clothes he is hastily stuffing into a roll bag. "We gotta get outta here they're comin' up the staircase now, they gotta have the elevators blocked up."

"Hhhmm, so it would seem. Both of you into the bathroom and shield your eyes. I will call you momentarily. When I do, come quickly, straightaway and without question. Follow my commands to the letter and we may yet survive this day as free men."

"What are you doin'?" Joe stammered excitedly

"We have no time Joseph! In there with you both, hurry!"

"Don't get no funky ideas, Doc. I'll crack you one if you try anything weird."

"C'mon Joe, give it a break." The Doctor replied with a nervous tinge to his voice, "I'm as much a womanizer as you are."

Both men complied. When the bathroom door shut behind them, Crys removed the small Chinese magic box from his pants pocket and sat cross-legged on the floor before it, as sounds of running feet thundered down the hallway towards him. He ignored them as he opened the box, and light as bright as a thousand suns poured out of it, filling the room, the hallway, the entire hotel and the street beyond with brilliant, utterly blinding luminescence. Everyone within a mile radius covered their eyes as the pure white light engulfed everything, and drove them all to momentary blindness.

Suddenly, the light was gone as fast as it came, and people in a mile radius suddenly could see again.

Many called it a miracle of God; others called it a curse from the pits of hell. Still others looked for alien perpetrators from the skies. But inside the hotel, only one man, Crystalon, knew exactly what had happened.

***

149

The door to Crystalon's room was savagely kicked open as the bewildered, yet still operating, police entered the room. There they found an empty room, devoid of all life, yet more perplexing and stranger still was the fact that the room was empty of everything. All the furniture was gone and the walls are stained a stunning white, that hurt the eyes to stare at.

The hotel manager entered behind the police, covering and squinting his eyes as he looked at the room.

"Mon Dieu! What has happened to them?" He stammered out nervously and in obvious awe.

Chapter 21

Amanda Serros followed silently behind the old oriental man who was sent to gather her, through hallways dimly lit by torches in sconces, and finally, after being silently bade by him to enter, into a great hall.

"Wow!" She exclaimed, in awe of her surroundings, even in deference to her predicament.

The oaken dining hall was huge; in fact she wasn't even sure she could see the end of it. Glaring light filtered through from somewhere, as a ceiling so high, as to be almost beyond comprehension how it was constructed, loomed in the distance overhead.

She swiveled her head from side to side, and up again.

"This place is enormous." She whispered.

"Indeed, and quite impressive. Wouldn't you say my dear?" A voice replied, she turned and saw the man who had greeted her earlier upon her awakening to captivity. Again, she saw him as if he were a blurry image, unfocussed, indistinct, undefined. He sat at the head of a tremendous dark wood dining table, filled with many people of all races and ethnicities.

"Yeah, you might say that I guess." She followed her escort to her seat near the head of the table, within easy speaking distance of her mysterious captor. The older man smiled at her, wisps of hair covering his face as if they were the remnants of a mustache. His wizened head was bald, and he smiled gently at her, as he pat her hand and shuffled away, his gold and red robes fluttering slightly with each step.

"Heh." The mysterious man at the table's head grunted with a sardonic smile. "He likes you. You remind him of his daughter I believe. Your strength of will I think mostly. He appreciates your defiance. I see you refused to wear the dress I bade you to join us in tonight."

"That's right. You may hold me here, but I'm not your slave or puppet." She defiantly replied.

"My dear Miss Serros, you are whatever I deem you to be." He snapped his fingers, and her clothing disappeared, to be replaced by the dining gown he had ordered her to wear.

"I-I." She stammered, stunned by what just happened.

"You would do well to learn your place here, woman. That place is whatever I require you to be, whenever I demand it."

"Why did you take me? What do you think you'll get out of this? Do you think Crys will do your bidding, or whatever, by me being your captive?"

"Hahaha." He laughed heartily. "No my dear, not at all. I mean to merely annoy him. To make him reckless from your loss. To make him angry. Men become sloppy when they fight angrily. They lose the fine line of reason guiding their attacks. By you being in danger I have thrown his inner center off balance."

"Don't give me that eastern philosophy stuff. If you think this is going to throw him off balance mentally, you don't know the man anywhere near as well as you think you do."

"That is definitely where you are mistaken, Miss Serros. I know him only too well."

Amanda realized she was sparring and getting nowhere fast.

"What is this place? Who are all these people?" What are they doing here?"

"This is my home. They, like yourself, are my guests. All of these people have come to see that the way of life I offer is superior to what their so-called governments and leaders offer them now. They are enjoying my

152

hospitality. As you yourself are. But if you continue your questioning of me, well, let us just say that things will become quite a bit less hospitable for you. Wine?"

He reached over and poured her a glass of wine, smiling as he did. She could see that, but still she could not truly see this man. Involuntarily she shuddered at his closeness.

He laughed at this aloud. "You have naught to fear Amanda Serros, as long as you do as you are told."

"Then why are you hiding your face? I have no idea who you are, even if I could see you."

"Ah but your lover Crystalon does, and perhaps he would see through your eyes."

She bristled with momentary anger, then relaxed when she realized he was goading her "He's definitely not my lover." She replied haughtily

Amanda heard laughter and a willowy snickering. She looked above her towards the sound to see dozens of the ghostly, ghastly Wraith lords hovering in the air high above the dinner guests, all staring at her, enjoying her fear and ill ease.

"Ignore those fools. If you cease your fear, they will depart. They are drawn to your frightened emotions and feelings. They can smell your fright." He leaned towards her as he spoke the last words, and she could almost see his face, but something was not right, something... then he recoiled back to his seat.

"Ignore them Amanda Serros, enjoy yourself while you are here. Obey the rules of my house and no harm will befall you. The rules are thus: You are allowed free reign to whatever part of the house you would like. You may even step outside and bask in the sunlight of any day you choose. You may eat and drink to your heart's content. But do not try to escape, or you will pay for your transgression horribly, painfully and instantly. That is the simple law here."

153

She stared upwards at the chittering things on rotted ghostly wings and sneered at them, practically spiting her defiance in their faces. They recoiled almost instantly and flit away, seeking new game to antagonize.

"Very good, my dear. Very good indeed." The mysterious captor congratulated. "Now, let us all enjoy our meal."

Chapter 22

"-e's c-min- -ro-. -ey Mr. Tal-n! W-ke up!"

Crystalon's head pounded mightily as he shook it to waken himself. He forced his body upwards from where he lay, holding his pained skull in both hands as he grunted, then rubbed his eyes before finally speaking.

"Enough, Joseph, I am awake, stop your caterwauling."

"Sorry Boss. But we're in some kinda trouble here. You gotta get us outta here, wherever here is."

"What are you- Oh, I see." Crys stopped himself and stared about them all. He could see himself, Joseph, and Dr. Walker all sitting on a small piece of rock about ten feet square, as similar chunks of debris floated by their perch. But beyond that, they were in a vast, black, empty void.

Walker turned towards Crystalon, fear etching his features. "What is this place? What have you done t-to us?"

"Relax yourself Dr. Walker. We are safe as long as you do not step off the rock. If you do, you will be lost forever in the void between worlds."

"Are you freaking kidding me? You say that like it's some matter of fact, daily occurrence. My God man, we could all be dead or drifting around here for all eternity for all I know."

"Again Dr. Walker, I implore you to relax. Calmer heads must prevail. I will bring us to safety as soon as possible."

"Boss, how'd you do this? How'd we end up here?"

Crystalon rubbed his throbbing right eye once more before returning Joe's gaze.

"Simply put, Joseph, I absorbed the magic we had placed in the Chinese box at the Cathedral, from the sword,

155

and used that new found power to move us to safety in a doorway dimension."

"A what?" Joe asked, his own relatively in-control demeanor shattering at Cry's proclamation.

"We are between worlds, between dimensions, gentlemen. These doorways exist throughout the fabric of reality. They are magical pockets of space/time, which a mage may use to traverse fantastic distances while between dimensions, to move from one place to another on his home world in blindingly fast time. They are doorways that shorten distances on a world."

"I'd rather take a plane." Walker offered quietly.

"This way is faster, but in my current state it is far more taxing. Though my powers have increased, I am still weak comparatively to my previous state of being. It will be several hours before I can take us back to our world."

"Heh." Walker mused with a slight, nervous grin. "You just referred to my world as our world." Walker replied.

"Indeed it is, at least for now, Doctor." Crystalon answered, with a furrowed brow.

"So whadda we do now?" Joe asked, tired and awed by what he saw around him.

"We wait Joseph. As I have said, I will have recovered sufficiently to return us to our world in short time, only a few hours."

"How come ya can't use one a these things to get you back to your Earth?"

"Because these doorways only exist for a particular world, not between dimensional duplicates."

"So you can step into one, when fully empowered and exit one almost instantly and be anywhere on the Earth?"

"Yes, Dr. Walker, but you are mistaken about one thing, A mage will not be limited to his world, I can exit one on any world in the dimension I am currently in, and

do not for a minute delude yourselves into thinking there
are no earth-like worlds in the great vastness of space.
There are countless worlds which would sustain human life
and have done so. Human life is the most populace in the
great tapestry of the universe, no matter what dimension
you travel to."

"Incredible!" Walker breathed, honestly humbled
by what Crystalon had revealed to him.

"Why are you so surprised, Walker? You yourself
are a magic user."

"What, you mean my playing with a few charms
and baubles to scare away Wraith Lords? Yes, I have a few
magical tricks up my sleeves, but nothing on this level! I-
I'm really finding myself way beyond whatever I can do
right now. This is very far above my head."

"You have set your own limits Dr. Walker. Only
you can expand them. Begin to think outside the box as it
were. Your own inner universe will expand exponentially.
But it all began here." He tapped the side of his head as he
spoke.

"So this place is magic, right?" Joe asked, with a
bemused look on his face, his short hair bobbing as he
raised his head up and down repeatedly, trying to goad an
answer out of Crystalon.

"Yes Joseph, it is indeed."

"Alright Mr. Big Brain, then answer me this: Why
dontcha use yer Chinese magic catcher box thingy to
absorb some a the power outta this place, ta make ya
stronger and get us home faster'n a few hours?"

Crystalon stared at Joe, his own face suddenly
perplexed and, uncharacteristically, his jaw dropped as he
replayed Joe's words over in his mind.

Finally, Crystalon prepared to speak, his jaw set and
after a moment he smiled at his friend.

"Joseph, I knew there was a reason I hired you to show me about your world. You are indeed, a brilliant man."

"Yeah, yeah the wife tells me that alla the time too. Not that I believe her either."

"Gather close my friends, we are about to leave this place."

Crystalon opened the small Chinese magic catching box, and summarily chanted in a language unknown to either man as colors as bright as any rainbow suddenly appeared and swirled, entering into its small confines. Then he closed the lid once more.

"Prepare yourselves gentlemen, this could be a rough ride home."

"Hey, whatever it takes boss, just, uh, don't put us back inta that hotel room with the cops an' all."

"Duly noted, Joseph. Now, let our journey begin!"

Crystalon opened the small bejeweled box as light washed over them all, as bright as a star, and then the lights winked out, and when they did, the men are gone. Leaving only an empty rock among many floating in inky darkness, and nothing more...

Chapter 23

Day turned to night, as the city of love became the city of light. A small burst of said light, not unlike a flashbulb going off, heralded the return of the three men, a block away from the hotel they had occupied, on an adjacent rooftop. They stared silently for a moment as all sorts of police vehicles appeared at the buildings front, followed by fire vehicles.

"They think we burned the room." Joe stated plainly.

"They do not know what to consider here, Joseph. This is beyond their understanding, and so they are taking every precaution."

Joe stared at the hotel a moment, then something else caught his eye as he turned his head quickly from one direction to another.

"What're these things?"

"Hhhmm? What are you talking about Joseph?"

"These glowin' lightnin' bug kinda things."

After a moments pause, he continued, "They kinda look like little people almost, but they're glowin' so bright it's hard to see. They kinda remind me o' pixies, at least what I think pixies might look like, if they were real."

"You see them?" Crystalon asked, obviously surprised.

"Yeah, otherwise I wouldn't be askin' would I?" Joe asked, slightly annoyed.

"They are called FyreFlytes. Magical beings that exist around us, one of many types I might add."

"An' you see this stuff all the time?"

"I have once more, since I began regaining my powers. On my world they were a common entity for many, many years until one day they simply disappeared."

"How come I'm seein' them now?"

159

"Because you must have absorbed some minor trace of magic from our journey to the gateway dimension. Are you seeing these as well Dr. Walker?"

"Uuhhh, you bet." The Doctor replied almost silently, with a semi blank look upon his face.

"What is wrong, Walker?"

"Nothing. I'm just starting to realize how deep I am into something that is way over my head. All I wanted to do was help people by being a Doctor. Now I'm involved in stuff I barely understand."

"Ahhh, but Dr. Walker, you are already deeply involved and more, you have an affinity to magic that is relatively untapped."

"So these FyreFlyte guys disappeared on your world when?" Joe asked, seriously.

"A few thousand years after I took control of my planet, when I began consolidating my power elsewhere in the galaxy. Why do you ask, Joseph?"

"You ever wonder why they left?" Joe inquired, his face grim.

"I-Joseph, what are you getting at?"

"That these little guys mighta split from your world causa you. Maybe you killed 'em off without realizin' it, or maybe you did it on purpose, or maybe they just had enough a your heavy handed stuff and split to somewhere safer, nicer."

"Joseph, I-I do not know. Perhaps you are correct in your assumptions, though you do know what happens when you assume?"

"Yeah I make an ass outta you an' me, but who said anythin' about assumin'? I was askin' a question. You're the one who got all defensive about it. Did you do somethin' to these little guys? Or did they leave on their own? An' if they did leave on their own, how come you never noticed it and wondered why?"

"Why are you haranguing me with these questions?"

"Cause I don't want you ta make the same mistakes here, that you did where you came from. Look Mr. T, I like you. I think you're an up an' up kinda guy, but what you tol' me an' 'Manda the other night, well it don't exactly make me wanna sleep any more comfortably. I'm askin' ya to watch yourself, an' not ta make the same screw ups you made back home here."

Crystalon turned away from Joe and stared at the hotel across the street from where they stood. He breathed heavily a moment, then turned back to his friend.

"Joseph, I am not the same man I was then. I assure you, I will make no mistakes here, at least none that would be in any way shape or form comparable to what I did to my own world. I promise you that."

"Just make sure you keep that promise. I don't wanna be the guy who helped a new Hitler inta power."

Crys said nothing.

Walker watched them both silently, until, "We had better get out of here. Crystalon, can you take us to our next destination, through the portals?"

"Yes, I have sufficiently assimilated enough of that dimensions magical energies to make travel between gateways easy enough. Let us be gone."

Joe stared at Crys, who returned the stare, in silence. Then both men looked away, neither trusting the other as much as they did mere moments before. With a wave of his hand and an esoteric gesture, Crystalon and the two men disappeared in a small pop of light, amidst an ever-expanding sea of darkness called night, that envelops the city of Paris.

Chapter 24

Amanda Serros exited the door of her room, and began exploring her captor's home. She paused a moment, listening and looking for signs of observation. But there were none. Amanda was alone.

She gulped hard and began walking; following the crude brick steps in the torch-lit hallway of the ancient castle. Her light footsteps made nary a sound as she descended to lower levels, exploring in silence. Outside a steady rain pattered against the castle's walls. Modern windows blocking the rains egress.

'*This place is a mix of old and new.*' She thought to herself. '*Ancient stone walls with modern plumbing. I guess this guy isn't that much of a stickler for details of the good old days.*'

She continued walking, losing herself in the adventure of exploring the old castle. Venturing back and forth between hallways. Most doors were locked. The ones that weren't were simple closets or storage rooms. The musty smell of age permeated this section of the castle Amanda found herself in. Dust covered the corners of the floor as small spider webs filled corners in the ceiling.

"Hhhmmmpph. No one's been here in ages. I guess I should backtrack and find another hallway to explore." She spoke aloud softly.

Her footsteps disturbed dust as she was about to turn around, but something made her continue on a moment more.

Hesitantly Amanda stepped forwards, and placed one foot slowly in front of the other, she made her way deeper into the slowly darkening hallway. The torches on either side of the walls grow more sparse and dimmer, but yet she continued further, driven by a feeling that told her she should not stop now, not turn around, but instead forge forward.

Ten minutes passed as Amanda slowly spiraled down a long winding hallway. She knew she was underground now, but how far beneath the earth's surface she knew not.

Reaching upwards, Amanda removed a flaming torch from a wall sconce, the last one in sight, and wrapping it with some cloth hanging in a small pile near the torch on the wall, she caused its flame to flare brighter and stronger, granting her much needed light. "Cute" she remarked offhandedly as she continued on, referring to the pile of material obviously left for a torchbearer to make use of.

Moving aside spider-webs with a subdued, "Ick," Amanda continued on as the tunnel leveled out and started moving in a straight line. The stink of mildew and wetness assailed her in this dungeon. She looked down and realized she was walking in inch-deep water in the darkness. "What else can this be but a dungeon?" She thought to herself.

Then she heard it, a light splashing sound, of someone swimming, or bathing. She snuffed the torch in the water at her feet, and soundlessly crept forward, till she could see around a stone pillar.

Before her was a wide, deep cavern, filled in its center with a huge fresh water pool being fed by a stream that ran in one end of the cavern and out the other. It had a high ceiling by way of natural stone formations and light filtered through many cracks in the stone from outside giving it an eerie, otherworldly effect.

In the pools center, a woman was bathing. Her long, black hair cascaded across her shoulders as she dove under the water's surface a moment, then resurfaced twenty-five feet away. Standing, she dried her naked body off with a towel that was lying there.

Wrapping herself in the towel, she made her way into a small room, naturally made by shifting strata that hid her from all eyes.

Amanda held her breath and hid, not knowing whether to run back the way she came or go deeper into the cave. A moment later she got her answer as someone exited the room the woman had walked into.

"Oh no..." She whispered so low she barely heard it herself.

From out of the naturally made doorway to whatever place the woman had went, the person who came out was decidedly not her. Rather it was Amanda's mysterious captor.

The man whose face could not be seen looked around, his visage as ever, was a hazy blur to Amanda. Then he made his way towards the staircase Amanda walked down on, directly towards Amanda herself.

Amanda quickly looked around, and spied an alcove in the rocks about her. Moving as silently as possible, (actually fairly easy with all the water dripping sounds about the natural cavern) she ducked between the rocks.

Without a pause, her captor walked past her and up the rock-hewn stairs.

Long minutes passed as Amanda barely breathed. Finally, some fifteen minutes later, Amanda stood and looking around herself nervously, she made her way towards the room the woman entered, the same room her captor had exited from.

"Is this what he has planned for me? Making me some kind of slave who lives in a cave? My God what have I gotten myself into?" She thought to herself.

Carefully she entered the natural opening that served as a doorway and peeked inside the small room. As she did she felt a shiver run down the length of her spine, for there was nothing within the rough-hewn space, save for the towel the woman had dried herself with.

"Where did she go?" Amanda thought to herself, *"How could she just disappear? What is happening? What have I gotten involved with?"* Amanda Serros began to quiver, almost uncontrollably with fright as she collapsed to the floor, holding her head in her hands.

Chapter 25

A small burst of light, and Crystalon, Joe Carboneri and Dr. Daniel Walker all stepped through a portal into a new, unfamiliar city. Water splashed from a marble fountain nearby, and all three men looked around themselves, taking in the scenery of a marble walkway in a wide, large plaza.

"Where are we?" Joe asked.

"Don't you know Joseph? Look around you then ask again." Crys replied.

Joe did as Crystalon bade him, swinging his head around, taking in the sights, until he saw a crumbling edifice in the distance. "Aw no, you took us ta Rome? I ain't stealin' from the Church again, Boss, no way!"

"You had no problem breaking into the church in Paris, did you Joseph? And as I have told you earlier, we are not stealing, we are borrowing energies from objects of power."

"Yeah well that mess in France kinda didn't sit right with me. Now I'm some kinda wanted international thief, or somethin' because a you."

"That is only temporary, I assure you Joseph."

"Yeah, right, till I end up in jail for the rest of my life you mean, that's the permanent part."

"Both of you be quiet." Walker ordered, "We're attracting attention, the unwanted kind. I have to make contact with some friends, they can help us out here, as well as with that mess in Paris."

"Your 'Knights of the Golden Dawn' you mean?"

"Yes, Crystalon. The Knights have many friends in high places. By the morning we'll be cleared of all charges in Paris. I just have to contact them."

"That will not be necessary." An unfamiliar voice speaking English with a heavy Italian accent replied, "Come with me, all of you."

As one, the three men turned and saw a tall, heavy-set man, with a bald head, dressed in blue and white robes and carrying a torch. How he appeared beside them so silently surprised even Crystalon.

"Come with me gentlemen, you have nothing to fear, I assure you."

"I am not going anywhere until you explain who you are, and how you know of us, let alone what it is you want of us. Who are you?" Crys demanded.

"I see this will not be easy. I have been sent by his Eminence to see to your needs. The Vatican knows many things in the world. We know good, and we know evil, and we know who stands with us and against us." He pointed at Crystalon. "You are a force to be reckoned with, sir, but we feel you are one who will fight for the good of mankind, when called upon. Nothing is writ in stone, but there is a greatness about you, a greatness you have not yet achieved ever in your life but still may, by making the correct choices."

"You're from the Pope?" Joe asked directly.

"His Eminence, yes." The robed man answered, bowing his head slightly as he spoke.

"This is so outta my league." Joe shook his head and muttered.

"I still have to contact the Knights."

"There is no need to, Dr. Daniel Walker, they have already contacted us."

"Oh, this gets better and better." Joe rolled his eyes as they followed the man warily.

"Know this sir," Crystalon began, "You will not lead us unawares into some ill-conceived trap. These men are under my protection, and as such any who seek to harm them will pay a terrible price."

"Do not seek to threaten me Sir. I am not your enemy. I seek only to offer you aid."

The men entered an old battered doorway at the back of a building and, after making their way down a long flight of steps with Joe grumbling the entire way, they emerged into a huge basement with many men working at modern tables under fluorescent lighting on objects not seen for centuries on Earth.

"What is this place?" Crystalon asked.

"This is a storehouse of dangerous artifacts. Objects deemed too deadly to be allowed into the wrong hands," their guide answered. "Here you will find what you need. I will assist you in your quest while you are among us. My name is Alfredo." He tipped his head slightly while speaking.

Crys looked around himself at the hundreds of men toiling tirelessly about him at the objects of power and somberly extended his hand to the man Alfredo, who took it strongly.

"Thank you. You and his Eminence have my sincere gratitude." Crys bowed slightly as he spoke.

The elder man nodded "You have grown much in your time on my world. From what I was able to glean about you from your arrival here, you are hardly the same man any longer. That man would not have shown the humble thanks you just presented."

"I am indeed not the same man, sir. My time here has changed me. I hope for the better. Meeting people such as these." He waved his hand at Joe and the Doctor, "has awakened something long dead within me. But there is one among our party who is missing. One who I must find."

"Ah, the woman you traveled with. We have people working on her whereabouts as we speak. We will find her for you, or at the very least point you in the correct direction to find her."

169

"Whatever you can do to aid us in our search for her would be greatly appreciated."

"Lemme ask ya somethin' boss," Joe began, "How come you can't magic us to wherever 'Manda is?"

"I cannot ascertain her whereabouts as of yet Joseph, I am-"

"Yeah, yeah I get it, you are 'not that powerful yet.' Understood. Just get all yer powers back will ya? I have a feelin' we're gonna need them."

"Your friend is correct." Alfredo interjected. "You will need all your resources for what is to come. It is like nothing seen on this world before."

"I ain't likin' the sound a that."

"Yeah I agree Joe." Walker added.

"Crystalon will regain his powers in full, soon. You see, one thing we know here is the difference between good and evil, between light and dark, and believe me, gentlemen, the coming dark is black as the deepest, foulest pit. Your role in all of this is more then you know, Crystalon. You are to be this world's savior in its darkest hour."

"How do you know all of this, Alfredo?" Crys stepped forward and asked, staring eye to eye with the man.

"I know because we have to know here. If we are not aware of evils plans and its attempts to grip power in this world, then no one will be. The Vatican is the last line of defense in this world against the rising evil."

"What about the Knights of the Golden Dawn?" Walker asked, "We've been up on this for years. Long before Crystalon arrived here the Knights have been standing in the way of the Wraith Lords. What about us?"

"Why are you upset, Dr. Walker? Your good deeds are always accounted for. We here know you are fighting the good fight, and represent altruistic pursuits."

"Then why are you acting like you guys-" He swept his right arm to his side, encompassing the people working

170

diligently at countless worktables on countless objects, "are the only ones to really do something about the coming evil?"

"You misinterpret, my friend. No one is belittling your organizations efforts. No, if anything you are to be commended."

Walker walked away and paced a minute before returning to Alfredo, "Just make sure you let the big guy upstairs know we're doing our best to make sure the world is safe, that is all I'm asking."

Alfredo smiled knowingly, "He already knows Dr. Walker, believe me, he already knows."

"Enough of this," Crystalon interjected, walking past Walker until he was once again staring at Alfredo, "What help can you offer me, Alfredo? Are there objects here I can draw mystic power from? I feel some, but they are somehow muted to me."

"That you can feel any of them at all is a testament to how powerful you truly are. All items of power are cloaked here. This is a safe house, of sorts, for objects that should never fall into the wrong hands, the hands of evil."

"What do you do with these objects here?" Joe asked as he picked up an ancient, tarnished metal disc from a table, as a white lab coated worker quickly grabbed it back out of Joe's hand, and shot Joe an annoyed look.

"After careful examination, some are hidden away at various facilities around the world, and some are destroyed." Alfredo answered.

"You mean hidden like at the end o' dat movie with the guy who has the whip an' the hat? Indiana Whashisname? In like big ol' warehouses?" Joe asked, not believing what he was hearing.

"Yes. Something similar to that, Joseph." Alfredo answered.

"Nevertheless," Crystalon once again interrupted, "What help can you offer our quest?"

171

"Yes, Crystalon, there are many objects here that can aid you, and I can send you to where many others are around the world."

"Then we will stop wasting time and begin. I must find Amanda."

"Do not rush this, sorcerer. Are you as powerful as you have been before?" Alfredo asked, staring Crystalon in the eyes unerringly.

"No, I do not know if I will ever be as powerful as I once was, but I know every minute we waste talking amongst ourselves is a minute more that may spell Amanda's end."

"Come with me, all of you." Alfredo beckoned. The three men followed without hesitation.

"Where're we goin'?" Joe asked.

"To meet someone who will be of particular interest, especially to Dr. Walker."

Joe, Crys and Walker all stared at each other quizzically, but followed Alfredo without hesitation. The robed man led them down several well-lit and austere hallways, until their surroundings slowly started to change and become more warm and inviting. Simple white walls gave way to mahogany moldings and artists renditions

Finally he beckoned them to enter an open doorway ahead of him. A man sat a desk, with three other men standing behind and next to him. He was looking down at the desk reading some papers he held in his hands. At the sound of them entering the room, he raised his head and stared over the edge of slim reading glasses. He was older, with short gray hair and a lined face. But there was great strength in his eyes, along with a youth and vigor well beneath his years.

The three men each had separate and distinct reactions; Joe looked at Crystalon and asked "Who's this guy?" Walker smiled when he saw the man and exclaimed happily, "Anthony!" smiling warmly. But Crystalon's reaction was altogether different. It was a reaction borne of anger and pent up fury. He literally threw himself across the desk at the man, his hands reaching for his throat. "You!" He shouted angrily, practically growling his fury. "You may have exiled me to this world, Sehr, but I will not allow you another chance at engineering my destruction!"

Chapter 26

"So does your plan proceed apace?" The mustachioed Frenchman Epine-Noir asked, as he brought a goblet filled with some liquor to his lips. Sun streamed into the room he sat in through a curtained window to his right as he languished in a richly appointed chair. Before him was a marble table, and on the other side of the marble table, Amanda Serros's captor paced. His always obscured visage was, as usual, undefined as he walked with hands clasped behind his back.

"Yes, yes it does. My enemy will be brought here soon enough. In response to the predicament of the woman, and when he does finally arrive, I will slaughter him."

"I do not understand." Epine-Noir commented, his French accent coloring the thin sorcerer's words, "Why you do not simply kill him now, while he is relatively weak. It is obvious he will not join our side in the coming war."

"My reasons are my own, Epine-Noir, and are not for you to know."

"Bah, I could have killed him four times over by now."

"Your last encounter with the man left you scurrying away like a rat with its tail between its legs." The obscured man answered with his back still to Epine-Noir as he stared at a blank dark wooden wall in thought.

"H-he caught me by surprise with the extent of his power, that is all. I could still have destroyed him."

"No my friend, I believe you are truly surpassed by him now, in terms of pure power. His might has grown tremendously, and continues to do so. If he cannot be turned to our side, which I believe now will be the outcome of all this, then I must destroy him, and will probably have to do so personally."

"You-I..." Epine-Noir hesitated, his obvious hatred for Crystalon had grown to be a palpable thing as he opened and closed his fingers, flexing his hands into fists that turned red as his grip tightened in fury. Then he re-composed himself and spoke once again, "You are about to make an error, my friend. Allow me to finish off this fool, if he does not join our forces. I can destroy him, I promise you that. The Wraith Lords hunger for his soul now. When I leave him a ragged ruin they will devour him and he will bother us no longer. I can do this thing, but you must realize that he has already given in to the side of light at this juncture. This world is unprepared for the inevitable rise of magic that has hidden itself for longer then man has been the dominant species on this planet's surface. If this Crystalon regains his powers in full he will shape this planet's, this dimension's, future. He must be under our control, he must do our will, or the Wraith Lords will descend back into the hell they were spawned from and all our planning, all our preparation will have been for naught. He cannot be trusted"

The big man whirled on Epine-Noir, his obscured face mere inches from the Frenchman's. "You would do well to consider with whom you speak, little man. I do not make 'errors'. Everything I do is well planned, everything. Crystalon's days are numbered, one way or another. He owes me...much."

"You know him? You know of him prior to this battle we now wage with him?"

"You ask too many questions, Epine-Noir. No more answers will be forthcoming from me. Leave now, or I will forget that you are my most trusted Lieutenant."

He turned back towards the wall and clasped his hands behind his back, contemplating his own deep, dark thoughts once more.

Epine-Noir opened his mouth as if to answer, then closed it once again and silently stood, and left the room with quick steps.

Chapter 27

"Boss! Whatta ya doin'?" Joe Carboneri screamed, as he tried to tear his friend off of the old man that Crystalon had by the throat.

The room exploded into chaos. The three men who were obviously the old man's bodyguards surged forward in an obvious attempt to pull Crystalon off the man, but with a flash of Crys's eyes they were flung away to opposite corners of the room, groaning miserably. Dr. Walker joined with Joseph, trying to pry Crystalon away from the man Crys had just called 'The Sehr.' but all efforts were failing as all could see the blood in Crystalon's eyes. Revenge and anger colored his every thought, and he saw and heard nothing else.

"Crystalon! Stop it!" Walker shouted.

Alfredo stood nearby, impassively, as he took in all the excitement surrounding him, and then he nonchalantly raised his staff up several inches and brought it down powerfully, its end slamming into the floor. All around them the room rumbled as if a great earthquake had just taken place. Everyone, including Crystalon, stopped and stared about at the frozen chaos.

"You will cease this stupidity now, Crystalon! This foolishness will end immediately!" Alfredo roared in a voice that seemingly made the room shudder with his presence.

"I will have my revenge on this man for what he has done to me, I will not be deterred!" Crystalon countered.

"This man does not know you. He is not from your world. In fact he has never met you before now. Release him!" Alfredo commanded.

Crys stared at the man who fearfully returned his gaze, and loosened his grip, all the while not taking his eyes off the man before him, as both Walker and Joe guided him away from the table.

179

"Crystalon, this is Amanda's father." Dr. Walker began, "He sent me to help you when he learned of her capture. He leads the Knights of the Golden Dawn."

"Circles within circles!" Crys muttered to himself as he sat at the table across from the man.

Everyone was nervous within the room. The three bodyguards returned to their feet, rubbing their necks and eyeing Crystalon nervously and cautiously.

Everyone's eyes were upon the sorcerer even as his gaze rested unerringly upon the man seated across from him.

"So," he began simply, "Amanda is your daughter. I must be an idiot, or my mind is more befogged then I originally thought from my journey here months ago, for I did not to make the connection between you and she. And yet something held me back from joining your 'Knights of the Golden Dawn' outright. Now I realize what it was. Or perhaps I always knew. So my greatest enemy in my own world would be my ally in this one."

The older man stared him in the eye, unwavering, his fear diminished now that he realized Crystalon was not going to murder him on the spot. Then in a heavily tinged Greek accent, the man spoke "I do not understand what you speak of, Crystalon, if that is what you call yourself. Dr. Walker called for assistance, telling us all of your predicament and that you needed a tutor. My daughter is accomplished at teaching adults; she lives in New York and was obviously the logical choice. That is all that was involved in this. No duplicity at all."

"So say you, Serros. I choose to reserve judgment on this, for now. What do you want of me?"

"I? I want you to find my daughter. She is trapped somewhere, bound by the web of madness and intrigue you have gotten her involved in." Serros punctuated this by pointing and wagging his finger at Crystalon.

"You presume much old man. You are the one who sent her to me. I did not seek to involve her in these affairs.

You used your daughter to keep track of my whereabouts and movements, to spy on me, so obviously know that I would slap myself across the back of my head for the sheer stupidity of it, if I were able to. Was she reporting to you the entire time? I have half a mind to leave you all here and simply continue my quest, leaving you, Amanda and Walker to your own destinies."

"Crys..." Joe began, uncommonly low voiced for him, as surprise colored his reaction.

Crystalon merely waved him away, and turned back towards Anthony Serros.

"But I will not. I left your daughter's doppelganger before, when I was thrown from my home dimension like a sack of spoiled meat to the curb, by your double there, only to arrive in this one. She was the love of my life, but she betrayed me, as your daughter did here. But I will not abandon her, no matter what she has done. I bear no blame for this. That is completely on your slumped shoulders, old man. But I will rescue her. When I do, I will be done with you all. I will also save your world from the evil that surrounds it now, like a bloody claw closing around it, to crush humanity until it no longer exists. But after that we are through."

He rose from his chair and turned to exit the room. The bodyguards stood in his way but a moment, then he stared at them with eyes that would melt steel, turned towards Serros with the same burning gaze, until the three big men warily moved aside at Serros' nod.

Crystalon moved quickly down the hallway, behind him trailed Joe, and several paces behind him was Alfredo.

"Crys! Boss! Where're ya goin'?" Joe shouted.

"To get some rest Joseph. Rest from this madness and from these people." He stopped and let Joe catch up. "You knew nothing of this, correct?"

"O'course not. I had no idea any o' diss stuff was goin' on." Joe answered, with a slight amount of indignation in his voice. Alfredo caught up, breathing heavily, and resting his weight on his walking staff.

"Crystalon, we have quarters prepared for you and your friends. Please accept our hospitality. It is not often anyone receives an invitation from the Vatican to stay on the grounds."

Crystalon sighed, heavily, and then spoke. "Very well Alfredo. I do need to rest. The past several hours have been trying to say the least."

"Come with me, both of you. You have quarters prepared and awaiting you. If you need food, the kitchen is ready and at your service. Please relax Crystalon. I assure you, no one meant you any harm in all of this."

"I have heard those words before, Holy Man. They are most always amended with a 'but' or a 'sorry' at some point."

"You are not a trusting soul, Sorcerer."

"And should I be? What reason should be given for me to trust any of you? Any of this?" He waved his hand about him in an arc taking in the entirety of the brightly lit hallway with paintings hung, depicting religious scenes.

"God loves you, Crystalon, and he has plans for you. When I say you are to be his greatest warrior in the coming battle, it is not a term I throw around loosely."

"We shall see, Alfredo, we shall see. For now, I need a warm bed and a night of sleep."

"Very well, follow me, both of you."

Chapter 28

Crystalon tossed and turned. He could not sleep at first, as the mere sight of Anthony Serros had driven him to anger beyond words. He moved first from his side to his back, and then to his stomach, trying to find a position on the bed where sleep would come. He punched his pillow trying to soften it, and finally just threw his head back and after many minutes of staring daggers at the imaginary image of Serros on his ceiling, he fell asleep.

And then the dreams came. Dreams of his parents, long dead. But somehow still calling to him...

"My son." his mother cries out to him across a fog-enshrouded land.

"Mother?" He answers, questioning his senses.

"And your father." another voice, male, masculine answers.

"Why are you both here?" He asks in his dreamscape.

"Because you need us." His mother replies.

"In all my years you two have never appeared before me, except for recently since I have been trapped on this maddening world. Why is that? Do you suppose to tell me I never needed you both before this"

"You closed your heart and soul to us, my son." His father replies from somewhere in the mist, but ever closer to him.

"Only now, since your banishment to this strange New World, have you opened it again." His mother adds, even closer still.

"What do you want of me?" He asks, suddenly he is a small boy again before them both, as they part the heavy fog and stand before him.

"We want you to be happy." His mother answers, fully human again and as he remembers her. Beautiful and young, full of life and joy.

"We want you to smile, and live, Crystalon." His father answers, no longer a dead man with an sword through his heart, but a strong, noble warrior, who stands larger then life before the small boy, a hero in his eyes.

"But why are you here, now?" Crystalon reiterates.

"Because you have come to a cross roads of your life." His mother replies. "From this moment on your destiny is your own, yet it will affect untold others. You can either join with these good people who have befriended you, and truly begin your quest in earnest, or you can turn back to your old, selfish ways, and do nothing."

"I already told these fools I would help them," Crys answers getting angry instantly.

"These people are not fools, Crystalon. They fight a shadow war against the forces of evil, against overwhelming odds. They will lose the war without you." His father stated matter of factly. "They very possibly could lose the war with your aid, but at least they will have a fighting chance with you by their side."

"But you must want to do this, Crystalon." His mother turns again. "You must want to do this, and not feel obligated to do it for no other reason then that you are about to fight evil. A corrupting, vile force that will tear this world apart."

He turns to face her, a recalcitrant child facing his mother and answers belligerently "I told you I want to do this, Mother, and Father. I told you I am doing this for the right reasons."

"Yes son, you did tell us, but are they only words? Or are they more?" His father asks.

Crystalon turns towards his father now, "I do this for the right reasons, Father."

"What are those reasons?" His mother asks.

184

He shouts his anger at them both then, his pent up fury at seeing himself as a powerless boy in a man's world. His long held in impotence explodes in the form of him growing to his full height and adulthood instantly, and erupts in the words he shouts violently as he confronts them both.

"I do this to make up for the mistakes I made in my own world! To not fall into the same patterns I did before; to save this world from an evil it will not comprehend until it is far too late. I do this because it is the right thing to do, and for no other reason. I do this because no one else can, and if I turn my back on this problem, this situation, no one will be there to take my place. I do this because I have to."

"And that, my son, is why you are now a hero." His father smiles as he touches his son on the shoulder.

"If you had said you did this to merely gain power, Crystalon, you would have been doing this for the wrong reasons." His mother continues. "But what you have said inspires us and makes us both proud to be your parents. We will watch over you, my son and pray for your success. Your trial is about to become far harder, far deadlier. Nothing is written for certain, so you must succeed on your own merits. You can still lose this battle and this world, this Earth will be plunged into darkness everlasting if you fail."

"Make no mistake, My Son," his father continues, "the fate of this world rests on your broad shoulders alone. But I feel you are more then up to the task ahead. But you must know that you will face foes you cannot imagine who will task you greatly, and one in particular who will cause you great anguish, no matter if you win or lose."

"I will do what must be done my parents. It is so good to see you both again." He speaks calmly, smiling now, resplendent in his full sorcerers uniform with flowing cape and mystic symbol upon his chest. The dreamscape around him begins to fade as his smiling parents begin to recede into the mist that surrounds them all.

185

"Wait my parents! I must ask you, what of my sister? Where is she? What is the fate of Shaleeya? What has become of her?"

But there was no answer, only the sounds of water lapping in the distance and then all turned to darkness...

End Part One

Part Two

Chapter 29

The four men ran through the overgrown forest. The *road* they are on, if that was what it could truly be called, was barely five feet wide. Their feet thundered through the dense woods, as they continually looked over their shoulders fearfully. Up, always up, their eyes travelled. To the treetops and just below, as the murky midday sky offered little consolation to the damp chill of the woods surrounding them.

"Are those things still followin' us?" Joe Carboneri asked.

"I-I don't know Joe. I just want as much distance between us and them as possible." Dr. Walker replied, breath ragged as he pushed himself harder then he ever had before.

"Be quiet you two. They will hear and come. They can smell our breath." Crystalon answered, hushing them both.

The fourth member of the party, Alfredo said nothing as sweat soaked his brow from exertion. He wore a black and white jacket and shirt, black pants, all rounded off by a black fedora with a white band around it, looking more like a well to do man out for a fancy dinner, then one running for his life through a foreign lands forest. He paused and looked behind him, then again upwards, searching for any sign of what pursued them.

"Keep moving, Alfredo." Walker admonished as he grabbed the older man by the arm and tugged him.

"I am Daniel, I am."

"Boss, Crys I-I hear them things, their freakin' jaws are snappin' like dogs goin' after a bone, 'cept its our bones they want to chew on!"

189

"I know Joseph, I hear them too." Crys replied as his feet pounded the ground as fast as his heart was pumping.

"Man, if you told me I'd be runnin' for my life in Transyl-freakin-vania four months ago I'd a told you, you were nuts!"

"Joseph, stop talking! They can smell our breath!" Crys reiterated angrily.

Joe raised his hands in silent surrender, and continued to just run.

Suddenly the men entered into a clearing, a large circular space with dead brown grass beneath their feet.

"We will have to make our stand here." Crys ordered.

"You got enough power from that magic you absorbed back at the Vatican?

"We shall see Joseph, we shall see."

"Here they come!" Walker shouted as he pointed skywards.

They all turned their heads in the direction he was aiming and as one, saw a black wave, a black cloud, a mass of ...something... headed their way. Over, around, under and through the treetop canopy beneath the murky, densely clouded sky.

"Are these freakin' things vampires?"

"No Joseph, they are creatures called *Arjul*."

"An' am I s'posed to know what the heck that means?"

"They are evil." Alfredo replied, "Considered by some to be the devils teeth."

"Another form of soul sucker?" Daniel Walker asked

"No. These do not suck the soul of a man, they devour his flesh. They are the piranha of the sky, and of this accursed place."

190

"Stand back, all of you. Now let us see if I am indeed becoming more and more familiar with the resonance of this worlds magic." Crystalon commanded as he steeled himself. He turned towards Alfredo then and spoke with a slight smile. "A prayer would not be unwelcome holy man."

"I have been doing so for some minutes already, Wizard. We have God's attention."

"Very well, be prepared to run gentlemen, for I have no guarantee that this will work."

Crystalon gestured then, in odd patterns and shapes about him, his fingers glowing white with fire as the very air burned at his touch, a glowing fire of intense heat that made the others turn away and squint their eyes hard, their hands swept upwards to cover their eyes. All except Alfredo, who continued to watch, seemingly transfixed by what was occurring.

The cloud of dark things suddenly descended towards the four men, jet black horrors with leathern, bat-like wings attached to a fat, plump body that were headless save for a mouth filled with rows of razor sharp teeth clicking and clattering noisily, looking for succor. So noisily, in fact, that the sound was deafening and maddening all at once. Joe and Walker dropped to their knees in apparent agony from the sound of it alone.

As one, the cloud of chittering monstrosities dove directly towards their prey, seeking to fill their bloated bellies on the flesh of the four men before them.

Then, at Crystalon's behest, the air exploded about them. As a huge circle appeared in their path hovering above the ground, a circle of glowing fire, ten yards across, that the hungry monstrosities flew headlong into, screaming in agony as they were all instantly immolated, turning to ash with a silent scream on their sharpened teeth.

Wave after wave of the chittering horrors entered one side of the disc shaped portal and did not exit. None

191

were able to stop their yearning hunger for man-flesh and control the descent towards doom.

Looking at the incredible site from on edge, one would see thousands of bloodthirsty beasts flying into what would appear to be a hovering flaming plate or saucer, and not exit the other side, where Crystalon stood, brow furrowed, dripping with sweat, and hands gesturing esoterically in manic concentration.

Uncountable numbers of the creatures, a veritable wave, a cloud of them, swooped and dove towards the men, all ending up being sucked into the ravenous maw of the fire portal, meanwhile the sound from the beasts screaming, clattering, and chittering was supplanted by a roaring from the portal itself akin to standing next to the raging engines of a space shuttle at full thrust. The men on the ground covered their ears and groaned in pain, while Crystalon soldiered on, holding the powerful portal open stoically until the last bloodthirsty creature dove in, teeth gnashing, and was devoured by the portal. Only then did he drop his hands and let the stand off end.

Alfredo looked at him then grabbed the mage as he collapsed momentarily. Joe and Walker were there an instant later helping him to his feet.

"You all right boss?" Joe asked, concern etching his face.

"Yes, yes Joseph. Merely tired-exhausted actually. Towards the end of their run, I was no longer even seeing them dive in; I was simply listening for their screams. When I heard no more, I closed the portal, hoping, no, praying, for the best."

"You did well, Crystalon." Alfredo praised as he helped to steady the sorcerer.

"Thank you, Alfredo. It was...exhausting to say the least."

"I'm impressed, I know that." Walker interjected.

"Impressed? Impressed? That was freakin'
awesome! I ain't never seen anythin' like that!" Joe
practically gushed with praise. "Man, that was the most
freakin' impressive display o' power I ever seen. I gotta tell
you, 'impressed' just don't cut it, I'm freakin' blown
away!"

"Thank you all, but enough praise for now, we must
continue on."

On unsteady feet at first Crystalon stood and
somewhat painfully along the wooded road, Joe in front,
Alfredo at the rear, Dr. Walker between himself and Joe as
the four men continued deeper into the woods.

"You sure it's this way boss?" Joe asked after
several minutes.

"Yes Joseph it is indeed 'this way'. I sense the
magic now. I can tell where a great repository of mystical
items is laying in wait for me. But we must hurry, these
woods will grow dark soon and I-..." He paused a moment
and listened intently, then he began to run, as they all heard
the dreaded sound of the Arjul once more, racing directly
towards them.

"Run!" He shouted once, then was off himself as
the sky turned black once more behind him with chittering,
teeth gnashing horror.

"More o' these freakin' things???"

"Just run Joe, hurry!" Walker grunted as he half
dragged Alfredo with him.

"Where're we runnin' to though?"

"There!" Crystalon shouted as a huge castle
suddenly appeared before them over a rise in the ground.
"Quickly those damned horrors will be on us shortly and I
have not the power left to open another portal, at least not
at the moment."

The four men sprinted mercilessly up the dirt road,
running for all their worth. Their breath was ragged,
especially Joe and Walker who are practically carrying

Alfredo with them as they ran, the old man looking almost perplexed at what was happening around him.

Behind them, the new mass of flying Arjul drew ever closer, as they sprung with all their remaining might the last few feet to the doorway of the castle before them, bounding up the ancient stone steps two at a time.

Crystalon readied his hand to bang on the door, slamming it downward towards the door's surface, when the door suddenly opened quickly from the other side and a man grasped his arm powerfully and hauled him within, beckoning the others to follow as he slammed the door behind them, a split second before the dire creatures slammed into the huge oaken doors with a wet thwapping sound, over and over.

"Greetings gentlemen, and welcome to my home. I am Baron Vorlas. I welcome you to my castle."

"Man this is just gettin' more an' more freaky. If a guy in a cape wit' slicked back hair steps outta a curtain, I'm outta here." Joe murmured.

Dr. Walker jabbed him in the ribs while maintaining a smile of his own.

"Welcome, I say again gentlemen, welcome to my humble home," Vorlas smiled, gesturing them all to follow him. He stood at the six-foot mark, with a jagged nose and short jet-black hair. He wore a suit and thin tie, all in black to match his hair. His was devoid of facial hair, and smiled warmly at them.

Still, the men could not contain a shudder when thinking of their last minute rescue by this mystery man.

"What brings you to my fair home this day, hhhm?" He asked in a heavily Romanian accented voice.

"We are here seeking... something, and were attacked by the Arjul after our driver left us on the side of the road saying he could drive no further. He complained of the road not being wide enough for his car to continue on." Crystalon explained.

"Indeed, these roads are old and meant for horse travel in this part of my country. We have not been modernized as of yet. I prefer it so, do you not agree? It keeps some of the Old World charm of the place." The men began to walk, following their host

In the distance a wolf howls, then another and another, Vorlas smiled at the sound.

"You mean charm like that?" Joe asked.

Again Walker nudged Joe, harder this time, and glared at him with ice in his eyes. Joe got the message and shut up.

"It is getting dark outside my friends. Transylvania at night is a dangerous place to be. I suggest you enjoy my hospitality this evening and continue your trip tomorrow. There are plenty of empty rooms here in my castle; my home is your home. Dinner will be served at seven PM, the staff will see to your needs, and show you to your rooms. I look forward to your company then." Volas turned then and walked away.

Joe looked at Crystalon and started opening his mouth, but a stern gaze by the sorcerer stopped him immediately as they followed several staff members to their rooms.

Inside Crystalon's room, Joe finally spoke his mind as Walker entered behind him. Alfredo was in his own room tending to his attire. "Hey Boss, I'm really not likin' this guy poppin' outta nowhere, castle an' all and savin' the day. I'm still thinkin' this guy is Drac's cousin or somethin'."

"The man saved our lives. I was spent after the massive outpouring of energy I used to destroy those nefarious creatures. If not for his timely assistance we would be dead and devoured by now."

"Maybe so, Boss, but I don't like the way this place just appeared out of nowheres."

195

Crys turned towards his friend and smiled. "It didn't appear out of nowhere Joseph. This is where we were heading the entire time. I sense a wellspring of mystic energy here in this castle, beneath our very feet. This castle was calling to me with its siren song of power. Now we must find the siren itself."

Joe sighed and collapsed in a thick chair, "Why'd I know you were gonna say that?"

Chapter 30

Tink. Plick. Tink. Plick. Tink. Plick. The sound, more of an annoying noise really, roused Amanda Serros from her deep slumber. Groggily her eyes regained focus as she realized she was in her room – or prison cell as the case may be – within the great castle where her mysterious captor was holding her.

"Where?" She asked as her eyes regained focus. Tink, Plick. Tink, Plick. The sound continued as Amanda looked towards the direction the sound was emanating from, towards the foot of her bed actually. It was an old-fashioned canopy bed she was asleep in, within a room decidedly made up for a young girl, full of frills and pinks and whites everywhere.

There, seated near the foot of her bed, legs crossed in an old rocking chair, sat a thin, mustachioed man with greased back, black hair and a black rose in the lapel of his powder blue suit. He was flipping a coin over and over in his right hand, catching it in his right palm, then slapping it down on the top of his left hand, then he pulled his right hand away to look what side it had landed on. He looked again, twisting his head slightly to the left and half smiled at the result, then continued to flip and catch the coin, repeating the same routine.

"Ah you are finally awake Cheri. Good, good."

"What do you want, Epine-Noir?"

"Ah you remember my name, very good, very good, so we can, as you Americans say, cut to the chasing, no?"

"The chase, cut to the chase." She pulled her sheets up over herself, realizing for the first time she was naked under the covers.

"Ah do not be so formal, Cheri. You say chase, I say chasing, oui?"

"How'd I get here?" Amanda asked, ignoring him.

"Ah, our master himself found you unconscious down at the hot springs bath beneath this mountainous castle. He bore you back to your room, where you have lain since."

"How long was I asleep?" She asked fearfully.

"Less then a day." He answered while continuing to play with his coin, never looking her in the eye as he did so.

"Okay. So what do you want? Why are you here Epine-Noir?"

Suddenly, and very much like a coiled snake, Epine-Noir leapt at her, landing atop her, pinning her hands to the sides, moving his face within inches of hers, all at once and so fast she barely had time to register what had just happened.

"I am here, Cheri, because I want you to know that you had better be nice to me. Very nice. Because I am your way out of this house, not the master. He will keep you here forever, at least until Crystalon finds you, and he will come here looking to rescue you, to free you from his enemies, myself among those. But all he will find here is death. His own is a certainty. Yours is up to you. You must decide, Cheri, who you will back when the moment of truth comes. The sniveling sorcerer from another world? Or the man who will soon be the master of this one."

"You're not going to be the master of anything, especially not the world. If anyone is sniveling it's you, you pretentious little man, now get off of me!" She kneed him in the groin as she spoke, sending him tumbling off the bed, holding his private parts while his face twisted in pain.

"Keep off of me you sick, little freak!" She shouted more out of fear then threat.

But he was almost instantly up and slapping her across the face savagely. She tumbled to the floor, as he brought his hand back and down across her face again, hard. "How dare you, pig. To attack Epine-Noir is to court death and pain. I will make you regret the day you ever met the fool sorcerer."

Amanda laid stunned on the floor, her cheek bruised, and her wits similarly wounded, as she watched the hand rise again, only to be stopped by a much stronger arm.

Instantly Epine-Noir's face went white as he saw who stopped his beating of the helpless Amanda. "No, m-master I-" he stuttered as the mysterious captor's powerful fist smashed into Epine-Noir's jaw, sending him careening across the room and out into the stone and brick hallway.

"Stay away from this woman, dog. She is under my protection, for now. If you touch her again I will cut off your hand, and then beat you with it." The Master growled, anger carving dark lines in his face, as he stormed towards Epine-Noir, who scurried backwards on all fours like a trapped rat in the hallway, sweat glistened on the smaller mans face as his back came up against a stone wall far too quickly for his liking. Amanda stood on wobbly legs in her room as she struggled to make her way to the hall to see what was happening, holding the bed sheets about her body tightly.

In the hall the larger man, her true captor, towered above the cowering Frenchman, and continued to berate him. "Do not touch this woman again Epine-Noir, or as useful to me as you are, I will still feed you to the Wraith Lords, piece by piece." He grabbed Epine-Noir by the collar and drew his face close. "Do not try my patience, wizard, for you will find it short and unforgiving." Then he hurled Epine-Noir from him, and stormed away with nary a backwards glance towards Amanda who stood in her doorway, one thought echoing in her mind. '*I almost saw his face.*'

Chapter 31

The dinner table at Baron Vorlas' castle was large enough for a dozen people, yet only the weary travelers and Vorlas himself sat about it. The dining room was relatively large, yet not so big one would feel lost in it. The room was made up of dark wood and hanging tapestried with candles all about providing lighting. The aroma of just cooked meat permeated the place.

Music filtered through from a small band of musicians across the room.

"Your home is indeed wonderful Baron, once again I thank you for allowing us to stay here temporarily." Crys started, before taking a sip of his wine.

"I thank you Mr. Talon," The Baron replied in a heavily accented English. He then stood and raised his goblet. "I offer a toast to my new friends the road weary travelers who have made our day here in the old mansion so much more...interesting."

They all stood and followed his example, taking a sip of wine as they did, then sitting, only after he did.

Joe looked at Crys, then Walker, and then back to Vorlas before he spoke. "So what is this place? Didja grow up here?"

"This was indeed my ancestral home, Mr. Carboneri. Though when I studied in the United States I never thought I would return here. The passing of my last remaining relative has forced that hand upon me. And now I sit in guardianship of this place." He drank his wine again and cut a piece of steaming beef that was heaped upon his plate by busy servants who milled about them all.

Alfredo sat next to Dr. Walker, merely watching quietly and eating in small bites, smiling pleasantly as he did at the servants, and nodding every so often.

"Where'd ya study Baron?" Joe asked between mouthfuls.

"Harvard University."

"Ah okay." Joe answered non-committedly as he continued to chew.

"I must ask, sir," Crystalon queried, "Why did you return? You do not sound as if you are pleased to be here."

"My...life, my stewardship of this mansion and the surrounding area are something I had no control over. It is my...duty to be here. A duty that was entrusted to me before I was born. It is not something I like to speak of, but tonight, with you, my new friends, amidst this talk of life and destinies forced upon one, well I sadly do not know or believe any of you can understand." He swirled his glass of wine around as he spoke, the contents of the goblet moving like a small vortex at sea within the glass, his eyes staring only at the red liquid within, his thoughts far away from where he now sat.

"In this you would be surprised my friend, how similar our stories may indeed be." Crystalon replied.

The man who could only be called the head butler appeared from an adjacent hallway, gray haired, mostly bald atop his head, wearing a black suit with a white ruffled shirt and red ascot, he approached Vorlas and whispered in his ear excitedly.

Vorlas quickly stood. "Gentlemen, please excuse me. Some...thing requires my immediate attention. I shall return quickly." He turned and walked away, fast, following the older man.

"What do you suppose that was about?" Dr. Walker asked.

"I do not know, Daniel, but I do not like the manner in which it affected our host." Crys replied, while watching Vorlas depart.

"You think its trouble boss?"

"I do, Joseph, and I believe it may pertain to us."

202

"What makes ya say that?"

"Because we are the newest things in town."
Walker answered.

"An' this town don't get anythin' new but once
every hunnert years or so, right?"

"Yes, Joseph that is indeed correct." Alfredo
answered, as all heads turned towards the formerly silent
man.

"I wondered when you would rejoin us in
conversation." Crys replied.

"I have been listening earnestly, magician. I believe
we should join our host at his front door immediately."

"Why?"

"Because, Crystalon, he is about to need our aid."

"Lets stop arguing and go help him," Walker added
quickly.

"You trust in Alfredo's word rather quickly,
Daniel." Crys stated. His eyes slit as he stared at the young
Doctor.

"Let's just go. I have a bad feeling about this."
Walker replied while avoiding Crystalon's gaze and
walking quickly towards the hallway Vorlas disappeared
through.

Joe looked at Crys and shrugged his shoulders,
turned and quickly followed Alfredo and Walker.
Crystalon merely walked after his companions an instant
later, deep in thought.

A moment later they followed the sound of voices
getting louder, one of them definitely the voice of Baron
Vorlas

"No, you may not enter here, Constable. I have no
need of your presence in my home."

"I believe you are in error, Baron Vorlas." A man in
a Transylvania policeman's uniform answered him.
Standing behind the officer were a half dozen other
policemen. All wearing seemingly antiquated uniforms, as

if they had stepped fully clothed out of the mid 19th century. The uniforms were red, with many buttons running down the front, and each was wearing a strange hat, not quite a cap, more solid and taller all in black. Each man wore polished black boots as well. "Strangers have come to our fair town, and it is my duty to welcome them. As well as to ask them what they are doing here."

"They have no need of your...services, constable. You should leave. You are not welcome here. They are merely weary travelers whom I aided when they were attacked by the denizens of these haunted woods."

"Ah but I would feel much better, Herr Baron, if I could speak with them myself."

"And what would you ask of us, Constable?" Crystalon asked as his party appeared behind Baron Vorlas.

"Ahh, you must be the road-weary travelers I have heard so much about. I am most...pleased you are well. I would like to come in and discuss your trip here as well as what you are exactly doing in our fair town."

"The only person who may invite you into this home is the Baron himself, and I distinctly heard him tell you no."

"But I would like so much to speak with you at length concerning your journey."

"Again I tell you no, Constable." Vorlas replied, anger coloring his voice and face.

"You heard the man, he said no." Joe retorted angrily as he pushed his way forward to the doors edge, where both Crys and Vorlas immediately each placed a hand in front of him, from either side, stopping him from walking out the door.

"Go now Constable. You are not wanted or needed here. Leave and do not return."

"Go, I will, but I shall return Baron Vorlas, and you will rue the day you refused me entry."

He spun quickly and walked down the stone steps, his men following suit as a mist quickly rose about them all and they seemingly disappeared into the night.

"What the hell was that all about? Talk about damned creepy!" Joe asked perplexed.

"We saved your life." Crys replied matter of factly, as Vorlas nodded once in agreement. Sergei, the gray haired lead butler closed the door behind them as they all returned to the dining hall.

"Saved my life from what?"

Alfredo snorted a laugh back as he looked at the others. "Do you want to tell him, sorcerer? Or should I?"

Crystalon waved his hand in a 'go ahead' gesture as he sat down once again at the dinner table.

Alfredo looked at Joseph and smiled like an elf at Christmas time before speaking, "We saved you from the vampires."

"What? That guy was the vamp?" Joe started incredulously.

"Indeed." Crys answered as he sipped more wine.

"Did you not notice the uniforms they all wore?" Alfredo asked.

"Yeah they looked old, so what? This ain't exactly Beverly Hills ya know. Mebbe they can't afford new ones."

"Those are the uniforms they all died in, Joseph. Well over a hundred years ago," the Baron replied. "They continue to try to do their policeman's duty, but with a nefarious twist. They do not protect and serve. They serve, but usually it is an unwary travelers heart and blood they serve to each other."

Joe involuntarily shivered then turned toward Alfredo "How'd you know what they were?" Joe asked Alfredo, who cut a piece of steak on his plate.

"Is it not obvious Joseph? They had no souls." He answered between chews.

"This gets freakier an' freakier." Joe mumbled as he pushed his plate away from himself, suddenly no longer hungry.

"What do they want here, Baron?" Crystalon asked their host directly.

Vorlas matched his gaze to Crystalon then spoke after a momentary pause. "The same thing that you do, Mage. They want the magic wellspring that this castle sits upon."

Chapter 32

"He wants what?" Joe started.

"The magic Wellspring." Walker replied without breaking his gaze on the Baron.

"How long?" Crystalon asked, as he pushed his chair back from the table, leaned forward and steepled his fingers upon its surface.

"Hhhmmm?" Baron Vorlas answered

"How long has that ...monster been coming here and trying to get into the castle?"

"You would not believe me, Crystalon, if I told you."

"You have no idea what I would believe Baron, trust in that."

"Over one hundred and fifty years."

"Waitaminute, how old are you?" Joe asked in surprise.

"I am forty four, Joseph."

"Then this is your families curse is it not?" Alfredo asked.

"Not our curse, our responsibility." Vorlas replied.

"So yer family's been watching this place for all that time. Sounds like hell."

"It is Joseph, it is. But we Vorlas's do not shirk our responsibility."

"You are a brave and true man, Baron Vorlas, but I fear you need our help in this endeavor."

"Why Crystalon? I have repelled the vampires for years. Why would I need your help now?"

"How many times have they come to your door, Baron?"

The Baron looked away and wiped his brow; his gaze falling upon a painting of a woman on his fireplace mantle. She was stunning. Blonde hair piled high, perfect features and a slight smile upon her exquisite lips.

"She was your wife, wasn't she?" Alfredo asked quietly.

"Yes, yes she was."

"W-what happened?" Daniel Walker asked, barely audible.

"They came here, ten years ago. I had never seen them brave the grounds before. Strong magic keeps them away from this place. Spells laid using the wellspring as a source of power that are an anathema to vampire. Yet they forced their way through. By magic of their own, or by willpower, I cannot say, but they were here. My Natalia knew none of this. She did not know what my duty was. She was not involved. The servants know; they are all trained what to do and what not to do. She was strong headed my Natalia. Her background was... none of this." He waved his hand around meaning to encompass the room. "No matter how many times I told her not to answer the door, we had servants to do that, she insisted on doing so herself at every chance. I was away from the manor that eve, on business in Stuttgart. Sh-she heard the knocking upon the door. Sergei ran to see who it was through the peephole, but she was a step ahead of him. She foolishly opened the door and Constable Trago was there. Smiling as if he were a suitor on a date. He asked her to step out of the doorway for he had to show her something that he and his 'police' found upon the grounds. Sergei ran to stop her, but she stepped through the door and instantly was taken to the sky, as the monsters changed to their man-sized bat forms and flew away with her screaming. Her screams echoed throughout the night. Sergei and the staff armed themselves properly and went in search of her, but found nothing. Her screams seemed to be coming from nowhere and everywhere."

"Baron, I-I'm sorry." Joe offered, as he looked at Crys.

"There was nothing you could have done Baron." Crys added, obviously uncomfortable with the role as someone who was trying to soothe another's pain.

"No Crystalon, you are wrong. I could have been here. I did not have to be away that eve. But I was. I should have told her about this place. Instead I let her live a life of lies. She had no idea about the monsters that live here. It is my fault my beloved Natalia is dead, and nothing can ever change that."

"Baron," Crys began, "You might as well blame yourself for nightfall or the coming dawn. Nothing you could have done would have prevented her death."

"You cannot know that Crystalon, you cannot."

"No, I cannot, but I can tell you that if those monsters did not kidnap and abscond from this mansion with your wife that night they would have another. Or perhaps she would have opened a window at the wrong hour and one of them would have hypnotized her from without, forcing her to walk out to her doom. You cannot know what would have happened, Baron. Mourn your beloved, yes. But do not destroy yourself over her fate. It is best to wreak vengeance upon this unholy fiend and his minions. Let that be your focus."

"But how? They come at night and run as soon as I prepare to destroy them. Over the years they have killed many in the village below as well as many on my staff who have tarried too late, and have been out past sundown. It is impossible to get to them; they fly away so swiftly. I have destroyed all of two of them these past many years."

Crystalon nodded his head thoughtfully, then answered, "That was before we arrived here. Now your situation has changed, dramatically."

"And all I must do is surrender the repository of magic energy this manor rests upon to you."

"I am not here for evil, Baron, as I am sure you already know. There are dire forces threatening the planet entire, that make these ...vampires pale in comparison."

"What could be so horrific as to make these monsters appear inconsequential?"

"Baron, the creatures we chase, and their enigmatic masters are called Wraith Lords." Daniel Walker offered.

"Wraith Lords." Vorlas repeated quietly as he stood and walked over to his fireplace mantle, staring at his wife's portrait hanging there. "What are they?"

"Soul devouring monsters." Alfredo answered.

"Indeed." Crystalon agrees. "But they are not our primary concern. There is a force driving them, a controlling figure who was vying for my power and allegiance, until I denied him, or it. Then this being captured and kidnapped one of our number. She is our concern at the moment, but I cannot attempt a rescue until I have gathered more magical power. Else I would be destroyed by the might I sense behind these creatures."

"So you would use the power selflessly, for the good of the world?"

"Yes, Baron, that is my only concern. Until I came to this world I was a vain, petty man who had all the power in the universe, it seemed. When I came here I was as nothing, and threatened from all about."

"But the concern for my well being by those I encountered here, even when I was an angry, self concerned fool made a mark upon me. From the moment I awoke in a hospital bed and was tended to by caring Doctors and Nurses, I saw something I had not seen in many millennia. People here cared about me, even if they did not know me. They wanted to help the amnesiac stranger. There is something special about this world."

Vorlas turned from the painting he touched tenderly and faced Crystalon. "You say 'This World' as if it were not your own. Are you truly mad?"

210

"Perhaps I am Baron, perhaps all of this is the product of a diseased mind and I am laying bound in some asylum, but I do not think so. No, I am a man from far away. A man who has traveled incomprehensible distances, distances as far as beyond the furthest star, yet as close as the next heartbeat. And now I ask your aid. I need your wellspring of magic."

"So you are he." The Baron stated flatly.

Crys, Joe, Daniel and Alfredo all looked at the Baron quizzically.

The Baron stared at Crystalon, his eyes bore into the sorcerers soul, questioning without words, seeking truths that only the eyes could silently tell, and then the Baron spoke once more: "There is an ancient legend Crystalon, a legend of a man who once wielded great power and who would become the only hope of the world's people against an unknown and malevolently evil and powerful enemy. One who will decimate the Earth and make it a feeding ground for evil."

"The wraith-things." Joe Carboneri stated flatly as he made fists of both hands and released them over and over.

"They are just the tip of this iceberg, I assure you." The Baron answered as he turned back towards his wife's painting again. Shadows flickered across it in the candlelight as he silently stared at it before returning his gaze to the men in his parlor.

"The legend also states that the man who comes to save this world may be worse of an enemy then those he seeks to destroy."

"I am no enemy of those who seek to protect this world, Baron. Our enemies are a common foe."

"So say you, Crystalon. But who would stand for you?" He turned towards the three men who stood behind Crystalon, Joe, Walker and Alfredo. No one moved, then Joe looked around and stepped forward.

211

"I'll stand for 'im. I had my doubts for a while, but now I know this guy's the real deal. He's shown me things the last few months that I ain't never knowed existed. Hell, I couldn't even imagine they existed." He clapsped Crys on the shoulder and continued to speak. "He's the real deal all right. I trust 'im, an' that's sayin' a lot comin' from a guy like me."

Walker stepped forward and stood next to Crys as well. "I stopped doubting him when he saved us from the Police in that hotel back in France. He hasn't steered us wrong yet. I believe he's the only chance this world has at survival. I'm in his corner."

"What about you, old one?" Vorlas asked Alfredo.

The wizened man smiled beneath his full white beard and spoke, "The man has performed miraculous things. But he has impressed me more with his sincerity and determination. He is also a brilliant protagonist, and strategist. Many other men would have charged after their woman blindly, running headlong into the jaws of death. This man gathers his forces for his attack, knowing to strike too soon would be disastrous. I have come to trust him as well."

"Very well," Vorlas began, "You have all given your reasons for trusting this man, but the questions remains, why should I?"

"Because Baron, you have no other choice." Alfredo answered stoically as the double doors to the parlor suddenly swung open and Sergei storms through them.

"Baron! This is most unforeseen! Trago has returned, but the dark cloud has returned with him! Even now they fly against the castles walls as we speak, seeking entrance, we are doomed Baron, doomed!"

Vorlas slapped his butler across the face, "Get a hold of yourself man! Nothing is written in stone. We will yet win this day." He turned towards Crys and nodded solemnly. "If I grant your request will you help us?"

212

"I will do better then help you Baron, I will rid this land of your enemies with true finality."

The Baron turned and walked across the parlor towards a waiting staircase leading down, then he stopped, faced them and spoke cryptically. "Very well, follow me."

Walker and Joe looked at Crystalon, who nodded to follow, Alfredo merely smiled slightly and dropped in step with them, his white suit and black tie reflecting the candlelight in the room as the four men descended the staircase.

The staircase was stone and rough-hewn. Vorlas plucked a flaming torch from a sconce on the wall as he descended, holding the torch aloft before him as he spoke, "This cavern has been here since before man walked this world. My ancestral home was built over it, for my forebearers knew the importance of what lie beneath."

"Yer bein' a little vague there, Baron."

"I believe he is trying to be, Joe." Daniel Walker replied.

Above them a sudden rumbling and a loud cracking sound reverberated through the castle walls, instantly Sergei was at the top of the stairs calling to the Baron, "They have breached the walls with explosives, Baron, they now come through!" He shouted excitedly and in terror.

"Get everyone down below here, man. Block the door!" Vorlas shouted back to him loudly, up the many flights of stairs they have descended.

"I thought vampires couldn't enter a house unless invited? At least that's how the story goes." Joe questioned.

"They've circumvented that, Joseph, by blowing the wall of the house down." Crystalon replied as he stared up the stairs, listening to the cries and screams emanating from above him.

"Monsters." Alfredo stoically stated as he shook his head sadly.

213

"Hurry my friends, I fear we do not have much time. The evil ones will soon smash that door down and kill all they find." Vorlas coaxed them on as they descended one level after another on a circular staircase cut of the stone beneath their very feet. After many minutes of walking, they came to a lower level and a crumbling stone arch. They walked through it towards a hidden pulsing source of light. Rounding a corner they came upon a huge rock, whose glowing, pulsing, golden light illuminated the entire buried cavern.

The men stared at the gigantic boulder in awe, which was as large as a small house.

But none more so then Crystalon, who finally, after many long seconds, offered wide-eyed, and in a barely discernible whisper, "I know what this is."

Chapter 33

"Well boss? You gonna enlighten us?" Joe asked sarcastically and with little patience.

"Yes sorcerer, what is this boulder? Why does it glow thusly?" Alfredo asked.

"It is... my lost power."

"Huh? Excuse me?" Daniel Walker stammered.

"Many months ago, When I was battling for my throne, my very existence on my own Earth, I knew that my time was ending, that all was about to be lost. Before that could happen, I harnessed a large amount of my mystic might and sent it into the void. I could not allow those who had defeated me access to my power. It somehow all coalesced in this boulder. I never expected to be able to regain it. And yet fate has once again surprised me." He stroked his chin with his left hand while touching the glowing surface of the boulder with his right, as his voice trailed off softly.

Baron Vorlas stepped forward and spoke firmly, "That cannot be, Crystalon. This boulder has been here for over a century. Yet you claim this was only sent by you a mere months ago. How can that be?"

"Time," Crystalon began, "its movements are fluid, and in my dimension it moved far differently then here, on this Earth, far slower. I am over one million years old, and in my universe there was no end in sight for my life."

"Oh man, so if you go back to your world, it may be completely different then you remember?"

"I do not know Joseph. Perhaps my own...compatibility with my home dimension will allow for me to step back to the moment I left, perhaps not. I do not have an answer to that query, my friend."

215

From above, Sergei's voice drifted down to them "They begin to breach our blocked doorway, Baron, we must retreat down below. We cannot hold them any longer." The elder manservant shouted.

Vorlas looked up into the darkness and replied "Do so and do it quickly old friend. I want no more loss of life for my friends and staff. Hurry down to our side, all of you."

"This ain't good." Joe quietly spoke to Walker, who nodded grimly.

"Crystalon, if you're going to do something, now would be the best time." Walker offered.

"Indeed Daniel it would be. I will begin the incantation immediately, but this will take some time at least, as well as considerable effort on my part. You all must hold them off. Baron, do you have any weapons stored here?"

"Yes Crystalon, of course. My family has protected this source of magical power for generations."

"Ok Baron, show us to 'em." Joe commanded, his brow set as if in stone.

The Baron didn't reply, he merely walked away purposefully, Joe and Daniel looked at each other quizzically and followed, Alfredo moved to join them, and was stopped by Crystalon.

"Not you Alfredo, I need you here."

"Why, mage? I want to help."

"You will. But I need you here in case they breach the defenses of the others. You may be my last ally should they fall before I can re-absorb my power from this bauble."

"What can I do? I am but a mere old man."

"We both know you are far more then that." Crystalon replied with a stoic glance from beneath a furrowed brow, before returning his gaze to the huge glowing stone before him.

216

"I know not what you speak of, but I will do what I can to help you." Alfredo turned away from Crystalon, pointing his back to the sorcerer and standing firm as if to break the tide of evil that would surely surge towards them.

"Indeed." Crys replied as he moved his hands in esoteric gestures, muttering lowly at first, each hand movement in cadence with his words.

"Swords an' sticks? This is what you got down here fer weapons? No guns?"

"No Joseph, These 'sticks' are made of the native oak from this land. They are blessed in holy water, and the smallest scratch will grievously injure, if not kill the vampire who is touched by it."

"How about the swords? Are they blessed as well?" Dr. Walker asked.

"Yes Daniel Walker, they are."

"Good, I'll take one." Daniel grabbed a sword from the wooden closet they stood at and hefted it about, making graceful arcing cuts through the air with its shining blade.

"You have some skill with a blade Dr. Walker." Vorlas commented.

"Yes I did a fair amount of fencing in college."

"This is more then a mere points competition, Dr. Walker. This is indeed life and death."

"You won't find my skills wanting Baron." The doctor held the blade outright before him sighting down its length as he measured its trueness.

"I pray not, Doctor. For your life, as well as ours, might depend on it."

Joe packed his pockets with short, sharpened sticks and then grabbed a sword as the sounds of fighting drew closer to them from above...

"I ain't likin' what I'm hearin here. Where's yer pal Sergei? I thought he was comin' down fast?" The burly former truck driver asked.

Baron Vorlas looked up into the darkness above, where the sounds of fighting emanated from, and shouted "Sergei! Run! What are you doing you fool? Get the rest of the staff down here where we can make a defense against those monsters!"

From above: "Master! I will hold them off for you! The rest of the staff has fallen, it is only I! I will AAAIIIIIEEEEE..."

Silence.

Thick.

Palpable.

Silence.

Then a sound.

Plip.

Plip.

Plip.

Joe and Walker stared in absolute horror as blood slowly pooled at their feet, dripping down the stone stairs in a small stream from above, as the sound of laughter drifted down to them. Their own blood pounded in their veins making their heads hurt as Sergei's screams faded to nightmarish memories.

"Ah Baron" Trago's menacing voice trickles down to them from above, so much like the blood at their feet, "your manservant tasted good! Hahahahaha! I also have a surprise for you. One I've been keeping for quite some time."

Vorlas' face went white as he tried to charge up the stairs, but now Joseph restrained him with Daniel's aid. "You ain't goin' nowhere, Baron. Sit tight. The Boss will get us outta this one."

"Let me go!" Vorlas raged. "I will destroy that monster for this! Trago must be destroyed! His evil cannot go on!" He fought against their grip, as they struggled to hold him fast.

Walker gave Joe a look saying, 'I hope so', wordlessly as the sounds of maniacal laughter wafted down to them from above.

Then another sound drifted down to them. A sound out of nightmare. Terrible for what it portended. The sound of a woman's voice, softly calling. "Vorlas my beloved, come to me." It whispered.

"N-no." He replied in a barely audible voice, as his eyes threatened to burst from their sockets. "It cannot be. That voice..." He trailed off to silence.

Crystalon watched the events happening nearby before he nervously turned once more back to his preparations, working quickly as sweat congealed on his brow. Alfredo stood nearby staring at the sorcerer.

"We must hurry Alfredo, yet I cannot rush this. If I prepare inadequately, I could destroy this entire region of Europe."

"Then do not fail, Wizard. It is that simple."

"There is much more to you than meets the eye, isn't there, Alfredo?"

"We all have our mysteries, our secrets, Wizard. You before any others know this only too well."

"Indeed Holy Man, indeed. But those secrets may die here with us both today if we do not repel these vile creatures."

"Yes I know Crystalon. Continue your incantations. I will be the last line of defense here for you." The old man continued loosening his black tie and opening the collar of his white shirt. He held his hand out to his right and suddenly, his staff appeared in a burst of golden light.

Crystalon looked at him and smiled "I see you possess more magic than meets the eye, eh wise man?"

"Did not Moses best the Pharaoh's magician in fair combat? Did he not part the Red Sea?"

"Ah, I see." Crystalon continued his spell, concentrating all the harder on the glowing rock before him.

***

"Oh God," Joe started in fear, "here come those things!"

The Arjul descended from above, the ravenous mouths on bat wings diving towards the men below, a veritable tide of ferocious screaming, yowling, ravenous, flesh devouring hunger. Joe, Vorlas and Daniel turned fearfully toward the wave of flying death, ineffectual swords turned upwards, knowing they would be devoured by these things; these screaming, flying piranha. The three men fought back their fear, almost simultaneously. Suddenly, a wave of flame blasted across their path, incinerating the flying beasts as their cries filled the caverns with madness inducing roars at a volume beyond sane measure.

"Where?" asked Joe as he turned and saw Alfredo standing there, the tip of his staff aimed at the burning Arjul.

"What th-?" Joe started, wide eyed.

"I knew I sensed it about him." Daniel whispered to him.

"What, you knew he had powers?"

"No, he uses power. He's different. Not a sorcerer, but a magical conduit from a higher source."

"Higher source? You mean like God?"

"That is for you to decide Joseph." Alfredo answered with a knowing wink.

"It will avail you little, humans." Trago's voice floated down to them. All their eyes turned towards him as they saw him seemingly floating on air towards them. With him, at his side was a woman dressed in a flowing white gown. He held her hand delicately as she fixated on one of them, wantingly, longingly.

Vorlas.

"Come back to me my love," she cooed.

"N-no Natalia. You are not my wife. You are an un-dead thing. My Natalia is gone, forever stolen from me. You are not her, vampire." The Baron bravely replied, tears

220

streaming down his noble face, as he pushed himself to his feet from where he collapsed upon seeing her.

"You are wrong Nikola Vorlas, very wrong. I am your wife, but I am so much more. I am forever freed of the cumbersome chains of human mortality. Now what I want, I take, with no thought or circumstance. Trago freed me, in both mind and body. If you deny me, I will simply kill you instead of turning you."

"Turning me? You would curse the man who loved you more than his own existence to a never-ending un-life? Surely you are not my Natalia. Of that you have just made me unabashedly certain."

"End this foolishness my dear. Kill this peasant dog." Trago ordered contemptuously floating above. Behind him five more vampires floated on wispy clouds of smoke, all attired as Trago, in mid nineteenth century Police uniforms. All laughed evilly amongst themselves, sneering at the men below.

"I ain't likin' this Dan." Joe murmured to his friend.

"I know Joe. Get ready, they are going to attack any second. I'm not sure how long Vorlas can hold them off by arguing with his *wife*."

Joe turned to Daniel Walker and looked at him quizzically, "Is that what he's doin'?"

"I hope so," was Walkers grim faced reply.

As if in response Trago suddenly grew bored by what he was seeing, "Enough of this foolishness. Kill them, now!"

The Vampire Police dove at the men below.

"Stand firm men!" Alfredo roared as he sliced his staff through the air in an arc, its length glowing in his hand as it slapped back several of the un-dead, their outstretched, clawing hands hungrily seek to tear at his flesh.

Natalia dove at Vorlas, slamming him to the ground like a broken toy found useless by its owner.

"Unnngggghh!" Vorlas groaned as he struggled mightily against her. He repeatedly hit her with blows that would stun a much bigger man. She laughed at his efforts, then slapped him away. He sprawled across the unyielding stone ground, bouncing several feet like a rag doll.

Vorlas struggled to his knees, than turned towards her contemptuously, blood trickling from his mouth. He wiped it away, a mixture of anger and repulsion etched across his features.

She looked at him and laughed, with a deep contempt of her own, before finally speaking, "I will kill you slowly, *Dear Husband,* and enjoy it very much. You are a useless man. You whine continuously, and refuse to release the past. The past which was my human life. That life is no more, fool. I am Vampire now."

"You are not my Natalia, you foul thing. She is dead, killed by that monster you follow. You will not besmirch my memory of her by your foul use of her body."

He threw himself at the woman who was once his wife, his hands outstretched as claws, grabbing her neck and tumbling to the ground with her, rolling over and over across the hard stone floor. He grunted mightily, she merely laughed as she backhanded him away.

"I am many times stronger than you, my dear," she chortled. "You cannot hurt me. You cannot even affect me. I will kill you slowly, breaking every bone in your body one at a time. Only then will my family and I feast on your blood, and you will beg us to do so!"

***

Across the cavern, Joe and Walker sliced their swords through the air maniacally, trying to stay alive, sweat soaking their bodies from sheer exertion as vampire after vampire attacked them.

"Unngghh, This ain't goin' so well Doc." Joe grunted as he sliced at a vampire's neck with his black blood-soaked blade, ichor pooling at their feet now.

"We're alive aren't we?" Walker replied with a loud grunt of his own.

"Yeah, for how long?"

"Hopefully long enough for Crystalon to finish."

"Yeah I hope that's fast cause I don't think we're gonna last much longer here."

"I know Joe, I agree. I can't feel my arms at this point."

"At least ya still have 'em." Joe replied as he sliced a Vampire's arm off in one strong downward cut. "Can't you do anything magical? With that thing around yer neck?"

"My neck? Oh the amulet!"

Walker immediately tore at his shirt and pulled the amulet free, backing up from the Vampire chasing him, he quickly murmured something as light flashed from the amulet in his hand, shining outwards as it engulfed the Vampire in glowing, golden radiance, setting the thing ablaze instantly. It crumbled to ash within seconds under the amulet's powerful assault.

"Whoa! And you didn't do that sooner? Why?"

"Ummm, to be honest, I forgot I had it. But its power is not limitless."

"Well just keep usin' it till its empty. These things are poppin' out of the woodwork and I can barely lift my arms anymore."

"You have to, we both do, otherwise we're dead!"

"Yeah I know!" Joe grumbled as another vampire screamed from above diving towards him with its fangs clicking together loudly seeking his throat. Joe slammed the blade upwards into the thing's chest to the hilt, as the blessed blade made the un-dead monster burst into flame, covering Joe in goo.

"Yuck." He moaned as he stared at his blood soaked clothes.

223

"Heads up, Joe!" Walker shouted as another vampire threw itself carelessly at the momentarily distracted man.

Walker leapt in the way, slicing at the thing with his own blessed sword, decapitating it, spraying Joe with even more blood and ichor.

"Thanks Doc, I think. What's with these things? Some a them explode inta dust. Others inta a gory mess?"

"You think I know Joe?"

Walker nodded as his eyes crossed the room towards Crystalon and Alfredo, who had gone back to watching Crystalon's back as he worked his enchantments over the glowing stone.

Joe awkwardly sliced at the thing in front of him, it's slavering lips and teeth chattering incessantly for his blood as he hacked at it.

"This ain't no good, Doc. No way we can hold these off much longer." He grunted as he hacked the thing across the face, bludgeoning it. It laughed as it smacked the blade from his hand effortlessly.

"Huuuuummaaaann. You will slake my thirst." It hissed with its clattering jaws mere inches from his face.

"Like hell." Joe growled as he pushed with all his strength against the monster's chest.

"You are funnnnyyyy huuuumaaaannn. I will ennnnjoyyy killing youuuuu."

The Vampire shoved him aside like discarded garbage. Joe rolled across the ground grunting painfully.

"This ain't no good. Boss! We're in trouble!" He shouted in Crystalon's direction.

The Vampire suddenly grabbed him by the back of the neck and whispered in his ear "Yes you are Huuuuummmaaaann."

"The sword," gasped Joe, "it's my only chance. I gotta reach it!"

He stretched forward, grasping for the hilt of the sword, his fingers grazed its leather wrapped hilt, but he could not grasp it.

The un-dead thing reared its own head back while suddenly forcing Joe's head forward. It bared its fangs and plunged its teeth towards Joe's neck, but at the same time Joe grabbed for his discarded sword with a last ditch effort, stretching himself until he almost popped a joint in his shoulder and shoved the point of the consecrated blade upwards, through the things mouth and jaws and out its neck.

The Vampire turned to dust immediately as Joe dropped to the ground panting in exhaustion.

"That was way too freakin' close." He grunted as he leaned back against the cold, stone wall momentarily.

***

"I cannot spare a gaze away from what I am doing, Holy Man. You must aid our friends." Crystalon admonished Alfredo.

"I am endeavoring to do so, sorcerer."

"Then endeavor harder." Crystalon answered curtly with sweat running down his forehead from exertion, as energy danced around each of his hands.

"What is taking you so long?" Alfredo asked as his staff slowly started to glow again.

"I hid my power behind massive protection spells so no one could inadvertently trigger them. To do so, well, it is actually quite possible the planet would have been obliterated if someone less skilled then I had tried to obtain this hidden mystic power."

"You, as usual, have a huge ego, wizard."

"Perhaps I do, or perhaps I speak truthfully and do not underestimate the power I once wielded, as perhaps again, you do."

"Bah. We do not have time for this, The Vampires encircle us and more Arjul are screaming their way towards us as we argue."

"On this we can agree, Holy Man. Go, aid our friends I will be fine here."

"Very well, Sorcerer." Alfredo nodded once towards Crystalon who returned the nod, and then doubled his efforts as his fingers sparked multi-hued energies that danced about the glowing boulder, his face contorted in grim determination and concentration.

***

Walker sliced at the Vampire before him as two more landed next to them, their hideous leathern wings disappearing as they touched down. They circled about Dr. Walker, teeth gnashing hideously and noisily, darting back and forth, and reaching towards him as he batted away their clawed hands.

"How many of these things are there?" Walker asked Alfredo as he sensed the old man by his side. Alfredo slapped one of the un-dead monsters across its face with his glowing staff, making it burst into flame and disappear while screaming painfully.

"I do not know Daniel, but I have to think over the course of more than a hundred years, quite a bit of the local populace has disappeared from here. I would think that some of them, at the very least, ended up as the Un-dead."

"Well isn't that great." Walker replied as he sliced at another Vampire, who hissed angrily and painfully as it retreated from his sword's bite.

"How's he doing?" Daniel asked with a nod of his sword towards Crystalon.

"As well as can be expected, I suppose."

"Meaning?" Walker hacked the formerly hissing Vampire in twain as two more descended to replace it.

"Meaning he will be finished with his enchantment when he is finished, Doctor Walker."

"Boy, you are a grouchy old man tonight, aren't you?"

"You have no idea how old I truly am, or how 'grouchy' as you put it."

"Yeah, whatever. Hey my amulet is charged up again, want to add your staff's power to it and maybe we can buy ourselves some time?"

Alfredo nodded affirmatively.

Down towards them vampires flew, now with more marauding Arjul between and about them. The noise was deafening, as the loud creatures screamed in unison.

"Here they come, Dr. Walker. Stand firm."

"I am Alfredo, I am," then Walker asked. "Now?"

"Now." Alfredo answered.

In unison, light leapt from Walker's Amulet and flames from Alfredo's staff which engulfed the roaring hoard of flying horror, destroying both Vampire and Arjul alike.

Their combined abilities incinerated the monstrosities, their screams of death echoing madly off the stone walls, making the cacophony within the cavern even more dreadful and mind numbing.

Long seconds passed as both men sweat with concentration, spreading their energies from one side of the swarm of flying death to the next.

But both men knew their efforts were too little, as they all too soon were tiring and their powers become spent, while the seemingly endless wave continued to bear down on them.

"We're not going to last, Alfredo."

"I know, my friend, I know."

Then, almost simultaneously with Walker's amulet giving out first, both men ran out of energy, the amulet and the staff both went dark as the two men drop to the ground, exhausted.

The cavern was clear momentarily.

227

"Listen," a sweat soaked Dr. Walker whispered to Alfredo, from where he had fallen on his knees,.

"I hear them. They come again." The older man replied solemnly.

As a whisper at first, then growing steadily louder, the horrific screaming of the Arjul returned.

Both men silently look upwards into the darkness of the cavern as the sound grew steadily louder.

Walker gulped hard.

The wave of darkness and death descended upon the two men from above. The shrieks of the hell spawn drowned out any other sound in the cavern, as the two men were once again lost from sight beneath the wave of flying darkness and death.

Chapter 34

Amanda Serros stared out the window in the tower she occupied, in a land unknown to her. Since the villain Epine-Noir' sought to attack her, she had been kept in her tower. Food and drink had been brought to her, but she had seen no one, save the servants bringing her meals, in days.

She turned from the window, overlooking the rolling green hills before her and beneath her window, shaking her head angrily and resignedly at her predicament.

"Just terrific." She muttered to herself as she flopped down on the bed.

"There's not even a TV up here."

"You are not here for your enjoyment, Amanda." A familiar voice replied.

She stood and turned towards the doorway as her captor appeared before her, his face obscured as usual behind an area she could not focus on. "You are, after all, my prisoner."

"I thought you said I was your guest." She replied hotly and sarcastically.

"And did you truly believe that, woman?"

"Not for an instant. Guests are allowed to leave. Why are you holding me prisoner here? I don't know who you are, I can't see your face, and even if I could, who would I tell? I know we've never met before this whole escapade, so why are you hiding from me?"

"You will learn my identity in good time. When it suits my purpose."

"Big deal, I still won't know who you are when you tell me your name."

"No, but another will."

"Crys..." She replied quietly, looking away.

"Ah, yes, your sorcerer friend. But you and he are more than friends are you not?"

"What business is it of yours? You won't even show me your face, why should I discuss anything with you?"

"Because your life is in my hands."

"And what? You'll zap me away to somewhere else?"

"You misunderstand, my dear. I am far less a mystic, and far more a warrior. My fighting is done by blade and fist."

"Not guns?" She asked while staring out the window at the verdant scenery stretching on seemingly forever.

"No, I have no use for them. They are too impersonal. I prefer to look a man in the face while I run him through."

"Puts you at a little disadvantage though, doesn't it?"

"How so?"

"One guy with a gun at a hundred yards has you dead to rights."

"I do not make much use of magic personally, but what makes you believe I have not those around me who do?"

"So you're just a *sorta* magical guy?"

"I am what I am, Amanda Serros. Do not seek to ask so many questions of me from this point forward. I won't be satisfying your curiosity again."

"And why is that exactly? You keep me trapped here for weeks on end, you give me no idea why I'm being held, and you refuse to answer any questions as to why you have ghosts floating around here looking to torture someone and suck their souls out of their bodies."

"Are you being mistreated?" The mysterious stranger paused an instant before adding, "At the moment?"

"No, you haven't mistreated me. Even keeping me locked up, you've fed me and kept me well. But still I have no idea what is going on, or why you trapped me here. All I know is that it involves my boss."

"Your boss. The way you say it, it almost sounds like you have no hidden feelings for the man."

"Who says I do?"

"Why, you do, in your every action, my dear. You hear mention of his name and your eyes widen slightly, your nostrils flare, you look away. There are many reactions that are telling of the hearts true nature, Amanda Serros."

"You're crazy." She spit out angrily as she looked away, towards the window once again.

"Ah, am I? We shall see soon enough, woman. Soon enough." He walked away, his footsteps trailing away down the steps of the tower.

'*Well, that was wonderful.*' She thought to herself, '*I try to get some information from him by prying, and he does the exact same thing back to me and wins. This guy, whoever he is, is manipulative and cunning like a fox. I wish Crys would find me already.*' She walked away from the window and circled back to the big post and canopy bed, sitting again on its edge.

She flopped backwards onto the pillow then added aloud in a whisper, "If he's even looking for me..."

Chapter 35

In a cavern deep beneath a manor in Transylvania, the battle raged. Joe Carboneri, after attempting to regain his breath, painfully pulled himself up from against the stone wall he sat next to. He was partially hidden from view by rubble and the dimness of the cavern itself, but what he saw now was painful to watch. Baron Vorlas was about to be killed, and he had to do something. The she-vampire that had been his wife in life had pinned the baron to the rough-hewn stone floor, and was about to slake her vampiric thirst on his throat. Joe stood in abject horror for only a moment, as shadows danced from flaming sconces on the walls. The vampire reared her head back, almost theatrically, and then her teeth descended towards the Barons neck. With that, Joe had had enough. He raced towards them both and tackled the monster, throwing a forearm block at the back of her neck. The attack snapped her forward, in total surprise. The hell spawn never saw him coming, and his two hundred plus pounds moved quickly enough that his weight, plus his strength and momentum, knocked her away from his friend, toppling the She-Vampire off the walkway they had been fighting on and into the cavern below.

Joe huffed painfully as he fought his way to his feet and grabbed the Barons shoulder. "Baron, you okay? Hey Baron Vorlas, speak to me." Carboneri prodded the limp and bleeding man within his grasp.

Then a horrific and unholy shrieking sound grabbed and riveted Joe's attention as he turned his head in time to see that on the far side of the cavern, Alfredo and Dr. Walker were using magical abilities to destroy both Vampire and Arjul alike.

But then, seemingly after only seconds, both men's magically spawned powers ran out, and after an all too

233

brief moment frozen in time, the flying wave of demonic death returned and engulfed them both.

It was at this exact instant that things went from terrible to bad beyond comprehension, as the Vampire who was Vorlas' wife suddenly ascended from the pit beneath them on giant leathern wings, to shriek her hatred at Joe's terrified form.

"Holy mother of God!" Joe stammered as the vampire floated straight towards him, wings beating the air slowly.

He backed up, at first slowly, then turned and ran, as the vampire shrieked her disdain and dove towards him, its clawed hands outstretched for his flesh.

"I will kill you little man, and feast on your blood!" She howled into the dank cavern.

She grabbed him by the back of the neck, and heaved him disdainfully against a wall. Joe slumped to the ground, stunned as the vampire pulled his neck up to her face, her fangs ready to rend his unprotected throat.

Suddenly a gold chain dropped out of Joe's shirt, and on the chain, a cross. The vampire hissed immediately and shielded her eyes, allowing Joe to tumble out of her grip to the floor. Instantly he rolled away from her and grasped the chain that had been hidden beneath his shirt, yanking it free, he brandished the cross in front if him, frantically moving it around before her terrified eyes.

"Wassamatter monster? You don't want any o' me now huh?" He growled in a combination of both pain and anger, waving his cross around in front of himself.

She hissed and shrieked, but now in terror, covering her eyes and cowering from the sight of the cross.

Then, in a stunning moment of power, an explosion rocked the cavern, literally knocking Joe from his feet and the vampire from the air with its pure force. Joe turned towards the explosion's origin and saw something he could not even imagine, as Crystalon now floated in the air above

234

the glowing boulder, light passing from the boulder into his body, like bolts of multi-hued electricity. Crystalon spasmed painfully, grunting in agony, but then he turned towards the vampires throughout the cavern disdainfully.

Trago shouted, "Kill him!" and dove towards Crystalon as all the other vampires followed suit, stopping what they were doing in mid movement and following his order without question.

Joe looked on, in shock and astonishment, as he swore he saw the slightest hint of a smile cross Crystalon's lips. Then the sorcerer spoke words too low to hear, but Joe was positive he would not recognize the words or the language even if he had heard them.

As if in instant and mind numbing response, the roof of the cavern above them exploded away from them all, blasting apart the mansion and the ground beneath it from within. Shattering the sky above as golden energy ripped from Crystalon's fingertips, effortlessly obliterating what was so far above them, revealing the star specked sky.

"Your time is done, Trago. You go to the pits embrace now. You, and all your brethren." The Mage spoke. His words appeared to be in a simple talking volume, yet they loudly reverberated through the cavern shaking it with every nuance.

The vampires dropped to their knees, covering their ears in agony, as their leader, Trago looked on, stunned by what he saw.

The vampire lord was momentarily taken aback, but recovered almost instantly as he streaked through the air towards the hovering Crystalon, his tattered shirt moving slightly in the powerful forces he had unleashed.

"Foolish mortal wizard, this will matter not at all! I will still rend your flesh."

"No, monster, you will not! Your time on this world is over! Hell awaits your presence."

"Bah, you fool, you simply have ripped the surface clear and allowed the stars to shine through. What good will that do you? It is still night. You have erred, and now you die!"

Trago streaked towards Crystalon, claws outstretched, teeth biting and snapping at the empty air when, to Joe's eyes everything seemed to slow to a crawl. Everything, that is, except the night sky which suddenly and inexplicably sped up getting brighter and brighter instantaneously, to reveal a very bright and large shining sun overhead in mere seconds.

"N-Nooo!" Trago stammered painfully. "What have you done?" He shrieked, as he suddenly burst into flame and burned to dust before Joe's horrified gaze.

"Oh my Lord, what am I seein'?" Joe stammered quietly in wide-eyed shock.

Turning, Joe feverishly scanned the now brightly lit cavern as all the Vampires burst into flame, one after another. The Arjul then took screaming flight directly at Crystalon who gestured at them, with contempt in his eyes and they in turn exploded into ash throughout the dank cave.

"Boss!" Joe bellowed "What'd you do?"

"I regained power my friend, true power. Now those that have harangued and opposed us will know fear!" He clenched his fist and slammed it into his open palm for emphasis.

Chapter 36

At the exact instant Crystalon destroyed the vampires, a beautiful woman's eyes opened suddenly, wide and fearful. Long black, wavy hair fell across her bare shoulders as she quickly sat up in her bed, throwing a silken robe over her body as she stormed from her room, throwing open a heavy wooden door and walking down an ancient corridor. Quickly and with definite purpose she threw open another chambers door.

"He has gained power, a huge amount of it."

There was a man seated at an old desk within the room, and seeing her entrance he turned towards her. His face was not obscured now, but still hidden in shadow as he spoke.

"It does not matter, we still have his woman. She is our bargaining piece." He refused to look up as he worked at something on his wooden desk, a map of some sort.

"He is powerful once more, perhaps as powerful as he once was," she continued.

"Again, it does not matter. The Wraith Lords will take care of him."

"The power should have been mine!" She shrieked angrily, slamming her hand to the desk for emphasis.

"You are powerful enough, my dear. Without you, none of this would have been possible. None of it."

"So you lied to me all this time, all these years. You told me it would be mine! He was to suffer and die at my hands!" She cursed.

"No my dear, not your hands, *our* hands. We both knew this was a possibility; that he would arrive at the repository of energies before we could find it. In truth, only his familiarity with it allowed him to find it. We could never have found where it was so well hidden if not for him leading us to it like so."

"And you expect me just to accept this? He is almost unstoppable now!"

"Indeed, but so are we. He has simply upped the stakes by attaining so much power now. He hasn't won the game. In truth he has no idea what the game truly is, or who the players are, or even why."

After a moment he continued, "Let me ask my dear, is he more powerful than you now? Do we truly need to fear him? Was our plan not all along to entice him to our side, to make him join us in subjugating this vile world, and then reveal who we truly were after he had helped destroy this vile world's way of life? And only then destroy him as well, once he learned of our true intentions?"

She softened momentarily, and then nodded her head in the affirmative, in a nervous almost chaotic way without any rhythm to the nodding, her mad eyes regained some composure after a moment as she mulled over his words, her fingers toyed on his desk as she looked down. "You are correct, of course. He does not even know why we have taken the woman, nor who we truly are, but now he will begin to look for her anew, and this time he will do so vigorously. I must be able to steal that power from him, the power that is rightfully mine!"

The man did not look up but continued working, his broad shoulders moving slightly as he continued to inscribe the parchment on his desk.

"And indeed it will be my dear, as soon as we suck the very life from him, and we watch him take his last breath. Then will you be able to claim what is rightfully yours. On this you have my word."

Chapter 37

"Help!"

Both Crystalon and Joe turned towards the ragged sound of Daniel Walker's voice, running hurriedly to him, only to find a small mountain of ash.

"He's buried under that!" Joe shouted as he hurriedly dug through the ash, all that remained of the former bodies of the vampires and the Arjul.

"Stand aside Joseph." Crystalon commanded as he waved his hands and instantly winds picked up and blew the ash into the yawning chasm beside them revealing Joe and Alfredo.

"He's not moving, when the monsters attacked I hacked at them as much as I could with the blessed swords, but they overwhelmed us, and he finally threw himself over me to protect me I-I think he's dead..." Daniel trailed off as he checked for a pulse and vital sign. Both Joe and Crystalon stood silently by as the Doctor went about his work grimly.

"Help me. Joe press on his chest when I tell you."

"You mean CPR?"

"Yes Joe, exactly." Daniel replied.

Joe did as he was told while Dr. Walker gave the old man mouth to mouth. Long minutes passed. But finally they both stopped, and turned towards Crystalon.

"Can't you do anything?" Walker implored.

"No, I am not God, my friend, only a wizard when it all comes down to it. Taking the lives of those who are your enemies to one such as myself is relatively easy, but restoring it, that is impossible. I am no deity my friend, I am sorry."

He placed his hand on Walker's shoulder sadly. The Doctor bowed his head and exhaled saddened by what had occurred. All of them were.

"What of the Baron?" Crystalon inquired, a fear coloring his words for what the reply may be.

"The same, Boss, the same." Joe shook his head sadly, confirming Crystalon's worst fears.

"We lost two friends tonight. We hardly knew the Baron, but to die like that, by his wife's own hand, after she had become an un-dead thing." Walker trailed off shaking his head grimly.

"That was no longer his wife, my friend. His wife was long dead. That thing merely wore her body, and used it for its own nefarious purposes."

Walker looked about them in the cavern. Piles of ash, a shattered ceiling of stone and rock, and above that an obliterated mansion, were all that remained of the once beautiful, Vorlas home. He turned back to Crystalon and asked "Was all this worth it? Our friends are dead, what did we accomplish in the end?"

Then, from behind them, an unexpected voice answered.

"Let your hearts be light my friends, you rid the world of an ancient evil, Daniel Walker. You gave this mighty wizard power. Power that will at least give him a chance at saving the very world you stand on, and of saving countless billions who do not even know he fights for them."

All the men turned towards the sound of the voice, and collectively catch their breath. Even the Mighty Crystalon was taken aback by what he saw.

Floating in the air before them, glowing like a star and wrapped in white robes, was Alfredo. He held his staff before him and wings adorned his back. He looked younger and healthier, far more powerful, more vibrant then he had

240

seemed to them before. His form was translucent to their eyes.

"Whoa." Joe began, "Yer an angel?"

"Indeed, my friend, indeed." Alfredo smiled warmly at Joseph.

"So there was far more to you then I originally expected, eh holy man?" Crystalon smiled as he saw the figure before him.

"It makes so much sense." Walker quietly mused aloud.

"I cannot believe what I'm seein'." Joe stammered in a stunned whisper.

"You have been saying that a lot lately, my friend." Alfredo answered him with a wink and a smile as his wings beat slowly behind him, surreally.

He turned towards Crystalon then and spoke.

"You have much weight upon your shoulders, Wizard. You have won my respect, and I have aided you as much as possible. But the forces of evil conspire against you. Know this, o sorcerer; you may have to make a most dire choice in the days to come, one weighing the suffering of the heart against the greater good for all. That will be your final test, and in your decision, the fate of the world will rest. I pray you make the correct choice, no matter how painful. I believe you will. Now, farewell, to all of you. You are my friends and my companions. I will be praying for your success. Have no doubt in your souls; you three are the world's finest hope for stopping the evil that is amidst us all. God be with you, my brothers."

With that, he faded away, waving to them with a smile and a wink as his body turned into sparkles that darted majestically out of the cavern above into the bright morning daylight and disappeared.

"That was cool." Joe replied with a slight smile curling the sides of his mouth, as his eyes stared in awe at the shattered caverns roof.

"Just like that, he's gone." Walker commented quietly, and in awe.

"Uh, by the way boss, how'd you do that?" Joe pointed overhead at the sun. "Last I looked, it was near midnight."

"Joseph, I simply sped up time." Crystalon replied, while smiling warmly at his friend, and slapping him on the back.

"Geeze, you say it like its pumpin' gas or somethin'."

"Not at all my friend. And Joseph, Daniel, do not doubt for an instant that I have taken the loss of our two comrades lightly. Their deaths weigh heavily on my mind and soul."

"Did this happen in the past?" Walker asked, "Were you this caring about people who fought under you in years past? When you ruled your universe?"

"No. Honestly my comrades, I became callused and hard. Life meant little to me then. It means so much more now."

"Why? Because you're no longer immortal?"

"Who says I am not, Dr. Walker? My powers are almost to the levels they once were, I feel like myself again."

"Hey guys, I got a question here. How do we get outta this pit? The mansion is destroyed an' most o' our gear is buried under tons of rubble. An' there's no staircase outta this place now. So unless we grow wings like Alfredo an' fly outta here, we ain't got no way to the surface."

"Well Joseph my friend, you will find that we do not need wings to attain the surface, but we will indeed fly!"

Crystalon threw his arms skywards, towards the hole in the ceiling of the cave, and he immediately flew towards it and away, as Joe raised his hand to protest suddenly, he and Walker both rose into the air and followed the wizard up through the hole into the daylight above.

"Man-o-man this feels great!" Joe exclaimed while the sun warmed his face.

"Indeed it does, my friend, indeed it does," Crys replied as they all set down lightly on the ground.

"I wish we had our clothes back though. We're a mess." Walker mentioned as he looked down at the bloodstained rags he's wearing.

"All in good time Dr. Walker, we have something else we must attend to first." Crystalon snapped his fingers and suddenly all their belongings were back in their suitcases and by their sides.

"I don't freakin' believe it." Joe muttered in awe.

"So now what? Are we going to rescue Miss Serros now?" Dr. Walker asked, as he suddenly noticed the blessed sword he wielded below, now hanging at his side in a scabbard. He pulled it free and it fairly sang in his hand.

He looked at Crystalon and grinned; "You pulled out all the stops didn't you?"

"You have no idea, my friend, no idea."

"So answer the man, boss. We gonna go save 'Manda now?"

"Sadly no. We have one more stop to make."

"What? What're ya kiddin' me, Boss? You got yer power back, what more do ya want? We gotta save 'Manda."

"We will Joseph, but she is in no immediate danger. Indeed her danger will begin when we go to her rescue. For now they need her to draw us to them. Now we must go to one other place on the Earth, an ancient nation where an equally ancient power is hidden and calling out to me."

"So where to now? You gonna tell us or keep us in suspense?"

Crystalon smiled, "We go to Egypt, my friends. A great source of power is calling me there. One that will ensure our victory. But first there is something we must do here, something for our departed friends."

He bent down and picked up one of three shovels that had appeared and now lay at their feet, turned and walked up the hill behind them, where bent low and commenced to dig. Joe and Dr. Walker looked at each other and nodded in agreement; each grabbed a shovel and joined Crystalon. They both knew that the Mage could magically place their friends in their final resting place in the cemetery overlooking where the mansion used to stand, but that would be impersonal, and just not right. These men died fighting side by side with them, and they should shed sweat and tears burying them. All three instinctively know this as they silently continued to dig. This was the final gratitude they could pay their departed comrades for the ultimate sacrifice, and it was a final debt they each paid willingly.

Chapter 38

"So where to now, boss?" Joseph asked, "You said somethin' about Egypt; is that fer real?"

Crystalon smiled. He jammed the blade of the shovel into the ground and turned to face his friend, "Yes, Joseph, that is for real. We travel to Egypt now, for an object of great power calls to me from there. It is an object that cannot be allowed to fall into our enemy's grasp, for if it does, the balance of power that now favors us could shift once again to his favor."

"You know it's him now?" Walker asked as he cinched the sword belt and scabbard to his waist, placing the mystic sword he had lain on the ground nearby, within it.

"I know nothing for certain my friends, something or someone is working very hard to block my sorcerer's sight in this matter. I cannot see our enemy's identity, but I know our journey is nearing its end, and I swear to you both, it will not end in defeat for us."

"You seem a lot more confident then you did only a short time ago, Crystalon."

"Ah, but I am not overconfident, Dr. Walker, if that is what you were inferring."

"Perhaps I was." Walker replied, his eyes slit slightly as he stared at the wizard.

"No my friend, I assure you I am not overconfident, and I am indeed being extremely cautious, even in this matter where I deem it necessary to obtain this object of power before our foes do."

"I trust ya boss." Joe affirmed, jamming his shovel into the earth at his feet, leaving it standing there.

"As do I Crystalon. You've brought us this far, and the road has been dangerous, but we're still here." Walker nodded his agreement.

"Let me repair your clothes my friends, as well as my own, and we will be on our way."

The Mage waved his hands and the now sweat and dirt stained clothes they all wore suddenly were swapped for a new set, except Crystalons...

"Hey! I know that outfit! It's what you were wearin' when I first, uhhh met ya. But wasn't it red then?"

"You mean when you nearly killed me with your truck, do you not, Joseph?" Crystalon smiled after a moment. It was a relaxed smile, and he clamped his friend on the shoulder powerfully, then walked past him to the hillside overlooking the woods and valley beneath the Barons home, or what was left of it. He wore the cape that he wore when ruling his reality, his universe. A tunic with mystic symbols emblazoned upon it, as well as form fitting pants. The color was purple, a lighter purple for the top and dark purple for the bottoms, with black, tall leather boots. A purple cape blew in the slight breeze behind him, lifting his cape about. His goatee was trim and his hair sharp. He looked like a new man, a man confident in his power but also wary, like a big jungle cat that was stalking his prey.

He turned back to his friends and smiling, spoke, "Yes my friend, it was red, Purple signifies change in my realm. I have changed; I am now a much different man then when I arrived here. But enough of that, are you both ready for the final leg in our quest?"

"Yeah, I know I am, Boss." Joe replied.

"As am I, Crystalon." Walker added, nodding his head.

"Then we go, my friends."

Suddenly the wind whipped up around the three men, plucking them from the ground, lifting them up and, flying them away like leaves from a tree.

246

Joe inhaled sharply, Walker slightly less so.

An instant later, they are flying at speeds almost beyond comprehension, across the sky, like three meteors.

"I-I can't freakin' believe this! Wait'll the wife an' kid hear about this one!" Joe stammered, surprised he could hear his own voice over the wind.

"You must not tell anyone about your adventure Joseph."

"I know boss, sorry. I'm just stunned by all this. Hangin' with you gets wilder by the minute."

"Yes it does Joe." Walker agreed with a smile as he spread his arms to his sides. He looked below him and the ground was far – miles, in fact – below them, and it was passing beneath them so fast as to be a blur.

"Crystalon, how are we able to talk and why aren't we freezing?" Walker asked, already knowing the answer, as the question left his stunned mind.

"Ah my friend, because it is magic." Crystalon replied winking, his own arms thrust ahead of him as his cape flapped in the wind.

"I still can't freakin' believe this." Joe murmured, feeling more and more like a child left to play in a toy store. He looked around him, as far as the eye could see. They are above the cloud cover now, flying through a cotton candy mist.

In the distance, a passenger jet approached them and then just as quickly they flew past it and around it; those within who were quick enough to look caught their breath as the three flying men went past. Most never even caught a glimpse of the men. Those that did either put down the drink they had or ordered another, stronger one.

All too quickly they were descending to the Earth, as the clouds parted and a golden desert lie beneath them.

They touched down lightly. Joe and Walker in stunned silence, but both are grinning from ear to ear.

247

"I would ask you why we didn't just pass through the dimensional corridor again, but I already know the answer after that flight. That was magnificent, Crystalon." Dr. Walker could barely contain his enthusiasm as he looked around himself at the sky, the sand and then...

"The pyramids!" Joe shouted in surprise, "We're at the freakin' pyramids! Do you two have any idea how far we just freakin' went? An' I'm serious about that, I got no idea, but I know it hadda be really freakin' far! I can't believe we were just flyin'! That was amazin'! Prolly the most amazin' thing I ever seen or did! To heck with the goin' through dimensions or whatever, nothin' beats the way we got here now! Nothin'!"

"Ancient Egypt, land of the Pharaohs, as well as so many more mysteries and magic." Walker stated plainly, all but ignoring Joe's rant, but smiling at him anyway, with a nod.

"Indeed my friends. Here an object of great power is calling my name like a siren song."

"Remember the sirens killed unwary fishermen, Crystalon."

"I know Doctor, and as I have told you, I am indeed wary."

"Well what's the plan, Boss?"

"This may be a simple mission Joseph. The object I am looking for is indeed ahead of us all in that pyramid." Crys pointed directly ahead of him at a magnificent structure looming and glistening in the sunlight.

"How can ya tell? They all look the same?"

"I know Joseph. Believe me, I know after being powerless for so long, my abilities have streamed back to me. My affinities for all things magical has returned and it is pointing me towards our destination."

The three men began walking towards the pyramid in the distance.

"You were never powerless, you know." Walker stated flatly, while staring straight ahead.

Crys turned towards him as they walk. "What do you mean Doctor?"

"You had remnants of power with you from the start."

"You know this how?"

"You practically ensorcelled that poor Nurse Debbie at the hospital. Of course you did not mean to, but you had magic about you. She was willing to do anything for you, and it was not some misplaced crush or something similar. Your nascent abilities attracted her and she was, I hate to say it but, she was seemingly under your spell, even though you did not realize you had put one on her."

Crystalon stopped walking.

"What are you saying? That I practically had this woman mystically bound to me? Without my even knowing it?"

"Yes Crystalon, you did. She was not the only one. Think about all the people who helped you out so willingly when you arrived, even Joseph was somewhat under your power."

"Hey! Watch it, Doc!"

"That detective who helped you so much, he did not have to go so far to aid you. All of this you make possible, subconsciously. The night the Wraith Lords attacked your roommate? How did you think I knew to come to your aid? You sent out a mystic 'SOS' that I 'heard'. You still had power, my friend, that's all I'm saying to you."

"How is it that I was not aware of any of this?" The Mage held his chin in deep thought as he stared at the sand at his feet, truly perplexed.

"I believe it was because you were so powerful for so long that you didn't realize you had any abilities left when you were so unceremoniously dumped in our dimension and stripped of the majority of your powers.

Only now it turns out you did a lot of the stripping yourself. You must have felt like a man who was blind for the first day in his life. Magic is a part of you, heck no one who's ever lived on this world has ever been more powerful, at least as far as I know, and I've studied this stuff. I can't say I blame you for feeling powerless, even though you still had some inherent abilities left."

"This is all incredible..."

"Now you know what I'm feelin'." Joe muttered as he kicked sand.

Crys looked at him sourly, then turned back to Walker and continued. "I feel like blinders were just removed from my very eyes, how could I have missed this?"

"In the long run, would it have mattered? Think about this, you're a more humble man now, because of this very circumstance."

Crys sighed and smiled at his friend once more, walking once again, both Joe and Dr. Walker at his side. "You are correct of course, Doctor. But I wonder, did I do all of this to myself on some level so I would learn this very lesson of humility?"

"Or perhaps a higher power, God if you will, did it to you, or at least pushed you in that direction, so you would learn that you were indeed a man, and not a deity."

"Intriguing, to say the least Doctor. This has been a very... humbling experience for me. In truth, I never supposed myself to be a God, even at my most arrogant of moments, though I admit to believing myself to be a level higher, or above other men. All of this has reminded me of my long, almost forgotten humanity. This entire journey it seems has been for that purpose, I suppose."

"It might well be Crystalon, but we'll never know until this journey is over."

"Speakin' o' which." Joe added as he walked up to the pyramid steps at his feet.

"So how do we get in?" Dr. Walker asked as he touched the stones of the pyramid, in obvious awe.

"Why through the entrance of course, Doctor." Crys replied as he walked towards the open and marked doorway for the guided tours.

Both men follow the sorcerer into the hot, ancient structure.

"There's gotta be another place in here that we have ta go to. No way what we want is on the beaten path."

"Do you mean like a hidden room, Joe?" Walker asked as he ran his hands across the wall's surface.

"Yeah, I think so Doc. That sounds about right."

"You're right, I'd have to agree. Crys, what do you think?"

"I'll find out right now gentlemen, please stand back."

Crystalon set himself and raising his hands up majestically, spoke in a language that was unknown to either man Both looked at each other in stunned silence, then back at the Mage as his fingers painted esoteric gestures in the air. Light spilled from his fingertips in glowing, sparking arcs, as his words grow louder and louder until they fairly roared. But then they were overtaken by a louder sound as the walls suddenly parted before the stunned men, revealing a long hidden antechamber, filled with dank air and cobwebs.

"Illumination." Spoke the wizard as suddenly the room was filled with brightness from no seen source.

"I ain't never gonna get used ta this stuff, am I?"

Crys smiled at Joe and walked into the room. Gold was everywhere, coins, jewelry, even armor made of the stuff, glistened throughout the entire room, but Crystalon headed towards one object, a belt lying on the floor half buried in the sand and dust. Once it must have glistened like the sun, but no longer. As Crys stooped to pick it up, the walls suddenly closed behind them.

"Run for it!" Joe yelled as he scrambled towards the closing walls, arriving an instant too late as they slammed shut before him, almost taking his fingers with them.

"Do not panic, either of you." Crystalon chided. "We are not trapped or in any danger, I assure you, I can release us from this makeshift prison at any time."

"Can you little sorcerer?" A new, female voice intruded and the three men turned towards its source. Suddenly a woman wearing a golden Egyptian mask stepped from the shadows, she also wore a golden breastplate and white metallic skirt, her midriff was bare and tight, exposing a muscular stomach bespeaking of a life of strength and training of some type.

"Who are you? Why are you seeking to entrap us here?" Crys ordered, defiantly.

"I am the one of the guardian of the Gods, thieves, and they have entrusted us with keeping this, and all of the tombs, intact and whole. You will not steal Ra's belt of power from this temple, defiler." She answered angrily. "For your transgression you will not leave here alive!"

"You said 'Us.', woman. So far I see only you." Crys growled as he faced her. She walked from side to side, inspecting jewel filled bowls and glittering ornaments that lay about the floor, as well as dusty wooden crates filled to overflowing with the stuff. Then she finally turned back to Crystalon, "Yes, thief, I said 'us'. For my servants will ensure none of you will leave here alive!"

She gestured and started chanting in ancient Egyptian as suddenly towering twelve-foot tall statues with horse-like heads seemingly wrenched free of where they had been standing for untold centuries, stretching and moving as they began to come to a semblance of life. Rocking side to side they stretched limbs unused since time immemorial with loud creaks and grinds of their metallic forms.

"I so ain't likin' this!" Joe whispered.

"My warriors, these defilers have come to rob the tomb of Ra, to steal the beloved belt of power he left here for our kinsmen, lo those many centuries ago! Go forth now, and destroy these that would sully the master's lair!" She shouted defiantly.

One of the giant statues turned towards Crystalon, Joe, and Daniel, a sharp sword in his hand and aimed directly at the three men.

And then the statue spoke, in a booming low voice, full of magic and dust and power that shook the walls to the foundations with its volume. "This tomb will be your final resting place thieves, of that I swear at the boot of Ra himself!"

And Joe gulped hard...

Chapter 39

"Has there been any word from them?" A gravelly voice asked with a heavy Greek accent.

"No Anthony, none." A man seated at a desk with a computer before him answered.

Anthony Serros shook his head and walked away out into the corridor of the plain, white walled office he was in. His daughter had been missing for some time now, and he had only the sorcerer's word that she was unharmed.

"*But how does he even know?*" The old man thought to himself as he continued walking, shaking his head.

"Mr. Serros! Mr. Serros I need to speak to you!" Serros turned towards the sound of his voice and he saw a young man in a white lab coat, with a hand full of papers, running down the hall from behind.

"Yes Giovanni?"

"Mr. Serros, you have to see this..." the younger man trailed off as he ran back the way he came, Serros walking as fast as he could to keep up.

"I'm coming, I'm coming Giovanni."

He walked into a room filled with technicians, each studying a computer or a chart.

"Sir look at this," Giovanni said as he sat down, and pushed a seat out for Serros to sit down next to him.

"What is it Giovanni, please?"

"Look sir, look."

Serros fumbled with reading glasses he pulled out of his pocket and squinted at the screen and papers Giovanni spread out before him.

"Mr. Serros, this is Romania, the Transylvania area, yesterday. These magical spikes, we were able to read and quantify the magical energies."

255

"How? How are you able to do this?" Anthony Serros asked angrily. "This is unknown to me? Why wasn't I informed that we were able to now scan for magic?"

"Sir, the sorcerer who was here told us how. Magic has a frequency. He explained how high it is, it's actually higher in the band of signal range than anything we've ever intercepted or searched for before. That we were able to scan for it so quickly-"

"Quickly? Those men left here over two weeks ago!"

"I am sorry sir, it's the fastest we could put equipment together to do this, this is a tremendous undertaking, and a tremendous achievement, sir."

"If you say so, Giovanni." Serros grunted unpleasantly.

"Sir, look at this. This is what I wanted to show you. In Transylvania there was a huge magical spike, completely off the charts of what we ever expected to read. That was earlier, but look at this sir, this just came in, it's in Egypt sir. Another huge amount of magical energy, it's almost as large as the one from Romania."

"So you believe our friends are there? Even that maniac, Crystalon? Why haven't we heard from Alfredo yet?"

"I-I do not know, sir. But something is going on there, and that's not all."

"There's more?" The old man asked as his eyes widened in surprise "Is there news of my daughter?"

"No sir. I'm sorry, there is not." The younger man sighed, shaking his head. "But this just came into our readings, more magical power, but it appeared as if out of nowhere, and it seems to be not just a vague energy spike, but it seems to be moving with a purpose over Europe, and heading southeast."

"Where does it appear to be going Giovanni?"

"Well, we can't be positive yet sir."

"Well, guess then, why even tell me any of this if you have no idea?"

"Sir, it appears to be going directly towards Egypt, where we believe our people are."

"Well, what is it? Do you even know?"

"I-I do not know sir, but our best guess is that it's the Wraith Lords themselves, and they are going to attack our people."

"Can we warn them?"

"We tried sir, there is no cell phone service where they are, and we had several mystics try to connect to them at least mentally, so we could warn them, but they are blocked somehow. There is some kind of mystic shield or barricade stopping us from contacting our people; even Crystalon himself, who we are assuming is the most powerful mystic source of energy there. It's like dialing a phone and getting a busy signal."

"I understand you Giovanni. I am not an idiot, or an old fool."

"I know, I know sir, but well what I'm trying to say is they may be in very real trouble and we can't do anything about it, at all. We can't even warn them."

"Well Giovanni, if I am to judge by your charts and computer screens here, our people were in trouble before the Wraith Lords were chasing after them."

"Yes sir. That is what I mean. But there's more sir"

"More still? What now?" The old man smacked himself in the forehead in consternation as he slumped into his chair.

"Sir, no you don't understand, this may be good."

"How? What are you saying?"

"We may be able to attune our search and find out where the Wraith Lords appeared from, where they began their journey from in Europe, and I'd be willing to bet that is where we'll find your daughter!"

Chapter 40

"Did you send them?"

The shadow-faced man was seated at his desk when he looked up at the woman in his doorway, She's wearing a green metallic breast plated shirt, which faded into black leather pants. The Green had swirls of gold and black throughout it and her long black hair lay across her shoulders as she stood in his doorway, impatiently tapping her foot with her arms crossed.

"Yes my dear, I sent them."

"How many of them did you send?" She asked, her creased brow coloring her obvious disdain.

"All of them. I sent all of them."

"You sent every Wraith Lord we had?"

"No, I sent every one of those soul sucking demons on this plain of existence."

"Is that wise? They may kill him."

"No my dear, I truly doubt they will. If by some chance he falls to them, then all the better. He has encountered something in Egypt, something powerful, some relic that he should not be allowed to keep. The Wraith Lords will either take it from him, kill him, or be killed. In any event, we win. They were becoming...troublesome."

"Pffhehh." She spit out as she walked across the room and stared out a window, before turning back to him.

"What about Epine-Noir?"

"He has been sent after the Wraith Lords. If they succeed in killing the wizard, Epine-Noir can obtain the relic. If Crystalon destroys the demons, then Epine- Noir can face him, and if Crystalon did succeed in destroying all the Wraith-Lords, he should be sufficiently weakened and easily defeated by someone of Epine-Noir's power. If Crystalon destroys Épine-Noir, especially if he destroys the

Wraith Lords first, we will know just how truly powerful
he really is, and we will be free of that little madman.
Again, a win-win situation for us all."

She paced back and forth across the room shaking
her head then finally speaking as she stared at the shadow
faced man again, "I hate him you know, very much so in
fact."

"So you have said, my dear." He replied with a bit
of tired resignation, as if he had heard this same mantra
many times over.

"What he has done to us both-" She began before
he cut her off with a sharp wave of his hand.

"Is of no consequence," He interrupted.

He stood from his desk and put his arms around the
woman, holding her as she started to tremble with
memories.

"Do not be concerned, my dear, our hour grows
nigh. Our revenge is almost at hand; it will not be much
longer now. All the pieces of the puzzle have fallen into
place, all our well-crafted plans and schemes are almost
complete. Soon the wizard's power will be ours, and soon
he will die by our hands. What he has done to us both will
be avenged, and he will know who has killed him. As his
eyes glaze over, he will stare us both in the face. It will be
glorious!" He roared heartily.

"And the woman? His lover?"

"She will be dealt with as well. But for now, she
will draw him to us like a beacon."

"I cannot wait." She purred as she hugged the big,
shadow faced man, "I will so enjoy his death."

"As will I my dear, as will I."

She pushed away from him, suddenly despondent
again. "What happens then?"

"What do you mean?"

She turned on him, a raging anger coloring her face
suddenly red. "Do not play games with me. What happens

when we destroy him? What happens to us? To the future? To this world?"

He smiled as he sat back down and leaned back in his chair facing her.

"What happens is that we rule for all eternity. This world becomes our kingdom, and none will survive who would raise a hand against us. We will be supreme, through our shared power, and Crystalon will be a forgotten memory."

"So we will rule together?" She asked like a child asking for more ice cream, tilting her mad head to one side.

"But of course my dear! Of course we will rule together! That is our destiny! Our purpose! We will turn this world on its side; all the trappings of their so-called modern way of life will be done away with. They will know that they are all but serfs to a single master. This entire world will bow before our might, and we will rule as the sorcerer never did on his own world. People will fear us for we will be ruthless in our judgment of those who would betray or deride us."

"Good. That is what I wanted to know. I go for a bath now." She turned haughtily, her head held high, her chin pointed upwards and she whirled out his door, slamming it behind her.

"Mad as a hare," he mumbled as he returned to the work at his desk.

Behind him, an air vent shook with the rumble of the door the woman had just slammed behind her. But through a long and circuitous route, an ear was pressed against that vent listening to the feint sounds that have made their way to it. With a startled expelling of air Amanda Serros pulled away from the vent behind her bed, she nervously pushed the bed back in place then sat upon it, wringing her hands nervously.

"I have to get out of here." She whispered aloud.

Chapter 41

"Die in Ra's name!"

The huge, golden sword came down incredibly hard, shaking the room as it contacted the hard floor. The three men scattered with its impact as they fought to jump out of its way. The golden horse-headed statue snorted ancient dust at them, as it reared its blade up again so far above their heads.

"Get away, both of you!" Crystalon ordered, as he unleashed mystic energy in a blast directly into the living statue's chest, blasting a hole straight through it.

"Ha! Do you think that will stop the Guardians, Sorcerer? Think again!" The woman with the golden mask gloated. In her hand was a scepter, with a glowing stone at its tip. She pointed it at the living statue Crystalon had just decimated, and immediately the gaping hole sealed itself in the un-living creature's chest.

"This ain't workin' out so good." Joe grunted to Walker, who nodded without taking his eyes off of the battle before them.

"Woman," Crystalon began with an angry glance in her direction, "you begin to annoy me."

As he spoke he threw both hands before him, unleashing mystic flames that burned so hot they turned the gold statue to a puddle of liquid gold instantly.

"You are powerful, wizard, of that there is no doubt. But you will not defile the temple of the Gods. You will not steal from those who walked this land eons before you were born!" She gestured with her scepter again, and immediately several more of the gigantic statues came to life and turned towards them.

"You underestimate me, woman, greatly. First, I am not as young as I look. Secondly, your toys here have worn out their novelty."

263

Crystalon floated in the air, above the heads of the statues and then chanted in a low voice before throwing his hands outwards, seemingly encompassing the entire room in his grasping hands, then he hurled his hands outwards, and to the sides. Instantly the statues stopped in their tracks and dropped to the dust and sand filled floor, lifeless once more, with a deafening thud.

"You would dare?" She stammered, her eyes bulging from her head behind her golden mask in disbelief.

"You have no idea how much I would dare, woman. Stand down and surrender or I will be forced to deal with you much more harshly. I do not have time for this foolishness, this is your lone warning."

"Bah, I will kill you myself!" She grunted and pulled a long curved dagger from within the many folds of her clothing, and then brandished it towards Crystalon in a no nonsense manner.

Then, as he gently touched down to the ground, she ran towards him swinging her knife wildly in front of her. "Aaaaiiiieeee! May Set take your soul!"

Crystalon tweaked two fingers on his right hand in a snapping motion to his left and the knife flew from her hand, imbedding itself to the hilt in the stone wall.

"Ra's eyes!" She stammered in disbelief, and then hurled herself headlong at him.

"Alright you crazy broad, dis nutso stuff is over." Joe rumbled as he tackled her in mid-air, dropping her to the floor in a heap as they both rolled across the dusty ancient pyramids floor, kicking up dust as she fought like a cornered tiger to break free.

"Whoa lady, Whoa!" Joe shouted, while trying to contain her and not injure her. But this strangely garbed woman had no such compunctions.

"Fool! Away from me!" She kneed him hard in his private area.

His face turned red as he dropped to the ground writhing in pain and let her get away.

She ran from Joe, but suddenly inhaled sharply and stopped in her tracks, her hands up and shaking.

"Freeze lady, I don't know who you are, or what you are even doing in here, but this has gone on long enough." Walker stood there, his sword pointed at her face.

"Indeed woman, this has gone on far too long in fact." Crystalon walked up and helped Joe up off the floor, who immediately shot the woman a seriously angry glance, before one from Crystalon quieted his demeanor.

"Now, as my companions alluded to, we do not know who you are, or why you are even here. Tell us please, what business you have in this pyramid?"

She spit at his feet, glaring menacingly at him, "I will tell you nothing, dog. You trespass on holy ground. The Gods will take your soul for this, you thief!"

"I am no thief madam, I am a seeker of truth and more, of magic. A terrifying evil faces the world, one of unknown and deep black power. One only my companions and I dare to stand against. And we are literally three against many. The numbers of which are truly unknowable as well."

"Why should I believe you?" She hissed.

"My dear woman, if I wanted to do you ill, I would have done so already, many times over. You are in no danger from us. Search your feelings; we are not men with evil in our own beating hearts. We, instead, mean to save the world from a terminal darkness that seeks to envelop it."

She paused a second as Daniel lowered the tip of his sword slightly, then with slightly less venom in her voice, she replied, "Why should I trust crypt robbers?"

"Why shouldn't I just skewer you where you stand?" Walker answered, "That I haven't as of yet should give you reason enough to consider that we are telling the truth. Crystalon here could, I don't know, burn you to ash in a heartbeat I guess, if he wanted too. I could just slice you open right now, if I was a bad guy, and Joe here," he tilted his head sideways to Joe, who growled menacingly, his eyes boring holes into the woman, "Well, right about now I know he wants to kick your scrawny behind clear out of this temple, but he's a good guy, so it's not going to happen. But none of us are here to hurt you. We're here to save the world."

"Words, only words."

"What would it take to convince you of our sincerity?" The sorcerer asked.

"You would have to prove your intentions to me, wizard."

"Ah, so to you, words are meaningless."

It was a statement, not a question, as Crystalon walked away from her with his hands behind his back, in thought.

Then he turned and faced her again. "Woman, come here. I know how I can prove my intentions to you."

She walked towards him in trepidation, but allowed him to place his hands on either side of her facemask, his fingertips touching her skin at her exposed temples.

Then he spoke to her in a soft voice as he stared into the eyes behind the golden mask.

"Woman, know me."

Her mind exploded in a cacophony of color and sound within abject, stark silence, images coalescing and colliding within her brain. Images of Crystalon's entire life, instantly playing across the scape of her brain like a drive in movie theater's screen jammed in her face.

"Ohhhhh..." She murmured as she dropped backwards into Joe's arms, clutching her forehead.

She looked up at Crystalon, as her Golden mask broke free from her face and tumbles to the ground, revealing a beautiful face with high cheekbones, wide, large blue eyes, and brown hair that cascaded down her back as it fell out from beneath the top of her helmeted mask.

"Your life..." She stammered in shock as she touched her face, spasmodically. "Everything you did, and saw... What a life you have lived!" She turned in awe to face him as her hair fell into her eyes and face, "You were a man who people feared, and with good reason."

"Yes, yes I know, but no longer."

"I know, I see that in your mind. Even before you were trying to do the correct thing, but your vision was...skewered. You went too far, but you have paid for your sins now. You really are trying to save the world. This world. A world not your own." She stumbled away; not able to walk on suddenly wobbly feet. As she fell, both Walker and Joe caught her.

She looked up at Crystalon, a mixture of awe and fear etched upon her face.

"Take the belt, it will help you. I see what you face, those...Wraith Lords are demons. You must destroy them."

"There are more than just those, of that I am now sure. They are the foot soldiers in this war, nothing more. Whoever is running this war is pulling their strings."

"You think it's Epine-Noir?" Walker asked.

"No, that fool is a toad, nothing more. He takes orders and enjoys murder and intimidation. He may be a lieutenant, but only because of his thirst for blood and sadism. That worm is a fool, but he is also a monster."

"Ah Monsieur," a voice answered from behind them, making them all turn around quickly. "I am so glad I have made such a lasting impression on you. It is good to know that the last thoughts in your life will be of the man who hates you without question, and is about to kill you."

Behind them, and blocking a new, mystically formed exit in the pyramid, was Epine-Noir, and literally an incalculable amount of Wraith Lords floating behind him.

"Now my brethren, the time has come to destroy these fools once and for all!"

Chapter 42

"You call demons your 'brethren'? Surely you are more demented and foolhardy a man then even I thought you to be, Epine-Noir!" Crystalon roared.

"Better them then a foolish sorcerer who should have joined the winning side months ago, Mon ami. Now you have made your bed as the American's say, and you can lie in it, oui?"

He pointed then, Epine-Noir did, and the bodiless, skeletal winged Wraith Lords skittered through the air towards Crystalon's party, their transparent bone arms slashing the air as they flew, their see through, rotted wings slapping the air horrifyingly, chittering sounds escaping their ethereal lips as they sped through the cavernous pyramids inner chamber towards their prey. "Kill him! Kill the Sorcerer!" Epine-Noir shouted.

"Kill the sorccccccerer!" They maddeningly whispered in unison as they flew towards Crystalon and his companions.

"What are those...things?" The mystery woman asked, her eyes wide in dismay.

"Monsters, who seek only our deaths – yours included now, whoever you are." Crystalon answered.

"My name is unimportant, but you may call me the 'Golden Scarab', sorcerer." She answered without taking her eyes off of the hovering, chattering, transparent monsters that floated horrifyingly before them.

"Very well, Golden Scarab, then get behind me, and if your constructs are useful against magically empowered foes I suggest you re-animate them, and do so quickly!"

She shot him an haughty glance, but immediately gestured and the golden statues come back to life.

269

Crystalon blasted green flames from his outstretched hands, skewering the Wraith Lords instantly. They faded away with screams of agony on their ethereal lips.

Nearby, Walker held his amulet and murmured an incantation and once more the pure white light from within the amulet poured forth majestically, burning the hell spawn to ash.

"I hate this stuff, I hate this stuff, I hate this stuff!" Joe repeated over and over again in a low voice as he swung one of the blessed swords he and Daniel had taken from Baron Vorlas' estate, The gossamer winged horrors hissed and spit and clawed the air for him, but they stayed back in fear, for many of their number have already fallen from the blessed blades touch.

"They're giving ground." Walker shouted at Crystalon.

"Indeed. They are no match for men who are prepared for them. These demons rely on fear. If you do not fear them and instead fight back with great power yourself, they are almost powerless."

Her back to the men, Golden Scarab orchestrated her gleaming colossuses as they attacked the wisp-like Wraith Lords, wrestling with the ethereal horrors. "These things are a match for my warriors." She shouted over her shoulder to Crystalon.

"Yes but your warriors need only delay them a few more moments. I will take care of the rest." He answered almost brazenly as he sprayed the air within the buried temple with mystic energies, dissipating their enemies like so much mist.

But the numbers of the Wraith Lords were great, as literally hundreds of them forced their way into the temple, each willing to end its own hell spawned existence if only to be able to destroy Crystalon.

"These things – they never give up." Golden Scarab shouted, as she was driven closer and closer to the men.

"I know lady, I know." Joe swung his sword yet again, destroying yet another Wraith Lord, as the thing screamed horribly, its pain echoing throughout the ruins.

"Crys, I think now would be a good time to get rid of these things once and for all."

Crystalon turned towards Walker and nodded in agreement. "You are correct, Doctor. Now is as good a time as any. We have diminished their numbers sufficiently Now all of you, drop to the ground!"

As he spoke, Crystalon heaved both arms forward, unleashing a terrible blast of energy that looked like purple lightning. It crackled and sparked, arcing across the room, bouncing from the walls to the ceiling of the buried pyramid and engulfing everything not hugging the floor. Joe, Walker and their new-found ally each breathed in sharply in amazement as the purple lightning crawled across the walls and up onto the ceiling, incinerating the Wraith Lords in groups, each screaming loudly in pain as their gossamer-like bodies slowly burned from top to bottom, leaving no trace of the monsters behind, as if they were never there.

"Now that was cool." Joe breathed in astonishment as he looked around the room.

His gaze circled the buried temple and then stopped at the far end where a maddened figure stood, his hands glowing.

"Uh-oh, I almost forgot about him."

"Thankfully I did not, Joseph." Crys replied.

"Sacre-Bleur! I do not know how you have become so powerful, Monsieur, but I will still destroy you!" Epine-Noir screamed in a high pitched, maddened voice. He hurled his hands forward, as balls of dark energy ripped from his fingertips, lancing through the air towards Crystalon.

271

"Back!" The Mage shouted shoving Joe Carboneri aside with his right hand as he whirled his left hand in front of him from his side. His fingertips crackled with energy as Epine-Noir's mystic blast suddenly sprayed around Crystalon and his friends, like water off the outside of a glass.

"Merde! What have you done? How did you do that?" He shrieked, his voice growing ever louder as he now very purposefully walked toward Crystalon. As he did, he was rapid fire speaking one incantation after another under his breath in a mumble that grew more frantic, as Crystalon merely slapped aside each spell the evil, white suited, little man threw at him, with complete and utter disdain.

Crystalon continued to step forward with growing determination and anger in each footfall until he finally growled "Enough!" As he backhanded the air in front of him and instantly Epine-Noir, who was still standing ten feet away, was flung across the room to slap against the pyramids ancient, dust packed wall with a dull thud.

Epine-Noir shook himself, trying to move away from the wall, and suddenly found he cannot. He suddenly, and very forcibly was shoved up the wall twenty feet, till he was dangling there like a puppet held by only its strings.

Then Crystalon was there as well, facing the dark wizard, nose to nose, his brow furrowed in anger and pent up frustration.

"Do you remember the first time we met? In the house when you were awaiting me in the darkness? You pinned me to the ceiling like a rag doll. How does it feel to be as helpless and more? Do you enjoy being powerless to free yourself? You are a despicable sadist, Epine-Noir, among your other sins."

He stared eye to eye with his enemy and then spoke slowly and surely.

272

"I shan't ask you this more than once, little sorcerer. Where is she?"

"W-who do you mean?" Epine-Noir stammered in a low, fear tinged voice.

"Do not play games with me, you strutting fool!" Crystalon shouted backhanding Epine-Noir, hard enough to draw blood from the man's lip.

He turned back and stared daggers at Crystalon, then raised his chin up, to stare Crystalon in the eye.

"Ah, you must mean the woman. I forgot about her, I killed her so long ago," he stated flatly.

Instantly Crystalon backhanded him again, snapping the man around fully this time. "Do not lie to me, Epine-Noir. I will not tolerate it from you or anyone. Where is she, damn you to hell's deepest, darkest pit, where is Amera?"

Epine-Noir cocked his head slightly to the right and stared at Crystalon, puzzlement written all over his face. Then he smiled wickedly "Who?"

"Amanda! Where is she? I will not repeat myself again, and be fully aware that what I have done to you thus far, is as nothing to what I am capable of!"

"Boss!" Joe shouted from the floor, as a vein on Crystalon's head visibly throbbed while he stared at the man held helpless mere inches from his own face.

"Boss, come down here, c'mon! What're you doing?" Joe implored from the dust covered pyramids floor far below. "You gotta stop this!"

Crystalon looked slightly over his right shoulder, as he answered his friends. "He knows where she is."

"Who? Amera? What are you talking about?" Dan Walker replied, surprised by Crystalon's ferocity.

"No, I-" He turned swiftly towards Walker then, "how did you know that name? That is my wife's name."

"You just said it, Boss." Joe replied.

273

"I did not." Crys answered angrily, as he continued to mystically hold Epine-Noir aloft.

"Yes, you did indeed, Crystalon." The woman known only as Golden Scarab re-affirmed.

"If I did then it was but an error. I meant Amanda."

"Awright boss, you gotta calm down, let the creep down easy, and lets all talk a minute." Joe implored as he patted the air down with his hands.

Crystalon turned back towards Epine-Noir and dropped him instantly to the ground twenty feet below, but the man stopped falling an inch from the ground, landing with a dull thud instead of with broken bones. Immediately Dr. Walker and Golden Scarab took positions around him, not allowing him a venue of escape.

Crystalon floated down, his cape fluttering behind him as he, likewise, landed gently.

"Boss, take a breath, this guy has you all worked up, you gotta think clearly, especially if we're gonna get 'Manda back."

"I-dislike this man much, my friend. He is evil for evils sake alone, and he is yet but a puppet, to a far more powerful enemy, one who has dogged my steps since I appeared on this world."

"Then maybe it's time we dogged his." Dan Walker stated flatly, while staring at the crumpled Epine-Noir.

"Alright, we gotta find 'Manda, no doubt, an' this here sleaze-ball knows where she is. Let's make him talk." Joe turned and took a step towards the evil sorcerer, cracking his knuckles as he did.

"You foolish ape." Epine-Noir whispered as he wiped blood from his lip.

He brought himself to his knees and faced the approaching Joe Carboneri. "Do you actually think you can intimidate moi?"

He threw his arms forward suddenly and surprisingly, as a wave of invisible energy leapt from his fingertips, leaving naught save a distortion in the air and a terrible heat in its wake. Crystalon turned towards them both as he raised his hands to begin a counter spell, knowing he was already too late. But then the woman only known as Golden Scarab threw herself in front of Joe, pushing him aside as the wave of evil magic enveloped her instead of Joe, instantly she screamed as the wave seemed to eat at her form. Dissolving it, disintegrating it slowly and oh so very painfully.

In an eye blink it was over. Golden Scarab was gone, as if she had never existed. Dr. Walker, Joe and Crystalon stared, stunned. Walker fingered the hilt of the sword in his hand, trembling slightly. Joe's lip quivered as he stared at the monster before him. But Crystalon slowly turned toward the evil man with rage and pain written all over his face. All the while Epine-Noir merely giggled to himself.

"Enough." Crystalon murmured. Then again in a roar, "Enough!"

Epine-Noir fired off a spell at Crystalon, the same one he had used but a moment before. Crystalon merely waved his hand, brushing it aside, rendering it useless.

He grabbed the madman by the throat with his left hand, lifting him upwards so that his feet were dangling there.

"You have earned this, you depraved, sadistic bastard." The master sorcerer whispered in his enemy's ear.

He jammed his fingers into the villains forehead, they become immaterial, no blood was seen spurting from his brow, but his hand was buried up to the knuckles as he spoke slowly and in a voice not meant to be heard by the others. A voice speaking in a language that has only been uttered from Crystalon's lips upon this Earth.

Epine-Noir's eyes stretched open as far as they could go without his flesh tearing, his mouth likewise in a silent scream of pure agony. He did not even breathe.

275

For what seems like an eternity they stood thusly, and then Crystalon quickly removed his hand, and his enemy crumpled to the floor, a puppet with its strings cut.

"I know where Amanda is." Crystalon offered to his two companions. "We will proceed there now."

"Kill you, kill you all," a ragged voice repeated. Epine-Noir crawled towards them, madness gripping his features. Madness and pain. He spit the words out over and over, saliva drooling down his chin and spewing from his lips.

"Out, both of you." Crys ordered as he beckoned towards the entranceway.

"What about him?" Joe asked.

"He is staying behind." Crystalon answered.

"Crystalon," Dr. Walker began, "Men like this, he may not seem like a threat anymore, but he could be again. He's the type that never stop until they kill you, no matter how long it takes."

"Daniel, I am well aware of who and what Epine-Noir actually is, and I am not done with him. Now go please, I will be right behind you."

Walker nodded hesitantly as he watched the vile man continue to crawl after them, and then he exited behind Carboneri.

Crystalon turned towards his enemy then and spoke; "This is good-bye scum, not good riddance. Evil men like you deserve no more than that. Your entire life has been built around others pain and suffering to advance yourself. At my worst I was nothing like you. You brought a new meaning to the word evil in my mind. There is a saying on your world, and I am paraphrasing here, as I do not remember it exactly, I have heard it but once. 'If good men stand idly by and do nothing against evil, then evil will always win.' I am a good man. I perhaps lost my way over my immortal lifetime, but I was ever a good man. It took much for me to remember that. It also took you. For that I thank you. Our time together is at an end. Oh, and Dr. Walker was indeed correct, I know exactly what and who you are. Your brand of evil ends here tonight, make no mistake on that regard. Adieu, Epine-Noir."

Crystalon exited the pyramid into the harsh heat and sunlight, behind him Épine-Noir continued to crawl, muttering over and over, "Kill you, kill you all."

Crystalon turned back one last time, waved both hands before him in opposite directions, and the pyramid toppled before their stunned eyes. Collapsing in upon itself, with a roar that seemed to shake the Heavens and the Earth, the structure disintegrated as hundreds of tons of stone buried Epine-Noir. He left their sight for the final time, ignominiously buried forever.

The three men stared at each other a moment before Crystalon finally spoke; "We go to a land called Scotland. It is there that our enemies and Amanda await us."

Joe and Walker stared at each other in the midst of the boiling desert sun, then silently nodded their grim approval to each other and then to Crystalon.

"Let's finish this." Dr. Walker agrees.

Crystalon threw the tail of his cloak upwards in the air, whirling it around the three men and they instantly disappeared in its folds in a puff of smoke.

Chapter 43

Within the castle where Amanda was being held against her will. The grim, shadowed, bearded man sat, brooding over something he was writing, when the wailing sound of a woman's voice assailed his ears. He slammed the book closed, and rolled his eyes heavenward. "Damned lunatic," was all he muttered.

He turned towards the door as the mad woman exploded into his room. She wore a diaphanous shawl, all in black, "He is dead!" She cried passionately at the top of her lungs.

"What? Who? Crystalon? Did that fool actually manage to defeat him?"

"Crystalon?" She questioned quietly as she fumbled with her fingers to her mouth, then wandered around the room staring at the corners of the ceiling.

"Yes, did Épine- Noir kill Crystalon?" He asked, obviously at his wits and patience end with the woman.

"Crystalon?" she repeated in a vague whisper. "N-no, no!" She blurted out. "He is alive, alive I tell you, alive..." Her voice trailed off as she stopped to study a spider web in one corner of the ceiling.

"Crystalon is alive. What about Epine-Noir? Is he yet among the living?"

"No, Epine-Noir is no more." She muttered with her back to the broad shouldered bearded man.

"So the sorcerer killed him. One less loose end to worry about when this is all over, I suppose."

"No loose ends, no loose ends." She whispered as her eyes meandered around the room, as if she'd never seen it before.

"Be gone with you then woman, I have work to do. Leave me to it." He ordered impatiently.

"They are no more as well. Them. Those things you love so much. The monsters..."

"The Wraith Lords? The sorcerer obliterated them as well? At that I am indeed surprised. I assumed they would give him some sort of a fight." He got up and slammed his left fist to the desktop. "So be it. Woman you had, at best, be as powerful as I believe you to be."

"Where goest you?" She asked tilting her long black maned head to the right with a blank stare.

"To practice what I do best. Swordplay." He got up to leave the room before turning back to her. "You there, come along now. Prepare yourself. Focus. No doubt the sorcerer will be here soon. We must both be prepared."

He moved her out of his office, and down the hall.

At the other end of the hallway, around a corner, but perfectly within earshot, and hidden in the deep shadows of the place, Amanda Serros finally allowed herself a breath. She heard everything her two captors had said, and she now knew that one way or another this madness was nearing its end.

Chapter 44

A burst of smoke and the three men appeared again, halfway around the world.

"Uh, I guess we're in Scotland now?" Joe asked, wide eyed.

"Indeed we are, Joseph."

"Funny I was kinda expectin' ta hear bagpipes."

"Well, things aren't always what we expect Joe." Daniel Walker answered.

"Yeah I gotcha Doc. I suppose most stuff don't live up to its hype."

He looked ahead of himself, scanning the countryside. "This place sure is pretty, that's fer sure. So, how're we gonna find this place they got 'Manda?"

"Already done, Joe." Walker replied quietly.

Joe turned around and faced the same direction as Crystalon and Daniel. Before him, some slight distance away, loomed a massive, ancient castle.

"Uh, this look familiar to you or somethin' boss? I mean the way yer starin' an' all."

"Indeed Joseph, it does. In my world, this great castle was my home."

"That's not good." Dr. Walker replied.

"No, it is not indeed," Crystalon acknowledges. "It portends familiarity with me."

"He means whoever is behind all of this knows him." Walker grinned as he spoke to Joe.

"I know what he meant, wise guy. What? Now you find a sense of humor?"

"I have to agree with Joseph, Daniel. Now is not the time for levity."

"Sorry guys, I was just trying to lighten the moment a little. I mean, chances are we're facing our deaths in the next few minutes."

"An' that's different from the last few weeks how?"

Crystalon ignored Joe and began, "I understand completely Daniel. That is why I am going to ask you both to stay here while I go and face our unknown foes."

"Naaah, no way Jose. I'm in fer a penny, in for a pound."

"The same, Crystalon. I'm a sorcerer myself, remember. Not anywhere near your league, but I am a magician. You might need me."

"In truth I need you both, of that I am sure. But I do not want to put either of your lives at any more risk."

"Now yer worried about our lives? C'mon boss, let's just get this over with."

"Really Crystalon", Walker began, "what could we possibly face here that could give you a problem?"

"Uh, maybe them?" Joe replied his voice wavering slightly as he gulped hard.

High above, on the ridge facing them, armored knights on horseback appeared, gleaming in the sun. At first only a few, then more, until the entire horizon in both directions was filled with men in armor, with spears, swords and bows drawn, all facing Crystalon and friends.

"That don't look good. What do you think boss?"

"As impressive as they look, they are not insurmountable."

"What are the odds? A thousand to one?"

"Yes Daniel, I believe so."

"Looks pretty damned insurmountable ta me, boss."

"What I do not understand is why are we facing men with bows and arrows, and not machine guns?"

"Things are done a certain way, Daniel, when it comes to sorcery and mysticism. This is something a young sorcerer like yourself must learn." Crystalon answered while staring at the surrounding horde.

"My point being that one man with a machine gun has as much chance at killing us as these three thousand do with their bows and swords."

"By as much chance, I assume you mean none?"

"Well, I guess you could interpret it that way, too." Daniel smiled wryly, glancing sideways at Crystalon, whose purple cloak floated in the breeze about him.

"Will you two please get serious? There's a couple a thousand guys, all wearin' all sorts a different kindsa armor pointin' arrows at our heads. Boss, you gotta get yer head in the game! We're about ta be killed!" Joe pleaded, obviously losing his cool at last.

Crystalon turned away from the massing army on the ridge before them and quizzically looked at Joe. "As I have told you before, Joseph, you are a brilliant man."

"Huh?" was all Joe replied.

"Their armor," Crystalon continued, "You are correct, none of it matches. Some is old and shredded, as if it has seen many campaigns, some not favorably. Some is bright and glistening in the noonday sun, as if recently forged and having never seen a day of battle."

"Uh okay you ain't so worried here so I'll go wit' this. Waddaya talkin' about?"

"They're pulled from different points in time." Walker barked out.

"Indeed they are Dr. Walker, as our good friend Joseph has deduced, these men are not from around here, rather not from this time period. They have been pulled through time, here to face us by our mysterious foe, one obviously schooled in the mystic forces. He shows his hand."

"Wasn't he this entire time though? Epine-Noir was a mystic and a powerful one, he commanded the Wraith lords, yet he in turn was commanded by this person whoever he is."

"Daniel, I have come to these determinations as well. I knew our foe was powerful, but make no mistake it could just as easily be a more barbarous warrior who is our foe, and merely one who has a sorcerer of great renown under his employ. Many possibilities still exist within our conundrum."

Joe suddenly turned back to Crys and Walker.

"Hey, uh, guys you better take a look at this. Things are happenin' here and it ain't lookin' good."

A voice curled across the field towards them, borne on the wind rustling their clothes "Ready!"

"Uh, guys, you really better look at this," he implored.

"Aim!" the same voice roared across the field towards their position.

"Boss! C'mon wake up!"

"Fire!" The voice thundered, as with an almost ear deafening snap fifteen hundred bows released as one, sending a shower of certain death arcing across the sky, aimed directly at the three men.

"BOSS!"

Chapter 45

The sky turned black, as a cloud of wooden and steel death flew towards Crystalon, Joe and Walker. Joe was staring wide-eyed and fearful at the certain death on the wind that was headed towards them.

"BOSS!" He reiterated.

Looking up from his conversation with Daniel, Crystalon snapped his fingers and the arrows all suddenly burst into flame and turned to ash instantly, long before they would have hit the three men.

"Don't do that to me next time!" Joe wailed angrily. "I thought we wuz gonna die there."

"Joseph," Crys began, "By now you should know better as to what I can accomplish, also a good barometer to go by is simply how concerned I appear to be. If there is no concern, as there was none just now, then you shouldn't be concerned either."

"What if ya make a mistake?"

"Hhhmm?" Crys replied quizzically, cocking his head to the side and furrowing his brow.

"You done it before Boss, back in yer own world, don't forget about that. Don't get cocky is all I'm sayin' here. Don't underestimate these guys."

"Again you are correct, my friend."

"Aim." came the voice from the top of the field again.

"Here we go again." Daniel grunted.

"Fire!" The soldier ordered his men, who released a second wave of the deadly arrows.

Crystalon snapped his fingers again, expecting the same result, only now, the arrows seemed to blur momentarily in mid-flight, then continued on unaffected.

Crystalon immediately waved his hands in an arc overhead, and a glimmering energy dome appeared just in time to block the arrows attack.

"Joseph, you will continue to admonish me when you see fit." Crys angrily retorted. "Enough of this. Ready your mystic swords my friends we go into battle."

The two men pulled the swords from their scabbards, and prepared.

Crystalon raised his hands, heaving them forwards as words spilled away from him, in the form of a spell that forced the warriors apart, like an invisible ram.

The entire three thousand-man force was driven to the ground by his powerful wave of mystic force, stunned by the sheer energy which propelled them like wheat before the scythe.

Slowly they regained their feet in stunned silence.

"Kill the wizard!" One ragged, red bearded, helmed warrior shouted as he brandished a sword in one hand and an axe in the other, charging across the field at Crystalon.

"Enough you fool!" Crys rumbled as he waved his hand at the man, stripping him of his weapons, which flew away from him to land a dozen feet away.

The red bearded man looked around like a mouse caught in a trap, eyes wide and frightened, then he pulled a dagger from his tunic and with a scream charged at Crystalon.

"I said, 'Enough!'" The angered sorcerer roared as he turned the dagger to molten steel in the man's grasp, who instantly sank to his knees clutching his burning hand.

"You men, leave now, and you will not be burdened by this war that is not your own any longer."

"Where would we go?" a heavily accented voice replied from within the crowd. "This land, it is eternal, but it is so different... We do not recognize this place, yet it rings familiar."

"You men were taken from your homes, from your lands, from your times by a mystic who does not care about you or your loved ones. This person merely seeks to use you against me. I can help you and return you to where you belong."

"Why should we believe you anymore then the master himself? He promises us to set us back where we belong once you're dead. Why shouldn't we believe him, an' just kill you now?" Another warrior replied in anger.

"Has he been truthful with you thus far? Has he earned your trust and obedience? Or has he demanded it? I will not harm you all if you merely let me return you to your homes once this is over. To do so now would take much time, time I do not have at the moment. There is a woman's life in the balance here."

The warriors, the knights, then turned to one another and conferred, in a dozen different languages. But then a new voice intruded from behind them all,

"You rabble! To the attack! Your master commands!" The voice was powerful and instantly commanded respect. It was a voice of strength and iron will. The voice of a man who did not take 'No' for an answer.

Instantly Crystalon's demeanor changed, he turned towards the voice with sheer, utter surprise etched across his features.

"That voice, it cannot be!" He almost muttered, his own voice so low as to be barely heard.

"Attack them! Kill them! Do it now, I command you all, you rabble! Kill them, but save the wizard, for he is mine! He must die painfully and at my choosing!"

"Boss! You know this guy?" Joe asked, as he held his sword tightly at his side, staring at the transfixed mob.

"I know that voice..." Crys replied, unable to believe he was hearing who he knew in his heart he was.

The horde hesitantly turned towards Crystalon, readying their weapons as the warrior king in their midst bullied his way through them all to the forefront of their line. His black mane and beard caused Crystalon to raise his eyebrows in disbelief.

Finally, Crystalon could see his tormentor, his enemy. He who had dogged his every moment for months. The large warrior brandished a gleaming barbarian's sword larger then any other in the horde of knights and warriors, and raised it above his head then pointed it down at the three men from his high point on the hill above them.

"Kill them now!" He roared as the men charged down the hill on horseback and on foot.

"It cannot be," Crystalon stated plainly in stunned amazement.

"Who is this guy, Crystalon, who?" Walker asked almost pleading.

"It is my mortal enemy, a man I banished thousands, upon thousands of years ago. The murderer of my mother and sister. A man I thought long ago done away with, condemned to a forever living hell of my own devising."

"Boss, enough! Cut to the chase, who is this guy?"

"His name is Maceyis, and he is the last person I ever expected to see alive again!"

Chapter 46

In the hills of Scotland, overlooking a great lake, three thousand sword wielding men in armor, both new and devastated alike descended upon three men in a small valley. Atop the hill behind the screaming, rampaging, roaring horde was an ancient castle overlooking the desperate melee.

At the head of the army ran a giant bearded man, his long ponytailed hair swung harshly with each step. He wore leather and steel armor and brandished a huge sword that glistened like the sun as he led the charge towards his immortal enemy, the mage, Crystalon. A grin cut across his savage face, the face of the hidden enemy, the face of Maceyis.

"Boss, do something!" Joe shouted, grabbing Crystalon by the arm and shaking him wildly.

"Y-yes, y-you are c-correct Joseph. Do something I shall!" He shook himself clear of his momentary shock, and then he raised both hands and unleashed a blistering wave of purple fire. The oncoming horde disappeared beneath its forty-foot tall flames, but almost instantly simply ran through it with Maceyis shouting, "Kill them! His magic cannot harm you! You are protected!"

"What?" Walker asked in shock himself. He turned towards Crystalon, "What does he mean?"

"I've no idea. He must have a sorcerer protecting him. But that cannot be! It would have to be one of equal or greater power then myself. It took over a dozen men of fantastic power just to subdue me, and that was while I was drugged by my duplicitous wife."

"Okay tell me yer life story later, just stop this army that's gonna cut us ta ribbons, now!" Joe implored.

"Yes, once again you are correct, Joseph."

289

He brought his hands down low then raised them up above his head, as suddenly the ground beneath the feet of the oncoming army suddenly tore itself to pieces, hurling the men skyward, then back to the earth with sickening thuds, followed by many moans of pain and agony.

"This is not over!" roared Maceyis as he climbed to his feet once more.

He hurled himself at Crystalon, who backhanded the air in front of him, a huge almost invisible wave of semi-clear energy flew from his hand and smashed Maceyis, but the bruiser merely stepped through it, his blade descending on Crystalon.

Suddenly another blade intervened and stopped the deadly plunge, Dan Walker's sword parried Maceyis's, saving Crystalon from a cleaved shoulder and arm.

"Ho ho, what is this? The little sorcerer has himself defenders, does he? Good, more to die at my hungry blade, and little sorcerer, after all those long, long years, it is oh so hungry indeed!"

"You ain't killin' nobody here, chump." Joe growled as he slammed the big man from his blind side, with a shoulder, tackling him over.

Maceyis swat Joe aside with a meaty fist, sending the smaller man tumbling. Joe rolled and was instantly back on his feet, drawing his own sword awkwardly.

Behind them the warriors gathered to their feet, unsure of what to do, or who to follow. They stared perplexed at the strange tableau taking place before them.

Below, Crystalon angrily threw his arms forwards at Maceyis, as lightning leapt from his fingertips, impaling the giant warrior.

Maceyis merely laughed.

"You cannot harm me, little sorcerer. I have planned well for this battle."

"Yes braggart, obviously you have. But that is of no matter. Know that when this is all over, this time, I will not merely imprison you in a timeless realm, I will destroy you, as I did your lackey, Epine-Noir."

"Words little sorcerer, merely words, you cannot harm me. But I can kill you!"

He swung his sword madly at Crystalon, who literally flew backwards, taking to the air to avoid the stroke.

"Do you think you are the only one who can fly little sorcerer? Meet my, as the locals say, 'Air Force'."

Suddenly, from behind the castle, a great whooshing sound was heard with volume like thunder, and then rising above the castle were six great beasts, leathern and worn, on wings that beat the air with a deafening roar. The ancient dragons rose up and flew immediately towards Crystalon.

"Okay," Joe Carboneri began, wide eyed and swallowing hard, "There's somethin' ya don't see every day."

Chapter 47

The six mighty dragons descended on Crystalon, forces of nature more than of flesh and blood. Their worn, holed, leathern wings beat the air with great gusts of heat, like unto standing before a blast furnace. Each beating of their wings pressured the air and the earth like a hellish thunder.

Joe and Daniel stepped back and covered their faces from the sudden overpowering heated onslaught. Crystalon said nothing and did not move. His purple cape blew in the fiery wind as it passed him powerfully. The six great beasts roared and pranced through the sky above as they circled him. Silently he stood, floating in mid-air, his arms at his hips, his face stoic and resolved, he stared at the beasts, at each in turn, into their great red eyes as flames played about their snouts with each exhaled breath. He stared into them, as if to tell them "You will not win here. I stand before you and I will stop you. Leave now with your lives."

The dragons each received his message and haughtily shook their great heads in refusal and disdain. They were mighty, powerful creatures and would not bow before some mere human sorcerer.

Crystalon narrowed his gaze and nodded slightly, as if to say, '*So be it. You have made your decision, and your grave, now prepare to lie in it.*'

As one, the great, fiery beasts descended on his hovering form like lightning, then simultaneously they spit huge gouts of flame at him, engulfing his flying body, seemingly vaporizing him where he hovered.

"No!" shouted Joe, as both he and Walker ran through blistering waves of heat, towards the spot Crystalon was hovering, heedless of their own safety.

"He's got to be alive!" Walker screamed to Joe, "He's our only hope!"

"At last!" Maceyis roared triumphantly. "At long, long last!"

Then majestically the flames around Crystalon changed color to a bright purple, matching his tunic, and they seemingly imploded upon themselves as if drawn in by some great vacuum, until all that remained was Crystalon himself, unharmed, his hands covered by smoldering purple flames, hovering in the same spot facing the dragons.

"Now beasts, know your own power!" Crystalon roared as he whipped his hands forward, purple flames burst forth from his outstretched palms, engulfing the six dragons, instantly immolating them, burning them to ashes in a heartbeat.

Their ashes rained down upon Maceyis as he looked on incredulously

"Madness!" Growled Maceyis as he thundered across the ground towards Crystalon and the others. "To hell with the plans, I'll kill you myself if I have too. I swear by all that's unholy I will!"

Behind them all, the three thousand, time displaced warriors moved away, not sure of where to go, but now knowing they didn't want any piece of Crystalon, judging at how he so easily did away with the dragons.

When suddenly a female form, gossamer with glowing eyes, as if a ghost, appeared before them all and commanded, "Stop."

As one, the men halted in position, instantly ensorcelled.

"Aid your master. Kill the sorcerer and his companions. Leave none alive. Go now."

Wordlessly, and without any obvious thought, the men descended, wooden like at first, then with some speed and then raucousness, brandishing their swords and shields. They howled like mad animals and rumbled the remaining steps towards Joe, Walker and Crystalon.

Crystalon slapped his hands together in mid-air, as hurricane force winds issued from them.

Instantly the men were blown backwards, some rolling up hill end over end.

Again, only Maceyis ignored the mystic power of Crystalon, standing steadfast against the elemental onslaught.

"He's holding his own, but how long can he keep this up?" Walker asked.

"Holdin' his own? Doc, the Boss should be stompin' all over these guys. He's fightin' this war on two fronts. We gotta help him, Doc. The Boss can't hurt this guy with the ponytail, somethin's stoppin' that, an I'm willin' ta bet its in that castle. Some other magic guy or somethin'."

"Yeah Joe, I think you're right. We're useless here. Maybe we can get into that castle and find the source of whoever is doing this to Crys."

"Other question is, Doc, do we really wanna take on anyone that can stymie the Boss this way?"

"It's more than that Joe, Amanda is in that castle, I'm sure of it, I can feel her presence through my talisman." He fingered the amulet at his neck beneath his shirt.

"Maybe it's time you use that thing for more then keepin' yer neck warm."

"Maybe you're right Joe." Walker agreed grimly as he lay the amulet on top of his shirt.

The two men ascended the hill, giving wide berth to the, once again, almost robotic forces descending towards Crystalon.

"Good," thought Crystalon, "They are heading into the castle to rescue Amanda."

The warriors loosed arrows once more at Crystalon, who shielded himself this time with mystic energy that deflected the arrows away.

"So you can hold my forces at bay, little sorcerer, but you cannot harm me. It seems we have a stalemate. Or do we?" Maceyis laughed as almost instantly clouds appeared in a formerly cloudless sky and the sky turned jet black with dozens of lightning bolts slashing down, most missing him, but a few striking Crystalon through the chest multiple times, dropping him from the sky like a broken ragdoll.

"Now you die, little man!" Maceyis shouted gleefully as he raised his sword above the wizard's prone form. "At long last revenge is mine!"

He drove his sword down towards Crystalon's chest, when suddenly Crystalon's eyes opened wide and glowed with untold power.

The sword impacted the ground, but there was no body impaled by it.

Crystalon was no longer there. Then almost instantly Maceyis realized something else, it had turned to night in the blink of an eye. Stars shined above, as did the full moon.

"Madness! What has he done now?"

He looked around himself as the gathered soldiers stood perplexed as well, staring at the stars above in awe and fright.

"You have erred Maceyis. You thought me easily defeated by a many pronged attack." Crystalon's voice echoed from everywhere throughout the small valley.

"Well no, I never thought *easily*," Maceyis grumbled in reply.

"Now, learn the error of your ways, fool."

Suddenly the sky exploded with the light of a million stars, instantly blinding everyone present.

"Your wizard is mighty indeed Maceyis! He wields the lightning with great power, but he lacks subtlety and precision in his power, he is untrained. I am not."

Lightning leapt from the sky at Crystalon's command, striking with pin point accuracy, scattering the army of men; driving them apart then striking at the ground beneath Maceyis' feet, tossing him from his feet and driving him into the air with the pure shock of its explosive power.

With a grunt Maceyis landed in a heap. He immediately struggled to his feet, snarling, and faced off towards Crystalon He gripped his sword so tightly the blood drained from his hand.

"You continue to impress, Little Wizard. After all my planning, all my sacrifice, still you continue to vex me." Maceyis wiped at his mouth with the back of his hand, clearing blood that was dripping from his lips.

"Oh shut up, you pompous ape." Crystalon replied, splaying his fingers wide and pushing them away from himself at the ground. Instantly the ground moved, rolling like a wave in the ocean towards Maceyis, tossing him into the air and away, then slapping down atop him with a thunderous slam.

Painfully the barbarian king pushed away the dirt that covered him as he once more struggled to his feet.

Crystalon smiled. It was not a happy or pleasant sight. It was one of a predator about to kill its prey.

"What has happened, Maceyis? Your magic guardian seems to no longer be protecting you. Perhaps you should look into that."

Suddenly, towering blasts of flame erupted from the ground, surrounding Crystalon, effectively separating him from Maceyis. The heat was like unto a blast furnace as waves of deadly fire emanated and encircled him. He covered his eyes and began a counter spell, when suddenly the flame behind him parted and he turned to face this new menace.

His eyes grow wide in recognition.

"No! You? How can this be?" He asked incredulously of the figure he sensed more than saw that was almost completely hidden behind a scorching wall of flame and smoke.

Then the flames parted, and a woman walked through, wearing a floor length, low cut, black gown, with a thick golden necklace laying across her chest. She seemed to float on air towards Crystalon.

"I hate, hate, hate you!" She howled insanely at him, taking the sorcerer aback, actually causing him pause as he stared in stunned silence.

"This cannot be." He stammered quietly, severely shaken by this woman's presence.

"Oh, but I assure you it is." A laughing Maceyis replied as he quietly snuck up behind Crystalon, and smashed him across the back of the head with his swords hilt, knocking the sorcerer unconscious with one powerful blow.

"Well done, my dear Shaleeya, well done. Never did this fool of a magician believe the weapon of his destruction would be his own long lost, presumed dead, darling sister." He kicked Crystalon's unconscious form once, then spit on him contemptuously. "Well done indeed, my dear." He reiterated, as he turned his back on the Sorcerer and trudged back up the hill towards his castle.

"You men," He bellowed at the nearest group of warriors who still stood shocked and unmoving, "Carry that fool inside my castle, and then bind him securely in my dungeon. I am not yet done with him."

He turned and walked away proceeding towards the castle's entrance in the distance, whistling and laughing to himself as he did. Behind him, several of the time-displaced warriors grasped the unconscious Crystalon roughly and dragged him up the hill towards the direction of the ancient and impressive castle.

"Today is a good day, a good day indeed!" Maceyis laughed to himself evilly as he ascended the hill.

Chapter 48

Crystalon looks about him. He stands in a white wasteland. No up, no down. No walls or scenery of any kind, in any distance, anywhere he looks.

"Ah, I am dreaming." He says aloud.

"No, my son." A voice answers from seemingly everywhere about him, "You are not."

"Father? Why am I here? I know I am not dead. What am I doing here?"

"You know the truth now, my son." A second voice, female this time, replies.

"Mother? Show yourselves, please. I wish to see you both again."

"As you wish my child." His mother replies as both fade into being before him. Both look markedly different from the last time he saw them. Both wear gold trimmed, white robes, and appear at peace.

"Again I reiterate, why am I here, my parents?"

"You have a decision to make my son." His father replies. "As you now know, your sister has been your enemy, as well as the madman Maceyis. Her power may well indeed be greater than yours."

"I truly doubt that." Crystalon scoffs haughtily.

"Do not let your own pride and arrogance be your undoing." His father scolds. "You will not be able to save her. You must come to terms with that and be prepared to make a difficult choice where she is concerned."

"You expect me to slay my own sister?" The sorcerer asks incredulously.

"You will have to do what must needs be done my son." His mother answers sadly.

"No! I can save her!" He roars.

"I believe not, boy. She is beyond redemption. For this world to survive, for all worlds to survive, you must do the unthinkable. Your burden will be most heavy indeed."

"Why do you tell me this? Both of you?"

His mothers shade answers, "Because you and you alone stand between this planet and its utter annihilation. Your choice when the time comes, will weigh heavily on every being on this world. Do you understand my son? You must not falter, you must slay Shaleeya, this day, or all will be lost."

"No! I refuse to believe there is no other way! I must be able to save her! I must!"

His mother smiles a smile filled with sorrow. "You will learn the truth my son."

"Please boy, keep your wits about you when dealing with your estranged sister. She will do anything she has to in order to complete her goal, your death. If these two lunatics actually do defeat you, all will be lost, my son. The world will be sent into unending peril."

"There has to be another way. I can save her!" He almost begs.

"There is not. She is lost to us all. You must go now my son. The fate of this Earth, nay this universe, rests in your hands. I pray you are strong enough to do what must be done when the time is nigh. Do not falter my son. This world's fate rests squarely on your shoulders. Do not fail. This will be your final step in redemption. You are ready to do what must be done, what only you can do." His father stopped talking as both his parents slowly faded from sight.

"Goodbye my son. Know you, no matter the outcome, you have made us both proud once again." Crystalon's mother calls to him as she fades into the ether.

Chapter 49

Crystalon awakened slowly, as he heard voices nearby.

"He's comin' around."

"I know Joe. I'm sure he'll be happy at the bang up job we did."

"Will you two stop bickering? If I didn't know better I'd think you were an old married couple." A third, female voice intruded. A voice Crystalon quickly recognized as he snapped awake.

"Ame- Amanda? You are alive? You are alive!" He shouted joyfully.

"You had doubts? Gee, thanks," she answered hesitantly.

Crystalon quickly took in his surroundings. He was chained to a wall in a dank, wet dungeon by his wrists, which were held above his head, as were Joe, Daniel, and Amanda. Water dripped from somewhere nearby in a slow and steady rhythm.

"What happened to you all?"

"Well," Joe began, "Doc an' I made our way into the castle, an' we were sneakin' around, headin' to the lower levels, lookin for 'Manda..."

"When that woman grabbed us. I tried to use my powers on her, but she laughed me off, like me focusing whatever mystic power I had through the amulet was a real joke. It had zero effect on her. Then she aimed her hand at us, I saw a bright light, and that's the last thing I remember." Walker completed.

"What of you, Amanda? How came you to this place? Or have you been held here this entire time?"

She hesitated then spoke with some amount of fear and trepidation in her wavering voice, "No they actually treated me pretty good, for holding me captive that is. I had a nice room and a comfortable bed. I was fed gourmet meals daily, as long as I played by the rules."

"Which you obviously halted doing." Crys added.

"Yes, I was trying to escape. I did some snooping around myself. I've been looking throughout this place for weeks, which by the way, thanks for taking so long to rescue me, nice job with *that* too. Anyway, I was trying to find a way out, but I couldn't find an unguarded exit, no matter where I looked. Then earlier today, the monsters, those Wraith Lord things were just...gone. I figured you did something to them."

"Right, but how'd you end up here then?" Walker asked.

"She tried to escape through the main entrance. Foolishly, I might add." A new voice intruded, from the doorway to the dungeon.

They all turned towards the sound of Maceyis' voice as the conqueror walked in, followed by Shaleeya, who floated along behind him, cocking her head spastically from one side to the next, eyes wide, practically bulging from her head, as she neared her brother.

"Hate you, hate you..." She murmured madly under her breath while staring at her brother.

Crys eyed her sadly, shaking his head in remorse.

"Yet another evil you must answer for, Maceyis." He angrily spit out in the general direction of his enemy.

Maceyis waved his hand nonchalantly, "Your threats are meaningless, Little Wizard. I have won here. Or is that not evident to you yet? Have you tried to escape your bonds? Shaleeya has made sure you cannot."

"What do you want Maceyis? If you are so in command, why have you not simply killed me?"

"Why waste my vengeance upon you, and not be able to savor it at length?"

"Yes, of course. So you intend to bore me to death then."

"No Crystalon, you will die painfully, but only after I succeed in my plan."

"Which is what? What could you possibly want here?"

"Very simply, to rule this world. What else does a conqueror require out of life? One must have goals my old friend, Surely you agree?"

"How did you escape the eternal prison I had bound you in?"

"It took me many years, I assure you. Thousands perhaps. But eventually my dear Shaleeya freed me from your insidious pocket dimension, where you left me unmoving. I owe you for that, believe me, I intend to collect on that debt, Little Wizard."

"Your threats are laughable, fool."

"Says the mage held captive by his wrists from the ceiling."

As the two antagonists continued to verbally spar, the mad Shaleeya fearfully stayed away from her brother, stealing furtive, frightened glances at him.

"How did you come to be here, dog?"

"Ha! Belligerent to the end I see. Very well. We will play this game to its inevitable conclusion. After you killed your mother..."

Crystalon visually bristled at this, as he struggled in rage at his chains.

"...and trapped me seemingly for all eternity in that hellish moment, I truly knew despair. There was no sleep; there was no rest. Just eternal damnation for myself. Trapped between instants, and made to watch the universe go by at an interminably slow pace. But eventually your beloved sister did manage to find me, as I had instructed her, though I truthfully admit I did not think it would take her so many years. But then again she is related to you, so she already has an inbred propensity for stupidity and failure damning her every step."

Joe leaned over to Dr. Walker and whispered "How is the boss able to listen to this garbage?"

"Shhhh. Keep quiet, Joe." Walker admonished him, trying desperately not to be noticed by Maceyis.

"Your attitude is, as always, refreshing, Maceyis." Crystalon responded, "It has been many, many lifetimes since I have heard someone so blatantly idiotic pretend to intelligence. You are bland and predictable as always, you Neanderthal, but then to call you a Neanderthal would be an insult to those beasts, for they learned from their mistakes whereas you keep repeating the same ones, over and over."

Maceyis laughed, it was a sick and twisted sound filled with venom and danger, "And yet here I am, with you and your friends chained to the wall of my dungeon."

"For now, ogre, for now. What is your intent here, Maceyis? What do you want with this world, how did you end up here to begin with?" Crystalon asked again.

"It can't do any harm to tell you, Little Wizard, in fact I want you to know my great plan."

He paced before them all, back and forth with his hands held behind his back as if in deep thought.

"As I have said, Shaleeya found me, after many years. But as you can see, her mind is not quite as it once was."

She stood next to Maceyis now, shaking spastically, her head tilting back and forth, drool running down the corner of her mouth, her eyes wide.

"As such, her decision making is... shall we say suspect."

"She brought you to this Earth by mistake, and could not find the way back to our own. Of course."

"Yes, and like yourself she was virtually powerless at first. Due to her mental... state... it took her much longer to regain her abilities than it did you. She eventually did reconnect with magic in this world, but it was a slow,

306

steady regaining of power. In that time I forced my way into power, killing, maiming, stealing, eventually amassing an illicit fortune over time."

"How much time?" Crystalon asked stoically.

Maceyis laughed, "Centuries. I was immortal before our first battle centuries ago, made so by my own wizards who sought to re-create your spell. Your sister is already as such due to her mystic abilities."

"Again, what do you want with this world?"

"And again I say, to rule it. Your beloved sister has created an 'Arc Imperillium' here. We intend to use it shortly. Then this world – and soon after, this universe – will be ours forever."

The blood drained from Crystalon's face as he listened to Maceyis. "You are madder then I ever considered, Maceyis. To even consider using such a thing is tantamount to damnation." Crystalon barely whispered. Next to him, Joe and Walker looked at him then at each other, not knowing what Maceyis just told Crystalon, but both knowing the absolute terrible implications it must have, only by the look on Crystalon's face.

Maceyis laughed again, waved the back of his hand disdainfully and exited the cells with Shaleeya following behind him, cooing like a bird as she floated along silently. "What worry does an immortal have for damnation? Think on this foolish Wizard. Then think again on how I manipulated those on the other side to cast you here, powerless and weak."

They both disappeared down a dank corridor and were gone; the only sounds, those of Maceyis' footfalls and his laughter fading into the distance.

Joe turned to Crystalon first, "Boss what the heck was that about? Whatta we facin' here? I know it ain't good, but what is that Arc Imperiliwhatsis thing he was talking about?"

"It is a mystic forge of dark and evil, devilish magic. It has but one purpose, Joseph. To steal the souls from an entire world's population and to use those souls to empower its user as unto a God upon the Earth."

Chapter 50

"He's going to steal the souls of everyone on the Earth?" Walker asked, horrified.

"Yes. He intends to use the 'Arc Imperillium' to siphon the soul of every living person on the planet, making them soulless zombies who will work for his aims. A mindless, merciless army if need be, with no moral core. They will build a great mystically powered fleet of star spanning vessels and because in my universe the stars are mapped and all populated planets are known he will send that fleet to the stars themselves, to those worlds he knows are populated, assimilating first the weakest of races, adding their might to his great armies already burgeoning power with the Arc Imperillium."

"You're just supposing all of this." Amanda spoke, fear coloring her voice as she stared at him.

"No, I am not. Many, many years ago there was a rumor he was trying to implement this very plan, but he failed, as he did not have a suitable source of magic."

"Does he now?" Joe asked, staring Crystalon directly in the eye.

"I am afraid he might."

"So he did something to your sister? How'd that happen?" Amanda asked.

"He captured her, and my mother, after the battle of Worlot, when my powers first exploded from my consciousness. I mistakenly thought them both dead, but I was just a child at that time, barely sixteen summers old."

She returned his gaze, her face betraying conflicting emotions.

"Okay enough o' this stuff. What do we do here? How do we get outta this mess?" Joe asked, as he strained against his bonds.

"Our time will come Joseph, believe me. I know this to be true. We will have our moment to escape."

"What if we don't?" Walker asked.

"Trust me, Dr. Walker. You have thus far, I will not fail you." Crys replied gravely.

"Our situation leaves a lot to be desired Crystalon." Walker replied hesitantly.

"It won't for much longer, believe me."

"Aren't you afraid we're being watched or listened to?" Amanda asked quietly.

"We are, but I have woven an illusion to our words and gestures, What they are seeing and hearing is not what we are discussing."

"Can you break us free of these chains?" Walker asked.

"As of now, no. My sister has ensorcelled them. It will take much to defeat her spell. I must bide my time until I am certain to be able to free us."

"Do we have time?" Amanda asked, fear coloring her voice.

"I pray we do." Crystalon answered quietly.

"I'm not likin' the sound o' this." Joe stated flatly

"He revealed to me he had my mother, but never my sister. I did not hesitate, and I attacked him. He and I did great battle, on his terms, and I bested him. But it was too late for my poor mother. He had transformed her magic...ca...ly..." He hesitated and trailed off, fear coloring his face anew.

"Crys, what is it?" Amanda asked fearfully.

He hung his face low in his chains, staring at the floor in disgust and despair. "They told me there was no redeeming her, they warned me. Now I see why." Crystalon murmured to himself.

"What is it? What're ya goin' on about boss?"

Crystalon raised his face up and stared at them all. Emotions played across his countenance as he prepared to answer, "I always assumed he had some nameless sorcerer – or a conclave of them, more then likely – perform the transformation spells on my mother that drove her mad, and ultimately led to her death. But I see now I was wrong."

"No, Crys you have to be wrong. Don't even think that." Amanda fearfully shook her head in denial.

"Amanda, it has to be. It answers so much. It explains why I could never find those responsible for my mother's transfiguration. It explains why I could never find my sister after that horrible, epic battle was over. Shaleeya changed my mother into the monstrosity she became. She drove my mother insane, after Maceyis had done likewise to Shaleeya herself. Maceyis is responsible for more evil against my family and I then I thought even possible... and he must pay."

Chapter 51

"Well, now what? We're hangin' by our wrists here in some dark castle dungeon like in an' old Dracula movie. How do we get outta here?" Joe looked quizzically at Crystalon, the emotional spectrum playing across his face as he sought answers. Next to him Amanda hung limply in her bonds, exhaustion beginning to take a toll on her. Daniel and Joe looked to Crystalon for guidance in the dimly lit darkness. "So boss? Whattaya got ta say?"

"Quiet Joseph, we are being...watched."

Joe and Daniel turned in the direction of Crystalon's gaze, and in the dim light at the dungeons door, they could see a furtive figure staring at them fearfully. It was Crystalon's sister, Shaleeya, barely discernable in the darkness.

"Enter Shaleeya. I will not harm you, no matter what he has said to you. No matter what lies he has told you all these many years."

She fairly flew into the room, quickly floating in front of them. "You are the liar, the great deceiver, the ev-il one, my bad, bad brother. I hate, hate, hate you!" she grunted madly, while floating around him, back and forth.

"Not so, dear Shaleeya. You do not know the relief I have at finding you alive and..." He hesitated, "Well. I am so relieved after many long, long years. My heart fairly sings to see you again."

"Pfeh, you have no heart. You have done so much ev-il to us all. You killed papa and mama. You left me alone for so, so long." She derided him.

"Hey lady that ain't so. The boss is a good man, a real good man."

She turned to Joe, cocking her head sideways again madly. "You shut up ugly little troll man, or I'll pop your head from your neck, and I'll smile while I'm doing it."

313

She spoke matter of factly, as if she were simply speaking of opening a can of soda or inserting a key into a door lock.

The words sent chills down everyone's spines.

"Shaleeya, look at me." Crystalon commanded.

"What do you want devil-man? That's what my love calls you, the devil man you know. He tells the truths about you, about all the bad you've done, forever and ever."

"There was a time in my life when what I did was considered 'bad' by many, but those days are long over my sister, and they were not in the manner you were led to believe. I am not the villain here. Maceyis is. You must understand that." He exhaled sadly and looked her in the eyes, "I am here to save you Shaleeya, not damn you. Let me help you. You can still be saved. This does not have to end sadly."

"I don't believe you, bad man. I am safe and my Maceyis loves me."

"He does not know what love is Shaleeya. Think back to our family, how our parents treated us, with kindness and decency, with love. Maceyis is a monster. He killed our mother. It is not too late for you to be redeemed. Let me help you."

"No, you are the one who needs help, bad, bad man. Maceyis will slay you, and when he does, this world be ours and we will rule it, and play with the toys."

"The toys? What mean you Shaleeya? What toys?"

"The people. The people left behind. When you die, they become our playthings. Our pets. Yes, this world will be ours, and only because of my Maceyis' courage will everything be made right. Not like you, who were scared and weak and evil. Our world could have been made right, could have been orderly, but no, you refused. Now Maceyis will do it here, and your death will be what makes it all work right, what will bring order to this place of craziness.

I can't, can't, can't wait!" She exclaimed gleefully before turning and floating out the door, mist trailing behind her.

"What's she talkin' about, killin' you ta make this thing start?" Joe asked, his eyes grim and set, with a furrowed brow.

Crystalon turned towards his friends, his face was almost ashen, as he spoke "He intends to start the Arc Imperillium with my death, the great explosion of mystic energy will be sucked into the Arc, starting it with a catastrophic burst of devastating power, and from there it will drain into itself every soul on the planet, and Maceyis will have won. He will be a dark God, and all creation will be his plaything."

Chapter 52

Silence pervaded the dungeon as the realization of what Crystalon just informed them of sank in. Nearby in the darkness, water dripped slowly but steadily.

"This all makes sense now," Crystalon continued. "The soul sucking demons were controlled by my sister. Those Wraith Lords are usually chaotic, barely articulate brutes, but she has become a succubus of sorts. Souls must be drawn to her for sustenance. I see that now. Yet another item to add to Maceyis' list of evil debt. The Wraith Lords were hunting for her. They used them in the Hospital to get my attention, and yet not draw attention to her or my old enemy Maceyis."

"Do you think they knew I was on staff there already?" Walker asked.

"Possibly Dr. Walker, though in truth, I doubt it. It would not have mattered if you were there or not. You are inconsequential to them. No, I was always their target. Maceyis as much as admitted it here himself when he spoke of manipulating the weak minded fools who sent me here."

"Yeah I wondered about that. That means your sis has some way of, at least, contacting your home world." Joe added.

"Indeed. That means I can as well, but I do not care to at the moment, or need to. I must release us from these bonds before we can make another step further in our war with this madman."

"He really is crazy, isn't he?" Amanda asked quietly.

"Yes, but in a different way as opposed to poor Shaleeya."

"He's trying to rule the world, or what's left of it when he gets through." Walker quietly stated.

317

"He will enslave this universe, then cross over into mine and literally destroy it for revenge upon myself and those that wanted him banished."

"I don't get it, why? Why do all that? He has everything he needs right here." Joe questioned.

"There is no sane thought process here Joseph, you must see that. There is no rational mind we are discussing. This man is a conqueror first and foremost. He sought to always be in battle; he sought to always rule and to always expand his empire and to subjugate. It burns in his mad veins. Further, he is evil personified. There is no redeeming him. He must be stopped, not because of what he plans for myself, but because of what he plans for all of creation. If he succeeds here, on this Earth, the whole of creation is doomed. He will be unstoppable. If it takes him a thousand years to create a fleet of star spanning vessels, and another thousand to conquer this galaxy and then this universe, it will not matter. He is immortal now. Time is of no consequence. Be it tomorrow or in a thousand, thousand tomorrow's, he will have won."

"That can't be allowed." Walker stated flatly, everyone turned towards him then and saw his eyes set grimly on his furrowed brow. "We have to get out of here." He stared at a wooden bench nearby them, where all their belongings lay scattered about on. And suddenly a pendant hidden in the midst of it all slowly and shakily rose.

"What are ya doin' Doc?" Joe asked wide-eyed.

"The inconsequential guy is trying to earn his keep." Walker answered, while gritting his teeth and slitting his eyes in concentration. "I saw Crystalon do this a few times, so I figure I should be able to after wearing it for so long." Sweat furrowed his brow, as the amulet began to float towards him. "Shaleeya is concentrating on you, she's magically trying to hold you in check. I don't matter. I'm beneath her notice. We have to use that to our advantage."

318

The Amulet floated to his hand, and he grasped it like a man holding on for dear life, which he knew they all are.

The amulet began to glow brightly, like a sun in his hand, and the chains that held their hands above all their heads suddenly and inexplicably shattered.

"Thank you Dr. Walker. The mystic chains are no longer draining my strength. You have provided us with a chance. It will not be wasted."

"So, what now?" Amanda asked, while rubbing her sore wrists.

Crystalon walked over to her, grabbed her in his arms and kissed her quickly before she could argue, or push him away. At first she resisted, then that quickly ended as she wrapped her arms around him and returned his passion.

She pulled back suddenly and slapped him across the face "That's for taking so long to find me!"

Crystalon was momentarily taken aback, and with his eyes wide in surprise, touched his face quizzically. Then she leaned forward and resumed kissing him.

Suddenly a huge explosion rocked the castle to its foundations. Dust and mortar rained down on their heads as Crystalon and Amanda broke their grasp. She looked around nervously.

"W-what's happening?" She stammered.

"This castle is under attack." Crystalon answered stoically.

"Yeah, but by who?" Joe replied.

Chapter 53

Now sounds of fighting could be heard, men shouting and grunting in rage as the battle outside seemed to be making its way into the castle itself.

"Let's get outta here." Joe ordered.

"Yes, head for the main entrance." Crys replied while attaching his cloak once again and walking out the dungeon room doorway and away from his friends.

"Hey! Where're you goin'?" Joe shouted.

"To find my sister, and to rescue her. Amanda, I shall return. Joseph, take care of her until I do my friend."

"Boss! She's gone! There ain't nothin' ta rescue there, ya gotta see that!"

"I have to try Joseph. I have to!"

He turned and disappeared down the dark basement corridors of the castle.

"Great. Let's get outta here. Whaddaya think's goin' on up there Doc?"

"I have an idea, and I pray I'm right as to who it is, Joe."

Joe swiveled his head and turned towards Walker as they ran past empty cells in the dank dungeon, and began to climb a stone staircase upwards. "Yer pals in the 'Knights O' da Golden Dawn'?"

Daniel Walker nodded quietly as they flew up the staircase, leaping sometimes three steps at a time, half dragging Amanda with them.

Several hundred feet away, and in the opposite direction, Crystalon raced through the blackness, unerringly guided by a mystic sixth sense drawing him to a source of great mystic power, which he knew was his sister somewhere in the dank depths of the castle ahead of him.

Suddenly, ahead of him bright light exploded from a roughly hewn stone entryway of sorts.

Heedless of his own fate, the Sorcerer hurtled through the opening to see a sight as if from nightmare. A huge, swirling circle of mystic energy, standing vertically before him floated in the air, multicolored hues filled the swirling abyss, blues, greens, yellows, reds, flecked throughout with stars.

Standing before the swirling miasma, with their backs to him were both Shaleeya, floating several feet above the ground with her arms held high, and next to her the madman Maceyis, grinning from ear to ear. Both turned towards Crystalon as he entered the room.

"You!" shrieked Shaleeya, suddenly twitching madly.

"You mad dog! You created it! The Arc Imperillium is complete and operational! You insane bastard!" Crystalon roared as he swiftly turned from the swirling mystical forge and towards his dire enemy.

"Ah my enemy! You deliver yourself before I even had called for you. Welcome to your doom." Maceyis laughed matter of factly.

"The only doom here will be yours, devil!" Crystalon roared as he suddenly flew into the room, floating feet above the floor, emerald energy erupting from his fingertips pinpointed directly at Maceyis, and just as instantly a shield of golden energy appeared between the two men as Maceyis laughed haughtily. Floating above them both, Shaleeya snarled at Crystalon, madness coloring her eyes a blood red.

***

In the main room of the castle, a battle raged on. Knights of the Golden Dawn armed with everything from handguns to swords, as well as amulet bearers like Dr. Walker, battled against hordes of ancient warriors from all eras that Maceyis and Shaleeya had stolen to the present day. Swords clashed against shields, magic amulet blasts of white light burned against enemy skin, and nearby, outside,

322

another explosion went off, shaking the castle once again. In response a roar, so loud it caused everyone to stop and cover their ears in fright, shook the building on its own accord.

"What the hell was that?" Joe shouted while running towards the door.

"Do either of you see my father?" Amanda Serros asked as the two men pulled her along with them.

"Not in here, Amanda." Walker replied. They dodged out the door, evading a sword wielding, giant warrior in burnished armor as a Golden Dawn knight intercepted the brute's sword and parried it with a resounding clang of his own gleaming blade.

"Hey did you two hear that thing a minute ago? Whaddaya think it was? Another dragon?" Joe asked as he ran.

Suddenly, from beneath the ridgeline a huge head rose up, serpentine eyes each as large as a car instantly struck terror in everyone present. Their unyielding gaze drove daggers of pure, unadulterated, primitive fear through everyone's quaking breasts.

Fear gripped them all equally as the combatants ran, shielding themselves as best they could. Horrific leathery wings beat the air and carried the incredibly huge beast into the sky, actually forcing everyone on both sides of the battle to give pause and shield their suddenly wide set eyes from the heat radiating from the dragon. Black, soulless, demonic eyes stared at them as flared nostrils spit heat and black smoke upon the entire field and a dragon far larger than the earlier ones rose up out of the valley, each flap of his tremendous wings driving everyone on the plain back from the pressure and heat that was generated alone.

"That's it," Joe gulped nervously, "When I see the boss I'm tellin' him I quit."

Chapter 54

Crystalon stood defiantly, floating in the air above Maceyis, out of reach of his sword, and across the cavern from Shaleeya, facing her, as energies ripped from both Crystalon's and Shaleeya's outstretched, straining hands constantly, being parried and blocked in turn as each tried to a find a weakness within the other.

"Stop this madness, Shaleeya! You are my sister, my blood! This filth," he motioned towards Maceyis, "has warped you in mind and body. I can help you, I can restore you. If you let me!"

"No!" She shrieked madly as she redoubled her effort.

Bright energy coruscated across the distance between Shaleeya and Crystalon, as he blocked it again, but the sheer force of the energy against his glowing mystic barrier forced him closer to the ground and he gritted his teeth as he prepared to strike back. Suddenly his ankle was grasped from below, and he was yanked to the ground, slammed onto his back by a grinning Maceyis, who instantly drew his sword and raised it above his head.

"Now I have you, Little Wizard!"

Crystalon's eyes went wide in recognition. He rolled out of the way of the quickly descending blade. Kicking out at Maceyis, he caught the bigger man in the groin, instantly doubling him over and sending him sprawling, the sword dropping from his grasp. Crystalon extended his hand and the sword flew into it. Simultaneously, Shaleeya sent a deadly bolt of energy from her hands, laughing as the blast arced towards Crystalon's head. Instantly he raised the sword, blocking the blast, and shredding the roaring flame asunder!

"The sword of Saint George the Dragon Slayer! We are reunited my friend!" Crystalon smiled as he stared at the gleaming blade in his hand.

"It flew to you! The blade has chosen you! Damn you!" Maceyis roared as he tackled Crystalon. The larger man punched Crystalon across the jaw repeatedly, stunning him, and knocking the sword from his grasp. Above, Shaleeya hovered closer, her hands sparking angrily as she smiled wickedly.

Crystalon kicked him away savagely. "Of course the sword chose me! It knows it is a blessed weapon to be used for good and not evil, and it knows I have chosen my side in this conflict. I have held it before, but a few scant weeks ago in France. Even a mystically blessed weapon knows you for what you are, a devil, a snake, an evil man who must be defeated for the sake of all creation!"

"Always it is you! Always, you stand in my way! Your never ending meddling will finally cease here and now, and your power will fuel my eternal reign! I will choke the very life from you!" Maceyis howled as he leapt back upon Crystalon and gripped Crystalon's throat tightly with both hands.

Then with an explosion that shook the very chamber they are in, Crystalon hurled Maceyis from him with a blast of pure mystic power.

"Away you murderous dog! This ends here, tonight!"

"Yes! With your death!" Shaleeya shrieked as she again attacked him. Energy gripped him, seeking to burn his flesh away.

Almost simultaneously, Crystalon pointed his hand at the ground beneath her feet and the stone suddenly came to life encasing Shaleeya from head to toe trapping her within.

Instantly Crystalon was free. Maceyis stood on unsteady feet, but then Crystalon was there swooping down from above hammering the larger man with his glowing fists savagely, again and again, driving Maceyis to his knees with his angry, barbarous assault.

"Very good, Little Wizard," Maceyis sneered as he fell to his back, wiping blood from his face. "You learned your lessons well. I have brought you down to my level, now finish the job, kill me." Maceyis almost laughed.

Anger and hatred roared through Crystalon's very blood as it pounded like a drum in his ears. He picked up the sacred sword and raised it for the killing blow. Without hesitation he rushed closer to the sprawled barbarian before him, seeking to end their centuries long enmity.

***

Outside, warriors on both sides of the battle scattered, as the dragon soared above them. It blasted flame from its mouth, turning men as well as the grass beneath their feet to ash instantly as it roared its anger to the heavens, sliding by in the sky gracefully.

Joe, Amanda and Daniel hid beneath a fallen stone archway, which blocked them from view from above.

"That thing is going to kill us all!" Amanda cried in fear.

"Sshhh, Amanda stop it! I have to think." Walker admonished her as he waved his hand in her face, palm up.

"Well I hope you got something good in mind, Doc. 'Cause we really went from fryin' pan ta fire this time."

"I know Joe, but I think I have an idea, I need my fellow magic users in the Knights."

"An' how the hell are ya gonna get them from here? We make one move out there an' we're French fried!" Joe retorted, his patience finally at an end.

Walker turned towards him angrily, barking back "I know Joe, I know! I'm trying to work this out!"

"Look!" Amanda grabbed Daniel by the collar and yanked him towards her, she pointed and he followed her fingers aim to see several Knights of the Golden Dawn gathered together behind nearby downed and burning trees.

"Can we get to them?" she asked.

"We have to try." Walker answered, "Together we might have a shot at this thing. Alone, spread apart like this, we're dead already."

***

Back in the vast dungeons and catacombs of the castle, Crystalon raised the sacred sword and prepared for it to descend when inexplicably the room commenced to rumble and shake; he turned quickly towards the source of the vibrations, the stone obelisk he captured his sister in. Instantly the obelisk shattered, spraying stone debris everywhere. Instinctively, Crystalon covered his eyes as Maceyis kicked out, sweeping Crystalon's legs out from under him.

Crystalon dropped the sword and fell. But before his head could impact the cold stone floor he stopped his plummet and turned floating in the air towards Maceyis, he swept his hand aside, as a blast of mystic power erupted from his hand like a glowing wave, slamming Maceyis backwards at reckless speed, to where he smacked into the stone wall with a painful impact.

Stunned, Maceyis slid down the wall grunting painfully with clenched eyes.

Shaleeya's eyes glowed like lightning and with a savage growl of hatred, she turned the air in the catacombs into a whirling maelstrom, sweeping up Crystalon within its swirling mass before he could fly free.

Nearby the glowing, swirling Arc of the Imperillium spun silently as if in silent judgment of the battle happening before it. Good vs. Evil, The Mad vs. the Just. Dark Vs. Light. The fate of the world, nay of the very universe in the balance. Shaleeya floated towards Maceyis, "My love are you hurt? Did he harm you? I will kill him;

yes I will, and eat his eyeballs on toast! I will, I swear it to you."

Maceyis fought to his feet with her help, holding on to her as pain wracked his body.

"He wounded me greatly, Shaleeya. My body is broken gravely inside. I can feel...things rubbing together." He turned towards the Arc Imperillium, then back towards her as he limped forward with her help, as he leaned heavily on her. "Is the Arc complete? Will it drain power and return it to me?"

"Y-y-yes my love. Let me heal you, let me help you and then we can kill the evil one, kill my bad, bad brother."

"No, my dear Shaleeya, this way, there is no winning this. His power is too great, too refined." He grunted, in obvious pain, "He has been holding back, trying not to harm you, and yet you are engaging him with all your magical might. Still he continues to stand against you, even with my own physical attacks upon him. Even now he begins to shatter your vortex. He will be free in instants and back upon us. I am sorry my dear, but it is over." He leaned forward and kissed her. Then her eyes went wide in surprise and pain, as the sound of a blade being driven to the hilt sickeningly permeated the room.

The maelstrom encasing Crystalon shattered, mystic energies flying everywhere as the sorcerer shrieked in soul felt agony at what he saw, "NOOOOOO!"

His voice reverberated throughout the entire castle and to the outside where everyone in battle involuntarily shuddered at the angst-ridden cry. Even the mighty Dragon turned its head towards the sound unexpectedly.

Maceyis held Shaleeya's limp form over his left arm, his dagger protruding from beneath her breast, her body twitched spastically, as she turned her head towards her brother, reason and clarity returning to her wet eyes, a tear running down her cheek plaintively "Crys...my dear brother, forgive me, please..."

"Feh," denounced Maceyis disdainfully, as he threw her still breathing, but limp body, through the Arc's swirling eye. She disappeared from sight and a blast of energy radiated outwards from the Arc, bathing Maceyis in power, throwing Crystalon's stunned body backwards. Crys crumpled to the floor in shock, as Maceyis, now glowing brightly, suddenly stood and flew upwards shattering the stone ceiling as he did, and burying Crystalon under tons of stone. But a soft glow of blue was there over Crystalon's form before the stone hid him from view.

Simultaneously Maceyis was rocketing towards the surface and the outside world. "Follow me, Little Wizard, if you dare!" He roared contemptuously at Crystalon.

The great sorcerer, Crystalon, rose from beneath the rubble of the catacombs as stone debris flew from him explosively.

"I will end you Maceyis, no matter how powerful you make yourself, murderer and usurper this I do swear!" And then he violently streaked skywards; stone chunks caught up behind him in his flight behind the now mystically empowered warrior.

Chapter 55

Maceyis flew free of the castle, bursting through its high roof and parapets, streaking towards the battle below. He raked the ground with powerful mystic energy blasts, killing men on both sides of the conflict with great contempt.

"So, that is how it feels to kill with *true* power!" He mused. "Wonderful!" Maceyis smiled eagerly.

***

"Look!" Amanda shouted to Joe and Daniel, who both turned to where her finger was pointing.

Suddenly, shockingly, Crystalon was there. He flew out of the castle's ruined roof, behind Maceyis, and in his wake, several tons of stone followed him. Crystalon pointed his hand at Maceyis and the tons of flying stone debris hammered the evil madman, pounding him to the ground and burying him under the tons of flying rubble.

"What am I seein'?" Joe murmured.

"What?" Daniel asked as he turned his head in the direction Joe was looking. And then he saw it too.

Wisps of smoke seemed to rise from each newly dead warrior on the field and floated to Maceyis.

"Oh God, no, he's absorbing souls!" Daniel whispered in shock.

"Crys you gotta stop him." Joe implored.

High overhead the dragon rolled and soared, beating its wings powerfully, sending waves of heat over everyone with each pounding flap.

Amanda inhaled sharply and collapsed to the ground, "I- I don't feel so...good."

Both men also suddenly dropped to their knees, holding their heads.

"W-what's happenin' to us?" Joe stammered in obvious pain.

"O-our s-souls, h-h-he's stealing t-them." Daniel answered haltingly.

Far above, Crystalon was driven back as Maceyis fired chaotic energy at him, haphazardly but still dangerous as the blasts had begun overpowering Crystalon's shielding spells, cracking them with each new assault.

"You see, Little Wizard? With each soul I possess I grow infinitely stronger! Soon I will be far more powerful then you are yourself! And then I will grind your bones to dust!" He finished with a smile and a flourish of his hand as he whipped the wind up into a frenzy, catching Crystalon within its grasp and smashing him to the ground.

Crystalon groggily looked towards his friends and saw them all doubled over in blind agony.

"No! This will not continue!" He grunted in stark determination.

He weaved a spell, moving his hands in esoteric patterns in the air, cutting glowing symbols out of the very atmosphere. Then Crystalon heaved his arms towards Maceyis as the sky exploded in agony. Lightning ripped into Maceyis with pinpoint accuracy, rock and stone suddenly flying upwards as wind whipped into a frenzy, and water flew, seemingly of its own accord, from the nearby lake. All attacking Maceyis simultaneously.

Crystalon tiredly faced his friends as his eyes glowed golden and then they were free.

"Boss! What'd ya do? Ferget about us! No matter what it takes, stop this guy!" Joe implored.

"Never again Joseph! Never again will I sacrifice my family and friends for any reason, ever! I will find a way to defeat Maceyis without your deaths on my conscience!" He replied, his voice booming above the roar of the tornado he had created.

Then Maceyis was free, turning Crystalon's own creation of the elements back at him.

"Ha! This is so easy now, Little Wizard! Using the wind, the water, the Earth and the sky as one, it is now so simple, and with each soul I possess, so much easier!"

"You talk too much madman." Crystalon replied as with a quick incantation, he turned the air around Maceyis to burning plasma that clung to him like glue.

But then the dragon streaked down from above, flames leaping in huge blasts from its open maw to engulf the sorcerer.

Maceyis broke free of the burning plasma, as instantly Crystalon was engulfed by burning Dragon's breath and disappeared from sight.

"You are losing ground, Crystalon. My powers continue to grow, while I freely admit I am not as precise or as skilled as you obviously are. But sometimes, sheer power is enough, and mine continues to grow. Now the beasts do my bidding, and soon, so will the rest of this world. Bow before your new master, Little Wizard!"

Crystalon merely gritted his teeth and murmured a spell that caused barbed vines to suddenly spring free of the Earth, streaking upwards to enwrap Maceyis, dragging him to the ground then pulling him beneath it. Streaking skyward, Crystalon exploded the dragon's flames from his own body, ignoring their burning heat.

'*My protection spells are hard pressed.*' He thought to himself, '*Between guarding my friends as well as myself from Maceyis' growing power and the dragon's magic charged flames, I am reaching my own nigh inconceivable limits.*'

Even as he thought, the dragon attacked him again. This time the flames that roared from the monsters maw caused him pain as he grunted aloud, "Arrgghh!"

"Crys!" Amanda shrieked below, as Joe pulled her back towards him.

"Ya can't help him 'Manda, none of us can. He's the only one who's got a chance against this guy now."

"No, we can't stop Maceyis, that's true, Joe. But we can definitely do more than just watch him fight for the rest of the world." Daniel replied.

Suddenly Maceyis burst forth from beneath the Earth, growling as he did, streaking skywards, flying on a slab of rock, spitting dirt as he re-entered the fray.

"Die wizard!" Maceyis' voice boomed as he unleashed a torrent of magical energy that hammered Crystalon, even as the dragon renewed its frenzied, flaming attack. Pinioned in mid-air between the two, Crystalon began to falter and then went limp as he dropped towards the ground. The dragon wheeled in the sky, swooping towards the mighty sorcerer's insensate form and caught him in its great jaws. Maceyis flew upwards on his rock, and then leapt off and onto the dragon's neck. Together, the two wheeled across the sky, Crystalon's body clenched between the dragon's teeth.

"At last!" Maceyis roared, "I have killed this fool! Crystalon is dead! The world is finally mine!"

Far below three compatriots and friends watched in stunned horror, the only sound, Amanda's gentle sobbing.

Chapter 56

Across the battlefield, men stopped fighting and continued to stare zombie-like as more and more lost their souls to Maceyis' wicked magic. The Arc Imperillium continued to force souls into the mad Maceyis.

From above a darkness began to cover the land, growing larger in all directions as souls were pulled from all living within that expanding circle.

"We're still ourselves. How come?" Joe asked Dr. Walker, quietly.

"He's still protecting us. That's the only answer," Daniel Walker replied.

Both men looked skywards as the dragon rolled through the sky, Crystalon's limp form hanging from its mouth, Maceyis riding on its back.

Amanda sat crumpled and sobbing on the burnt grass. She'd had enough. The long weeks of incarceration, the threats, and now seeing Crystalon killed finally broke her.

"This is not over." Walker vowed.

He turned and looked around, finally spotting that group of amulet wielders he found earlier.

"You men, over here." He waved at them. Half a dozen men rushed to their spot beneath the fallen stone archway.

"We need to help him. Crystalon is still alive. That's the only answer as to why we're still ourselves, and have not lost our souls to the enemy. Follow my lead." They nodded in reply. Most were weary and wounded. Dirt and blood covered their faces as they struggled back to their weary feet.

Amanda looked at Joe and whimpered plaintively, "It's the end of the world isn't it?"

"No 'Manda, not yet. It may be the bottom 'o the ninth wit' two outs, but we ain't done yet. We got another ace up our sleeves, we're jus' tryin' ta find it."

High above Maceyis continued to bellow and laugh as he rode the great beast through the sky. "Do you know what this creature is, Little Wizard? It is the very Dragon St. George slew. Your beloved sister called it back from the abyss. This is the father of all dragons! A beast of legend and fury!"

Maceyis' voice boomed out over the rolling hills of Scotland, followed by his maniacal laughter.

"Together, Knights of the Golden Dawn, let this beast from the abyss feel our fury!" Walker commanded, as seven amulets blazed to life in seven hands, bathing the dragon in golden light, from far, far below.

The dragon suddenly pulled up painfully, and began to fall haphazardly from the sky and slamming into the ground as if it were a meteor. The very ground shook horribly, and knocked all those standing from their feet. Dirt and dust filled the air, blocking the sun.

From somewhere within the now cloying miasma, the great monster bellowed in rage and pain. Men covered their ears and dropped to their knees at the horrific sound.

"You men, cover us. Joe, lets go find Crystalon. If he's still alive, we have to get him to safety so he can regroup." Daniel ordered again.

"I'm right behind ya Doc."

Walker looked over his shoulder at Joe who grinned back at his friend. Then the two men disappeared into the pea soup fog-like cloud of dirt that covered the ground as far as the eye could see.

Nearby the dragon roared again, as it tried to regain the sky. But this time, it was a pain wracked growl, a mix of rage and agony.

Carboneri and Walker quickly walked towards the spot they saw the dragon go down, both praying inwardly that Crystalon was okay.

Suddenly, a time lost knight ran toward them out of the thick cloying fog, raising his sword above his head and howling madly as he attacked.

Joe rolled to his left, avoiding the downward stroke of the swordsman, then Daniel took his own blade, and slashed backhand with his left, cutting below the helmet line to the exposed neck, decapitating the man in one stroke.

The knight dropped to the ground in two pieces. Both men moved forward without another thought to the fallen enemy.

Then they are upon him. Crystalon was unconscious at the least. His body lay in a painful pose, his legs twisted horribly beneath him in positions no mans should ever be.

Joe grabbed the sorcerer by the collar of his tattered cape, and Crystalon groaned painfully.

"He's alive Doc! Whadda we do now?"

"Now you both die." A powerful voice roared behind him. Joe turned quickly, lifting his sword instinctively, as another blade bounced against it, then slid down to bang hilts. Joe stared eye to eye with Maceyis, bloodied and maddened. "I don't even need my powers to take care of a dog like you!"

"Give it yer best shot, you ugly bastard!" Joe growled through grit teeth.

The larger man grunted with effort as he tried to push Joe back. But Joe was no weakling or pampered man. His strength was the strength of one who had worked all his life with his hands, and he knew how to use them.

As well as his feet.

Joe kicked out; catching Maceyis hard in the groin, the larger man's eyes bulging in pain and surprise, as Joe followed up with a quick roundhouse left punch, which spun Maceyis around. Then Joe swung his sword with his right hand, Maceyis managed to parry it, easily, wiping the blood from the corner of his mouth, and nodding approvingly.

"First blood to the short, fat man."

"I ain't fat, dumbass, I'm stocky. An' yer still ugly." Joe rushed in, striking at Maceyis again and again with his sword, Maceyis' parried easily at first, then with more concern as Joe's angry, frenzied attack put him on the defensive.

"Get the boss outta here!" Joe yelled at Walker.

"Not without you, Joe."

Walker ran up towards the combatants, circling Maceyis from the side, his own sword brandished menacingly. Somewhere in the fog the dragon roared again, this time more powerfully.

"Danny, get the boss outta here! He's the winnin' card."

"Fool!" Maceyis spit venomously, "your *winning card* is broken and near death, a death I will gladly give to him. With a smile I might add." Which he did.

Joe roared as he ran in hacking and slashing left to right. Maceyis parried easily then threw his hand forward as a blast of light knocked Joe from his feet and sent him end over end for 20 feet.

"It seems I was wrong about having to use my newfound abilities against you. As much as I am enjoying our manly battle, time is constraining, and I do not have enough of it left here to continue our duel. Well played, little man."

Then Maceyis ran in with his sword raised for the deathblow, as suddenly a bright, powerful light blinded him.

Walker's Amulet, guided by his hand continued to pour the mystical light of purity into the powerful warrior's eyes. Walker used his free hand to grab Joe by the collar and dragged him to his feet.

"Get up! I can't carry you both! Shake it off and help me with Crys. We have to get back to relative safety, hurry!" He half dragged the stunned Joe Carboneri to where Crystalon lay, then they both threw Crys' arms over their shoulders and ran, while Walker used one hand behind him to continue to blind Maceyis as they disappeared into the now settling fog.

"Do you fools think this will hold me for any amount of time? I was toying with you both, enjoying a few minutes of honest fighting. I could kill all of you with but a thought."

Neither man replied as Joe bit his tongue, fighting back the urge to return a taunt, but knowing their enemy was correct.

Joe turned towards Walker as they dragged the softly moaning Crystalon with them and grumbled, "I hate this freakin' guy. You know that right?"

"We both do, but all the hatred in the world is not going to beat him. Only Crys can. And that boat may have sailed at this point."

"He's hurt bad, ain't he?"

"Yes, very bad. How he's still alive at this point has to be willpower alone."

They lay Crystalon down behind the stone archway as the other six amulet bearers encircled him. Walker looked at them all.

"Follow my lead, our magic is minor compared to his, but we can do one thing positively, I'm a Doctor by trade, and under my guidance we can heal!" He held his amulet in his right hand, closed his eyes and bathed Crystalon in the golden light the amulet emitted. Instantly the other six men did the same, nodding at each other then staring at the sorcerer in their midst.

"Come back to me Crys." Amanda murmured as Joe put a burly arm around her.

Above and behind them all, the dragon roared again, this time from the air.

"That thing's back in the air." Amanda quietly spoke to Joe.

"It don't matter. If the boss don't make it, we're done." He turned and looked her in the eyes, "All a us, everywhere."

She nodded knowingly, obviously frightened and filled with despair.

"Nothing is over, my friends." Crystalon intoned weakly as he was helped to his feet. He was together and whole, the amulets light having healed him.

"Boss, don't take this wrong, but you look like hell."

"It is good to see you as well, Joseph." Crys replied.

The master sorcerer closed his eyes and concentrated a moment before opening them. "He is absorbing souls on a large scale. For many miles around us he is leaving walking dead, and the circle is growing. His power now eclipses mine. He uses necromancy of a sort, coupled with my sister's succubus abilities, to push souls into his own body by way of the Arc Imperillium."

The dragon roared again as flames could be heard now, bellowing from the dragon's mouth, attacking the Knights of the Golden Dawn once more.

"That monster must go, even before Maceyis." Crystalon angrily grumbled.

"Boss, you said he's more powerful then you now?"

"He is Joe, there is no denying it. The souls of the helpless empower him greatly."

"Can you do the same thing?"

Crystalon looked at Joe incredulously, as did Amanda and Walker.

"Joseph, what are you asking?"

"Look boss, I got a wife an' kid. I want them ta live and to have a good life no matter what. If you can use my soul ta take this guy out, then do it. I'm willin' ta sacrifice for the win. This is fer all the marbles. I mean how many do ya need? You're already more powerful than anyone in history. Would our three souls be enough ta put ya over the edge? Ta make you more powerful then this goober?"

"You do not understand what you ask! I do not know if I can restore you once this is over."

"It doesn't matter, Crys." Walker answered as he placed his hand on Crystalon's shoulder, "We, the world, need this. It's the least we can do. If our sacrifice will win the day, then I know I will make it willingly."

"What say you, Amanda?" Crystalon asked as he turned to this woman he has only begun to explore his feelings for.

She walked over quietly, filled with fear as she placed her arms around Crystalon's neck, and kissed him passionately. Then she withdrew.

"Do what you have to, I trust you, and I believe in you."

Crystalon swallowed deeply, filled with fear himself now. "Very well." After but a moment, he raised his head and stared them all in the eyes, one after another. "My friends, there are no words. What you entrust me with...I cannot say with enough humility what this means."

Amanda raised a hand and stopped him. "Just shut up and do it, before I change my mind." She rattled fearfully.

"Very well, know that I...I love you all. Now sit on the sward beneath us. I do not want any of you to fall when I do this...thing."

"What's a 'sward'?" Joe asked Walker.

"The grass, Joe. Sit down on the grass."

Then he said no more. He raised his hands and began to make patterns that burned the air with bright

341

golden light and energies, burning the very air with arcane power. Above their heads the energies encircled them, descending upon them and then as one they all dropped quietly to the ground, as if they were but puppets with their strings cut, Amanda's last sight was of Crystalon. She smiled at him as her eyes closed.

Crystalon turned then towards the sound of the dragons roar. Tears filled his eyes, before he collected himself, pulled his mouth pulled back in a sneer, followed by a roar of anguish and finally unbounded rage.

"You are done monster I send you back to whence you came, with nothing but disdain!"

He held his hand out and far beneath the castle, buried in the rubble of the keep's stone walls and ceiling, the great sword of St. George stirred, stirred and flew of its own volition up through the hole in the ceiling to land in Crystalon's hand as he soared up and above the dragon. Maceyis once more rode upon its back, brandishing a sword of his own.

The dragon's eyes went wide in recognition.

"You know this blade, monster? You should. It felled you once, and is about to do so again! The mighty sword is named, Ascalon, and it has tasted your blood and your hell spawned evil before, and will do so again for a final time. Your time here is over, there will be no resurrections past this one, foul beast, the sword Ascalon and myself will see to that!"

Crystalon rocketed through the sky at fantastic speed towards the dragon, Sword held before him, pointed directly ahead, his tattered cape trailing behind him.

The dragon pulled back and exhaled flame, engulfing the streaking Crystalon, with the largest, deadliest blast of mystic flame it had expunged yet.

"Beast! What do you?" Maceyis cried in surprise. Trying to hang on and not get bucked off.

What happened then, did so in an instant. So quickly that no one, either on the ground or in the air, saw it take place.

Crystalon disappeared within the fearsome flame blast emanating from the dragons mouth, but then the dragon pulled up hard and began to shake violently, its wings beating the air without rhythm, as time seemed to slow about the great beast. Then the monster was split asunder explosively, as Crystalon and the sword of St. George shredded the beast's body from within, exiting from his tail, tearing the monster apart. Guts and gore – as well as one man – fell towards the ground far below. But this time the man who fell was Maceyis, and not Crystalon, who followed the conqueror and burned the sky with his flight as he dove down towards the would-be warrior king. Maceyis slammed into the ground, and was instantly stunned. Only his own hastily prepared shielding spell having saved him from a crushing death.

"Now this is between you and I, and you and I alone, brash windbag. We will end this once and for all." Crystalon bellowed loudly as he slammed his sword towards Maceyis' head, the larger man parried quickly, with desperation guiding his hand.

"So, Little Wizard," Maceyis grunted with effort, "you seek to end this as it began so many, many millennia ago? Man to man, sword to sword?"

Crystalon smiled as Maceyis redoubled his effort, his sword pressed against Crystalons. "No." Crys replied, with a smile, like a tiger playing with a mouse.

The great sword of St. George burst into mystic flame then, engulfing Maceyis' blade, melting it to ash in the blink of an eye.

Maceyis screamed in agony as his hands burned.

"I defeated you all those years ago on your terms, now I will do so yet again upon my own!" Crys spit, as he placed the sword in the scabbard hanging at his side and forced green flame from his hands, smashing Maceyis back, like a ragdoll.

"I-I'll kill you!" Maceyis howled almost incoherently as he threw raw mystic energy at Crystalon, flames of varying colors, light and then electrical arcs. But all failed to touch the mighty sorcerer, each breaking on his glowing mystic shield, which now failed to crack, or even discolor, with each blast thrown upon it.

"How? How is this even possible? I had you defeated, beaten, near death. And yet you now turn aside my mightiest attacks as if they were gossamer?"

"How? Through the selfless sacrifice of the three most wonderful friends a man may ever know. What they have done, what they have given of themselves, cannot be measured. Know you Maceyis that people of better quality, of better lives and of better... souls then you will ever understand, or be of, have defeated you, while I am but their instrument of your destruction!"

Then Crystalon threw his all into one final, blinding, deafening, mystic onslaught. He heaved his arms forward, stepping likewise with his right foot, his face a twisted grimace as catastrophic mystic power ripped from them, engulfing Maceyis, smashing his powerful shielding spell to bits instantly, Maceyis disappeared screaming beneath the powerful attack. All around Crystalon, people were blown back from the sheer power of this final assault, like leaves in a powerful hurricane. Warriors on both sides of the battle covered their ears; some began to bleed from the incredible volume of the attack.

The ground quaked and shattered beneath their feet as the sky turned black and hail as large as softballs dropped from the sky all at once. Through now present fissures that had suddenly burst groaning from the hard rock and soil beneath their feet, flames licked upwards scattering all those present haphazardly, and still Crystalon pressed his horrible, unrelenting assault.

Minutes passed when those present and hidden behind walls and beneath fallen rocks and trees prayed for an end to it all, praying, for it was as if hell has been unleashed on Earth The castle behind them all suddenly shook, and literally crumbled to pieces all at once before stunned and frightened eyes, and yet Crystalon still continued his attack.

Beneath the castle in the catacombs the Arc Imperillium was crushed to dust beneath untold tons of stone, its evil magic forever silenced.

And still Crystalon continued his final attack.

"This is for you all, my family and friends, my entire insanely long life has been about this one moment, I see that now. Everything I have become, everything I am and have been, has been about defeating this power mad tyrant! I pray I live up to your faith in me." Crystalon wept almost silently, as he paused and swept his hands back once more behind his head, energies gathering as if sucked into a vacuum in his hands, as the world about him grew deathly silent, and then he unleashed it all, in one last ditch effort of unbelievable, unknowable, incalculable mystic power.

He hurled it all directly at the beaten and fallen Maceyis, who lay on his back, the last ebb of magic he possessed consumed in keeping himself alive. The madman struggled to a kneeling position with one knee, his hands weakly held up defensively, as blood – his own for once instead of untold innocents – covered him from a myriad of wounds. The last thing Maceyis saw was that final, awesome, horrible blast of Crystalon's, all roaring towards him as he raised his hands instinctively to cover his face, fear dripping from his every pore.

"I end this now and evermore!" Crystalon bellowed with finality.

And then, it was over.

Crystalon shuffled painfully towards the spot Maceyis fell, and found the man's ashes burned into the now barren ground, permanently etched into the now steel hard, glass smooth Earth beneath his feet.

The Wizard Crystalon did not smile at this; instead he spit his disdain at the spot his most dire enemy has finally, after an incalculable time, fallen.

Then he turned and began to painfully walk back to where he left his friends.

He finally arrived and found them all still catatonic and unmoving. He sank to his knees and wept openly. "I am sorry my friends, I can do no more."

With that, the mighty sorcerer Crystalon dropped to the ground unconscious himself, to lie there unmoving next to those who willingly empowered him to victory over the greatest evil man has ever known.

Chapter 57

"*Awaken my son.*" *A soothing female voice softly warms Crystalons ear.*

He opens his eyes and sees bright white all about him. He lies on his back on the ground seemingly made of the same bright whiteness.

"*Am I dead then?*" *He asks quietly.*

His mother and his father shimmer slowly into view, both smile as they glow with a golden light from within.

"*Only if you so desire, my son.*" *His father answers,* "*Though none would fault you if you chose to join us now in the hereafter. The choice is yours. Your trials are over. The Redemption of the Sorcerer is complete. You are redeemed. You are complete. Come back to Heaven with us my son, you have earned your place.*"

"*I-I do not know.*" *Crystalon answers hesitantly.* "*My friends, I need to help them and tend to them. I do not know if they are yet whole.*"

"*Trust in yourself, my dear child.*" *His mother replies leaning forward to gently kiss him on the forehead.* "*All will be well.*"

"*Crys?*" *A new voice intercedes, as they all turn towards it.*

Crystalon's eyes go wide with recognition and his smile beams broadly as he sees her walking towards him in the bright place.

"*Shaleeya!*" *He shouts enthusiastically, grasping her around the waist and hoisting her skyward, spinning her round and round before finally setting her down. She leans forward smiling, and kisses him gently on the cheek.*

"*Thank you.*" *She says with a beautiful smile. She is wearing a white robe with golden trim, as are his parents he notices finally.*

She steps back besides their parents; all smile at him proudly.

"You have done well my son, so very well indeed." His father intones as he clasps his son on the shoulder and then shakes his hand with a grip like iron. Crystalon smiles in return and grasps his father, hugging him as if he will never let go.

"I have missed you all, for far too long to put into words. To be with you all again, to see you and hold you...there are no words to express the joy within my heart."

"Then stay with us!" His mother pleads as she grasps his hand. "Let someone else save the world from whatever doom may come its way. You have done your part and more then any could ask. You deserve to rest."

"Aye mother, I do. But I must say no, I am sorry. My power is greater then ever before, and I have a responsibility to use that power for the good of the universe, for the good of all universes. I feel my song is not yet complete, my story is not yet over. I beg of you all, do not think the less of me for my choice. I know it is the right thing, the responsible thing to do. It is what I must do."

"Think the less of you?" His father asks, his face twisting quizzically, "On the contrary my brave and powerful son, I could not think more of thee. You exceed all my expectations and those of the very universes themselves. God himself smiles upon you; there is no doubt. Go now my wonderful, brave son, go now and continue to make us all proud of you, we will be with you and watching you always."

His father, his mother and sister then walk forward and hug him as one. Tightly with unending love.

And then the world about him grows bright once more...

Chapter 58

"He's comin' around I think."

"Thank God!"

"He's opening his eyes, Crys! Crys you made it back to us!" Suddenly the bright white light gave way to sunshine as Crystalon felt himself hugged and flung from the ground by a familiar female form.

An instant later his eyes cleared as he lay back on the grass and Amanda Serros continued to hug and kiss him madly, as if she never wanted to let him go.

He smiled warmly and enwrapped her with his own arms, returning the warmth of her embrace and redoubling it.

A moment later they both stood as Joe and Daniel shook his hand and clapped him on the shoulders.

"What has happened? When last I saw, you were all still insensate. How did you come back?" Crystalon asked, while smiling broadly and thankfully.

"I-I dunno boss. We all woke up at the same time, but you were out cold next to us. We all thought you were dead, I swear you weren't breathin'."

"Right," Walker continued, "Then you suddenly inhaled sharply and we knew you were coming back to us."

"So it's all over then." Walker looked around himself, quietly reflecting.

Joe Carboneri walked up behind him and pounded him on the back playfully, almost knocking Walker to the ground "What Doc, you wanted more?"

The four of them smiled at this and at each other.

Then Joe looked at Crystalon, A question coloring his face, "Hey Boss, when'd you get a chance to change yer duds?"

"Joseph, what are you-"

Crystalon looked down at himself and suddenly realized, as did Walker and Amanda, that he was wearing a different uniform, a white one with gold trim. His cape was whole once more and similarly adorned. He smiled instantly and looked heavenward; he mouthed *Thank you*, to the sky as his three friends looked to each other and then to him with puzzled looks upon their faces.

"Amanda! Amanda!" A frenzied voice called from across the field as an old man ran towards them all.

They turned as one towards the harried voice.

"Daddy!" Amanda replied, rushing to meet him. The old man hugged her almost painfully. "I thought I had lost you my dear, I thought you were gone from me forever..." He trailed off as Crystalon, Dr. Walker and Joe approached.

"Sorcerer, I cannot thank you enough for what you have done here this day. You have saved us all. The entire world! I know you may hate me, but I-"

Crystalon silenced him with a wave of his hand, "No Mr. Serros, I do not hate you. You are not the man who exiled me here, but simply his lookalike. I owe you much for what you have done for me. In fact I owe him as well, for without you both I would not have been able to find myself. Without any of you, none of this would be possible. I am humbled by your trust in me."

The great wizard Crystalon then did the unexpected. He dropped to one knee and bowed before all his friends and companions in humble thanks.

"M-my boy, p-please stand, please, I... we do not deserve this. We should be honoring you!" Anthony Serros replied, almost in shock.

Crys rose; smiling as he shook the older mans hand.

Serros returned his handshake in absolute stunned silence.

"We need a party." Joe stated simply, smiling like a cat from ear to ear.

"But we are so far from Rome, it will take us days to return there." Serros replied.

"Why not have one right here then?" Crystalon answered.

"What? Where?" Walker replied, his brow furrowing quizzically.

"Right here." Crys replied again, now smiling himself. He turned and waved his hand at the remains of the castle and instantly, as if time were rolling backwards, the castle rebuilt itself, brick by brick, before their stunned eyes, until every brick was in place as it belonged. The great castle shone as if new in the sunlight.

Crys turned to Joe, Walker and Amanda, and smiled again "I did tell you in my world this is my home."

Later...

The party was in full swing within the now freshly re-made halls, rock bands played continuously on a brightly lit stage, each not knowing how exactly they made it there, but somehow not questioning it, or their pay, too deeply. Food of all types was shared on large steaming platters by the staff of one of the very best restaurants in Manhattan, who also did not question how they arrived, where they were, or the thickness of their wallets, as Crystalon and his friends, along with the remaining Knights of the Golden Dawn celebrated cheerfully. At the head of the table, Crys, Joe, his wife and son, Walker and Amanda sat closely together, and next to Amanda sat her father. All relaxed and enjoyed the moment, for it was well earned.

Dr. Walker leaned towards Crystalon, "Crys what about the Arc Imperillium? Are you sure it was not rebuilt when you reconstructed the keep?"

"No Daniel, I made sure of that. It is forever gone, as are all traces of Maceyis' evil."

"Hey boss," Joe began somberly, "Look I know she was a bad egg an' all, but I'm really sorry about yer sister. I wish there was a way ta save her."

Crystalon smiled with a touch of melancholy before answering, "Trust in me Joseph, though she is not here with us she is in a much better place, I know it. She was driven to do the things she did by the evil Maceyis, whose deviltry has indeed ended forever. Of that I am sure." He stood then, and spoke in a louder voice, "A toast then, to friends and loved ones lost in our great quest. To our friend and companion Alfredo, to the tragic Baron Vorlas who nobly fought for his cause, to the woman only known to us as 'Golden Scarab', and to my sister Shaleeya, as well as to those Knights of the Golden Dawn who fought bravely and made the ultimate sacrifice. May they all rest peacefully in the better place they have all assuredly gone to!"

The people all toasted at once, to their victory as well as to their lost comrades. They all grew silent as they put their goblets down on the long table, reflecting pensively of battles won and friends and loved ones lost.

Walker was the first to break the silence, "Crys, you sent all the time lost knights back to their own eras?"

"Indeed my friend, with no memory of what they had encountered here. Those who did not survive will be thought lost in one war or another, which they in fact were indeed."

"Hey boss, I been thinkin' what do ya think ever happened to the guy from this side? The Chris Talon guy you replaced when you got here?"

"Honestly Joseph I do not know, and can only hazard a guess, but let that be a question for another day, my friends. Tonight let us celebrate and enjoy our well-earned victory!"

Goblets noisily clanged together as the next band began to play in the great hall behind them, filled with the

Knights of the Golden Dawn and their guests, dancing and reveling long into the night...

Epilogue

Another when, another now... A land we have seen before. Bodies and weapons of war lay strewn about on a burned, battered plain. The sky was filled with black smoke, blotting out the sun itself. Great ships lay smashed and crushed about the steaming soil as if by an even greater hand. Carrion birds pulled at still warm bodies, as insects flew about colder ones. A great castle we have seen before lay in the distance, smoke rising all about it.

Inside the castle's gates, and into the castles very great hall, bodies were scattered about as if a great and mighty battle to the death had taken place and indeed it had. For now the victor at last sat upon the throne. His head was down, and he wore simple clothes. Surprisingly they were sneakers and jeans, with a white button down shirt, now stained with blood. Nearby a very familiar woman with golden hair knelt on the floor and held a likewise familiar old man's body in her lap as she sobbed pitifully, clutching his head.

The man upon the throne looked up and smiled, it was a face frighteningly familiar, but twisted, evil, and cruel. His eyes glinted balefully as he looked about, and then Chris Talon leaned back, pausing a moment to run his hands over the comfortable padding on the arms of the throne and the fine wood that made up its body. He then raised his eyes up and looked around maliciously, finally speaking, "So it *is* good to be the king! Ahahahahahahahaha..."

The End?

Other books by Ralph L. Angelo Jr

- Redemption of the Sorcerer, The Crystalon Saga, Book One: A mighty sorcerer and ruler of his world is deposed and exiled to a world identical to his own, save for one difference, magic doesn't exist there. Now he must fight against seemingly insurmountable odds to regain his powers in time to save both parallel universes from utter destruction. ISBN# 0615763030

- Torahg the Warrior, Sword of Vengeance: In a land before recorded time, a world of warriors, monsters and wizards, a young prince is framed for the death of his father by his own evil brother and riven to exile. For twenty long years he wanders the world, until finally he is coaxed into returning to his homeland seeking justice for his father and bloody revenge for himself.
  ISBN# 1490516263

- The Cagliostro Chronicles: In the depths of space awaits danger for all mankind. When man's first faster than light space flight begins, it opens up a whole new universe for mankind. But it is a universe filled hostile enemies as well as a century-long conspiracy against humanity. Will mankind survive? ISBN# 0615854427

- Help! They're All Out to Get Me! The Motorcyclists Guide to Surviving the Everyday World: A Non-fiction motorcycle safety and instructional manual for the new and returning riders. A 'Must Read' for those seeking to better their motorcycling experience. ISBN# 0615756786

- My Enemy, Myself, The Crystalon Saga, Book Two: It has been two years since Crystalon defeated the mad warlord Maceyis. Much has changed in that time. Crystalon has become his adopted world's hidden mystic guardian, protecting the Earth from those who would threaten it with evil, sorcerous intent. Until a visitor from his past, one he never expected to see again would appear within his very home. Now he and his companions must travel between worlds to his home dimension, a universe where he is hated and feared, to face a threat that dwarfs any challenge he has ever faced before. The challenge of an enemy who wears his very face. The challenge of 'My Enemy, Myself'. ISBN# 149950523X

- The Cagliostro Chronicles II: Conflagration The star cruiser Cagliostro must land on an unknown alien world to make repairs after an almost disastrous battle in space only to discover a new threat to Earth and humanity. But alone and unable to return to Earth until they can complete repairs will they be enough to stop this new threat by the Agalum empire? And what of the strange new foes they encounter upon this world of prehistoric monsters and aliens? It's more fast paced, interstellar action in the sequel to the best-selling 'The Cagliostro Chronicles'. ISBN# 978-0692255506.

- Hyperforce
  A team of fledgling superheroes must join
  together to face a threat from the stars as a young
  alien prince crash-lands on Earth seeking aid
  against a terrible enemy. The team that will
  become known as 'Hyperforce' will face this and
  many other threats in their debut novel. Join
  Captain Power, Solaron, Dragonfly, Starbolt,
  Creature, Silver Shadow and Stryker as they seek
  their place in a strange new and ever evolving
  world. An action and adventure lover's paradise.
  If you loved silver and bronze age comics, you're
  going to love Hyperforce! ISBN# 978-0692302156